LUCY CRUICKSHANKS

The

ROAD
TO
RANGOON

HERON
BOOKS

First published in Great Britain in 2015 by Heron Books
This paperback edition published in 2016 by Heron Books
an imprint of

Quercus Editions Limited
Carmelite House
50 Victoria Embankment
London EC4Y 0DZ

An Hachette UK Company

A CIP catalogue record for this book is available
from the British Library

PB ISBN 978 1 78206 347 6
EBOOK ISBN 978 1 78206 346 9

· 10 9 8 7 6 5 4 3 2 1 ·

Typeset by CC Book Production

Printed and bound in Great Britain by Clays Ltd, St Ives, plc

Praise for Lucy Cruickshanks and *The Road to Rangoon*

'Pleasingly ingenious . . . Full of effective surprises . . . There is a raw energy'   *Guardian*

'Beautifully written, immensely atmospheric, the characters are unforgettable . . . This is a compelling story that will touch your heart'   Kate Furnivall, author of *The White Pearl*

'Authentic, beautiful and highly accomplished . . . all novels should aspire to be this good'   *Bookbag*

'A beautifully atmospheric novel'   *Woman's World*

'There are very carefully observed mannerisms amongst the local people, and the oppressive times in which the people of Burma were living are acutely portrayed. [Recommended] for anyone who wants to gain a sense of Myanmar today'
                                                                                           Trip Fiction

'An intelligent and incredibly impactful read that stays with the reader long after turning the final page'   *Novelicious*

'Vivid, startling and absorbing'
                                          Matthew Plampin, author of *The Devil's Acre*

'An enjoyable and well-written novel'
                                                                  South China Morning Post

About the author

Lucy Cruickshanks' love of travel inspires her writing. A great fan of the underdog, she's drawn to countries with troubled recent histories, writing about periods of time when societies are at their most precarious and fraught with risk. She's fascinated by their uniqueness and moral ambiguity, and in capturing the people who must navigate them. Her debut novel, *The Trader of Saigon*, began life after she sat beside a man on a flight who made his fortune selling women. It was shortlisted for the Authors' Club Best First Novel Award and the *Guardian* Not The Booker Prize, longlisted for the Waverton Goodread Award and named a Top Ten Book of 2013 by The *Bookbag*.

Lucy was born in 1984 and raised in Cornwall, UK. She holds a BA in Politics and Philosophy from the University of Warwick and an MA in Creative Writing from Bath Spa University. She lives on the south coast of England and divides her time between writing and caring for her young family.

For Miles

'You must always beware the five enemies of man:
fire, flood, thieves, people who wish you ill and
whoever it is that rules you.'

Burmese proverb

'This is Burma, and it will be quite unlike any land
you know about.'

Rudyard Kipling, *Letters from the East*

PROLOGUE

Shan State, Burma
March, 1974

Thuza's father placed down his pencil and folded the map with trembling hands. Her mother was sitting by the stove, a blanket spread across her pregnant belly, staring into the flames with tear-swollen eyes. At her side, the letter was open on the table. She stroked it with her fingertips and mouthed a soundless prayer. Thuza was curled on the floor by her feet, listening to her mother's slow, deliberate breathing and worrying the frayed edges of the rug through her own fingers, closing her eyes and then opening them again and again in the dimly lit room, trying to squeeze the last day into focus, to force it to make sense in her aching mind. The curtains were drawn, apart from a crack that her father could watch through, and the night outside was still deepest black. She could hear the wind shifting through the dense teakwood forest, stealing down the mountainside, disturbing the leaves. The muted cry of an owl shuddered through the air and she shivered at its hollowness, and the chill of her fear. They were far from the town and her stomach was knotted. Her muscles had stiffened from the hours she'd been sat there, afraid to move or make a noise. Her stare wandered from the letter to her father. He saw her looking and tried to raise a smile, but it fell away before he had steadied it, like a pebble that tumbled from the top of a cliff.

We know you're a smuggler. We've taken your eldest.
He'll come home alive if you do as we say.

It had only been a matter of time before the war reached Thuza's family. As the battles for land, power and money had grown more ferocious and the mountains of Shan State – Burma's rugged highlands – had slipped into lawlessness, Mogok became trapped. Everyone in the remote valley town feared the rebel fighters who hid in the forests as much as they did the men in charge. The Tatmadaw military government ran the country with stubbornness and maliciousness but, so far from Rangoon, their hold was brittle, and each side was as terrible and desperate as the other. They were both controlling. Just as mean. Now, with every road in and out of the valley stalked by bandits, the forests strewn with landmines and a relentless season of rain that had flooded the rivers and drowned the crop fields, the people were famished as well as afraid. The combination was costing new lives. A few months ago, Htwe Zaw, a friend of Thuza's father from the gem mines, had gone missing with his sons. Frantic with hunger, the men had ventured far inside the forest to hunt, much further than they all knew was safe. The rebels had snatched them. Htwe's wife had nothing but grit and gravel with which to pay the ransom, but the rebels called her bluff and, one by one, the bodies of her boys and her husband were returned to her, their throats slit, dumped at her door. Thuza had seen the blood that stained her step; four times fresh and bright, and then the slow fade. She still heard the sobs as she passed on the way to the market each morning. It made her teeth clench, they were so hoarse and raw. Yet despite her dread of it, this night had still shocked her. She had never expected to suffer the same.

The rebels must have known for a while that her family were smugglers. Her father was only a small-scale pilferer, selling just enough gems to trade for food and clothes, but rumours abounded through the town like mosquitos and the brokers in Mogok were shrewd and disloyal, and it was inevitable that, sooner or later, one would be bribed or bullied into giving up their more disposable suppliers. Her father was just the sort of man the rebels were after; someone unimportant to command and coerce. He worked at mines across the district and the rebels didn't care how or where he secured his gems from, just that sacrifice was necessary, either voluntary or forced. The future would justify their methods, they argued, and when the people of Shan State were free of their Tatmadaw oppressors, they could all live in peace and be happy and free. For now, however, there were battles to fund, weapons to buy and medicine and uniforms, and nothing mattered more than a constant flow of cash. Thuza never knew which of the town's dealers gave her family away, but around the market squares, she noticed men watching her. They were thin and toothless, rotten-gummed and twitchy, and untidy circles of blue-black ink were tattooed across the pleats of their knuckles to ward away the bullets and knives. They had stayed in the shadows when they followed her and were not wearing uniforms, but she knew they belonged to the insurgent fighters of the Shan State Army. The same withdrawn, malarial stare hung on the faces of all forest dwellers.

Thuza felt a rush of sickness at the memory and she shuffled across the rug and wrapped her arm around her mother's leg, huddling in. Now her brother was somewhere in the forest, caged in their camps like Htwe's family had been. The thought made her insides liquid with fear. Kyaw was seventeen, six years older than Thuza was and too busy to play together like they used to do, but still, she was in awe of him. In the rains before last, her father had been injured when a flooded mineshaft collapsed, and he walked with a limp that made her wince. His chest creaked from decades of inhaling the coarse, underground Shan State dust. He didn't earn as much as he used to. Her mother worked every hour she could to make up the shortfall, but the baby was big now – almost big enough to meet them – and Thuza saw her grimace and stretch her spine when she thought no one was watching, staggering on her trotter-like, bloated feet. The Tatmadaw had drafted Nanna to work in the poppy fields and she was barely allowed home from one week to the next. Her family relied on Kyaw. He was as brave and strong as a tiger, foraging for their suppers in the forest, sinking himself deep into her gullies in search of untouched fruit trees, scaling the highest faults of flaking granite to pluck eggs from the fragile cliff-side nests, scouring her caves for snakes and scorpions, roaming where the landmines were densest and the fewest men dared hunt.

So often, Thuza felt frightened of the forest, of its vastness and fickleness, but Kyaw never seemed scared. He would bring her wildflowers from his journeys sometimes, propping them in river-water in her favourite teacup by the side of her bed.

'How can anything that shelters such beauty be worthy of fear?' he would ask her, smiling, and she would smile back and feel bolder and lighter. It made everything seem safer, whenever he spoke.

When the rebels had first said his name, it had startled her. She could still hear the rasp of their voices. Their sickly croak. As her father had finished work at the gem pit outside Lay-Bauk the evening before, they had ambushed him, dragging him from the moonlit road into the thick, dark trees. Thuza had been with him. After she had visited the bazaar to fetch yams for her mother, she had waited in the shanty teahouse outside the mine's entrance as dusk fell so that they could walk home together, and then six men had jumped them, all speed and stealth and strength.

'*Pappa!*' she screamed as two brawny arms engulfed her. They seized around her body and lifted roughly, their power binding her limbs to her sides and completely useless. The soldier clasped his hand across her mouth and she coughed and snatched a breath, her voice and struggle fleeing her, and she watched in silent, trembling terror as three men rammed her father to the earth and pressed a blade to his windpipe.

'We've been watching you, brother,' one hissed. 'We've heard stories.'

Thuza's father glanced through the forest, finding her. His chest was heaving like hers was, madly. She could feel the soldier's breath in her hair, smell his sweat. Tears pricked her eyes, blurring her vision. Her father looked away and shook his head, panicked. 'There are no stories of me in Mogok, sir,' he said. She could hear the fear in his throat. 'You have the wrong man.'

'Spare us the pain and be truthful quickly. You're a rustler. We've ears like the elephants and hear every secret, and now there are jobs that we need you to do.'

'Please, brother. No! I dig the pits. Look at my hands. It's granite powder. Nothing more! I'm a miner, not a fighter. I've no skills that you need.'

The rebel leaned in closer and a grin leaked through him. 'Your son disagrees,' he whispered coolly. 'He says you're smart and noble and resourceful. We caught him walking this same road this morning. When we tied him up, he sung out your praises. He said you'd do anything we wanted to save him. We hope his faith has not been misguided. Don't doubt the state we'll hand him back.'

Thuza thought her heart had stopped at the mention of Kyaw. As she listened to the rebels' threats and demands and saw the thin line of blood trickling from the flesh of her father's neck, her head was giddy and she couldn't catch a breath. She didn't know how long they were kept there, how long the agony in her chest had crippled her, or her mind had spun and spun like a whirlpool, before the rebels drew back their blade from her father and threw down the letter, and then spat in his face and stole away. At home, her father read the letter to her mother slowly. It had the same threats but more details. Procedures. It was signed by the general of the rebels' largest jungle encampment. They had cried together, Thuza and her mother. Her father had set to work right away.

Across the room, Thuza's father scraped his chair away from the table and lumbered to the birdcage, his limp looking worse than it had before this evening, his body looking frailer in the skittish stove light. The rebels had ordered forty carats of rubies in exchange for Kyaw. They had also insisted on her father's mind. Everyone in the town knew that the war was escalating and that petty thieves would not sustain the rebels for long. The Tatmadaw funded their own power with the spoils of the gem trade, and they guarded the mines like rabid dogs. The rebels had set their sights on taking them. How else could they hope to win against the government? Besides, whoever owned the rubies didn't just have the money – they had the world of the spirits on their side. With the letter, the rebels had given Thuza's father a map of the district. He had lived in the valley all his life, cracking rocks in the quarries since he was a boy, and his knowledge of the land was as fine or finer than any Mogok soul, and they wanted him to draw on it, to mark every shaft and A-frame, every entrance, guard post and gunman, to detail the times that the shifts changed over, the moments of weakness when their ranks could attack. Her father had studied the map all night, scribbling frenziedly and clawing at the lump in his neck as he swallowed hard and it vaulted up and down. If the Tatmadaw found out that he had given such important facts to the rebels, they wouldn't care for his reason. He'd be arrested and jailed for aiding insurgents, but what choice did he have? Thuza knew he couldn't bear the thought of her family without Kyaw any better than she could.

He wriggled his hand through the door of the birdcage and chipped up its metal base, dragging out a small navy pouch.

His satchel was open on the back of the chair and he dropped the pouch inside, and Thuza heard the soft chime of rubies, jostling. He placed the finished, folded map into the bag too, and wrapped his scarf around his face. The strained crack of his cough jolted Thuza's mother from her stupor.

'You can't go out there, Sai,' she said. Her eyes snapped to him, sharp and worried. They were as bright and blue and rare as Thuza's own. 'That hack's enough to wake the sun.'

Thuza's father slung the satchel over his shoulder and shook his head, walking to the door. 'The baby's too heavy for you to do it, Nang. You know you wouldn't make it by dawn.'

'But your lungs won't carry you.'

In her chest, Thuza felt her muscles tighten. Her mother was right. Pappa couldn't control his cough when he got out of breath, and the pain from his shattered kneecap would have him panting before he reached the end of their path. And Mumma was so pregnant, ready to burst. There wasn't a way she could have walked through the forest in the dark without tripping, without the enormous effort seizing her own breath too. Neither of them could move as quickly or as quietly as Thuza could. She unpeeled herself from her mother's leg, standing up.

'Pappa, I can do it.'

Her parents looked at her, shocked. Her mother heaved herself up, the blanket falling to the floor. 'No, Thuza Win,' she said, shaking her head. 'There are landmines in the forest. And robbers. You can't.'

'I can, Mumma. I know my way. I'll be faster than either of you. I won't make as much noise. Please.'

A nervous glance flitted between the adults and her father stepped back from the door, easing to his knees and gripping Thuza by the shoulders. He stared into her eyes, his appearance grave. She had barely passed her eleventh birthday, but they both knew that little about her life was still childish. She hadn't been to school for years, and she understood without it needing to be explained that she would never go again, and that her family's secrets and their survival were her life. She had grown used to the hunger and anxiousness that swilled in her belly throughout the day and night, and the knowledge that the love and loyalty of her blood was all that she had to protect of any worth. Now her family were relying on her as much as she had relied on them.

Her father took hold of her cheeks and kissed her forehead. His hands and lips were rough and warm.

'Will you find your way, Thuza Win? You won't have the moonlight beneath the trees. The paths aren't obvious.'

She shuddered at the thought of the forest closing in on her, but smiled through her doubt. She had to be brave, like Kyaw was. She wanted to make her family proud.

'I can, Pappa.'

Thuza's father glanced back at her mother. One of her hands clutched the curve of her stomach. The other was pressed to her mouth. Her eyes were slick with tears. He took the satchel from his shoulder and hooked it around Thuza's neck, drawing her arm through the strap and knotting the leather shorter, and then he gripped her hand and pulled her towards the stove. From the mantle, he picked up her family's dagger, slipping it into the bag too.

'Stay off the road, my blue-eyed warrior. Stop for nothing. Tell no one what you're doing. Do you understand?'

Thuza nodded and her father kissed her again, before he opened the door and she slipped inside the night.

Thuza walked with her hand bedded deep inside her father's satchel, gripping the dagger so firmly that her bones ached, feeling the worn, velvety teak against her skin with its reassuring solidness, and aware of the little round divots where the jewels had sat before her father sold them and the florid engraving of her great-grandmother's name. Beneath the canopy, it was as black as anything she had ever experienced, no matter how wide she stretched her eyes and strained them. Her legs were cut by thorns and thick grasses. Her stomach hurt with fear. She was shivering, in part at least from the effort of trying to hold back her panic, and her clothes were soaked with the moisture that dripped from the trees above. In her calves, her muscles were ablaze and with their heat and the brittle snap of the dead leaves beneath her, she felt like she walked through a crackling flame. To find the highways, her father had told her to always move downhill, but the earth was uneven, perilous with sinkholes and hidden ravines, and sometimes to go up was down, and down was a trick. The hiss of the underground streams disorientated her, and she craned her neck upwards and searched desperately for a break in the trees so the stars could guide her, feeling her dread continue to rise. She didn't dare stop and collect her breath and her bearings. Soon the sun would be up, exposing her. She told herself that the dark was gift.

She stumbled on, each of her senses alert, and fumbled in the bag for the map, pulling it out and unfolding it frantically, holding it in front of her, trying to see her father's drawings, trying to blink the shadowy landscape into crisper lines, but she couldn't see a thing, so vast was the district he had scrawled on and so engulfed as she was in featureless black. She bit her lip and fought away the tears, cramming the map back inside the bag and turning to her left again, which she thought was downhill. She was almost running, tripping over tree roots, when at last she saw the road.

Her heart quickened, her whole body simmering with relief. She crouched low and edged towards it through the thinning trees, feeling the air start to dance around her and the darkness ease as the star-strewn sky began to appear between the boughs. She scanned the banks for the banyan. It was on the side that she was, thankfully, and she released the dagger from her grip and ran to the base of the giant tree, dropping to her knees. The road was deserted. In the moonlight, she scrabbled at the cool dirt between the banyan's roots with both hands, her breath shrieking in her ears, searching for the disturbed earth, finding it and tearing at it with her fingers, digging furiously and glancing over her shoulder until she hit the metal box. She swept the mud from its top and stared at it for a moment, her mind spinning. She had found it! The strength of her elation stole her breath.

Just as the letter had instructed, she hauled the box from its hollow, prized the clasp apart and levered it open. The hinge groaned as she peered in. Empty. She took the satchel from around her neck and dug for the rubies, throwing the pouch inside the box. What was it that her father had called her this evening? His blue-eyed warrior. She was usually his *Suhpaya* – his dear little princess. She liked being the warrior much better. So many times before, for as long as she remembered, she had felt ashamed when she walked through the town with him. She had dipped her stare to the dust, aware of the whispers of the women around her, how they gawped at the brown girl with such water-blue eyes. Though she looked the image of her mother and her nanna, Thuza felt she wore it much worse than they did. She couldn't help but worry that her father was embarrassed. The people of the town were superstitious, ruled by spirits and myths and rumours. Her appearance made them nervous. They avoided her family. It was safer to stay separate. Her blood was a curse. When her parents heard that she had done what they needed today though, everything would be different. They would be so pleased with her, like they were with Kyaw. She allowed herself the slightest smile and was about to reach for the map to add to the rubies when, suddenly, she froze. Adrenaline spiked through her. Her body was rigid. There was a noise behind, something irregular amongst the constants of the night.

She turned abruptly, scanning around. The forest was shivering. In the pale moonlight was a figure, the silhouette of a man in the misty distance, long and thin, marching towards her. She screamed, feeling a shock as though a snake had bitten her, and scrambled up, every thought in her head bellowing at her to run, but she hadn't done what she came to do yet, and she snatched at the map. It was no longer neatly folded like when her father had given it to her, and she felt the paper rip in her panicking hands, but she crammed it into the box anyway and kicked it shut and into the hole.

Grasping her satchel and sprinting away, her lungs seared and her ankles jarred on the uneven tarmac, but her terror kept her moving, kept her tracing the treeline for minutes and minutes, fleeing towards the shelter of the town. On the horizon, she could see a few wisps of smoke coiling from the chimneys, but there weren't any lights. She could go to the temple. It was just beyond the nearest checkpoint. She could slip by in the forest, unnoticed. Hide there! She wouldn't stop, not look back either. If the man was chasing, he couldn't ever catch her. She was running too quickly and he'd been too far behind. At the temple, no one would trouble her. It would be quiet, too early for crowds. She would wait until the sun was up, calm herself, then creep to the market, pretend she was only out to buy potatoes, and then she'd go home and everything would be fine. Kyaw may even have been back before her. Yes, he would be! It would all be OK.

Through her tears, she spotted the checkpoint ahead and darted from the road, dodging through the trees until she had passed it, then dipping into a slit of an alleyway between two buildings and emerging at the opposite end to throw her sandals from her feet and tear through the temple's front gates without breaking her stride.

In the courtyard, she stopped sharply. A hundred monks or more were lining up on the tiles outside the refectory, waiting for their breakfast with bare feet, the trail of their robes slung over their forearms and the earliest dawn light glinting from the alms bowls clutched to their chests. Men and women from the town were ladling rice and *mohinga* into their bowls, bowing with each scoop, or dodging through the crowds to pay their respects. Thuza gasped and looked at the sky. A blush of purple was starting to form. It was later than she'd thought.

'By the spirits, Thuza Win! What are you doing here?'

Sayadaw U Zawtika hurried from the line of monks and across the courtyard, spotting her. His face was anxious, his long years of life scoring his brow. At the sight of him, Thuza felt a sob escape from her lungs. The monk had known her nanna since they were children. He was a wise soul, caring, kind and always measured. He was her family's most trusted, most enduring ally. In a cynical valley, he was a solid friend.

'Someone chased me, Sayadaw,' she cried, staggering towards him. Her mind felt addled by exhaustion and fear. 'In the forest! I was lost.'

Zawtika's face dropped, horrified. 'Why were you in the forest, child . . . before dawn? Is it the baby? Is your mother OK?'

Thuza nodded, unable to speak.

'Your clothes are filthy. Is that blood?'

Another cry burst from inside Thuza and she dropped her satchel and slumped to the bench behind her, burying her face in her hands. She couldn't tell Zawtika why she'd been in the forest. Her parents had made her swear to tell no one of the letter and, aside from her promise, to drag Zawtika into her family's secret would endanger him and his temple too. Her words were snatched from her.

The monk bent to the bench, leaning in. 'Please, Thuza

Win,' he whispered gently, 'tell me what happened. Who chased you?'

Thuza looked up and wiped her streaming nose on the cuff of her sleeve, staring at him.

'The baby's fine, Sayadaw,' she muttered. 'It was Pappa. His legs were terrible – and his lungs hurt again. I wanted to buy him some medicine. The clinic ran out last week. I wanted to be the first there. I'd heard there were new landmines on the path by our home, so I tried to cut through the trees, but I lost my way. No one was chasing me, Sayadaw. It was my imagination. I was afraid, that's all. Don't worry.'

The monk shook his head and fussed inside his robes, pulling out a handkerchief and handing it to her. 'Oh, Thuza Win. You know the temple keeps aspirins. You should have come to me. I'd always help.'

Thuza nodded, rubbing her nose again and trying to force a smile. Zawtika glanced over his shoulder, through the bustle of townsfolk and towards the row of waiting, hungry monks. A few were watching them, narrow-eyed, but most talked amongst themselves, oblivious. He reached back into the folds of his robe and pulled out two small white pills. He placed them on the bench beside Thuza.

'Here,' he said. 'Your father can have these. I keep them for my headaches but I'll go without today.'

Thuza shook her head, lips puckering. 'Oh, Sayadaw. No. I couldn't.'

'You must. Tell your father to rest. Let his lungs settle before he works again. I'll send your family a supper this evening. The mines can wait a day.'

Thuza glanced at Zawtika and then picked up the pills, sniffing guiltily. She tucked them into the pocket of her blouse, her fingers groping with the button as she choked down her tears. She knew as a monk that he couldn't touch her, but she felt so tiny and drained and lonely, and wanted so much for Zawtika to gather her into him, to hold her the way her mother and father would have done if they were there. As if he knew, he smiled at her, closing his eyes and bowing for a long moment as if in prayer, before giving her a nod and walking away.

Thuza sat silently, her thoughts welling up as she watched him leave and rejoin the line, and then she dragged her heavy body from the bench and stumbled back towards the temple's entrance, lost inside the grogginess of guilt and shock. She was outside the gates and all the way along the street before she realised that she had forgotten her satchel. When she went back, it was gone. The sun had risen enough to lighten the sky between the dormitories, and the courtyard was bathed in a rosy, misty glow. The monks who had finished their breakfasts were milling, talking to the town. The flower girls were skipping at their feet. She couldn't see the bag anywhere – nor Zawtika – and her mind was aching and the crowd was fuddling her, its sounds and its movements. She would find the bag another morning, she thought. Come back later. Anyone could have picked it up, hoping for an apple to eat or jewellery to sell. They'd bring it back when they saw there was nothing. She couldn't think through the pain in her head.

Thuza's daze carried her home slowly, through the forest, up the hill. Her mother leapt up from her seat at the table when

Thuza opened the door, rushing across the room and pulling Thuza into her arms, pressing her against her body, weeping. Her father was crying too, asking where she had been, breathless with relief.

Thuza didn't mention the man who had chased her. She didn't mention the satchel. Instead she cried too, and she sat and ate the soup that her parents had made her, and she slept, curled in her mother's lap as though she had never slept so desperately before, dreaming of nothing but fields bright with wildflowers and waking only when the sun had crept high above the mountains' peaks and the warmth of yellow stroked the bones of her face. As she roused, her father carried her to the basin on the hearth, and she let her mother strip her to her knickers, ladle fresh water over her shoulders and sponge her clean. She eased the forest burrs from her tattered skin, rubbed the mud from her scratches and lathered the soap in her long, wiry hair. She closed her eyes and thought of the orchids that Kyaw would bring her this time, imagining their scents and their white silky petals. She would press them in a book and keep them for years.

Then, she heard the door open. The crack of a hinge. Her brother was home. She had done it! Safe!

'Kyaw!'

Thuza scrambled up and ran from the hearth, naked and dripping. In the hallway, she stopped. Kyaw wasn't at the door. He wasn't anywhere. Sickness rolled like a wave through her gut. Instead, Tatmadaw soldiers were spilling into her hallway, swift and strapping with fever in their eyes and their guns upheld. There were easily a score of them. It felt like more.

They were shouting, screaming at her parents to drop to the ground. An officer stepped through the door behind them, his eyes skirting the corridor, settling on Thuza. In one of his hands, he was holding her satchel. In the other was the dagger and a torn scrap of map.

Thuza didn't move. She stared at the map, her muscles turned to rock. She must have left a fragment in the bag when she'd panicked. She had led them here. She had given them away! Even from this distance she could see her father's jottings; how he'd circled the guard post and written '*ATTACK*'. Her mother and father were on their knees already, yelling at her to lie down. Their hands were above their heads. They were pleading with them.

'Sai Chit Aung and Nang Aye,' said the officer coolly. 'We are here to arrest you for wilfully aiding insurgent activity and destabilising the sacred and noble Union of Burma.'

Distressed, Thuza's father shook his head. He had seen the map too, and their family's dagger. There wasn't any point in lying. 'They've taken our son, sir. We had no choice. No choice!'

'We've no record of a kidnap.'

'We were threatened. It's the truth!'

The officer nodded to one of his soldiers and the boy lunged forward, grabbing Thuza's mother and pulling her up, thrusting her against the wall, belly first, and cuffing her hands behind her back.

'Let go of her!' Thuza screamed, her voice injured, frantic.

A second soldier grabbed for Thuza, and she kicked at him with all her might, and her mother shrieked and threw herself forward, hands bound, trying to block the soldier's rebuke. Thuza cowered instinctively, but instead of going for her, the soldier spun the butt of his rifle and thrust it into her mother's vast stomach. Thuza's mother cried out, crumpling. She lay on the floor, open-mouthed and gasping, her eyes giant with pain and fear. Thuza could hear herself screaming and her father scooped her up, trying to drag her into him, but she was still slippery with soap and dregs of bathwater, and she thrashed against him, terrified. Through the corner of her eye she saw the rifle coming towards her, and she turned away again, burying herself into her father's neck. She felt the impact of the strike like a gunshot, not on her own bones, but on her father's, firing into his jaw as the wood exploded through his cheekbone, cleaving his flesh and shattering his face over hers. She heard the break as if it were her own skull, felt the pain as sharp and bright.

Her father released her as he fell. The soldiers took hold of his ankles and dragged his wilted body from house, carrying her mother behind him and, as they took him, Thuza scrabbled on the floor for the fragments of his teeth that had landed with her, scooping them urgently into her hands, collecting them.

'Pappa!' she called after him, staggering down the steps and holding out the handful of teeth as if her father needed them, as if he couldn't leave without her and them.

At the end of her path, a Tatmadaw jeep was idling, and the officer opened the back door for his men to push her parents in, and at the sound of the engine gunning and the thought of the last unjust moment she had before their theft, Thuza snapped suddenly, springing forward without any clear idea what she was doing and sinking her teeth into the officer's forearm. She was aware of the warmth and bitterness of his blood in her mouth and of the tears streaming down her face, of the rage that had formed them, but not of what she meant to do next. She hung from his flesh as hard as she could, and he struck her, tearing her free from him. Thuza's balance was lost and she was thrown to the path, spitting the chunks of his meat from her mouth and trying to writhe away and run as he clambered over her. He pushed his knees onto her biceps, pinning her, and she squinted at the grey sky above her, petrified, feeling the gravel puncture the bare skin along her back and behind her head. The officer's grip was strong on her throat, and she tried to beg for him to release her, but she couldn't breathe and the words wouldn't come. The officer called for one of his soldiers and the boy bounded into the peripheries of Thuza's fading vision, and she saw in horror a glint of silver from her great-grandmother's dagger as it flashed through the air. She tried to scream again and turn her head, bucking as the blade sped downwards towards her, but the soldier found the gap between her gritted teeth and prized open her jaw, then all she knew was a pain like lightning, and the blood in her throat, pooling and pooling, then a boot on her temple and the cavernous, cold black.

NINE YEARS LATER

ONE

The heat prickled across Michael's skin the instant that he stepped from the cool, tiled hallway of the British Embassy residence and into the searing Rangoon sun. The gardens were glistening beneath the remnants of a brief dawn rain and crisp light skidded from the surface of the lotus pond and struck the ache in the middle of his forehead like a pebble being flicked. He squinted at its suddenness, pulling his sunshades from his head to his nose as he skipped down the steps and along the path. There was nothing lining his stomach but a slick of treacly coffee, and he could feel his hangover leaking through his skin. On the lawn beyond the bright-white gazebo, the gardener was kneeling beside a flowerbed, his shirt already slicked to his back by the humidity, and he waved at Michael, nodding warmly, then bent to the ground and turned his head, examining the thick stems of pristine grass with his good eye and his fingers before snipping the edge to a military line with his old secateurs.

Behind him, the sharp, speared bars of the metal fence peeped above the rhododendrons. A sluggish breeze tugged the clouds across the sky, streaking the radiant blue with strips of torn white, and Michael dried his face in the crook of his arm and dodged towards him. At his feet, the insects shrilled and from somewhere invisible a thrush was warbling, and the drawn, wheezy sigh of a horn from the Central Railway Station dragged itself through the listless air as it summoned the stragglers to the nine-fifteen train. He rummaged in his pocket and pulled out a half-full pouch of rolling tobacco and a packet of Rizlas, placing them down by the gardener's trowel. The old man nodded again with a broad, gap-toothed grin and Michael patted his shoulder, smiling back. When he visited Rangoon, he never finished his tobacco. Zaw Htay loved Old Holborn. He always got half.

There was a voice from the house and Michael looked up, shielding his eyes. His parents didn't approve of his smoking, but they never complained when he gave the staff a cut. This morning, the ambassador had risen later than usual and was still sitting with Michael's mother at the breakfast table on the upstairs veranda, spinning his glasses by their arm and leafing through the pages of the morning news. A fan revolved beneath the shade of the deep stone arches, ruffling the paper, and the thin-stemmed, swaying palms that towered above the red-tiled rooftop of the old colonial villa rippled the shadows that fell on their faces.

Michael raised his hand and waved to them. There had been a terrible fuss at the embassy the last few days about a British loan that the Tatmadaw had squandered on a bunch of French locomotives. Eight months his father had spent, persuading the Burmese government to fix the railway line between Rangoon and Mandalay and getting them a deal softer than a kitten's paw, and they'd blown it all on rolling stock in less than two weeks. Now, it would still take twelve hours to go four hundred miles because the tracks were nothing but rusted nails and rotten wood. *I'll be damned if there wasn't a greased hand-shake in that meeting room somewhere*, his father had muttered as they'd eaten brunch in his office the morning before. Burma should have been the richest country on earth. She had oil, teak, a sea full of fish, every precious mineral and gemstone known to man. It was an act of genius by the Tatmadaw that she wasn't. The county's failure frustrated his father. Whatever the ambassador did, however much he wooed and pressured, his impact never amounted to more than a wrinkle on the gloss of a murky, vast lagoon.

From a shuttered doorway, Daw Mar waddled onto the veranda and placed down a fresh rack of toast, then wiped her hands on the bulge of her apron and chatted a few friendly words with his mother as she topped up the ambassador's tea. He caught Michael's stare as he thanked her. The cook slipped away and he waved back, tapping his watch with an overblown grin and yawning dramatically.

'What time did you haul yourself in last night, Mikey?' his father called down.

Michael shrugged. 'About twelve.'

His parents shot him a knowing look. 'You fibbing hound.'

Michael shrugged again and grinned back widely. He hadn't found his way home until gone 3 a.m. In a steamy teahouse on some alley off the south bank of Inya Lake, he had whiled away the hours drinking bitter rice wine and playing cards until he couldn't count the clubs in his hands. When he'd finally arrived at the residence, he had clattered his bicycle into the gates as he'd opened them and then tripped on the porch steps as he fumbled with his keys. He knew he had woken his parents. He heard his mother pad along the landing and the flush of the chain. There would be a token word about it later – another warning to be cautious in the Rangoon nights.

There were only a few weeks left now before Michael was due to return to London and start looking for work after the long, post-university summer, but he didn't feel keen for October's arrival. Claudine's aunt had a flat in Battersea that she'd hardly stayed in since moving to Monaco and she had said that Michael could have the first month for free, and he was grateful, of course, but there was nothing that stirred him about working in London. The blue suits, black suits, grey suits. The overcrowded underground. The overcrowded office blocks. Those thin fluorescent lights that they suspended from the ceilings that made all the faces at the desks look lilac and gave him an ache behind his eyes. Here in Burma, he felt so much fresher. There was a freedom to each morning, a lush anticipation. He could lose himself in its timelessness and foreignness, and plunge inside its colours, so much richer than his own. Something here was moving like he'd never felt in England; the tow of a current, ready to pull him wherever he pleased.

He crossed the path and chucked his parents a last wave before opening the gates and stepping outside. On the opposite kerb, Sein was waiting in the shade of an enormous padauk tree, leaning on its trunk in his tatty corduroy trousers and too-large, dust-brown blazer, and reading the copy of *The Little Drummer Girl* that Michael had given him. The tree roots had lifted the pavement beneath him and he tapped the toe of his brogues against them absently as he read. He looked up and smiled, flicking his chin and his cigarette ash in unison.

'You look paler than ever, white boy,' he said as Michael approached. 'How's your head?'

'No worse than yours, I'd imagine.' Michael snatched the book from his hands, cuffing him with it. 'You want to be careful, reading that in the street.' They had used two English pennies to scratch le Carré's name and the title from the cover, and the soft, worn cardboard was still powdering in his hands. He thrust it at Sein's chest and Sein rolled it up and crammed it into his blazer pocket.

'I can't put it down,' he grinned. 'The intrigue! Besides, my father won't let me finish it at home. Says nothing good can come of reading spy novels in a city full of spies.'

'He's right,' said Michael. 'I wouldn't have given it to you if I thought you were stupid enough to be reading outside in the bright light of day. If the MI takes it off you, there'll be more to suffer than your dad's clipped ear.'

Sein shrugged, his lips pursing. 'The Military Intelligence has juicier mangos to gnaw at than me.'

Michael gave his friend a stern look. 'I heard they want all the mangos, Sein. Big, small, ripe and juicy, or as mouldy as they come. You know that. And my father says they're watching the students more closely than ever. He's heard rumours of them organising trips to the north to help the insurgents, or something like that. The Tatmadaw's twitchy. You need to be on your guard. It won't take more than a dodgy book in your pocket to get you on a watch list, and once you're on, you'll never come off. What are you doing here, anyway? I said I'd see you at the Lotus. You look like a spy yourself, hanging out on the corner.'

Sein shrugged again and his grin broadened. 'No problem then, is it? The spies are less likely to bother a spy. Besides, I was passing. I knew you'd be late. I thought the ambassador had locked you up.'

Michael rolled his eyes and felt his own smile start to crack too. 'And what was my crime?' he said. 'A hangover? That's unlawful imprisonment. The English courts are fairer than the Burmese ones.'

'Ah yes, my friend,' Sein laughed. '*Touché!*'

Sein threw his arm around Michael's shoulder and steered him along the broad, leafy street. Michael untucked his cigarette from behind his ear and sparked up. He knew that his friend was vigilant really, but it was hard not to feel more responsible than he should. The boys had met more than three years before when Michael was visiting his father for the Easter break, and though many times since he had nudged aside the feeling, there remained the sense of an unbalanced debt. That night, Michael had staggered from the Sailing Club after a spat with some Italian intern over the rules of *chinlon* and thrown up in an alleyway near the People's Park South Gate. Sein had been watching from a dingy downtown teahouse as Michael dropped his roll-up in the gutter and had wandered over to offer him a fresh one, practise his English and hold his light steady.

It was an unlikely friendship that had formed, but a strong one. For Michael, Sein and the Rangoon university boys were far more interesting than all the expat kids rolled together.

So many of the Burmese boys and girls he had tried to talk to before had been scared of him, muttering nothing more than a polite *mingala-ba* when he greeted them, never meeting his eye. Sein was ambitious though. Bright and near fearless. For him, Michael was his portal to a world of possibilities, to stories of privilege and justice and freedom. They shared the same dreams of adventures and thrills.

He took a drag on his cigarette, feeling his hangover ease with the nicotine, and squinted ahead down the tree-lined street. It was quiet in this part of town and they walked in shade on the wide, uneven pavement, quiet too, absorbing the peace. Around the tree trunks and at the bottom of the fences, stray dogs were slumbering, and the boys stepped lightly over their scrawny, sprawling limbs. The ageing British mansions cast long, ornate shadows and Michael glanced up at their tightly shuttered windows, and the archways that flaked with shards of ochre plaster and paint. Each of the balustrades was dark and deserted, and vines twisted through their wrought-iron bars and the fretwork that dripped from the cornices above, giving the sensation of long-time abandonment, though he knew the city's elite wined and dined and schemed inside. In the distance ahead, the mansions turned to townhouses, crowding closely together and crumbling, and he saw the towering gold and white Buddhist temple stupas begin to peep between the buildings and felt the same wonder that he did every morning as they shimmered in the heat-haze as if they trembled with excitement, promising him the clamour of downtown Rangoon.

Michael's love for Rangoon had been forged the moment he

had first emerged from the single, dilapidated terminal of the city's International Airport, five years earlier. He was travelling alone and had been meant to search for his father's driver in the chauffeurs' ranks, but instead, straight ahead as he left through the exit, he was met by the most imposing tree he had ever seen. It was an ancient, yawning banyan, he later learnt, taller and broader than a double-decker bus, and its boughs were so laden with crows that it gave the appearance that the leaves were black and shuddering, and it sounded like the loudest, most fearsome monsoon rainstorm, and he felt the sound in the hollow of his chest. Awed, he had stood for what must have been minutes, all other voices and the engines of the cars lost to the birds and this new, thrilling magic, letting the thickness of the air and its heat, its dampness and his anticipation settle onto him, and wrap around him and seep deeply in.

When he had gathered himself, he had asked the driver to take a long, snaking route through the city, and in place of the tiredness he should have felt after his journey, there was an energy more spirited than he'd ever felt before. Through the open window, he marvelled at the Burmese men in their skirt-like *longis*, and the pagodas that glittered at the split of every crossroad, at the iridescent lakes and the monks in vibrant orange, and the peddlers selling flatbreads and cheroot cigarettes as thick as sugarcanes, the spittoons on the doorsteps and the puddles in the potholes and the strings of grey-white washing, and the trees that tugged at power lines, and the dogs and the dirt. The checkpoints had soldiers who looked younger than he was. The roundabouts were lined with tiny concrete cubicles and the queues that stretched from each were astonishing as people waited to have their fortunes told. The women had painted their cheeks with straw-coloured paste – *thanaka*, his mother had told him, the creamy yellowness that all Burmese girls wore to keep their skin from burning in the sun, swirled into circles or scored in the image of leaves and flowers. Hardly another car passed them on the journey, but the bicycles were constant, hissing and trilling like birds at a stream. After centuries of war and nature's wrath, and what his father referred to as a deadly combination of ineptitude and neglect, the grand colonial buildings that lined the streets were lilting slightly, succumbing to decay. For Michael, this only added to the majesty. Rangoon had a melancholy, injured charm.

He had said as much to Sein one suppertime as they sat together in a riverside cafe. His friend had laughed and shaken his head.

'Those buildings are a sign, Michael Atwood,' he replied, with his characteristic broad grin. He took a pinch of *laphet* from a saucer on the table and stuffed it into his mouth, shooting his eyes pointedly to a Tatmadaw soldier patrolling outside. 'There's nothing melancholy here. Not a tealeaf! Can't you see it? Those chipped bricks and peeling archways are here to remind us. They're here to buoy us, to keep us hoping. All regimes will eventually fall.'

He nodded at Michael, waiting for agreement, and Michael smiled back, though he didn't feel sure. He wanted to believe it, but after all he had read and heard from his father, the grip of the Tatmadaw seemed fixed and ferocious. The press was stifled, opposition outlawed. The people were watched, afraid and suspicious. There were hardly enough jobs and food to sustain them. He hadn't the stomach to hope like Sein.

On the street, he looked at his friend, feeling a gust of sudden helplessness, but Sein had a smirk that stretched from ear to ear. He was rambling about some girl he had met at the university, about how pretty she was, like a spirit draped in jasmine, and how he'd lost at a game of Scissor Paper Stone with Ohn over who would go and speak to her, but she'd laughed at his friend and smiled at him instead. Michael grinned too, despite himself. Sein's good humour always lifted his mood.

With the weight of Sein's arm around his shoulder, he hastened their walk. They were reaching the centre of the city, travelling along the road to the west of the Zoological Gardens, and the people and the noise were thickening fast. The buzz of it shifted the last of Michael's hangover and he drew a lungful of the humid air, tasting the thick, forceful farmyard stench on his tongue, and between the intermittent pummel of a struggling generator, he heard the macaws as they shrieked from their cage. An elderly monk passed with a newspaper tucked beneath his arm and an umbrella for a walking stick, and the man bowed his head to them in a silent greeting. Beyond him, the kerb became crowded with vendors selling deep-fried vegetable fritters and sticky scented doughnuts, and a girl hawked her goldfish, the tiny creatures flitting their long black tails inside plastic bags that she swung from each wrist. Beside her, a mother squatted in the gutter with a row of dented tin teapots and her child. The baby grizzled and fidgeted, and white smoke soared from the teapots' lidless openings and perky spouts as the woman swayed on her haunches and poured water inside them from a perilously heavy-looking, bubbling vat.

The boys crossed through the centre of the roundabout onto Bahan Road, and from the far bank of the Kandawgyi Lake a loudspeaker crackled with a high-pitched song. There was a rally of some sort in Bogyoke Park, and on the horizon Michael could see a row of Burmese flags and Tatmadaw banners, and a longer row of soldiers – fifty of them perhaps – each with their rifle held aloft, goose-stepping before a languid, clapping crowd. Sein dodged into the heaving Bahan Market and Michael followed him, feeling the hot air congeal in the cramped passages and moisture drip on his face from the awnings above. There were children scurrying about him with flower garlands and little booklets of gold leaf for sale on silver trays, buzzing between them, searching for people on the way to their morning's chants and reflections, and the rich aromas of spices and incense, musky-sweet cheroots and freshly cut meat swamped him as he listened to the chatter of the sellers and their sandals in the dirt.

They emerged from one edge of the market and cut across the top of Bahan Road before dipping down a side street – then another, then another – to avoid the throngs. The crisp, rhythmic clack-clack of a loom greeted them, and Michael glimpsed the workers through a fissure in a doorway, dust dancing in the air around them, suspended in the glow of morning light, blurring their edges and casting their silhouettes with a silvery sheen as they bent over their benches and weaved robes for the monks. Ahead, the glorious golden peak of the Shwedagon Pagoda was radiant against the sky.

It towered above every other building, above even the tallest wind-swept palms, above the bravest freewheeling blackbirds. He sucked a breath and watched them soar.

The Lucky Lotus Teahouse was in a tiny square just north of the temple's complex, away from the crowds but with the market still visible, and they cut along their usual alleyway shortcut to reach it when Sein stopped suddenly, gripping Michael's arm.

'We'll go the long way round,' he whispered, flicking a look ahead as he towed Michael back.

Partway down the alley, four men were standing in the gloom, blocking their path, three of them wearing Tatmadaw uniforms and positioned in a crescent facing a fourth, nervous-looking man. They were talking at him, their faces held close, voices low and with threatening stances. The prisoner was nodding with his back to the wall and he appeared to be hurriedly re-dressing, knotting the string of a blue-checked *longi* around his waist and slipping his feet inside tattered puce-green sandals. A large tattoo stretched up his forearm, a coal-black orchid with an eye in the centre, crudely out-lined like a child might have drawn it, the petals hanging down to his wrist like fangs. The Tatmadaw men had turned at Michael and Sein's unwelcome advance and were shooting them stares, and the prisoner snatched his shirt from the railing and threw it over his shoulders, buttoning it up and scowling too.

'They were officers, Sein,' said Michael as they averted their gaze and backed around the building. He had seen the stripes on their sleeves and the dough of their bellies, so different from the lowly, undernourished ranks that usually patrolled this part of town. 'What were they searching him for?'

Sein shook his head. 'We don't want to know.'

Together, they doubled back through a bigger, busier market street, then entered the square, and Sein raised his hand as they stepped inside in the teahouse.

'*Mingala-ba*, brothers,' he called across the room.

Maung and Ohn already had a table near the back of the shop, and were sitting on their stools with their knees up, sipping tea and smoking. They were talking to two girls, who were smiling coyly.

Michael scanned quickly around the teahouse. His father had warned him about places like this more times than he cared to remember. Only sit in the centre. The spies chose the walls. Trained by the KGB, they were. Ruthless as hell. He threw a cursory glance at the seats along the edge. All empty. He shouldn't worry. Sein's father was a professor at the university, well enough connected by Burmese standards and careful with it, and Sein always knew the best places to meet. He picked the cafes away from the main drags, the ones where the light was poor and the smell of the milk was sickly sweet and slightly turning, but where the proprietors made a point to look the opposite way.

Maung and Ohn nodded a welcome and Michael and Sein zigzagged through the maul of densely packed tables that crammed the thin shop, strip-lights flickering above them, the air dank with steam. At the sight of Michael's approach, the girls said a hurried goodbye to Maung and Ohn and slipped to a table across the room, excuses made.

Maung groaned and sunk his head into his hands. 'You cost me, white boy,' he said to Michael. 'You scare them off. Every time.'

Sein laughed and pulled out a stool, slumping down. He slapped Maung's shoulder, then helped himself to a glass of green tea from the metal flask in the centre of the table. 'Your ugly face costs you, brother. And your lack of charm.'

'Nonsense!' cried Maung, his expression awash with overstated shock. 'I've more charms than the soothsayers. Those little petals were one sugar lump away from marrying me, I swear it.'

'Both of them?'

'Both of them!'

Michael took out the stool beside Ohn and sat too, picking up the flask and grinning, wide. 'I'm sorry, Maung,' he said. 'I didn't mean to spoil your fun. I'm sure you were in there.'

Maung shook his head and glared across the table. 'I was. Why do we hang out with this boy, Sein? What do we get for it? Nothing but grief.'

Sein shrugged, selecting a sponge cake from the platter on the table, unwrapping the cellophane and tucking in. 'You can hang out with whoever you like,' he said with his mouth full, 'but nothing but soap and water will fix the sewage that spills through those lips. What was it you said to that pretty one last week? Eyes like a sunset? What does that even mean, brother?'

'*Your eyes are as red as a devil's,*' laughed Ohn. 'That's just the kind of romance to make a girl weak.'

'You jokers don't know what you're talking about,' said Maung. He smirked, suddenly, and stroked the line of fluff on his upper lip. 'Anyway, once my moustache is finished, I won't need the pickups, will I? I'll look just like Lionel Richie. I'll be fighting them off. Endless love. That's what I'll be getting. Endless bloody love.'

The boys laughed and Maung examined his reflection in the flask's sticky-printed, tarnishing shine.

Across the floor, the teahouse's proprietor was returning from tidying the tables at the front of his shop, with a cluster of water glasses pinched by their rims between his fat fingers and a grimy rag in the loop of his belt. His name was Khun Zaw Ye, but the boys called him *Saya*, or Teacher, for short. Teacher was leathery-skinned and his front teeth were missing. The back of his head was latticed by scars. He looked at least forty, with a solid, round belly that strained above his waist-band, and though clearly his skin had started to loosen, the muscles beneath it were strong and persistent, and gave him the look of a fighting bear. His lips and the tips of his fingers were stained maroon by betel, and where his sleeves were rolled back, his forearms bulged inside a blue tattooed net. Michael had heard it whispered that he'd once been a soldier with the Shan State Army – the SSA – and had fought in the mountains against the Tatmadaw for years; rumours that Teacher had neither confirmed nor denied. Michael doubted it was true – why would the Tatmadaw leave him be if anyone knew it? – but he could see how the rumours might have begun. It didn't take much vision. Teacher was a brawler, vast and powerful. The look in his eye was commanding and stern.

Maung reached out and tapped Teacher's wrist as he passed his seat. 'What do you think, Teacher?' he said, throwing a look at Michael. 'Those girls . . . they liked me, didn't they? They were just as hooked as little fish.'

Teacher belched a humourless laugh. 'I've got better things to do with my time than watch you fail to get a girlfriend, Little Mouse.'

He placed the glasses down on a table behind the boys and whipped his rag across the greasy Formica as the sounds of a motorbike engine leapt into the air. In the cave-like shop, the noise was deafening, drowning Ohn and Sein's snickering and Maung's outraged protestations, and Michael turned to the doorway to see a bike sitting there, the driver revving it so heavily that smoke coughed from its tailpipe and the wheels spun. He couldn't see his face, but his *longi* was checked and the straps of his sandals were a grotty leather puce. Jammy bugger, thought Michael. Whatever he'd been stopped for, they'd let him go. He smiled, watching as the man lifted himself taller to peer down the street. He was straining, looking for something, and a moment later a truck pulled up beside him, directly opposite the shop by the outermost row of market stalls. The truck's driver hurled himself from the cab and mounted the back of the waiting motorbike, which revved again and sped away, and Michael barely had the chance to turn back to Sein and remark on the oddness, when the sound and shock hit him: a terrible blast.

At that instant, the explosion felt like a jet engine behind him, but bigger and more painful, and he felt the weight of the air thrown into him, the powerful thrust of a shovel against his body that forced him into the table and winded him, and then the rush of dust. The ferociousness of the noise that followed punctured through his eardrums and rang inside his head as it rocked the walls and shattered the windows, showering his body with debris and glass. He heard a scream as the dark billowed over him, coating him instantly, blinding him, dust searing in his eyes and lungs. He staggered to his feet, blood in his mouth, hot and metallic, and trickling from his chin as he unclenched his jaw. He couldn't see for the smoke, but through the shrieking in his ears and his blaring panic, he could hear people shouting. Maung's voice. Ohn's. Ones he didn't recognise. *A bomb*, they cried. *A bomb! A bomb!*

Michael scrambled towards the doorway, groping for his way, coughing hot, painful hacks that tasted like bonfires and aware of the other people scrabbling desperately around him, of chairs and tables scraping the floor as fleeing bodies threw them aside. Outside, it was clearer of dust and smoke, but debris floated down like confetti, the leaves and fragments of ash and plaster, slowly, slowly, sinking through the air. He gasped for breath. The fear in his mind was screaming *Run, run! Don't die here!* The power of the blast was still reverberating inside him, beating in his chest, ringing in his head, unsteadying him, like his body was a bell that had just been struck. From somewhere, there was a hiss of water escaping – or gas – the pressure of it piercing the fug, and people running, panicked, amid the bodies that lay on the floor.

He looked around for Sein frantically, but his mind felt dizzy and he didn't know any of the faces. Ahead, the market stalls had been decimated, and directly in front of him where the truck had pulled up and the motorbike had fled was the carcass of the vehicle, tipped on its side, the bars of the back pickup blasted outwards, its khaki coverings tattered and ablaze. He clasped his hand to his mouth, aghast. All around was chaos and terror. A frightened crowd. People were tumbling from the market's passageways and falling to the ground, bloodied and burnt, shards of metal embedded in their skin.

'Sein!' he heard himself cry. 'Where are you, brother?'

He turned and saw Maung and Ohn across the street. They were helping a woman who was lying in the gutter. They had scratches on their skin and shock on their faces but otherwise looked fine. He called out again and started towards them, but then he caught sight of something through the corner of his eye, there, on the ground at his side, stopping him. There were stains on the pavement, red blood not red betel, and in one puddle Sein was lying prone, still clearly breathing but his body full of fragments, his teeth tightly gritted and a yawning, streaming gash along the length of his cheek.

'Sein!'

Michael dropped to his knees beside his friend, afraid to touch him, but Sein looked at him, eyes piercing, terrified and desperate, his lips quivering in a soundless plea, and Michael shook himself and scooped him up, staggering. He looked around for someone to help. There were military police — scores of them — and soldiers brandishing their guns and shouting, but no ambulances, just disarray.

'The rebels will pay! The rebels who spill innocent Burmese blood are enemies of our people and our Union and all humanity! They will be caught!'

'We will punish them. Punish them!'

He could hear the soldiers' voices, feel their useless presence.

Then, through the smoke, Michael saw Teacher's lumbering silhouette. He was propping up a boy with an arm around his waist and hobbling towards a waiting car. The boy was hanging from his neck, his feet dragging behind him, and Teacher opened the car door and bundled him inside.

'Teacher!'

Michael forced himself forward, calling to him, running as best he could manage beneath Sein's limp weight.

Teacher looked at him, grabbed his shoulders. 'Are you alright, Michael Atwood?'

Michael peered beyond him into the car. Two bloodied bodies had been dumped on the back seat and were knotted together and two more curled in the footwells. The driver looked horror-struck, his shirt drenched with blood as he tried to knot a *longi* around the chest of the bleeding girl in the front seat. Michael looked at Teacher, giddy. Sein was a weight in his arms like lead.

'Sein needs to get to the hospital, Teacher,' he cried. He could feel his panic turning solid in his throat.

Teacher wiped his mouth, glanced around momentarily, then sped to the back of the car as the engine fired to life. He wrenched open the boot, tearing out the bags and baskets and a fishing net from inside, and then snatched Sein from Michael's arms and thrust him down.

Michael rubbed his own face, reeling. 'What happened, Teacher?' he muttered weakly.

Teacher slammed his palm against the side of the car. He stared at Michael, so hard that his heart skipped. He shook his head. His face was a thunderstorm. Michael staggered backwards, and the engine gunned again and the car started moving, pushing inside the confusion and uproar, its horn blasting, shrieking a warning, and Teacher strode away and left Michael gawping, watching one scuffed brown brogue below one corduroy-covered ankle, swinging from the back of the open boot.

TWO

Thuza opened the door to the birdcage and peered inside. The last sparrowhawk clung to his perch and scowled at her, his bright orange eyes swivelling furiously in their sockets. Though the light that leaked through the morning mist was thin and sickly, it caught his stare and set it flaming. She licked her lips and glanced outside. It was less than an hour since dawn had crept over the mountaintops, and the air was still sodden with dew and the damp scents of earth. The path that led from her home to the forest was puddled slightly, dragonflies flitted above pools of silver water, and the gravel glittered like a trail of spilt gems. She smeared her quivering hands along her *longi* to dry them and sniffed hard, drawing the cage a little closer to the window. The sparrowhawk puffed his breast at the jolt, flexing his talons to retighten his grip. With slow and careful movements so as not to make him startle, she rolled her cuff from her wrist and reached out, and then quick as the snares she had set in the forest, she snatched her fingers suddenly shut on his fragile neck.

'Don't struggle, little precious,' she whispered as she dragged him from the cage. The lilt of fear in her own voice struck her. 'Don't fight me.'

The bird shrieked and thrust the hook of his beak at her.

Thuza stiffened her grip, laying him back in her small, scarred hand and scooping the last of the paste she had made from the saucer on the table. Opium seeds, cayenne and richly perfumed clove oil clumped to her fingertip, slate-black and sticky, and she forced her nail through the crack of the bird's mouth and prized it open. She smeared the mixture on his rough, pink gums and pushed her knuckle into his throat, rubbing until she felt a stubborn gulp and swallow. She glanced outside again, feeling nervous. The vultures were watching, she thought. They were waiting. *They knew*. There hadn't been this many in months.

She shivered at the thought and at the freshness of the morning. It was the end of September and the rains were abating, and it wouldn't take long for the sun to fully rise, to sear through the haze that shrouded the mountains and settle on the valley a steaming, heavy mass. She breathed deeply, her stare lingering on the end of her pathway where it snaked inside the trees. Earlier, she had watched from the same window as the monks filed down the steep, rocky slope in long, neat lines. Half hidden as they weaved through the dense tangle of firs and bamboo, their robes were invisible against the darkness and moonlight struck the curves of their freshly razored scalps and the metal of their alms bowls so they seemed to drift through in the air like spirits. Their chants had coaxed her awake before sunrise and for a moment she had lain still, suspended in the last blissful instants of her sleep by nothing more than a spider's silver thread. Then the fear had sliced back to her consciousness, sharp as a knife blade, and dropped her into the day ahead. She should have felt excited, she knew.

She had worked so hard for so many years and everything was poised on the cusp of where it should be. There were just two more tasks – so small and so simple – and all she had longed for would then become true. Her mouth went dry. Everything about her life would change if she held her nerve and kept to her plan, but though she had tried to focus on this clearly, her fear had formed a metal cage around her. She didn't yet dare to set her hopes free.

Thuza glanced outside again, baring her teeth to the vultures and hissing, steadying her breath. She saw the monks walk the same route from the mountains to the town every morning, though they chose not to notice her. She understood why. Her house had once been grander than any in the valley, but it was old now, too big and expensive for her to maintain, and the two-storey teakwood frame leaned towards the forest until it was almost swallowed by the folds of the land. One hundred years old, it was left from the days when the British ruled Burma, the jinxed bequest to her family from a manager at one of Mogok's biggest ruby mines. Over the years, the Tatmadaw had seized every other British building that Thuza could think of, but they'd always left her home alone. It was bad luck, they said. Too much had gone on there. She could have it. Item by item, her family had lost almost everything from the time of the British, either sold for food or burnt to keep out the winter ice, and now, the giant rooms were cold and empty. The windows were smashed. In the shade of the forest, it never quite dried, and creamy-white mould streaked the dark wood, inside and out. Thuza didn't mind though. For all that had happened, she was glad to still be here. More than anywhere, she felt the presence of her parents and their love and encouragement, and it put her at ease, being close to the mountains. This was her home. She could never leave here. She'd be nothing without it. Her back to the wall, she liked to think, so the town could never sneak up.

There was a curl of wind outside, rustling the leaves, and a spider started along the window frame and then froze, watching her, light snagged on the hairs of his body and his thick legs, like dew on grass, sparkling him. Thuza stared and he weighed her for a moment before starting again in a hurried, high-kneed sprint to the broken glass at the corner of the windowsill, then a sideways skip, and a look and he was gone. She wriggled in her seat and tried to ignore her stomach's groan. She hadn't eaten breakfast and instead the nerves were filling her, churning inside. Biting her lips together, she pushed the feeling away and steeled her concentration. Food wasn't deserved until she was done.

In her hand, the sparrowhawk had slackened, and she looked down and loosened her grip, testing him. The bird's neck lolled back so she laid the limp body on the table and smoothed his feathers with the side of her hand. She had kept this bird until last on purpose. He was only a baby, with downy tufts still clinging to his haunches and peeping out from beneath his wings, but he was bigger than the others and the mottled brown and white stripes that stretched across his muscular breast were beautiful and sleek. The look in his eye had been so defiant that she couldn't help but smile. From beneath her finger, a steady heartbeat kicked. She grabbed the spool of cotton from where it was waiting, snapping a strand and running it along the length of her tongue. The drugs wouldn't keep him sleeping for long. Briefly, she glanced at the mirror on the wall, first to check the doorway behind, then at her reflection. Some days, she swore the fork in her tongue grew sharper and deeper. As if it knew and wanted to steel her, it was always the days she had most work to do. She dragged the cotton through the long split of fleshy pink, smoothing the frayed end with a skilful coil of the pointed tips and threading the needle. Like water in oil, her bright blue eyes stood out in the half-light, immiscibly shrill and out of place on her dark-brown skin.

She cast her attention back down to the table, lacing through the skin above and below the sparrowhawk's eye, tugging just enough to draw the lid closed, one glistening eye and then the other. It was important to do this properly, she knew, so that not a shard of light could spit in. Then when the drugs wore off, the bird wouldn't panic. He would think it was night and go back to sleep. He wouldn't make a sound or struggle and give her away. Her mother and father had made sure she learnt that. She tied the last knot in the corner of his eye and broke the hanging thread around her finger. The sparrowhawk's head lifted momentarily and then dropped to the table with a fragile thud. She tied another thread around his beak and then picked him up and nudged him into the last plastic tube. Then, she opened her satchel and slotted the bird in beside the rest of her drugged, disabled bounty.

'*Thuuuuuza!*'

From beyond the door to the back room, a mattress spring creaked with the strain of shifting weight. Cursing, Thuza dragged herself from the table.

Her nanna's voice came again, moaning. 'Where are you, Thuza Win?'

Thuza unlocked the door, covering her mouth with her sleeve to stop from retching and holding back an answer. Inside, the old woman had rolled from her bed and was sprawled on the floor, her limbs twitching and a pool of urine glinting on the wood as it slowly spread. Her thin arm reached out towards Thuza's footsteps. The look in her eye was half pleading, half rage.

'Bring me my pipe, Thuza Win,' she whispered, stretching out to her more keenly. 'I need my pipe.'

Thuza picked up the tray from the dresser. 'Can't you see I'm doing it?'

Her nanna stayed with her head on the floor, but her stare jerked impatiently as Thuza crouched just beyond her reach and unwrapped the pipe, the lamp, the bicycle spoke and the jar of tacky brown opium. Thuza peeled a rock in half and skewered it, lighting the lamp and holding the drugs above the flame to soften it, and a line of spittle rolled from the bone of her nanna's chin. Snakelike, the old woman wriggled and grasped for the pipe. Two feet of broad, straight bamboo, it was light for Thuza, but its weight was unwieldy in her nanna's hand. Thuza grabbed it back, moulding the rock into the walls of the earthenware bowl that hung from its shaft, then she pieced the hollow with the spoke and turned the pipe above the flame so the opium simmered. She held it steady to her nanna's lips.

Her nanna drew a breath until her eyelids fluttered. A cloud of smoke hissed out through her nose. 'Another.'

Thuza licked her fingers and snuffed out the lamp. 'There isn't any left.'

'I saw it.'

Thuza stood up and placed the tray back on the dresser, dropping the remaining half-lump of opium into the jar and screwing the lid shut. There were two full rocks already in the glass — enough to last for the rest of the week if Thuza took care. Her back to the room, she opened the top drawer and hid the drugs and the tray inside.

'I can see what you're doing,' said her nanna. 'Do you think I can't reach them?'

Thuza tucked the box of matches from the tray into her pocket. 'You can't light the lamp.'

Her nanna belted her palm to the floor. 'You *Naga-ma*, Thuza Win. You slippery serpent!'

Thuza winced like the spoke had pricked her. More and more, her grandmother was judging her as coolly as the town did. The spikes of her temper were making her cruel. She stepped to the top of the mattress to avoid the puddle of urine and hooked her hands beneath her nanna's arms, dragging her back up more roughly than she needed. Her nanna tried to clasp the string of Thuza's *longi*, but Thuza shifted and slapped back her wrist.

'You should eat something,' she said, without looking at her. With her foot, she shoved last night's bowl of untouched crackers closer to the bed.

'Give me my medicine, Thuza Win, you torturer!'

Thuza scrambled for the key around her neck and hurried from the room, locking the door, darting back towards the window and snatching up her satchel. Through the wall, her grandmother swore and sobbed and spat, and Thuza mouthed a prayer to the forest to protect her, and then she slipped on her sandals and rushed from the house.

The walk to Mogok town took almost an hour and Thuza was more than halfway when she thought of the trapdoor. With the time she had wasted already, she couldn't turn back. Her nanna had distracted her, the whining old jackel, and she'd forgotten to see whether the hatch was still locked. Of course, she knew that it would be. It was never left open if it wasn't in use, but checking again before she went out had become an obsession. Beneath the trees, the path was steep and dark, and a sudden, distant explosion set the crows shrieking around her. She jumped and fumbled in her satchel for a cheroot, glancing behind. The blast could have come from the ruby mines. Now that the rains were done, the miners would be lighting dynamite to drain the flood waters and clear the shafts. It could also have been from the rebels, she thought, as she looked back again and struck at her matchstick. The fighting was closer than ever before. Time was short. It was getting much worse.

She quickened her walk and pinned her stare to her feet, treading lightly and scanning the earth ahead for any signs of disturbance, any new, suspicious mound of leaves or hint of metal that might betray a landmine. She was always careful, staying to the paths she had worn herself and away from the rebels' routes in and out of the town, but the rumours and her vigilance still made her check afresh each day. Around her, the insects sang, urging her on. She drew on her cheroot and hummed a song back to them, as much to drown the pounding of doubt in her head as anything else. It had taken her a while, but Thuza had learnt to love her forest home. So much had changed since her parents were taken, but the trees remained the same. Despite the whims of the seasons, the shifting of the shadows and the colours throughout the day, the forest was a constant, as vast and powerful as the day she was born. It was same as the years when her parents had roamed it with her, and every moment since she'd been on her own. When all else around her had been a landslide, the forest was an ally, tall and proud. There was something about knowing that the heaving teakwood trees surrounded her on every swell and eddy of the earth for a hundred miles or more that made her stand taller too. The red soil, damp and supple beneath her feet, absorbing her footsteps, their shape and their sound, made her feel hidden. The relief of the shade let her ease her mind and think, and she was indebted to the caves and their secret treasures, beautiful and dangerous, alive with the spirits. From whatever way she looked at it, the forest had become her most treasured companion. It kept her free and it kept her safe.

Thuza was never such a fool as to believe that the forest was solely loyal to her, however. Its allegiances were troublesome, strained at the seams. She glanced behind again, stumbling over a tangle of raised roots, scanning through the trees and pulling hard on the cheroot in her hand. For all she under- stood the peculiarities of the mountains, the people within the forest around her were an unknowable force. On her every side, Shan State was hostile. The trees teemed with insurgent army fighters. They were swinging in hammocks, cooking by campfires, polishing rifles, biding their time. There were more now – wherever she turned but concealed beyond the limits of her vision – than even the day that they first took Kyaw. Throughout the town, the whispers were that a battle was coming, one larger and more ferocious than they'd ever seen before. For weeks, the market had been running low on water and tins of soup as families filled their cupboards, stocking up. Mothers scolded their children from the streets long before the sun had dropped, and security around the gem mines was as thick and determined as Thuza had ever witnessed. More than ever, Mogok was on edge.

Thuza had watched the soldiers amass with a practical interest, but she didn't spare as much time worrying about the war as the rest of the town. Far inside the forest, her home would be safe from the bullets and fires, and it made little difference to her who it was that had control. Neither the rebels nor the Tatmadaw would be as just, honourable or forgiving as they promised. For Thuza, the sole care was that nothing now stopped her. There was too much at stake to allow disruption. The threat of attack only made her more focused. She was sprinting against the days and hours. More than anything, she would need to be quick.

This was the thought that had been playing on her mind for weeks now, goading her beyond the extremes of what she felt sure about. Making her do things that she hadn't done before. She finished her cheroot and snuffed the butt into the trunk of a rubber tree before raising her walk to almost a run. The forest was thinning, but she was still high on the slopes above the town, and a ransacked landscape of vast open gem pits and a chalky maze of alleys and dishevelled, low-rise shacks was appearing below. In gossiping clusters, they clung to the lips of the mud-filled craters and along the river's silver brim.

She hoicked her bag a little tighter to her side. Today was no different, she thought, her heart racing. She could do this. The risks had been weighed and the prize was pure gold. A thin white mist skulled across the rooftops, and her eyes scanned them, then checked along the barren, unpaved roads that stretched from the town's rim towards the lawless borders of Thailand and Laos in the east and China to the north. She could hear the rumbling convoys of trucks as they carried their granite, marble, guns and drugs along the rutted tarmac, see them juddering onwards like insects and the smoke that rose as they laboured up the hills or freewheeled down. The smell of the dust and the dynamite from the mines was swilling over her, making her breathing feel slow and tiring, and the valley seemed cast in shades of muted green and grey. There was some farmland below, just a few flattened squares of paddy concealed within the hazy depths of the morning, but it struggled to grow amid the decimated land. Sharp-boned cattle drove slowly through the seedlings and an ibis circled above the lake, searching for fish that didn't exist. Since the Tatmadaw had begun using cyanide to leech the gold from the ground, the rivers and lakes had emptied of life and nobody stopped to fill their urns. Still, women waded along the banks, thigh-high in the muddy brown water and digging sand to sell for building, aware of the poison but with no choice to make. There were barricades across the roads behind them, checkpoints on the corners and banners above them with block-printed threats, and the bustle of the town was growing beneath, busy but silent, the flow of strained life.

Thuza emerged from the last of the forest's shelter, watching the people below and shivering with the new breeze, running her hands along her arms to smooth the prickle of her skin. The gravel path crunched beneath her hurried footsteps. Had she looked at Mogok and known nothing more than her eyes told her, she would never have believed that the rebels could fight so fiercely for such an ugly, lonely land. That was the truest fact about Mogok though: *secrets*. How life appeared might be a deception. Her beauty lay beneath her crust.

As it was, everyone knew there was no reason ever to come to the valley, let alone fight, except for the gems. It took little more than a scratch to her surface to see that Mogok was glowing. She was Rubyland. Thuza knew that gemstones had been mined here for a thousand years or more, since as far into the past as any story stretched. Their history was so riddled with myth and conflict that it was hard for anyone to know what was true, but one thing that Thuza knew for certain was that for as long as rubies had been desired, blood had been spilled. As much as Mogok was Rubyland, she was also a frontier. For every stone that found its way to royalty, a hundred lowly souls had been in chase, desperate to better their miserable lot. There were once so many gems in the valley it was said that if you looked up, you could see the crows overhead with rubies clamped in their claws having mistaken them for meat and plucked them from the earth. There were fewer stones now.

Every mine and every miner was owned by the Tatmadaw, but each inhabitant of the unhappy district still had that same destructive dream. Neighbour against neighbour throughout the valley, men squabbled for the land. As slowly and slyly as age crept upon them, they all became cheats, liars, thieves and informers, murderers, arsonists, gangmen and smugglers. After each rainy season downpour, the streets would suddenly be crowded with people, all finding jobs to do and journeys to take that would otherwise never have crossed their minds. They wandered through the alleys with their heads crooked down, scanning for splinters of sluiced-up treasure, because rich as it seemed, Mogok could not afford to be proud.

As soon as Thuza entered the town, she felt the muscles in her body tighten. She never felt as welcome here as in the trees. Though the warmth of the morning was rising, the mile-high peak of Spider Mountain cast a shadow through the streets, and the breeze was hissing through the alleyways around her, whipping up the chalk. She glanced towards the sun as it seared through the cloud. She would never normally cut through the bazaar, choosing instead to stick to the backstreets, but she was running late and she didn't have much time. Annoyed at herself for letting it happen, she turned left and headed towards the central square. The approach streets were crowded. Ageing Shan hawkers lined the kerbs, selling opium seed cakes and cheroots, Shan snacks with *nagpi* and peanuts, and *thanaka* roots, and rice and peas.

A military jeep crawled past with a broken taillight, and her chest seized and she glanced away from the soldiers' prying stares and dipped beneath the low-slung awning and between the stalls, feeling nervous. There were tables selling pickaxes, shovels and sifters, bamboo *byôn* baskets and ropes, cheap diamond polishing powder, and oils, scales and red Indian dyes. She passed the apotheca's stall, catching her breath on the heavy scents of aniseed and caraway, ginger and anise.

As she moved, she could feel the eyes watching, peering onto her from behind their stalls, dark and glossy in the dimness beneath the awnings, making her heart sprint. She was sure the voices dropped as she passed. The thump of the generators was beating in her head, and the smell of their petrol was making her nauseous, and she found that she was rushing, pushing past the meandering buyers, desperate to escape from the stifling tracts. She gagged at the blood on the ground by the butcher's table, shoving aside a small boy and bursting from the market into the open sun. She gasped and clung to her satchel, looking back just in time to see the boy's mother shoot her a stare and gather the child into her legs.

'*Naga-ma*,' the woman hissed, scowling.

Thuza bit her lip and rushed away, the memory of her nanna's insult scolding her anew. She didn't care when the town called her a serpent, but it hurt when her own family spat at her in the same way. Long before the world knew that Mogok was the Valley of the Rubies, it had been the Valley of the *Nagas* instead. In the forest's biggest, blackest caves, those vast, slick-skinned, long-clawed beasts had lived, tails beating the earth as they dozed there, licking their teeth and guarding their gems. Their ghosts still slept in the mountains. Everyone knew. They had stayed long after their dense flesh rotted, summoning the spirits to punish any soul who dared to venture into the forest to steal their rubies or disturb their slumber.

Thuza gripped her satchel tighter across her breast and sniffed hard, wiping her nose. It had been so long since she'd gotten her title that she couldn't remember the first person from the town who had said it, but she'd sworn at that instant to take it from him, and she made it her own – there to protect her – holding it close and helping it grow. If the town were afraid of her blue eyes and her forked tongue, it could never be a bad thing. They wouldn't risk crossing her. They would keep from her way. Sometimes, she almost believed the whispers. A serpent was as much as she deserved to be anyway, after how she had betrayed her own family. Perhaps that was why her nanna was so cruel to her. The old woman knew that Thuza was plagued.

She turned again, emerging onto the long, straight road that led from the town to the Lashio-bound highway. In the distance, the checkpoint was looming and already Thuza could see that the guards had spotted her. She spat a curse at the ground and gripped the strap of her satchel across her chest. She recognised the boys on duty today, though she didn't know their names. One was a Mogok boy, not an import like most of the other checkpoint soldiers, but he was Burman too, not Shan like she was. Though he was buck-toothed, gangly and nervous-looking, little more than thirteen perhaps, she doubted he'd miss a chance to put her in her place. She had heard that the other boy had a brash southern accent. He must have been a few years older, with paler, smoother skin and a shrewd, diamond-hard glint to his city-boy stare. She wished they were older. Men not children. The young ones scared her more than the men did. The Tatmadaw were their only family and it made them rash and unpredictable. She understood what it meant to be vulnerable. They had more to prove to them. More to lose.

Thuza arranged her eyes straight ahead and steely, and drew in a long, slow, steadying breath. The city boy was watching her. He had recognised her too. She would need to stay calm. Above the checkpoint, a row of charms was hanging from a rope that stretched across the road like a gateway. She swallowed the lump from the back of her throat. Her great-grandmother's dagger was lynched in the centre, its tip knifing downwards, rocking in the breeze.

'Hey!' The city boy called to his friend as Thuza came nearer. He was leaning against the barrier that blocked the road, picking his teeth and eyeing her coolly. 'The serpent's back.'

The buck-toothed boy was inside the checkpoint's shelter and he leapt up and scurried outside at the shout. 'Stop there, little blue-eyed serpent,' he barked, holding up his hand. He had unslung his rifle from his shoulder and was jabbing it towards her.

Thuza stopped in the middle of the road. She was less than ten yards from the booth, but could feel the boy's hostility broiling through his stare. '*Mingala-ba*,' she replied, bowing her head. 'May auspiciousness be upon you.'

The soldier wrinkled his nose and looked back at the city boy where he leant on the barrier, then crept a few wary paces towards her, the barrel of his rifle wobbling in the direction of her feet. 'Are you leaving the town again?' he asked, suspicious. It seemed less an enquiry than a vaguely aimed threat. 'We've heard you've been out three times this week.'

'I'm allowed to leave, aren't I?'

'You're allowed if we say you are. What's in the bag?'

'Just birds.'

'Birds again?' he glanced back again and then brandished his hand at her. 'What on earth do you do with all these feathered rats?'

'She eats them,' said the city boy, standing from the barrier and sauntering toward them. He spat on the tarmac and looked her slowly up and down. 'I heard she stashes them in a cave in the forest until winter and then guzzles them – bones, beaks and claws and all. Like a real *naga*.' He made an enormous crunching sound and slapped buck-tooth's shoulder. The boy giggled nervously.

The wind gasped and Thuza cast her stare briefly upwards. The dagger was circling above the boy's head. It was the only real weapon that was strung at the checkpoint. All the others had been carved by the soothsayers – rifles, blades, bows and arrows – and slung on the town's threshold to warn any passing evil away. She sucked her lips and swallowed drily. There might have been a few people left in Mogok who remembered how it got there, but not many, she supposed. She doubted the checkpoint boys knew what happened; that the officer who cut her tongue had hung it there as a warning. It would remind the town to respect him, said the whispers, and act as a talisman. For a while the sight of it might have shaken the town into compliance, if any more fear was needed to do so, but now it was Thuza's reminder and curse – and her curse alone. Not that it mattered. The truth was always a secret in Burma. Rumours were as powerful as rubies. She flicked her tongue against the back of her teeth. *That's right*, she thought. *I am the Naga-ma. I am stronger than you. I'm faster. I'm smarter. I could crunch you up too, in one giant bite.* She clenched her jaw. 'I sell them,' she said, standing straighter, hardening her stare against the city boy.

The soldier frowned. 'To who?'

'The farmers in Lashio. They catch the rodents.'

'You take your birds all the way to Lashio?' The boy looked sceptical. He crept a few more yards forward and prodded her thigh with his rifle. 'Let me look.'

Thuza flicked her bag open. The crests of speckled heads lined up in their tubes for him.

'There are lots today,' he said, peering in. 'A serpent's feast. Did you know you can't take birds from the forest without government permission?'

She nodded.

'Then why don't you lie to us?'

'You're clever. You'd check.'

The city boy paused and clawed the back of his neck, looking at his friend, who shifted on his feet, then shrugged.

'Alright,' he said to Thuza, holding out his hand. 'Eighty kyat to pass.'

Thuza breathed a small, invisible, relieved sigh and dug to the bottom of the satchel, and the soldiers watched greedily as she pulled out a little pile of folded banknotes.

Buck-tooth grinned as she passed them the money, suddenly

bolder. 'We'd let you go for less, you know, if you gave us a flick of your serpent's tongue,' he said, and he grabbed his crotch and thrust at her.

The city boy smirked, taking the bundle of money from Thuza and rolling his thumb through the tatty black edge. 'You're a braver man than me, brother, unbuckling your belt for a serpent like her. She's a whore as well as a bandit, you know. All Shan girls are the same. Whores, bandits and traitors to Burma.'

Buck-tooth laughed, but his head was shaking. 'Her mother might have been a night-owl, but this Thuza Win isn't. She doesn't leave the forest for long enough to let a man sniff at her. By the spirits, I've never seen a dog sniff at her. Who'd dare? I bet she's as white as a prayer flag if you peeled off her knickers.'

Thuza screwed her hands into fists inside her pockets and tried to quiet the hiss of hot breath as it flew from her nose. She didn't need men. She didn't need anyone from the town to be her friend. She had done just fine until now, hadn't she? She was happy on her own. She was safe on her own. Not anyone at all. Not for anything. Not ever.

The city boy tucked Thuza's money into his pocket and stepped aside. Thuza scurried forward and ducked beneath the barrier.

'Why do you go to all this trouble just for birds, Thuza Win?' he called down the street as she began to stride away. 'Do they not have hawks of their own in Lashio?'

Thuza shook her head, but she didn't turn round. 'The Mogok ones are fiercer. They catch more mice.'

She hitched up her satchel and kept walking forward, her

heart madly pounding, still staring ahead. As she reached the dogleg, she stole a glance back. The soldiers had slipped inside the booth and were no longer watching. She followed the road as it curved to the left, out of sight of the checkpoint completely, and then she darted from the path.

Hidden in the scrub, the truck was waiting. The engine was off, but clearly still hot, and the bonnet steamed from where it had cut through the cool, moist trees.

'You're late,' said the driver.

Thuza didn't answer as she climbed into the cab. Before she had managed to pull the door shut, he had started the engine and she grabbed the dashboard as the truck hurled itself across the rocky undergrowth and through the tangled forest maze. They arrived at the clearing in less than ten minutes and the driver reached across her lap and shoved the door open, pushing her out. He jumped from the truck beside her, pulling her up and dragging her to a small bamboo building a few feet away.

'You're late,' said a man sat at a table in the middle of the room.

'She knows,' replied the driver.

Thuza tore free from his grasp and threw herself into a chair. She took off her satchel and thrust it down, ripping open the clasp and pulling out the biggest, fattest sparrowhawk – the one she had saved as her favourite before. She yanked the bird from its tube and he thrashed his wings and growled through his tethered beak, and she tucked his body beneath her fingers and held him tightly in just one hand. With her other, she flicked her penknife from her pocket and in one swift movement she split the hawk's belly, dug her fingers into the warm, wet flesh, and pulled out a fistful of small, rough red rubies. She shoved them into her mouth and sucked the stones clean, then spat them into her palm and held them out to the man sitting opposite. They glistened in her hand like seeds of ripe pomegranate.

He rifled through them with a fingertip and selected the largest gem, examining its pallor against the grey window light. 'How many birds?'

'Five,' replied Thuza.

He slipped the ruby into his own mouth, then rolled it to his cheek and stared Thuza in the eye. The best ones were cold and hard when you touched them with your tongue.

'Not bad,' he said at last. 'I'll take them.'

He nodded to the driver who reached inside his jacket, pulled out a wad of cash and handed it to her. She counted it quickly and slipped it away, then pulled the remaining birds from her satchel, laying them on the table in their tubes, one by one. She finished and looked at the man across from her, shifting nervously in her chair. He hadn't moved, but was watching her carefully. She would usually leave now. Perhaps he'd forgotten. She didn't know what he wanted her to do. She waited for as long as she could bear the silence, her hands tucked beneath her thighs and her shoulders hunched, holding his stare until the moment she was sure he wasn't going to do it, then he cracked the slyest, softest smile and pushed his chair from the table, bending down. There was a box by his feet, a not large one but heavy-looking, and he lifted it onto the wood and peeled up the lid.

Thuza swallowed, staring down. She had known it would

be dangerous, but she hadn't foreseen this. The box was filled with bricks, sixteen at a quick count. They were creamy-white and clay-like in consistency, wrapped in clear plastic as though they were nothing more than big blocks of soap. She didn't need to have seen any before to know that they were explosives. She didn't move. They looked so harmless, so completely innocuous, but their value was enough to banish her past. It made her heart flutter at the thought of it. She was so nearly finished. All she needed to do was deliver them and collect her payment, and she would double almost a decade of savings from smuggling tiny rubies. Everything she had done since the day her parents were taken had built to this moment. She could use the money to travel to Insein Prison. More than five hundred miles south of Mogok in Rangoon, Insein was the country's biggest jailhouse — and by far the most notorious — but in Burma, anything could be bought with money and nerve. There she could bribe her parents free. With the rumours in the town that a battle was coming, she didn't dare wait any longer. That's why now, why her patience had splintered, why she had to take the extra risk.

She was perfectly prepared though. She had planned with such care. The routes to take were plotted in her mind, the trucks to stow away on picked. She had stockpiled water and food for her nanna and put it in a box in the corner of her room. The old woman would be sick and seething without her medicine, but Thuza would bolt the door and she'd already bought the wood to board up the windows, so she couldn't escape and at least she'd be safe. She wouldn't be alone for long, regardless. A week, perhaps. Two. Only long enough for

64

Thuza to search out the men who'd could unlock the jail cells and discover the values to tease out their keys. So many years before, she had formed this plan to keep herself breathing, and if she held her strength, it would all have been worth it. Her life could go back to the way it had been when she was little and happy. She could say she was sorry for losing the map and her great-grandmother's dagger, and beg her parents' forgiveness, and not be terrified and not be alone.

She gulped again, summoning her focus, and picked up the first solid brick and placed it into her satchel. Her hands were shaking. The dealer was watching her. He slipped an envelope across the table.

'You take them here. Meet this man. He'll give you your money. No questions.'

Thuza took up the envelope and tore along the top seam, tipping the note contained into her hand. She held it open, just long enough to read the name that was printed across the pale-pink paper in light, fuzzy pencil, then snapped it shut again and stuffed it inside her satchel, feeling her heart shoot spears through her body and trying to keep her face from betraying her, trying her best to stem the shock. The Thai. Of all the people she had expected to be sent to, she hadn't considered that it might be him. He was the most infamous arms dealer in Shan State and they had met before, more often than she cared for. The rumours said he was a hundred and fifty years old, and he'd lived that long on nothing but snake bile. Though she knew it wasn't true, she could see where it came from, and the tales left a shadow that made him more than simply human. With his gold teeth, staunch black stare and blistering indifference, he could menace a man without anything but a look. She licked the back of her teeth and looked to the window, longing to run from the bamboo hut, away from the men that watched her, and hide in the forest with a cheroot, and wrack her mind for what she could do. The Thai would recognise her. As if there hadn't been enough danger already. Not that she was surprised he was up to this too. She'd have guessed as much if she stopped and thought.

The dealer was staring at her. 'Is there a problem, Thuza Win?'

She shook her head.

He leaned back, still staring. The hint of a smile sat behind his calm expression. 'Why are you doing this? I'm curious. When you come to me with your rubies, I know what to expect. Good quality, fair price, sealed lips. I understand how you think about gems, Thuza Win. But when you asked about this . . . when you wanted . . . *work*? I was wary. I'm grateful of course – I can't be seen to do these things myself – but I wasn't sure I'd be wise to trust you. What is it that's making you take such a risk?'

Thuza shoved the next brick into her bag, turning away from him. She felt her heart jolt. She busied herself with her stacking, avoiding his eye.

'Is your brother still with the rebels? They'll be furious if they find out what you've done. They'll punish him.'

'I'm only a courier.'

'Don't fool yourself. You've betrayed the rebels. You're working for the Tatmadaw.'

'I'm not hurting anyone.'

'Whatever lets your conscience sleep.'

She stacked the last of the explosives into her bag and fastened it shut, still not looking at him.

He clapped his hands together and grinned, then slapped the table. 'You're braver than I gave you credit for, Little Serpent. If nothing else, you've got some mettle.'

She flipped the bag shut, standing up and looking to the driver. 'We're finished. Take me home.'

The dealer shrugged and nodded, and the driver stood too and lumbered towards the door, keys jangling. Thuza followed him, her head feeling woozy. *Step one finished*, she thought, and her heart gave a skip-step. *I've only got one more to go.*

THREE

Than rocked back in his chair, his boots on the desk and licking his fingers. Crumbs of flaky yellow *palata* spotted the breast of his officer's uniform and he peered down and frowned. The bread had been good – still warm and sticky with egg when the girl had delivered it – but it dripped with grease from where it was fried and it might leave a stain. He brushed the crumbs away, and the pack of kittens that circled his feet paused momentarily, before looking up. He'd have to tell Marlar to stop being lazy and wash the shirt quick, he thought as he heaved himself forward and plucked another brown paper package from the morning's stack. *For Aye Zaw*, the handwriting said in smudgy blue ink. He couldn't remember which one Aye Zaw was, but the girl who had left the box was a beauty, with shiny black hair to her waist and a bosom like a pillow, so Aye was a lucky bastard, whatever. Than ripped open the package and tossed the paper in the direction of the rubbish bin. Inside, he found three green apples and a bag of pre-packed tofu crackers. He selected the largest, least bruised fruit and rubbed it along the length of his thigh before taking a bite, then he clamped the apple between his teeth and tugged open the crackers, emptying them on the floor by his seat. The kittens leapt in and crunched at them greedily. Two dozen skinny prisoners glared from the overcrowded cell behind his back.

Than rather liked it when the jailhouse was busy. Aside from the fact he ate much better breakfasts and enjoyed the parade of wives and daughters that brought the food for their men each day, it was a far easier task to supervise criminals that were already locked up than to catch any new ones. Of all the duties he had in Mogok District, this was clearly the best. He didn't much like overseeing the mines (too many thieves to keep an eye on), and he didn't like manning the outposts (too risky), and he didn't like recruitment (too many tiresome, sobbing mothers). What he did like, however, was strolling a few hundred yards along Mogok's main street from his home to the station and sitting quietly, warm and safe. Sometimes, he would come to the jail on his day off too, just for the peace of it. He preferred to listen to the mutterings of the prisoners than the squabbles of his youngest children and his nagging wife. Perhaps when he was promoted, he'd ask to keep his jail-house duties. He was due a promotion. He'd done everything that his superiors said he needed to. His day was coming soon. In his bones, he could feel it.

Across the desk, Min was sitting quietly, concentrating on his notes. A history book was open in front of him, its musty odour rising from the lightly mouldering pages, and he ran his finger along the line of text and tapped the rubber of his pencil on his teeth. He often came here too when his homework needed finishing. The boy was seventeen now, his black hair thick and scruffy and his face lightly pocked by the remnants of pimples and doughy with the last traces of childhood, but his limbs were as long and lean as if he were fully grown. He reached the bottom of the page he was reading and mumbled to himself as a thought formed behind his eyes, then clicked his fingers and scribbled into his jotter with a slight, private smile. Than smiled too, though Min wasn't looking. Whenever he saw his boy so engrossed in a task, he still felt the same excitement and pride as the day the soothsayer had chosen his name. Min Soe Khaing was born on a Tuesday, which made him a lion; an honourable leader, powerful and strong. It was the ninth day in August and the number nine foretold of good luck and long-lasting prosperity. August – the eight month – commanded respect. Together, Than had been told as he shivered with eagerness, these factors would make his son a man to admire and fear in equal measure. The stars had marked him auspicious at birth. Than had no doubt that Min was destined to be great.

He grabbed a second apple and rolled it across the desk. 'Have some breakfast,' he said, jabbing his finger and nodding at the fruit. 'An officer's boy must be strong if he's to be an officer one day too.'

Min looked up, catching the apple, but his eyes darted briefly to the cell beyond Than's shoulder. His expression twitched and he shook his head, placing it down beside his textbook and returning to his work. 'No thanks, Dad.'

Than felt his grin crisp and he glanced back at the prisoners, all squatting down, silent and scowling. He knew what was on his son's mind. For all Min's talents, his mood sometimes turned soft. He snatched his feet from the desk and threw his weight forward, brandishing his own half-eaten apple in the air around Min's face.

'Listen, boy,' he said, tipping up his son's chin with a stern flick of his finger. He lowered his voice, partly instruction, partly threat. 'Don't let them stop you. If you're going to join the Tatmadaw, you're going to need to stiffen that spine. It's a soldier's prerogative. You'll get yourself into far more trouble if you don't take the fruit. One: the prisoners will think you're a pushover. You pass an apple through those bars today and when you go to pass one tomorrow, they'll snap your arm off, clean above the wrist. Two: your commanders will think you're a woman. Do you know what happens to women, boy? They're slow and weak and they don't think straight. They get themselves killed or captured and they run their mouths at the whiff of danger. The generals can't risk loose lips in the ranks so they'll send you to the front and let the enemy kill you before you have the chance to give anything away. Three: your brothers will think you're a snitch. Nobody wants to bunk next to an honest man – trust me – and you can be sure as the day that no one will take a bullet for him. Four: you really will go fucking hungry. Do you understand? The Tatmadaw will watch your back, son, but only a fool doesn't watch his own back too. Besides, if you didn't take that apple, I would, and if I didn't take it, the next officer on duty would. Those dogs aren't getting it, whatever you do. Why should they?'

Min stared at his father, his teeth clamped around the pencil and expression uncertain, and then he glanced above Than's shoulder again. 'What are they here for?'

Than shrugged. 'Robbing. Brawling. Gossiping. Does it matter? Don't waste your time being interested in crooks. Interest leads to pity. Pity leads to weakness. Weakness leads

71

to defeat. Only men who tempt the fates end up behind bars. I know what you're thinking, but you shouldn't. There's no shame in being hated. You have to be important before you're hated. Being hated is a sign you've achieved something. Those men are envious. They want what I have . . . what you'll have one day if you do your duty right.' He craned further forward and held his son's stare, picking up the apple and pushing it into Min's hand, closing his fist around it. 'Now, self-preservation is a much smaller crime than insubordination, boy,' he whispered. 'Eat the fruit. That's an order.'

Min took a breath slightly deeper than he should have, and raised the apple in his hand to his lips. He cracked his father a self-conscious half-smile. Than gave him a nod of approval and slumped back, throwing his feet to where they'd started on the desk. Min really was a good boy, but things like thinking were going to cause him trouble. He dug his fingernail behind a molar and dragged out a fragment of waxy apple skin. In a way, he supposed the fault was his own. Min was too used to having things easy. When Than was a boy, there hadn't been time for thinking about anything but the next hot supper or somewhere safe to sleep for the night.

He finished the last bite of his apple and tossed the core into the bin. Nearly every one of the memories he had from before his own parents died was tattered now, ripped and frayed and strewn apart by the years that followed them, but he remembered being very small and sitting in the steamy heat of his family's kitchen, the plates not yet rinsed and the scents of fish curry still in the air. His father would have understood exactly what Than meant. He was a wise and honourable man, so proud of Burma's noble past. He had hung a picture of Aung San on their wall and in the evenings he would pull a book from the shelf and take turns with Than's mother to read. Than would tuck into her lap and peer at the pages, following the scribbles with his fingertip – like Min did – and listening in wonder as they thrilled him with accounts of the great general's courage and cunning in ridding his people of the British and Japanese, how he'd played both sides and encouraged their fighting, and wooed and outsmarted to set his people free.

Those childhood memories still coloured each of Than's many doubts and daydreams, though he rarely saw them as clearly as when he fretted for his son. Individuals must master their own fortunes, said Aung San. Fortitude, resilience and persistence were crucial. If a man had these, he'd hold such power, and when you had power, you were worthy and valued. Only with power could you ever be safe. Than's eyes drew themselves to the brown and white photograph on the hook beside the jailhouse's window, to Aung San's flawless military uniform and the quiet but certain determination to his stare, and the words struck him anew, like a hammer to a gong. Aung San had that rarest balance of *ana* and *anza*: the might to coerce but charisma men respected. Delicate and prized, it made him magnificent. His spirit transcended his death like no other. His influence survived in every wish and hope in Burma. He was as close to a god as any man could be.

A shudder rippled through Than's body, a different memory snaring him, far colder than his last. The dusk before his parents had died, little Than had pretended to be the great Aung San. No older than he was when he'd huddled in his kitchen, he had felt such desperation at the sight of his parents' wasting, at the hold of their sickness and how it had worsened, and the muddle of their mutterings and the glaze of their eyes. As the night thickened, he had searched the streets of Rangoon, begging for medicine at the clinics and temples, trying to be persistent – trying as hard as he could to have fortitude – only to be told there was nothing to do. When his parents were gone and Than was alone, he had slept in the kitchen, curled up with his books. Though he could barely read them, they still smelt of his parents. Their fingerprints were smudged at the edges of the ink. He had whispered to Aung San and said he was sorry. He had let his family down, completely and terribly. He had shamed the general too with his failure. Though he hadn't been aware until many years later, those were the days when his edges started blurring. His own existence and Burma's began merging. One became the other, gently. They were seeping together; his blood, her soil.

Than couldn't even begin to comprehend how his life would have turned out if the Tatmadaw hadn't been there to offer him shelter. When they picked him up from the streets of Rangoon, he was only just nine. That day, the Tatmadaw had become his new family; his mother, his father, his protector, his home. He looked at Min across the desk, still scrawling in his jotter, his forehead lined. It frustrated him that the boy struggled to see his own potential. He'd wave away his father's praise, dodging any remarks that Than made about joining the military, no matter how pointed, wittering instead about school and keeping at his studies, or moving to the capital to get a job in an office. He didn't understand the world like Than did. He clicked his tongue and drew his cheeks inwards. Min could be as great as Aung San was – and when Min was a star, Than would be a star too.

He pulled his beret from his head and spun it across the wood. 'Put this on,' he said, taking a mirror from the desk's top drawer. He slid it over also, grinning. 'Tell me how you feel.'

Min gave a sigh, almost invisibly, and arranged the too-big beret on his dense-haired head. He picked up the mirror and wiped it with his sleeve before staring down. 'I don't know,' he said, frowning. He looked at Than and shrugged. 'I feel important?'

Than clapped his hands and laughed. 'That's right, you do. It's going to be great, Min. As soon as you join the Tatmadaw, we're on the fast road to success. You'll be up through the ranks quicker than a cheetah and I'll get my promotion, and we'll earn enough to move the family to the lakeside and we won't be bothered by all the town's frauds and tricksters, and everyone in Mogok will know we've arrived.'

'You can't be sure of that, Dad,' said Min. 'I've never fought before. I might not be good at it.'

'A boy as smart and strong as you? Nonsense. The generals will respect you, Min. They'll respect us both. A father and son renewing their allegiance to cause and country . . . Besides, you *are* important. The universe has said so. You, my son, are destined to be a grander legend than the ancient Burmese kings.'

A snort of laughter erupted from the cells.

Than's fists clenched and his stare spun to the prisoners behind. He stood up and scowled through the bars, keeping his distance at more than an arm-reach and scanning the sunken-cheeked and sullen faces for a culprit, feeling the hatred pulse through his arteries but aware of their numbers and the hatred they cast back at him, and glad for the deadlocks that kept them apart. He cracked his knuckles and tapped the gun in his holster with a fingertip, grimacing at them in his strongest, meanest, silent warning, then turned away and sat back at the desk. A scrape of phlegm followed from the lining of someone's throat and splattered on the floor. He gritted his teeth and pretended not to hear. The other reason that Than liked the jailhouse was that it was the only place in Mogok where all the Shan mongrels were firmly contained. It was almost twenty-five years since the Tatmadaw had assigned him to the district, but it didn't feel like home. It never would. The mountain people were too different from how he was. All the filthy minorities were. The lowlands of Burma were where the real Burmans lived, the smooth, beautiful core of the country that spread through her middle and kept her alive like a beating heart. That was where he felt comfortable. Not here. Here, the air was too thin for proper breathing. Wherever he went, he was always being studied. There was always someone scheming, always some new and obscene rebel plot afoot to destroy the Union of Burma and steal her mountain riches as their own. The constant vigilance gave him a headache. Mogok had been quiet for the last few full moons now and the quiet was more unnerving than landmines and gunshots. It was only a matter of time before the next attack came. The whispers said it was coming soon.

A frown settled over Than and he picked up his unfinished District Report, flicking to find the last completed page. He'd write those idiot prisoners up as insurgents, the lot of them, not pickpockets or boozers or whatever they really were. He'd make sure they got a fitting punishment. That would teach them for being so rude. He reached across the desk and snatched Min's pencil from his hand.

'How do you spell *resplendent,* boy?' he said, dabbing his tongue on the tip of the lead. He slammed Min's textbook and jotter shut and shoved them aside, then turned his file and pushed it towards his son, pointing at the page. Min pulled Than's beret from his head and smoothed his hair, reading. Mouthing the words he had written from memory, Than puffed out his chest and waited.

The Tatmadaw forces continue to be resplendent in their ongoing efforts to vanquish all traitorous foes in the Mogok valley, thanks entirely to the critical intelligence gained and acted upon by key officer staff . . .

Min let out a breathy smile and looked at Than. He rubbed his chin. 'A bit obvious, isn't it?'

Than shrugged and shook his head. 'Authoritative, I thought. Anyway, what's the point of being the man who writes the reports if I don't get the perks?'

He tapped the page again and Min took back the pencil and rubbed away the letters, rewriting them neatly.

'There's another error, Dad,' he said, returning to his own books. 'At the bottom. It says there were fifty-four prisoners in the jail at last headcount. You did it this morning. There were only twenty-six.'

The corner of Than's lips curled to a smile and he pushed his finger to his temple. 'The rest are in here.'

Min looked up, his face focused suddenly, concerned. He glanced to the cells and then set his attention on his father, dropping his voice. 'You're fixing the figures?'

'I'm being strategic.'

'The general will be furious if he finds out. You'll be hauled in.'

The slope of Than's lips steepened and he reached out and took hold of Min's collar, tugging him around the desk to stand at his side. His son was a good half-foot taller than he was, but he pulled him down and hooked his shoulders beneath his arm. In his chest, he felt his heartbeat quicken. He loved any chance to share a secret with his boy. It wouldn't be long before Min was writing the reports instead of him. It was time he learnt how the Tatmadaw worked. He leafed through the file's pages with his free hand, stopping near the end, then patted Min's ribcage and grinned, pointing down.

'See this list?' he said quietly. 'This is the number of men arrested in Mogok this week. This is how many were done for thieving, how many turned up late for work at the gem mines, how many were stopped without their papers and how many were caught with poppy seeds in their carts, and this . . .' He drew a wispy grey line beneath the largest figure. 'This is the only number the general cares about.'

Insurgents prevented from terrorist activity, they read in silent unison. *Forty-three*.

Min stared at the page for longer than he needed. Than waited patiently, the thrill of it brewing, and then Min looked up as if he almost had a question, but his lips were puckered and he didn't form words. Than nodded, winking. He drew Min tighter in.

'That's right, boy,' he said, and his grin was still growing. 'The general doesn't want to know that we only caught a mango rustler at the market. He wants to be able to telephone Rangoon and tell them that he's cleaning Mogok up, that he's burnt the opium fields and caught the dealers and stopped their cash before it reached the rebels and they bought their guns and fired a single shot. He doesn't want to have to tell Rangoon that he's not achieved a thing. He doesn't give a monkey's cock what's really happening. That's how a sprinkling of cleverness can help us. Every smart soldier knows not to embarrass his superiors. The reports are just the start of it. You play up the good, you play down the bad. You let them know they're doing well. Bad news is like sewage. You can't pass it on without getting a little of the stink on your skin. If it has to be done, leave it to another man. It's all about payback, Min. Understand? A good solider is loyal. That's all you need to know in Burma. Whatever anyone tells you, the only way to be a success is by being loyal to the man above you. Whoever he is and whatever he does, put him first and in time you'll get what's due.' He moved his face closer to Min's and prodded his finger into his chest. 'Say it, Min. *Loyalty*.'

Min wriggled in the vice of his arm, his eyes darting to the floor. 'Loyalty,' he muttered.

Than released him and shoved him back from the desk abruptly, straightening and stamping his boot on the concrete, saluting. 'Louder, Private!'

79

Min laughed, stumbling back and rearranging his collar, catching his breath as if he'd been holding it and slumping to his seat. 'I'm loyal, Dad. Alright? I'm loyal.'

Than tapped his head with his finger again and threw Min the last green apple from the desk. 'You see what I mean?' he said. 'It's paid off already. *Strategic*.'

Min tucked the apple into his schoolbag and Than slapped his shoulder as he sat down too. He loved that look the boy got in his eye when he said something clever – just the littlest hint of amusement and awe. Whatever wormy troubles were nibbling Than's innards, having Min on his side made them feel OK. He scratched his nose and scanned through the pages of the file again, checking the work he had done one last time. The report needed to be extra special this time. He heard that the general had not been pleased last month. Than could not afford to disappoint him again. Not when he was so close to securing that promotion. It was just beyond the tips of his reach. A good district performance and Min joining up was all that was needed to nudge it to his grip. His stare flittered to Aung San's photo on the wall.

'Are you ready for the recruiters, Min?' he said, his hands clasped together. He felt suddenly anxious. He wanted it done.

Min frowned and rubbed the nape of his neck, his eyes wandering away from Than's and across the desk. 'Mum still isn't happy.'

'Your mother's never happy. What did she say?'

'Come on, Dad. What did you tell me about snitching?'

'I told you something about loyalty too.'

The boy groaned, sinking back in his seat. 'She didn't say

anything. She was only talking about university again. About me going to Rangoon.'

Than winced and held up his hand as if to block the stony insult's hit. He shook his head dismissively. 'Forget that. You need to put those brains of yours somewhere they'll matter.'

'She might be right though,' said Min. 'I looked into it. I could go to university and sign up afterwards. There'd be benefits. I wouldn't have to join as a private on the meat rack. I could start as an officer straight away.'

Than took a short, sharp breath so he didn't scold him and ground his jaw, calming down. Marlar was a gabby old hen. Relentless. He shook his head again, more firmly.

'Let's just stick to things as we know them, eh, son?' he said, trying to sound cheerful. He stretched forward and squeezed his son's shoulders, holding the boy's stare and supressing the twitch of his nerves. 'We'll be a mighty team, you and me. We've planned it. The army life, Min. There's no better on earth.'

Min gave a weak smile and Than smiled too, though he felt too tense to be sure it looked warm. He kept tightly squeezing until his message bled in. He meant what he'd said. He meant it more than anything. What was any life worth as a civilian? Even as a child Than had known the comparison; how the soldiers had potatoes with meat for supper and he had nothing but stale blue bread. There was no life more secure. More vital. It wasn't only the new job that he wanted so badly. It was what the job showed him: he wasn't alone. Min was bound as his son to help him. The thought of his weakness, of him failing again like before, made Than panic, like a trap had his ankle and he struggled and struggled as it stiffened its grip. The Tatmadaw had become so much more than his family. He was them and they were Burma, and with all of his spirit he would work to please them, to defeat all her enemies and keep her together, because if Burma dissolved, he would surely die too.

He shuddered at the thought and released Min, gathering himself, fussing to tidy the papers on his desk, then looked at the clock. It was almost ten thirty. An idea appeared in his mind at that moment. He licked his thumb and found the last page of the report, pausing before signing his name at the bottom, and then snapped the file shut and shoved back his chair. Min was pretending to work but watching, and Than kicked the leg of his chair and grabbed his schoolbag from the floor, ramming it into his lap.

'Headquarters are expecting the report by noontime,' he said as he plucked up the file, tucked it deep inside his armpit and marched towards the jailhouse door. 'Run home and get your blazer and I'll meet you at the river bridge. We'll deliver it together. Don't tell your mum.'

FOUR

Michael sprinted down the broad, straight runway of Sule Pagoda Road, sweat streaming from his brow and into his eyes, and the shock of the blast still pealing in his ears. At the end of the street, the Rangoon River was running high, swollen with the season's rain and ragged beneath the swarm of boats that carried their teak, silt and granite towards the Irrawaddy or the Andaman Sea. The sky was a dour, pregnant grey and the wind was whipping the palms to a frenzy, but the air was broiling hot and humid. It throttled his breathing and his body felt ablaze.

Turning onto Strand Road and tearing along the pavement, the embassy building came into Michael's view. The street was emptier than usual, as was the waterfront and every alley and thoroughfare he had raced through since he'd fled the chaos of Bahan Road. The vendors had closed their peanut carts and hurried them away. A few boyish soldiers paced on the corners and along the promenade, wide-eyed with nerves and smoking incessantly, glancing at each other and talking into their walkie-talkies. There were rarely any cars on the roads of Rangoon, but the buses, bicycles and rickshaws were missing now too, and in place of their constant whistle he could hear the distant sirens still wailing, and feel their resonance through the soles of his feet.

Inside the embassy's foyer, the guards leapt up at the sight of Michael and the crash of the teakwood doors as he threw them apart. His footsteps struck the polished parquet flooring, echoing in the vast space as he ripped across it and thundered up the staircase, ignoring the calls of his name, their concern.

'Is my father here?' he shouted to no one in particular.

The first-floor corridor was narrow and dingy, and office doors were cracking open to enquire about the commotion, streaking the runner of worn carpet with gauzy light and foggy silhouettes, and he trampled over them, not breaking his stride. Horrified faces were peering at him, firing him questions, and he struggled to steady his vision through the haze.

Barrowman, his father's Second Secretary, grabbed hold of Michael's bicep and was trying to stop him from charging past, but Michael was stronger than the overfed diplomat, and he yanked himself free and seized the handle of his father's study door, shaking it hard, shoving at the wood. It was locked.

'Where is he, Barrowman?'

Barrowman shook his head, flattening his tacky, thinning quiff across his scalp. He was out of breath and his cheeks were ruddier than ever, the thread veins meshing across his face. 'I don't know, Mike. Jesus, what happened? You're bleeding.'

'I'm not.'

'Your clothes are drenched. Let me take you to the sick bay.'

'I need to find my father.'

'Michael?'

Michael turned and saw his father descending from the staircase at the far end of the landing. He was striding towards them, his expression grave.

'Dad!' Michael cried, stumbling to meet him. 'There was a bomb at Bahan Market. I was there. It was carnage!'

The ambassador nodded and wrapped a protective arm around Michael's shoulder, steering him towards the study. He could feel himself shaking and breathless too.

'I know,' said his father in his calmest voice. He glanced along the corridor and waved his staff back into their rooms, then unlocked the study door and ushered Michael and Barrowman inside. The study was cooler than the corridor had been, and less stuffy. The windows behind the desk were open and a squally breeze flitted through them, stirring the air, and Michael stole a breath and tried his best to control his nerves. His father placed his hands on his shoulders and stared at his face, searching him. Their tension was shared in the firmness of his grasp. 'Are you OK? We didn't know where you were. Downtown's in turmoil. The military are trying to lock it down. I've had the drivers looking for you. Your mother's a wreck with worry.'

Michael felt a new roll of sickness through his gut, and he shrugged his father away and slumped into the armchair by the bookcase. He sank his head into his hands. His mind was reeling. 'Sein was hurt,' he said, rubbing his face.

'Badly?'

'I don't know. I think so. He could hardly breathe. There weren't any ambulances, Dad. I put him in a car but I don't know where they took him.'

'Barrowman?' The ambassador turned and raised a finger to his secretary. 'Call the hospitals. Have them check for the boy. Try the Western General first. The number's in my drawer.'

Barrowman nodded and scuttled to the desk, opening the top drawer, pulling out a roller deck and leafing through. He plucked up the telephone's receiver, dragging the circular dial so it trilled. Michael watched him framed against the window, dust flashing through the grey light around him. One hand on his hip, Barrowman waited for a few long seconds before his lips creased and his nose wrinkled, and he tapped the cut-off and tried again. 'The line's busy, sir,' he said, placing it back down.

'Try the Eastern. Then Insein District.'

Barrowman found the numbers and dialled again, two more times, then shook his head, leaning heavily on the vast dark-wood desk. Thick streams of sweat were dribbling from his forehead, and he mopped them with a handkerchief and released a wheezy sigh. 'Half of Rangoon will be calling them, sir. We won't get through. We'd be better to visit. Starmer's delivering the sanitation proposal to the Aussies, but he left hours ago. He won't be much longer. I'll get him to take the car and do a round of the emergency rooms when he's back.'

The ambassador nodded. 'It's a good idea, Barrowman. Call the boy's father too. He might know something – and if he doesn't, he should. He's a professor at the university, isn't he Mike? Starmer can pick him up if he needs to. They can look together. Faculty of Mathematics, I think. The switchboard will put you through. I don't know his name.'

'Economics,' muttered Michael into his lap. 'He's a professor of Economics. Win Myint Cho.'

As he spoke, Michael heard a crack though his voice. The thought of Sein's parents not knowing what had happened to their son, or even where he was, of them not being able to sit at his bedside, struck Michael hard. His family were such gentle, generous people, so welcoming to Michael despite his foreignness and the risks that they faced for having him at their supper table. They had worked harder than any parents should have to, protecting their children, providing Sein and his younger brothers with the education that Michael took for granted at home, instilling ambition, forcing opportunities where they seemed impossible but were so dearly cherished, even though they amounted to barely a fragment of the ones Michael had within his reach. Imagining Sein's absence in their lives – in his own life – seized him for the first time since he'd held his friend's sagging body in his arms. Death was unthinkable, but here it was, teasing him. Sein's family would be broken if they lost him. His place as the eldest and most hopeful was unfillable. *You're all of our future, Sein Lay. We honour you.* He had heard them say it so often, so proudly. *When you succeed, all our souls shall be blessed.*

Michael took a deep, trembling breath and wiped his nose along his sleeve, trying not to cry. His father spotted him.

'Leave us please, will you, Barrowman?' he said, throwing a look to the door. 'Take the numbers. Get the third-floor girls to help if you need to. Come back when you find out something.'

Barrowman nodded again, gathered up the rollerdeck and its loose cards from the desk and left the room. Michael squeezed his eyes shut, listening to the latch click and Barrowman's brisk footsteps as they faded down the hall. Of course he had always been aware that his Burma wasn't real in the way that Sein lived it, but he hadn't expected her to shatter so abruptly, or so completely, before his eyes. Guilt was hot in his stomach, bubbling. He knew that despite his protestations and his pretence of compassion, the thrill of being here and being Sein's friend had in part been from the danger. How selfish he felt. How young and naïve.

His father was at the cabinet beside the window, a decanter in his hand and pouring a drink. In the cabinet's mirrored backboard, Michael caught his reflection. No wonder the embassy staff had stared. He was staring too, dazed and bewildered. Across his face, streaks of blood were smeared like war paint. His hair was grey and matted with dust. He looked like himself, but a hundred years older. The black of his eyes had become a well. He flicked his head and looked down at his clothes, as much shocked at what he had failed to notice about himself before as the sight itself. His shirt was ripped, stained darkest maroon, and the slick of colour that shouldn't have been there spread from his chest to his chinos below. He could smell himself suddenly too, like tarnished metal, the heat and the redness of Sein's insides mixing with the choking musk of concrete turned to powder, bitter burning plastic and smouldering wood.

His father dragged a chair from the beneath the desk and sat opposite Michael, passing him the glittering gold drink.

'We'll find him, Mikey,' he said, reaching forward and patting his son's knee. 'We'll make sure he gets the best care. I promise.'

Michael clutched the glass with both hands, frowning into it, dizzying himself with the fumes. 'I shouldn't have left him, Dad.'

'What else could you have done?'

'I don't know, but he was terrified. You should have seen how he looked at me. He couldn't speak, but I felt like he was begging me to fix it all for him, or to explain what had happened at least, and all I did was dump him in the boot of a passing car. I didn't even ask who the driver was. How do I know they've taken him to the hospital at all?'

'Of course they have.'

'I should have checked.'

'We're checking now.'

Michael's father nudged his chair forward, dropping his head to find Michael's eyes and pushing the glass of whisky to his lips. 'Listen, Mikey. I know you feel responsible for your friend, and lord knows you should do sometimes with the things you get up to, but this . . .' He shook his head. 'This isn't your fault.'

Michael shook his head too, feeling the tears forming again, the blockage choking in his throat. 'You don't know that,' he said, whispering. He looked up, his heart starting to sprint again, panicked by his thoughts. He was back in the bedlam of the Bahan Market courtyard, hearing the tyres of the motorbike shrieking, remembering the man with his blue-checked *longi*, feeling the burn of his scowl on his face. Guilt struck him, hard as a flint. He gripped the glass and his knuckles whitened. 'We saw the man who did it, Dad. Me and Sein. Before it happened. He looked right at me. The Tatmadaw were questioning him in an alley by the Lotus and I thought they were getting a bribe from a pickpocket or something, but they must have had a tip. They let him go though. Incompetent bloody imbeciles. I saw him again outside the shop. I swear it was him. What if he followed me, Dad? What if he targeted the teahouse because I was there? There's no better place to plant a bomb than where foreigners hang out, is there? The headlines. Coverage outside Burma. Get the British doing something.'

The ambassador's eyes narrowed. He flicked his head, staring. 'Don't be ridiculous. He can't have planned all that from a look.'

'Perhaps he'd seen us before. I'm there all the time, aren't I . . . by the market? Someone could have reported me. You know how the rebels think.'

'I know they have bigger things to worry about than you.'

'Then maybe it was karma, for all the times I've put Sein at risk.'

'You don't believe in karma, Michael. Besides, if it was, that blast would have hit you, not Sein, wouldn't it? I've told you. It was terrible luck what happened and equally terrible luck that you were there to experience it, but that's all it was, son. You're not to blame. It was luck in the same way it was that you were born with white skin in a drizzle-soaked Western democracy and that Sein was born here, under a scorching sun and smack in the centre of a wicked civil war. It was luck that you escaped today and he didn't.'

'But it wasn't luck though, was it, Dad? It was deliberate. Someone did this. Someone *chose* to do this.'

Michael stood up, staggering to the window and wrapping his hands around the open frame, resting his weight on it, straining outside, gulping at the air. He couldn't hear the sirens any more but his stomach still felt sick. Below him, Strand

Road had started to busy again. The buses were running. A handful of fishermen had returned to untangle their nets on the river's shore. On a bench opposite, an elderly man was having his shoes shined, reading the paper while the buffer-boy worked his rag in a blur of cream chamois and blue-black dye. A vendor was wheeling her cart along the promenade where he'd strolled so often with his mother on Sundays, and the bell that hung from the front of her barrel-shaped vehicle was calling to the street like a sparrow at dawn. Michael watched her amble towards the jetty, soup-smoke trailing behind and dogs trotting after her in a line of three. Already, the city had regrouped. Moved on. He lifted the collar of his shirt and buried his nose inside it, holding his breath.

The ambassador was standing at his side.

'Sein didn't deserve what happened to him, Dad,' Michael muttered, wrapping his arms around himself.

His father nodded, but a shrug escaped from him too, just a slight, mournful heave of his chest that gave him away. 'Burma's a warzone, son,' he said, quietly. 'We don't think of it sometimes, swanning between the safety of the embassy and the residence as we do, but she is. We watch selectively, hoping, pretending to help, wanting to be charmed by her exoticness and beauty, but we're on the outside, Mike. We can't ever fully understand or support her. It's a sorry thing to think of. The world has picked a fight with Burma for a thousand years of history. Every time her bones start setting, someone comes and breaks them anew. All these rebels, coming from the north and the west and the mountains and the borders, wielding their weapons and demanding spoils that the Tatmadaw won't ever give them . . . They're nothing new. What hope did Sein have to live the life he wanted, even if this hadn't happened? What hope does anyone have here with the Tatmadaw in charge? And heavens, I know what you're thinking. It's impossible to feel anything but completely bloody useless. No matter what we do, there's nothing we can change. This isn't the first bomb that they've planted in the city. Though I wish it would be, it won't be the last.'

'How can you stand it, Dad?'

'I've no choice. I can't intervene.'

Michael looked up, pleading. 'We should try though, shouldn't we? There must be something we can do.'

The ambassador pushed his glasses to his forehead and pinched his eyes between his fingers, the way that he did when his patience was failing, when something beyond his control had him snared. He let out a sigh, so long and drawn out that his shoulders rose then fell. 'I've tried and I've tried, Mike. This country's not for fixing. I'm afraid some problems don't have a solution, and this isn't the time to be cursing the rebels. This is the time to save your wishes for your friend.' He wandered back to the table slowly, and picked up the whisky glass and held it out to Michael. 'Now drink that drink, son, and let's get you home.'

FIVE

'What the fuck is this, Thuza Win?'

Thuza scraped the last crust of hawk's blood from beneath her fingernail and stared at her brother, disbelieving. They were hidden in the scrub to the rear of the Buddhist temple, out of sight and safe from the reproach of the Sangha by the high white wall and leafy tamarinds. The town was on the far side of the large, sprawling complex, safely distant beyond the labyrinth of alleyways, dormitories and miniature pagodas, and the mountains formed a shield behind them, with Taung-me the highest, steepest peak. The wind was light but turning in circles and the bells atop the stupas were swinging. Ribboned clouds streaked across a luminous sky and hot sunlight arrowed through the raggedy leaves. Chimes sang from inside the temple, and from the treetops a fever bird called breathlessly back to them, whistling a warning without respite. The sharp, sour remnants of pickled cabbage were just traceable in the air, lingering from the kitchens and the monks' lunchtime spread.

Kyaw was crouching on the ground beside an old British tombstone. It was cracked and overgrown with weeds and moss, and he balanced himself with his shoulder to it as he sorted through the pile of crumpled money that Thuza had given him, flattening each note against his knee and examining it closely. The look on his face was as though she had chucked him burnt paper.

'What's the matter?' Thuza asked.

Kyaw batted a mosquito from the air around his face and glared up meanly. 'You said you'd sold five birds. That means you must have had twenty carats of rubies. Where's the rest of my money?'

'There's more than four hundred kyat there, Kyaw.'

'It should have been more.'

'I got the best price I could. The stones aren't as clear as they used to be – or as big. I've already sold the good ones.'

Kyaw creased the neatened stack of notes in half and jammed them into his pocket. He stood up and dried his dribbling nose with the back of his hand. 'Then you'll have to get more.'

Thuza bit her lip. She didn't have time for this. He was looking ill again, she thought, and more irritable than ever. He had lost another rotten black tooth and the sores on his skin were freshly weeping. His eyes had withdrawn deeper behind his brow, and their whites were riddled with coarse red veins. The clothes on his back stank of sodden earth. Kyaw was twenty-six now, but almost a decade of living in makeshift jungle camps, exposed to the extremes of the Mogok mountain weather, and the hunger and vigilance, had taken its toll. He looked as old and tired as any man could. Thuza was tired too though and this wasn't her fault. His sickness was not her problem.

She buried her hands inside her pockets in the hope he wouldn't see her shake and glared at the ground to hide her scowl. As she had walked here, only the thought that this would be the last time he could threaten her had kept her feet moving. Tomorrow, when she'd delivered the package that the dealer had given her, she would have enough money to do what she needed. She wouldn't be bound to listen to Kyaw. A cautious, fragile hopefulness had borne her through the forest; the knowledge that her days of hunting gems were behind her, that the pound of her heart – the terror of discovery that trailed her everywhere and that each new moment could be her last – would soon be nothing but a fading shadow as she strode away and raised her head.

A part of her had considered not coming at all this morning. She had wanted to stay at home by the trapdoor, sitting on the rug so that no one could find it, counting away the moments that were left before she could rid herself of the sixteen dead-weight C4 blocks that lay inside. It didn't matter that no one but her knew what was hidden there or what she meant to do with it – or that no one stopped by her house ever anyway – she still felt a searing desire to guard them, like they might disappear and leave her with nothing, or somehow cry out and give her away. The dealer's words had reverberated in her skull all night. *You've betrayed the rebels. You're working for the Tatmadaw. They'll punish your brother. They'll punish you too.* At first she had been furious that he had the nerve to accuse her of disloyalty. How could she betray the rebels when nothing she did for them was through her own free will? She didn't even know what the Tatmadaw meant to use the explosives for. It was true what she'd said. She was a courier. Nothing more. She told herself that she didn't care. The doubt had seeped in though, slow and determined. It filtered through her slumber, a light, constant nag. For all that Kyaw bullied her, she didn't want to harm him. Though her motives were justified and she'd make the same choices a thousand times over, she didn't want him to know what she'd done. In the end, this guilt was what forced her to meet him. It was always the guilt. Always the memories. She didn't know if she would ever feel rid of it. She had worked so hard through the years to protect him, but all he seemed to say was *more*.

She felt her shoulders tremble and gathered herself, staring at her brother and shaking her head firmly, feeling impatience twitch in her core. Now she was here, she didn't want to prolong things. She didn't feel sure she was acting normally. He would read her unease and know she was treacherous. She wanted to leave and sprint back home.

'I can't get any more rubies, Kyaw,' she muttered, as solidly as she could. 'It's too dangerous. It's not how it used to be.' *It's not like when you were with me*, she wanted to say.

Kyaw shrugged, pulling a scraggy, half-smoked cheroot from behind his ear and relighting it. 'Nothing is as it used to be, sister,' he said, blowing a scattering of ashy grey from the tip and then planting the butt between his splintered lips. 'We work with what we have.'

'You're not working though, Kyaw,' she said. 'I am, and it's too big a risk to continue. I'm done.' She paused and looked him over. 'Besides, I've bought you enough money this month to feed an entire company.'

'We don't need *rice*, Thuza,' said Kyaw, shooting her a withering glare. He was folding his hands restlessly together as though trying to wring out his thoughts through the cracked, calloused skin. 'We need bullets. I promised the officers that I'd contribute. They're expecting more than a sniff and a chit.'

'You shouldn't keep making promises like that, brother. You knew the gems wouldn't last forever.'

'And nor will the war. We're making progress.'

Thuza screwed up her face. 'I heard the explosions this morning. They were landmines, weren't they? They were close to the town.'

'Of course they were close.' Kyaw grabbed Thuza by the shoulders. His eyes were flickering, wild with impatience, a mix of excitement and rage. 'We're winning.'

Horseshit, thought Thuza, shrugging free of his grip. The war would never be won. She looked at Kyaw's hands, still twisting together, at the stains on his knuckles, the same scrawled midnight-blue tattoos as had marked the men that followed her when she was a girl, through Mogok's squares and markets when her parents were smugglers, and had struck her with such immutable fear. They had struck Kyaw with fear too back then, she knew, though he'd never admit it now. Try as she had done, again and again through the loneliness that followed, she could never understand why he'd chosen this life. Once her parents were taken, somehow the Fifteenth Division of the Shan State Army had become more of a family to him than she could manage to be herself, and despite how they snatched him, he had bound himself to them. It was fury, she suspected, and pride, more than love or respect. He hadn't stopped to consider what they stood for or how they meant to get things done. It was enough that they were opposed to the

Tatmadaw. She stared at him, feeling suddenly angry. He had chosen to leave her – and for what? Not justice. How foolish he was. How short-sighted and childish. She wouldn't give him a kyat more than she needed to.

'I'm sorry, brother,' she said. 'I can't help you.'

'My commanders will reprimand me, Thuza. Do you want that?'

'It's your doing, not mine.'

He paused suddenly and scratched his head. 'Did you stop buying drugs for the ghoul, like I told you?'

Thuza spat at the dust by his feet. As much as her grandmother provoked her with her begging hands and ungrateful dependence, Thuza could never abandon her. 'Don't call her that.'

'She's dead already, sister. Don't waste our money.'

She shook her head again. 'She needs it.'

'I need it more. Hand it over.'

'I've spent it already,' she lied.

'Then give me the money you've saved for the monk.'

'Fuck off.'

Kyaw dived forward and stole Thuza's satchel, barging her to the ground so she couldn't grab it back. He turned the bag out and collected up the few small notes she had left at the bottom, and then he seized her arm and yanked her towards him, thrusting her against the crooked tombstone and turning out her pockets too. Thuza stayed quiet and stared stubbornly ahead. Just let him take it, she thought. Ride it out. She'd left the money in her bag on purpose; she'd known he would search her. Her heart thudded against the spiral of banknotes that were tucked in the pocket she had stitched so carefully to the inside of her blouse. She had enough money rolled up and hidden to buy the last of the opium that her grandmother needed before she left for Rangoon, and to make the payment she'd promised to Zawtika. There would be enough left as well to buy some potatoes to make a fresh curry that would last her the week and, afterwards, it wouldn't matter. She thought again of her hidden explosives and the scrap of paper that was tucked between them. The face of the Thai flashed up in her mind. A shudder spat through her.

Kyaw crammed the money into his pocket and Thuza snatched her wrist back from him, gathering up her satchel and slinging it over her shoulder, turning away. As if he had seen inside her thoughts, he skipped ahead of her through the trees, blocking her way.

'What's the matter, Thuza Win? Where are you going?'

'Home.'

'We're not finished.'

'I've given you everything I have.'

She stepped aside, ducking to the left of a bamboo thicket, trying to dodge past. Again Kyaw shifted to obstruct her escape. Her heart was sinking like a stone through water. She knew what was coming. Usually it caught her off guard, but not this time. It was why she had dreaded coming here with such strength today, she realised. No other reason came anywhere close. She had known since yesterday that she wouldn't avoid it, though she'd hoped and wished and begged the spirits that she could.

Kyaw spread his hands on the bamboo either side of him,

webbing her in. 'There's a job I need you to do, Thuza Win,' he whispered, leaning forward. He grinned, and a thread of betel-red saliva trickled from the corner of his mouth.

Thuza shook her head and stumbled back from him, wincing. 'No, Kyaw.'

'It's not a choice.'

'Get someone else.'

'There's no time. I've told my general it's covered.'

'I won't do it.'

'You don't know what it is.'

Thuza stared at him, trying to contain her rising terror, choking back the rebuke that was wedged in her throat. Her brother was right. She shouldn't know what it was that he would ask her. If she said that she did, it would give her away. She had known from the instant that she opened the dealer's note, however, and saw the name of the Thai glaring back. If he'd come to the district, he'd be here for the rebels as well as the Tatmadaw. Killing two birds. Make the trip more lucrative. They'd have made a deal. They'd demand that she help.

'What do you want, Kyaw?' she whispered. The weight of despair in her chest was a rock.

Kyaw's grin widened. 'The Thai's in town,' he said, creeping further towards her, enjoying the conspiracy and her discomfort. 'He's arranging a shipment of munitions to be delivered for the Fifteenth Division. It's a big one. We've got plans. You're going to meet him tomorrow night. The usual place. The payment's been made, but we need to know the date and the location of the drop. Have our men ready. You'll get the details and report back to me, OK?'

Thuza shook her head again. She couldn't do it. Not this time. Without reprieve since she'd opened the letter, her mind had tortured her with visions of what might happen if the Thai recognised her. He would, of course. She knew for sure. In the last few years, she must have carried over fifty messages for the rebels, and her bright blue eyes and serpent's tongue were far too distinctive to let her slip through his memory. He had called her *Naga-ma*, like everyone else. If it wasn't for Kyaw, she could have told him she'd defected, invented some story or another about loving the Tatmadaw, and then hoped and hoped he'd believe it was true. What hope was there now though? She was trapped, like her birds. If it weren't so terrible, she might have laughed at it. What was she supposed to do, exactly? Trade her explosives on behalf of the Tatmadaw, then spin her chair and barter for the rebels?

Her pulse pounded in her head, deafening. She couldn't see a way to escape. What if the Thai told the rebels what she was doing? They would hunt her down. And Kyaw? It didn't bear thinking. Everything she had worked so hard for would be lost. Perhaps the Thai would understand though. He was a traitor too, after all, far worse than she was. Did the rebels know already? The Tatmadaw couldn't possibly know. If they did, he'd be quartered and strung from a tree. Perhaps she had leverage. Would she dare to use it? Or perhaps he'd have sympathy. Respect her bravery. Everyone does what they must to survive. But the Thai was rich. He was well above survival. It made her tremble, her heart start racing. It wouldn't matter which side he gave her up to. If the Thai muttered a word, she would never free her parents. If he chose to give her up, she was dead either way.

She shook her head again, more weakly, feeling the tears start to form in her eyes. She could see her parents' faces in the fog of her vision, pleading to her. There was too much at stake to run away from this. *Uncover a way to make it work.*

'Please don't force me, brother,' she whispered. 'He scares me.'

'Don't be weak.'

'You're not listening to me—'

'No, Thuza Win.' Kyaw's face blackened and he seized her by her throat and pushed her backwards suddenly, ramming her body into the thicket, pinning her. She stood on her tiptoes, scrabbling for some solidness of earth beneath her, gasping, grabbing at his wrist and uselessly straining to pull him off. He held his face just a breath from hers. On her cheek, she could feel the heat of his cheroot. 'You're not listening to me. I've told you before, haven't I? If you don't do as I say, I'll make certain the Tatmadaw finds out what you're up to, about all those precious rubies you've stashed away over the years and where you get you get them from, and then what will happen? Do you think they'll show sympathy, Little Serpent?'

He drew a deep breath and squeezed tighter for an instant before releasing her. She crumpled downwards, coughing at the rush of air, but he pulled her up and held her face in his rough, dirty hands. His skin smelt of mould and faintly sweet cordite.

'I don't want to threaten you, sister, but this is important. It isn't just about our parents any more. This is about the future of our people. Don't you understand? We all need to make sacrifices. You're not just being disloyal to me. You're being disloyal to the whole of Shan State. We're being exterminated. Is that what you want, Thuza Win . . . the death of your people? Is that what our parents would want?'

She pushed him away. 'Don't, Kyaw.'

It made Thuza furious when Kyaw spoke of their parents. He might have been doing this for them at the start – when the anger inside him had been as hot as a flame and he needed to fight, and he didn't care which direction – but she doubted they ever crossed his mind now, except when he wanted to bully her. She didn't doubt that he'd give her up though, if he thought that he had to. Though she didn't know how, she would need to find some other route to navigate this.

'Fine.' she hissed, scrambling up and dusting down her *longi* and blouse. 'I'll meet the Thai.'

Kyaw dusted her down too, adjusting her shirt awkwardly across her shoulders, nodding to himself, and then backed away. 'Tomorrow night,' he ordered, pointing. 'Eight o'clock. Don't be late.'

Thuza let out a groan, thin and beaten. 'I won't, Kyaw.'

'You better not. Then you're back here the next day with the details for me. Sunrise. Understand?'

She nodded.

'And don't forget the gem money you owe.'

★

Thuza pushed hard against a knobbled, thick tree trunk, holding her breath and stretching her limbs so tightly that her eyes and her head felt fuzzy, and her fury escaped from the bottom of her stomach, rumbling out like the growl of a bear. She dried her eyes, bitterly, moving away. She considered taking a minute to gather herself before walking around to the front of the temple, but realized it wouldn't matter how long she waited. She wouldn't be able to relax after that. She slipped her sandals from her feet and pressed her soles to the cool white tiles in the walkway entrance, willing herself to feel lighter and calm. The shade in here was different from the forest scrub, clean and fresh, but still without relief.

She took her time crossing the courtyard, glancing into each open-fronted building and along the network of empty passageways that laced between them, her eyes skipping over the red and white walls and bottle-green roofs, all edged in delicate fretwork gold and covered with dazzling fish-scales of glass. The image of a young Buddha stared out from every alcove. The statues weren't smiling, but they watched her pass with a look of serene acceptance, lavish garlands of frangipani draped around each slender neck. She let out a long breath. Here, she never normally minded what Kyaw or her grandmother or the women at the market or the checkpoint soldiers or anyone else in Mogok chucked at her. Inside these walls, she wasn't the *Naga-ma* or the smuggler or trapped by her brother. She was Thuza Win as she had been before. Every upward slope, sideways lurch and twist of her existence made a little more sense. As she looked at the Buddha, she knew that the long years of her life would pass no differently from the fleeting moments

Kyaw frisked her. She had to ride it out, she knew. Just ride it out. If she did her best and endured her fortune, her next life would be a more merciful gift. The temple had kept her going – its tranquillity and its faith in her – buoyed her whenever she felt heavy. This morning, with all she knew was about to happen and all she didn't yet know how to solve, she felt more grateful than she'd ever done to be here. The spirits were on her side for trying. They would watch her walk and keep her safe.

Sayadaw U Zawtika was at the East Gate of the temple grounds when Thuza found him. The old monk was sitting on the top step at the entrance to a pagoda, with a boy of eight or nine at his feet. The child was not in his robes, but was clearly a novice. He wore just underpants and a frown as Zawtika drew a shaving-blade across the crown of his small, pale head. They were almost done and locks of severed black hair clung to the boy's wet torso, arms and chubby brown cheeks. Zawtika smiled broadly and waved at Thuza's approach, passing the boy a towel and tapping his shoulder with permission to leave. The boy didn't waste a second in jumping up and scurrying away, and he rubbed his scalp, still pouting.

'*Mingala-ba*, Sayadaw,' said Thuza as she came to the steps. She pressed her palms together and bowed.

Zawtika heaved himself up to greet her. '*Mingala-ba*, Thuza Win,' he said, beaming. 'How wonderful to see you.'

'And you, Sayadaw. I'm sorry it's been so long.'

The monk flicked his hand. 'Oh, Thuza. You have enough weight on your shoulders without adding another stone relic like me.' He eased himself back down and beckoned for her to join him. 'Tell me, how are you?'

She bit back her tears, turning away. 'I'm OK.'

'You look tired. Are you eating well? I can never be sure when I see you. You're a little hummingbird.'

She nodded. 'I'm fine, Sayadaw. I promise. You don't have to worry.'

'I was told you were lurking in the forest again. In the foothills?'

'You have eyes in the clouds, Sayadaw.'

'Yes. And novices on the ground. Were you poaching again? I wish that you wouldn't.'

'I'm sorry, Sayadaw, but I have to. I can't make enough money doing anything else. The birds are all I have to sell.'

Thuza almost believed her own lie as it slipped from her lips. She always meant *rubies* when she said the word *birds,* and though she knew that her friend would forever be loyal, it could never be known who was listening in Burma, or what comment may pass to trip a man up without shred of intent. At any rate, it was good for Zawtika not to know the truth. There was only one real crime in Burma: to act against the Tatmadaw. It would make him her partner – an accomplice and target – and after all he had helped her to wade through her darkness, she couldn't do that.

'You need to be careful in the forests, Thuza Win,' said Zawtika. 'Nobody owns the law on that land. If the Tatmadaw catches you, they'll string you up for stealing, and if the rebels catch you . . .' He shook his head and exhaled a pained breath.

'I know, Sayadaw. I'm careful.'

'And the war's getting nearer to the town, you know. There

are whispers that the rebels are planning an attack on the old British outpost. They think if they take the land at the edge of the mines, the Tatmadaw is done for. The rest of Mogok will fall in days . . . and then the district. Such nonsense.'

'The temple will be safe, Sayadaw. The rebels won't trouble you.'

'It's not the temple I'm scared for, Thuza. What will Mogok do if the battles reach the town?' He paused. 'Have you seen your brother lately?'

Thuza shook her head, a new rush of anger and dread welling in her chest. She felt guiltier about this lie than the one for her rubies, but she couldn't bear to speak Kyaw's name. He'd been left outside the temple walls, in the scrub where he belonged. She didn't want to let him in here, to have him spoil the stillness and peace.

Zawtika scratched his chin and swayed a finger towards the mountains. 'Is he still in the forest?'

'I think so.'

He gave a worried, critical tut. 'I don't know how he keeps his strength. All the stories of sickness I've heard from beneath the trees. A man can only escape from the fever so often.' He frowned and bowed his head to catch Thuza's eye. 'You'd tell me, if you knew of his health, Thuza, wouldn't you?'

'Of course, Sayadaw.'

'I could get him medicine. Mercy, maybe a dose of penicillin and a night's soft rest would help him think straight. Kyaw was always such a headstrong child, but he left so little time for thinking. He doesn't have that spark of smart behind the eyes like you, my little serpent.' Zawtika leant in and winked at

Thuza affectionately. 'I wish he'd talked to me before he made his decision to stay with them.'

Thuza smiled back, just a dash. It was different when Zawtika called her Little Serpent. He was the one who had encouraged her to use it, to harness its spirit and let its power keep her safe. 'You couldn't have stopped him, Sayadaw,' she said, and she meant it. Kyaw was never a boy to be told.

'But I'd like to have tried. For you, Thuza Win, as much as for him.'

'It's so long ago, Sayadaw. Please forget it.'

'If you see him, tell him to visit me. He can come at night if he needs to. I'm always here to talk to. I'll keep him hidden.' The monk rubbed his face. 'Oh, you children,' he said, grinning at once and slapping his knee with his fragile hand. 'Such headaches you cause me. You're just like your parents were. And that nanna of yours. The very first time I met that woman . . . ha! She was a scoundrel. It feels like a thousand lifetimes ago. It was the first day I'd ever been to school. She was older than me. Much naughtier. Had me hauled before the headmaster for stealing orchids within ten minutes of my arrival. She'd taken them straight from the old man's garden and placed them on his desk before the morning class. Pink as the sunset, they were. I snorted so loudly that he thought it was me. Of course, your nanna was always as noble as a fir tree. She marched herself right into the headmaster's office and batted those beautiful sapphire eyes of hers and demanded I was pardoned. We both ended up with clipped red ears.' He laughed and looked to the clouds above him. 'Did you know that, Thuza Win?'

Thuza nodded, smiling sadly. Zawtika always like to talk about her nanna, though he never asked after her health any more. He had stopped a while ago, Thuza noticed, when her answers seemed to have too sharp of a prick. She wondered sometimes if they had loved each other before he joined the monkhood. Through the years, she had heard their meeting relived many times. She wasn't sure if it had been the first time, but she remembered watching from her kitchen window one afternoon when she was very small as her father and Kyaw returned from the market and stopped to pick a fistful of flowers at the top of her path. Zawtika had been visiting, sharing a saucer of *lahpet* with her nanna like he did so often, and they had all laughed so hard at the memory of how the headmaster had twisted the children's ears so they wriggled like fishes that their eyes had gone shiny and her mother had needed to find them a handkerchief to wipe them all dry. Kyaw had given the flowers to Thuza later. When she was sleeping, he had put them in a teacup beside her bed, and when she awoke, she had knotted them up in her thick black hair. It made her ache, to think of those days.

She clasped her hands together tighter. She was so close now, she almost didn't dare ask. 'Have you heard any news?'

The monk's expression fell. His eyes skirted the courtyard. A younger monk was sweeping the tiles on the furthest side of the yard, kicking the dust into the air with a stiff wooden broom and talking to a flower-girl who scampered round his feet. To one side, a woman was sitting on the steps and cradling her baby, her eyes closed and lips signing a prayer. On a rooftop, a stub-nosed monkey plucked seed pods from the overhanging branches, peeling them apart and sucking out their insides before dropping the shells to the tiles in a mess. No one was watching them. Zawtika lowered his voice.

'I've heard a little more than usual, Thuza Win. We managed to find a laundry girl who would speak to us. She says she saw your father at the well in the prison courtyard. The scars on his back were healing. He looked healthy.'

'Did she speak to him?'

'No. But she was sure it was him. She overheard the sentries talking.'

Thuza frowned.

'It's good news, Thuza – as good as we can hope for, anyway. He must have made friends with a guard at last, to be out of his cell.'

'And my mother?'

'The girl never saw her. She asked a few of the other laundry maids, but no one had news she could verify. She left the cheroots you sent with the postmaster and gave him our payment. With luck, your letters will get to her.'

It had taken Thuza from dawn until dusk to make those cheroots, rolling and re-rolling the tobacco into tighter and tighter coils until she was certain that no one would see the notes she had buried inside. They weren't letters really, just a few words scribbled in her tiniest print to let her parents know that she was well, that her grandmother was well, and that Kyaw was well. She said she hoped they were keeping safe and she'd see them soon. They'd been in the prison for almost nine years, but it was all she ever managed to write. They didn't need to know anything else.

'Is that all she found out?' said Thuza, feeling suddenly panicked. It was the same every time that she spoke about her parents, and more so today. A hot wind spread through her. To fail would be treason. Unthinkable. It whispered taunts that she might have forgotten things, and pawed at her doubt that it all might go wrong. She had felt so sure before that she'd done all the right things, that her eleven-year-old self had been clever, brave and triumphant, but still her best had not been good enough. What was to say it was different now?

Zawtika shook his head and smiled at her sadly. 'That's more than most people have been able to tell us, Thuza.'

'There are rumours of another cholera outbreak though, aren't there? Did she mention it?'

'Who told you that?'

'I heard it at the bazaar. Some porters were whispering about the cholera and lice. They say there's an epidemic.'

'The maid didn't mention anything like that.'

'But the Tatmadaw gets their porters straight from the jails, don't they? They'd know. I heard that inmates were made to stand in the yard too, and to stare at the sun for hours on end, even if they were old or ill, and if they moved an inch, the guards would set the dogs on them. I heard that some days, they aren't even given water, and they lie in their cells in the dark, like rats.'

'Please, Thuza Win. Stop.' Zawtika held up his hand, flinching. 'Don't torture us both with such terrible things.'

'But what if it's true?'

'Whether it's true or not, you can't control it, and you'll

never know so you mustn't ask. These rumours start with the government, Thuza. They want to make you fearful.'

Thuza bowed her head and fiddled with a button on her blouse, trying to stop her dejection from overflowing any more. Poor, tired Zawtika, she thought as she looked at him. He had worked so hard to track her parents down. It had taken the monk a year or more of hushed questions, risks and favours, but he never gave up. He was the one that had found they'd been taken to Insein Prison. Through the years, Zawtika and her rubies had been her two beloved lifelines, creeping her closer and closer to her future, but now her patience was worn paper thin. She looked at Zawtika again and felt a new pang of guilt. She could never have done this without him. It was Zawtika who had found Thuza too, that first terrible new dawn. She was where the Tatmadaw had left her, lying on the gravel path. It was a day before he came for alms and she'd bled so white she was almost dead. When Kyaw came home, he went straight back to the rebels. It was all he could think to do through his anger and fear. All the things that her brother should have done for her, Zawtika did instead. Every day he visited – for years. He brought her food and medicine. He talked to her, taught her reading and numbers when the schools wouldn't take her. He was there to comfort her when they found out about the baby: Thuza's younger sister, born in the prison, lifeless and blue. They had lit a candle on the altar to bless her. He let her cry at the foot of his robe.

It didn't seem fair that Thuza hadn't told him what she was doing, that she'd kept such a vast, important secret from her friend. He knew she'd been saving and that one day she hoped to travel to Rangoon, but there were so many reasons why she couldn't tell him how close she was now, or what she had to do to seal the deal. She had never dared to let him know the tasks the rebels made her undertake before, so to tell him that now she was working for the Tatmadaw as well . . . that beneath her house were hidden explosives? He'd be furious. And it wasn't any different from when her parents were taken. To tell Zawtika the truth was to put him in danger. She couldn't do it.

'I'm sorry, Sayadaw,' she said. 'I know you're doing the best that you can. It just all feels so distant. Little fragments of gossip that I never know are real. Do you think you can arrange for my parents to send a message back? I want to hear it from them that they're doing OK.'

Zawtika shifted on the step and smoothed his maroon robes over his thin knees, shaking his head sadly. 'Thuza,' he whispered. 'I know I haven't given you much. I wish I could do more, but it's just too dangerous. The guards watch too closely, and if your parents were caught with so much as a pen, they'd be sent to the gallows or hotbox for certain. We just can't ask them to take the risk.'

'We could pay the guards more money?' she said, though she knew it was almost pointless.

'It's finding anyone who will take it, Thuza. You know that.'

She picked at her fingernails and looked at the ground.

The monk sighed. 'OK, Thuza Win. Give me what you've got and I'll get the messengers to ask some more questions.'

Thuza pulled out the money she had hidden from her brother and handed it to Zawtika. 'There's a few kyat in there for the temple too.'

Zawtika peeled aside a couple of the notes and turned them over in his hand thoughtfully. 'Are you still going to Rangoon?' he asked her.

She felt herself blushing. Her eyes skipped downwards. 'Not yet. Nanna needs me.'

'Have you saved enough money, for when the time comes?'

She shook her head, not wanting to lie any more than she had to.

Zawtika paused and then placed the money back down by her side. 'You keep this,' he said, patting it gently. 'The temple has a hundred souls to look after it.'

She hesitated, and then took back the money, tucking it away. She wiped a small tear from the side of her eye.

The monk rubbed his bare head – just a sharp, brief flick – and he hitched up his robe and tidied it over his shoulder as though shrugging his body free of an unfriendly thought. 'I miss them too, Thuza,' he said, staring into the distance. 'But you mustn't lose hope. Remember your mother and father as they were, as you all were together, and how you will be again one day, I have no doubt. Stay strong, Little Serpent. You're doing a wonderful thing for your parents. When they come home and see it, they will be so proud.'

SIX

The Mogok Military Headquarters was on the outskirts of town. It was not a single building, but an entire street of ageing British mansions that perched officiously along the southern bank of Mogok Lake. At the junction where the highway split and its tributaries threaded away between the mountains, south-east to Lashio and south-west to Mandalay, it was the perfect place to watch for strangers creeping in through the town's back gate – and for the scores of foolhardy thieves that tried to steal their rubies away in the opposite direction.

Than strode purposefully, but his head was bent down. The road was broad and empty, treeless and bleak. It always made him feel slightly uneasy, and with the thoughts in his mind feeling stickier and heavier and hotter with every step that he'd walked from the jailhouse, his doubt and his queasiness were making him sway. The buildings around him were all owned by the Tatmadaw now, a few as residences for the highest-ranking officials and guests, but most as offices, war rooms or courts. A long, tall wall lined the length of each pavement to hide their dealings, pocked by bullet holes and with chalky stone cracks spidering from their impact, and it was topped with a coil of tarnished black razor wire. Speckled grey plaster crumbled from the brick, and only the sharp peaks of rooftops peered out from behind. Telegraph poles tilted from the fractured paving, knotted weeds at their bases and knotted wires at their tops, and they sparked and buzzed where threadbare ropes were lynching them up. There wasn't a civilian in sight; not a hawker on the kerb, nor a school-child, nor the spinning wheels of a passing bike. This was the quickest route from the city by far, but the shrewdest men took the long way.

Min touched his arm. They had barely spoken since leaving the jail. 'Are you alright, Dad?'

Than pulled a packet of cigarettes from his pocket and lit one quickly, drawing hard. He looked ahead at the enormous two-storey structure of white stone and dark brown teakwood, ringed in a garden of cracked concrete slabs. It had been the Old British Club once where Imperialists gathered to drink gin on their evenings off and sneer at the natives, and was by far the most imposing building of any around. It occupied the exact plot of land where the highway forked, and though the gates were guarded they were open wide and two rows of vast featureless windows squared up against the street. The general always sits at the head of the table, Than thought as he spied the large, lean frame of Bo Win striding along an internal corridor. He couldn't be sure if the sight was a blessing. When he'd sat in the safety of the jailhouse and his idea had struck him, he had mouthed a prayer to the spirits that he'd find the general waiting and welcoming, but now he was here he felt hasty and reckless.

He gnawed on his cigarette and the tip flared, then he glanced behind at the road that led away. He could leave, he thought, be in and out swiftly. Just ditch the report with the clerk as he usually would. No one would know what he'd planned. He shook his head, twitching. No. This time was for seizing. Today he could be the master of his fortune. He'd have courage and persistence and reap his reward.

He spun around and grabbed Min's shoulders, tugging at his blazer and brushing the lapels so it sat square and clean. 'Are you ready?' he said.

Min's brow creased. 'Ready for what, Dad? Why am I here?'

'Your speech!' cried Than. He prodded his son's chest. The child was being petulant. Of course he knew. 'Is it memorised?'

Min's face dropped. 'You want me to do it now?'

'There's no reason to wait.' He held out his cigarette.

Min paused and then took it from him, staring at the ground. He wiped his mouth with the back of his hand and then looked along the empty street, to the open gates at the head of the road. He shook his head, just slightly. 'Dad, I'm not sure about this. Do we have to see the general? Can't I just enrol with the recruiters in the town like everyone else?'

Than stepped in, shaking his head as well. 'You're not like everyone else, Min,' he whispered. He bunged the trembling cigarette stub between his son's pink lips and took hold of him tightly. He could understand that the boy was nervous. The sun was rising higher in the milky blue sky, singeing through the last of the morning's mist with hot, bright light, and they'd walked here fast and they were starting to sweat, and both of them knew that this moment was important, but he needed him calm and thinking straight. He stared into his eyes and nodded as reassuringly as he could. 'Do you trust me, son?'

Min brushed his fringe from his eyes and nodded.

Than nodded too. 'Alright. Then let's go.'

Than kept hold of Min's elbow as they walked along the street, though he couldn't have said who he did it for most. He had the feeling that the boy might have stumbled, or tried to turn and scarper. His own legs were feeling unstable too. The pitch of his gut was getting worse. He didn't feel guilty. He had no reason. Min would see this was in his best interest. All of his family would realise soon enough. He was doing this for them. For everyone's safety. Progress was necessary to protect Burma's Union. Protecting the Union protected them all. Min could keep up his studies in his own time if he wanted. If that's what was bothering him, no one would stop him. No one would care if he still read his books.

They walked side by side and Than flashed his ID to the privates who guarded the gate, ignoring their exchange of uncertain, timid glances, and then he darted up the front steps and strode inside. The corridor to the left, down which Bo Win had passed, was long and cool. Their footsteps echoed on the tiles and the thud of the fans twisting above like distant, looming helicopters filled Than with the sense that something was coming, some unseen foreboding, a battle creeping up. At the end of the hallway, the Operation Hall was waiting. For an instant, he lingered in the doorway. In the huge, high-ceilinged room, there was row upon row of flimsy wooden desks, every one piled with books and brown folders, and with uniformed officials working busily behind. The air vibrated with the tap of telegraph keys and murmured conversation. He gripped the file beneath his arm. General Bo Win was standing beside a table towards the back of the room, a telephone receiver clutched to his ear. He clocked Than's entry but didn't acknowledge him.

'Rangoon, again,' said Than, leaning towards Min and whispering. He gave a small, authoritative nod as though he knew for certain. In his chest, his heart was beating madly. The sight of the general always made him restless. At times he knew it was envy that drove him. Today he knew it was wholly from fear. Though he couldn't have been much older than Than was, the general's skin and his pride were much better preserved. He was tall and wiry with muscles strung together tighter than ship-rope, and it was the way he stood with his hand on his haunch and tapping his fingers that Than found the worst threat, and the slight iridescence to the green of his shirt that let you know it was always brand new. His eyes were deep-set and dark and narrow. They sat behind aviators that he'd shipped in from Thailand, and the lenses were tinted a light, glossy red. There was grit to his jaw that never quite eased and a slant to his shoulders that couldn't be copied; he pushed them down and held them back in the way that only came to men with a lifetime of worth.

Than's mouth was dry but he licked his lips anyway as he guided Min through the sprawl of desks. They stood to attention before Bo Win, just far enough away that with the noise of the room, they wouldn't intrude. Not that the general appeared to be saying much. He was nodding, however, scribbling on a notepad and grunting what sounded like it might be agreement. As always, the lines of annoyance that scored his forehead were deeper than tyre tracks in Irrawaddy mud.

'*Mingala-ba*, General Bo Win,' said Than, stepping forward

and saluting as the general hung up the telephone. He untucked the file from beneath his arm and placed it on the edge of desk, turning it to face him, nudging it straight. 'I've bought you the latest District Evaluation, sir. I think you'll be satisfied.'

The general returned a brief salute. '*Mingala-ba*, Officer.' He pulled the file towards him. 'Isn't this supposed to be delivered to my clerk?'

Than levelled his shoulders and swallowed. 'He was not at his desk.'

The general hesitated, his vision skipping over Min too before settling on Than. He drew his aviators to the end of his nose and tipped his head forward so his stare came cool and undiluted, and then he took a sip of water and sat down. 'Very well,' he said, slipping his chair beneath the table and flipping open the report. 'What are the facts I need to know?'

Than let out a slow, slight breath. 'Forty-three insurgents captured or killed this period, sir.'

The general looked up. 'Forty-three?'

'Yes, sir.'

'Soldiers or financiers?'

'Both, sir.'

'All Shan?'

'Yes, sir. The dogs.'

'Who compiled the report?'

'I did, sir,' said Than. He paused. 'Officer Than Chit.'

The general unhooked his glasses from his nose and tapped his teeth on their thin wire rim. He squinted at Than, a ticker tape of unreadable thoughts running behind his expression, but then his eyes sunk back to the report and he leafed through the pages without saying a word. His head began to slowly nod. Than clasped his hands together behind his back. The general was happy. His face was as impassive as the misty morning sky, but inside he was rejoicing. Forty-three. A truck-load of cattle. He had to be. Than waited, trying to keep his feet from fidgeting, until the general had reached the last page. Closing the file and slipping it into a drawer at his desk, he sat back, refocusing his attention on Than. He had linked his hands together across his stomach but he raised one finger and pointed at Min. 'Who's this?'

Than puffed out his chest, proudly. This was it. 'His name is Min Soe Khaing, sir. He's my son.'

The general's lips pinched, barely visibly. The point of his stare was as sharp as a knife. Than felt his breath catch at the top of his throat. He glanced at Min. The boy was still standing stiffly upright, staring ahead and looking smart like he should. He rebalanced himself, his hands gripping tighter together, slicked with sweat. 'He's wants to enrol in the army,' said Than, drying them surreptitiously on the back of his shirt. 'He'll be an excellent recruit. He's just the type of boy you're looking for, General. He's hardworking, strong and smarter than a professor, and he'll take orders.' He shot a look at Min again and nodded eagerly.

'General Bo Win, I would like to join the Tatmadaw to help make Burma great,' said Min, almost shouting. He was scared. Than could tell. 'My father inspired me. I'm driven by the Tatmadaw's cause and loyal to her every wish. I pledge to serve in any way requested of me to keep our nation united and advance the Burmese Way to Socialism by embracing

Buddhist concepts and ridding ourselves of pernicious economic systems that exist for man to exploit man and live on the fat of such appropriation, which will in turn free us from the shackles of civilian corruption, foreign dominance and internal aggressors.'

The general held up his hand, cutting the boy short. Than's heart was hammering as hard as a machine gun. His belly was a bubble of excitement and pride. The child was a wonder. He'd memorised the policies Than had given him word for word. The general shifted forward, his hands spread on the desk. He looked up. 'I'm certain the boy will make a first-class soldier, Officer Than Chit,' he said quietly, slowly and deliberately. 'But please explain what he's doing *here*.'

Than looked at Min. 'He's my son.'

'He's a civilian, Officer. Do you think it's appropriate to bring your wife with you when you're on Tatmadaw business? Or perhaps your grandmother?'

Than shook his head. He could feel his cheeks were reddening. 'No, sir.'

'Do civilians have clearance to be in this building?'

'No, sir.'

'And have I ever requested to meet your son?'

'No, sir.'

The general nodded and then picked up his aviators. He wafted them in the direction of the door before swinging them back on his long, slender nose. 'So tell the child to wait outside.'

Beneath his collar, across his chest and in the hollow of his back, Than felt the sweat burst suddenly through his skin.

With his shirt glued to his torso and eyes averted, he winced and chucked a half-nod at Min. The boy was pink-faced and drenched with sweat also, and he dodged away through the ranks of desks, crashing into more than one as he hurried to flee. What must they have looked like, thought Than, not just to each other but to every soldier in the whole of the room? The town would be talking. Behind his back, they'd be mocking him. Jeering. If it reached Min's mother, Than would never live it down. He balled his slippery hands to fists and tensed his muscles to stop himself from shaking. His legs felt as though they were sinking in sand.

The general waited until Min's silhouette had been eaten by the giant doors of the Operation Hall's entrance before plucking a piece of paper from the top of his filing tray, writing briefly and then looking at Than. 'Sit down, Officer,' he said, gesturing to a chair.

Than didn't move. He didn't trust his legs to carry him. 'Please, sir,' he said. He wanted to leave as quickly as possible, to run and hide in his shame and think. 'I have duties to attend to. May I be dismissed?'

The general shook his head. 'No, Officer,' he said, gesturing again. He cracked a smile; the first Than had seen. 'I hadn't planned it, but since you are here and you and your family clearly value the Tatmadaw and our objectives so highly, there are things I feel that it's right to discuss.'

The throb of blood in Than's head hastened. Had the outburst at Min just been to throw him? Had the arrow he'd fired flown straight all along? His head was spinning. By the spirits, he hadn't expected this as quick! Oh, the general was a riddle to fathom, but if nothing else it showed how close he had been all along. It was true, time and again, Than had seen long-term officers finally getting their promotions when their sons were signed up. Perhaps Bo Win would make him a captain and he'd get his own office somewhere on the street. Or perhaps he'd skip ahead and go straight to major. It wasn't unheard of in exceptional cases. He edged himself into the chair and bit on his cheeks to stifle his grin.

Bo Win placed down his pencil and pushed the paper he'd been writing on towards him. 'The generals in Rangoon are displeased,' he said, sipping from the glass of water at his side.

Than stayed quiet. He didn't look at the paper. The generals in Rangoon were always displeased.

'You're aware that the insurgents are moving closer to the town?'

'Yes, sir. Two more outposts were attacked this week.'

'Three. Another was targeted this morning. We held our ground, but they've taken the land to the north of Spider Mountain. Their line is less than half a mile from the city's perimeter and we're certain it won't be long until they attack again. They've been shipping in boys from across the country to bolster their ranks, and they're keener, fresher and stupider than the bastards who've been in the jungle for years. Their commanders don't care how many they lose and they're making progress. They're better armed than they've been for a decade too – though I don't know how since we're watching every road in and out of the district. We certain they're planning something. It's time to crack down, Officer Than Chit. We can't have them urinating on the edge of Mogok town. Rangoon wants a new push on the Four Cuts.'

Than tensed in his seat, frozen, and stared past the general at the blank grey wall. The sound of telegraph keys was rising, a barrage of noise like rain on a rooftop. This wasn't his promotion. Not anything like it. It had not even crossed the general's mind. *Hpyat Lay Byat*, he thought, feeling nauseous. The Four Cuts. They were nothing new to him. The Tatmadaw had been peddling the same tired, ineffectual strategy for as long as he'd served. To sever the flow of food, funds, intelligence and recruits to the rebels, they said, was like severing their limbs and leaving them stranded. All that was left was to watch them die. It wasn't a bad idea in theory, but no matter how many men the Tatmadaw arrested or killed, how many lines of supply they chopped and how many messages they intercepted, the rebels still found a way to battle on.

'What do you want me to do, sir?' Than muttered through his sickness. He had more than an inkling about where this would go.

The general scrawled again on another sheet of paper, then signed his name and passed it to Than. 'I had marked the job for someone else,' he said, 'but you've just got yourself reassigned to disrupting insurgent finances. Mogok is leaking rubies, Officer Than Chit. Every gem taken from a government mine, cracked stone or any scrap of earth in the district without my permission has the potential to be funding criminal activity. Those jungle monkeys are rich, and they're getting help from somewhere in the town. You are now responsible for finding the thieves and bringing them to justice.'

Than stared down at his orders with all his strength so his face didn't wince. He had a good idea who the robbers would be – everyone did in a town this size – but nosing around was the way to make enemies. There were too many deals, favours and distant cousins in Mogok to make it wise to do anything but turn your head and walk away. He swallowed a lump from the top of his throat. He wanted to be back in the jailhouse with his feet on the desk, not skirting along the edges of peril.

The general was glaring at him, waiting for a response. 'Do you understand your assignment, Officer?'

'Yes, sir.'

'Excellent,' said the general, and he waved to dismiss him. 'Then gather your men. You'll start straight away.'

Than shuffled the papers together in front of him; one of instructions, one branded with his name. He picked them up and staggered away, creasing them in the clutch of his fist, following Min's track through the desks in a daze. The rebels were ruining the country – he knew it – holding the oil fields, gem mines and forests to ransom, draining her dry. If it weren't for those selfish rats and all their wars, Burma would be rich. She'd still be a mighty power like she was when the kings were sat on their thrones. He felt a stone of dread in his stomach. Something had to be done, but he was not the man to do it. He didn't want to. This had not been his fortune. And yet, his own acts had conspired to force it. He could feel Aung San's stare searing down from the entrance, from the softly hued picture that hung above the door. He had known it was there. It was everywhere. *Everywhere*. The same disappointment. The same disgust even. Little Than, such a let-down. The miserable coward. Always inadequate. Always the fool.

Outside the gates, Min was waiting on the kerb. 'I'm sorry, Dad,' he said, leaping up and rushing towards Than as he marched down the steps and along the street. He skipped at his father's side, trying to catch his eye.

Than strode past him without a look. 'You should be,' he said, fumbling for a cigarette. He could feel that his skin was hot with embarrassment. He wasn't going to stop and chat.

'You were in there ages,' said Min, chasing him. 'What were you talking about?'

'It was military business.'

'You didn't get in trouble, did you?'

'Don't be stupid.'

'But the general was angry. Dad? What happened?'

Than stopped and spun to face his son, furious suddenly. Why couldn't he leave it? He should know to let it go. With trembling hands he stuffed a cigarette between his lips and then felt his finger jab the boy's shoulder, and he watched and seethed as the child stumbled back. '*You* were the one that looked like a fucking retard, Min. Not me. You didn't even finish your speech.'

Min stared at him, hurt. 'Well, he stopped me, didn't he?'

'Of course he did. You were stammering like a little girl in a whorehouse.'

'I wasn't.'

'You were. I could hardly listen for cringing. You told me you had it nailed.' He grabbed the scruff of Min's shirt and pushed him against the wall, ramming him there and closing in.

'I should have known, Min Soe Khaing. You're an ungrateful little weasel that doesn't know he's born. I must have told you every day of your privileged existence. By the spirits, I've had to! You don't fucking listen. Every day as I've toiled to keep a roof over your head and supper in your bowl and clothes on your back . . . If you spent less time being so fucking selfish with your tripe about fucking Rangoon and fucking university and more time planning for a sensible fucking future, you wouldn't keep letting your family down.'

Min's face was hard, but a slick of tears appeared along the line of his eyes. Than felt his body slacken beneath him.

'What can I do, Dad?' he whispered, beaten.

Than released him and spat on the pavement. He turned his back. 'Just fucking go home.'

Than's mind was still a blizzard when he reached the market. It was lunchtime and the yard outside the hall was teeming with vendors and their passing trade, and he swept through the mob with his shoulders and elbows, barging aside anyone in his way. The moneylenders were out, and the brokers and their spotters, each milling around, seemingly aimlessly with their hands hidden in their pockets, doing their best to pretend they didn't exist. As Than threaded through them, his military stripes clear on his bicep, they dipped their gaze and meandered away. He didn't care. They could tout their stolen gem-dust if they wanted. He had bigger things to concern him now. The stink of gasoline clotted the air, rising from the old water bottles that their sellers had filled and lined up on the edge of the pavement like skittles, and a boy as thin as a wisp of riverweed spread his eucalyptus leaves to dry beside. In the gutter, a Shan girl was feeding her baby, butter-yellow flowers in her headdress and her whole body rocking the child that hung from her breast. A young nun passed them, twirling her paper parasol above her head to shield herself from the sun and singing, the train of her robes, the colour of candyfloss, fluttering behind her, draped over her arm.

Than shunted his own eyes away, as furtive as the black-marketeers who thought that they'd dodged him, and cut inside the warren of overflowing stalls. He turned right, scattering a gathering of fishwives who blocked the aisle as they gutted their catch, slipping on the tiles where the wet blood pooled. As he passed the fruit kiosks he was almost at a run, and he knew that the merchants were watching and muttering, but he wound his way through them, quicker and quicker, to the furthest, darkest corner of the hall.

He stopped, his urgent breath slowing, and feeling the pressure in his chest release. Here the tables were bare and the stalls were boarded up. The air was cooler and stiller, and the cries of the traders had dropped to a hum of inaudible words. He wiped his mouth and glanced behind. It wasn't the money that was making him anxious. This wouldn't cost more than a box of cheap cigars. No, it wasn't guilt. It was anticipation. Marlar would chide him for coming if she knew, but where else could he hope to find any clarity? Where else would anyone sit and listen? Who else would tell him it would all be OK?

'*Mingala-ba*, Officer Than Chit,' said a voice from the gloom.

Than stepped forward. The wall ahead was lined by a row of curtains and the one at the end had been neatly pinned back. He wiped his face in the crook of his arm and crept towards the propped-up sign. *Palmistry and Astrology Fortunes*, it read in blocky lettering. The outline of a hand was drawn beside it, fingers spread and coloured light blue. He rubbed his face again and peered inside the tiny concrete cubicle. Two dark eyes stared back from the gloom. The candlelight caught their wetness so they shimmered like black flames.

'*Mingala-ba*, Daw Su,' said Than. He heard his voice stutter and he bowed, feeling awkward, then ducked beneath the curtain's swag and pulled it shut.

The ancient woman motioned for him to sit. Than eased himself to the floor on the opposite side of her little wooden table, mirroring her body, cross-legged and compact, and clawed his neck with a quivering hand. Daw Su was waiting patiently, assessing him gently, but as his thoughts slowed and he turned them over, he couldn't decide which one was the best to offer up first. She always had this effect to begin with. A shock to look at, her face was covered by thickly tattooed lines and the ink laced up and down through the deep crevices of her skin as though she'd been swathed in a heavy purple web. Her crumpled cheeks billowed and rolled as she puffed on the cheroot that was plugged between her lips. Thick as a gun barrel, so broad and round that her mouth couldn't shut, she held it in place with her toothless gums and smoke spilled through the gaps each side, like smoke from a dragon's nostrils.

'You look troubled,' she said quietly.

Than clawed his face again, much harder. He did feel troubled. He always felt troubled when he came here. He wriggled on the floor, his eyes skirting away. Daw Su knew why he was here. It was always the same. They had talked it through until he was raw. 'I've been given a new job,' he muttered.

The old woman nodded and a familiar, knowing look settled over her. She reached beneath the table and pulled out a tiny cheroot and slid it towards him. 'But it wasn't the job you were hoping for?'

He shook his head and picked it up. 'No.' He bent forward and she lit the cheroot. Its sweet, musky smoke sank into his lungs. 'It's worse than the one I had before.'

'A test?'

'It feels like a punishment.'

'Do you deserve to be punished?'

'Of course not. I follow the orders I'm given.'

Daw Su reached across the table, plucking up his wrist. Her hands were cold and heavy, her fingers ringed to each rough knuckle in rubies and gold. She turned his palm upwards and dried it on a silk, then squinted down, leaning so low and examining him so closely that he felt her rattling breath and her cheroot's glow on his skin. In the distance, he could hear the gongs from the temple pealing. 'Your body follows orders, Officer,' she said, 'but your mind is impatient.'

Than yanked his hand away and scowled. After all he had been through and how long he had served, he had every right to be feeling impatient. This morning's dishonour was hardly justice. It was as though the general had wanted to scorn him.

As though he'd been sitting and hoping for prey. Than Chit was his joke. He'd enjoyed it, the vulture. 'I've waited long enough for reward,' he said, feeling his cheeks burn afresh, swallowing his bile.

The old woman sat back and smiled, her cheeks softly blowing out. 'Reward isn't earned through time spent trying.'

'What more do I need to do?'

'Commit to the path you have chosen.'

He slammed his fist to the table. 'I am committed.'

'Then you'll do the task that's required of you.'

Than dipped his head and pressed his thumbs to his temples. The ache in his skull was as dense as treacle and, though small, the strength of the cheroot that Daw Su had given him was making him reel. The task required of him . . . He didn't even know what that meant. Did the general want him to succeed? It was hardly a secret that Bo Win didn't get his shiny Mazda on a government wage. Throughout the town it was common knowledge that he took tea money from the opium growers despite the fact that their profits funded the rebels, but Than wasn't sure about the thieves from the mines. If his pockets were filling from those bandits too, then his orders were a sham to keep Rangoon sweet and he wouldn't really want them found. Perhaps Than was not even supposed to try, but just to pretend to try, and succeed, like with the District Report? Perhaps his suppleness was what had dragged him to the fore. Or perhaps the general would win no matter what. If the rebels were stopped, Rangoon would reward him. If they weren't, Bo Win would still get his cut. Perhaps whatever Than did, he'd be laying himself across the train tracks and waiting for the wheels to roll over his neck. There were prob-ably more gangsters in Mogok to make an enemy of than there were honest men in the whole of Shan State. He closed his eyes tightly and tried to stem his nausea. 'I'm trapped between misfortunes, Daw Su.'

The soothsayer shook her head and took the cheroot from him, stubbing it out and hiding it away. 'Only a weak man finds himself trapped,' she said. 'A strong man will move the boulders. Perhaps you have been given this job because you are trusted?'

Than bit his lip. Much as it pained him to admit it, he could have named two dozen men he knew the general trusted more. Try as Than did, over and over, he could never excite the gen-eral's approval. It wasn't that Bo Win had ever articulated any specific grievance against him, but whenever they met there was an air of indifference, like everything Than did was a touch underwhelming. Like he might be forgotten with the change of the wind. It made him feel invisible, like he had been all childhood. Expendable. It made him feel forgotten. The Tat-madaw didn't care.

'You don't understand,' he said, scrabbling in his pocket to find his own cigarette and striking a light. 'Whatever option I choose is dangerous. I've been given a task that's impossible to win.'

The old woman shrugged. 'You can only complete your orders to the best of your ability. Winning will follow if it's just and right.'

'But, Daw Su, I'm not even sure what constitutes the best of my ability. What if it's best that I cheat and fail?'

'Only you can judge what is best. What is best for you may not be best for others.'

'Then what do I do?'

'It depends on the outcome that you want to achieve.'

Than threw up his hands. 'I want the general to notice me. I want him to recognise my loyalty . . . I want to be *inside*. I want what he has, Daw Su. The respect the town gives him.'

'Power is finite, Officer. Act carefully. The Tatmadaw understands that. It's not suitable for sharing.'

'Are you saying I should do nothing? That I must wait for the man above me to die?' He shook his head. 'I don't want to sit and wait.'

Daw Su kept staring, calm and straight-faced. 'All guns will smoke if you're brave enough to fire them, but a man can only hit where he aims. I am not telling you whether or not to act, just that power is fiercely prized.'

'Please, Daw Su!' cried Than. He reached across the table and grasped at her hands, bundling them together and pressing them in his. 'Speak plainly. Tell me what I have to do.'

Daw Su puffed again on her cheroot, sucking the smoke deeply and then letting it go. Two thick plumes rolled out through her nostrils and she peeled back her hands and tapped a long fingernail on the table for payment. 'Move one rock at a time, Than Chit,' she whispered, as cool and slippery as freshly cut ice. 'Move one rock and then move another. If you do what you have to, your day will come.'

SEVEN

Thuza crouched on the floor by her fireplace and rolled back the rug. The lock in the wood beneath it resisted as she wedged in her key and forced it to turn, and the bolt strained and jolted open with a firecracker snap. A season of rain had swelled the floorboards so the trapdoor was sticky, and she braced her heels to the lip of the hearth to heave it up. As the smell of saturated earth and the cold air gusted out, she shuddered, then unhooked her torch from where it was strung on the underside of the hatch, knocking it to life with the ball of her hand. With the torch clasped between her teeth, she glanced to the windows and door impulsively, and then she cast her feet down, lowering her body into the darkness as though slipping into an icy black lake.

The beam of weak yellow light trembled in the tunnel as she dropped to her knees, catching the sixteen blocks of creamy clay destined for the Thai and illuminating them. They were stacked along the wall, narrowing the tiny space even further, and she wrinkled her nose at them and squeezed past carefully, holding her breath. Though she knew they couldn't ignite from her touching them, their sight was enough to fill her with terror and she didn't want to knock or dislodge them, lest she have to stay in their presence any longer than she needed to. With her heartbeat sounding in her head, she began to crawl down the shallow slope, away from the trapdoor and her secret, dreadful, necessary stash. She hadn't had anywhere safer to hide it, but it didn't seem right that something so violent should be held anywhere that reminded her so acutely of her parents. She couldn't wait to have it gone.

Thuza wriggled forward, banishing the blocks from her mind, and the space thinned to no wider than her shoulders. She stretched onto her stomach and dragged herself along by her elbows, straining so hard that her neck and arms ached. There was a curve to follow and the last of the glow from the entrance faded, and she felt her chest tighten as she clawed past the black tributary stumps that ran from each side; the aborted channels that she'd toiled to burrow but met nothing but stone. The tunnels were weak from the rains and the walls were sagging, and a few of the props she had placed had toppled, so she dug them back into the soft earth, ramming the mud around them and packing it as tightly and cautiously as she could with her knuckles, trying not to imagine the roof crumbling down. From somewhere above, she could hear the drip of water leaking. A bucket was tied by a string to her ankle and it chased in her wake like a scuffling rat. She hadn't wanted to be down here again – she hadn't thought she would ever, ever need to – and her anger at Kyaw had been rising steadily, heating and heating until it burnt like a poker, and it jabbed in her ribs and made her grimace. What a dog he was, always biting her ankles, always gripped to her bones and dragging her back.

Ahead, the ribbon that Thuza had pinned to the wall was still in its place, and she bent her body and coiled around the sharp bend that it marked, into an alcove where she could almost sit up. She took the torch from her mouth and twisted it into the ceiling so it sat like a spotlight. There was a penknife, a cooking ladle and a miniature pickaxe piled at her feet where she'd abandoned them and she untied the bucket and placed it beside the tools, taking up the axe and beginning to scratch at the dirt in front of her. Lightly, her house was creaking above her, the weight of it bearing down on its weakened foundations as the wind blew through. If it fell, she wouldn't be the first soul to have been reclaimed by the Mogok earth. A dozen or more houses had succumbed in her memory, giving way to the warrens that lay beneath. Their owners – if they lived – were then carted away for thievery and deception. The skill, Thuza knew, was to move along gently, to not get too greedy and always go slow. She forced her heart-rate to calm, breathing hard and trying to ease her quick, angry hands. From the quarries a half-mile away, the drills sent a quiver through the ground to find her, so subtle that had she not known where the tremble came from, she might have believed it to be from herself. She pulled back the axe and scraped the clots from its hook to her bucket, holding it up and examining the brown lumps in the dismal light. From the bottom, a glint. Her chest tightened, disappointed. Not a ruby, but a crystal of some sort, the size of a wheat grain and milky white. She wiped it clean on the hem of her *longi* then tucked it in her mouth and carried back on.

For all the dangers of being in her tunnels, Thuza used to

feel at ease whenever she came. Whilst setting the forest traps for her birds and the bribes through the checkpoints and the negotiations with the dealers that followed were always perilous, there was something to the work here that focused her thinking; a rhythm to the digging that made her feel tranquil. The town was far away too — further in her mind than the bridges and pathways — and just for a while it let her relax. Beneath the ground, she was hidden from judgement. No one could watch her. Not a whisper could be heard. Tonight she had hoped she would feel the same mercy. She wouldn't have been able to sleep anyway, and she didn't want to listen to her nanna's wheezing through the wall. Even if Kyaw had not demanded that she bring him more money, she might have found herself here all the same. She wanted to feel a little closer to her parents — to the best bit of her history. She needed the past to keep urging her on.

Her father had said that he had the same feelings of calm the very first time that he lifted her down. She must have been seven or eight years old, and had sat at the brink of the trapdoor and stared at his smiling face as he reached up and took hold of her waist. To begin with, she'd been scared of the cold and the blackness, and the spirits that had to be living within. Her mother had breathed comforts in her ear, smoothing her hair and following after, and the sound of her bracelets jingling behind let Thuza feel sure that no souls could creep up. They had only travelled ten yards or so from the entrance when her father turned into a side-passage and Thuza saw Kyaw. A few feet away, he was sitting in a chamber that was big enough for the four of them. They wriggled up, sitting with their bodies pressed together, and Thuza felt the thinness of the air and the sprint of her heart as it beat in her chest.

'Do you know where we are, Thuza?' her father had whispered.

Thuza remembered she had shaken her head.

'We are sitting in the avenues that lead to our future, Little Princess. The turns of fate that gave us this house have not always been kind, but our family finds ways of making things right. For as long as we've lived here, we've been digging these tunnels. Mogok may be Rubyland and fought for by everyone, but these will always be only for us. They are our most precious secret. They are our opportunity for change. Though I pray it comes slowly, a day will arrive when you learn that life is not always fair and kind, but as long as we continue what our ancestors started, you must remember that we always have hope.'

'I don't understand, Pappa,' said Thuza, feeling nervous. Her father's cheekbones had been knifed by the lamplight so he looked more thin and old and afraid.

Thuza's mother picked up her hand and held it. She smiled, and Kyaw smiled too. 'The stones that you'll find in this earth are powerful. They are our gift from the spirit world, and if you tell them your dreams and fears – if you trust them as much as we trust you – they'll grant whatever wishes you may have.' She leaned forward and Thuza saw a flicker of blue in her eyes, like her own. 'We can trust you, Thuza, can't we? Will you keep our secret safe?'

Thuza had felt such tremendous pride that evening, for her parents to have shared such a very special thing. The memory was one that she clung to more desperately than any other. As she lay in bed at night and listened to the growl of her stomach, her grandmother scratching at the door frame and the finger-taps of rain on her roof, she would try to remember the taste of the first cold ruby she held on her tongue, or when she had bathed after leaving the tunnels and the water had browned to the colour of her skin. Hardest, she tried to remember the togetherness, and when hope had meant more than an ache as thick as tar.

Too soon, she learnt that her father was right. That day had come when she saw life differently, and it seared so much hotter than she ever thought it could. Over the years, she had taught herself not to dwell on the moment of their parting. She could wish away the images of the officer and the jeep and the guns, push the details of the words that were spoken from her mind, deny them. She could even forget the pain of them cutting her. What she could not rid herself of, however, were the feelings that were left there, the shadows of the memories that she'd blocked out so well. They were the grief, the confusion, the fear and her guiltiness. The realisation that survival was fragile. That her parents weren't as solid or strong or as permanent as the forest. They were flesh like her, and vulnerable too.

It wasn't always as simple as Zawtika said it should be when he asked her to cherish thoughts just as they were. More and more, whenever Thuza pulled out a memory from before it all happened, she found each one had a slash through its centre. It was a deep cut, the length and breadth of her great-grandmother's dagger, and through the parted folds bled the terror from where it had all gone wrong. It left her sweating when she woke every morning, and checking her back as she walked through the forest, and the hurt was as fresh as the day it was done.

In the tunnel, Thuza dug the pickaxe into the wall again and a chunk of mud the size of her fist fell out in her hand. She crumbled it into the bucket and tilted the neck to the fading torchlight, sifting through with her fingers. Above, the light gave a final weak spit and disappeared, and she cursed and slumped back, plucking it from the ceiling, wiping the handle and tucking it away in the pocket of her shirt. One pitiful gem and not even a ruby. Kyaw would be seething if she didn't find more. She'd have to come back and finish this later with a candle or the lamp from her nanna's room. In the darkness, she fumbled to retie the bucket to her ankle before crawling around the corner and into the passage that led to her home.

As she squirmed up the slope, the air freshened and the dark softened, and when she was almost at the exit, the hollow of the chamber came into her view. Since she'd returned from the temple, her brother's threats had been on a reel inside her head. She was tired and hungry, and she'd been thinking of Insein Prison and the dogs and the beatings, and with all of her worries her stomach was churning. She paused for a moment, staring into the dark. From inside, the past was winking at her, beckoning with a finger and calling her in. She closed her eyes and edged forward, placing her hands on the ground and digging in her fingers as if hoping to uncover some warm, sleeping skin. Like she would have done if she'd been at the temple, she bent her head and rested her brow on the cool, wet earth. She didn't know why, but she thought of her sister. She had named the baby Suhpaya; her beautiful princess. She didn't know if her mother had named her too, but she somehow felt like the title fitted perfectly. It had once been hers from her father – and so special – but now she was grown up and too old to be a princess, so if she had to be a serpent, she would be the fierce protector, and Suhpaya was her soul to love and defend. She trusted the spirits and the stones, like her mother had. It was more than trust. It was hopeless devotion. She dug her fingers deeper and her body starting shaking. Though she couldn't feel the answers, she had to hope they waited. It was too late to give up, to let anything stop her. She was ready, she knew. She would never be more so. What choice did she have but to carry on now?

'I miss you, Mumma and Pappa,' she said as a whisper. 'I miss you, my whole family, and I'm trying, but I'm scared.'

EIGHT

Michael stood in an upstairs east wing corridor of West Rangoon General Hospital, listening to the useless air-conditioning units labour against the heat, shuddering at the dusty, lukewarm blast across his shoulders, and staring at Sein through the blue-tinged glass. He hadn't ever been to a Rangoon hospital before, and though perhaps he could have imagined it, the reality of seeing it now was a shock. This was nothing like the place he had hoped he'd find his friend in. Not at all like the institutions that he'd visited in England when his grandmother had pneumonia, or when Stephanie Smithson had her wisdom teeth out. Somehow, here, he felt like time had tricked him – it had thrown him back to a distant, sorry past. The room looked worn out and utterly miserable. It hardly had any furniture within it; just a bed and a chair and an intravenous drip. Bare concrete covered the floor and white tiles stretched halfway up the walls, but they were chipped and grubby, separated by dark-grey grout. Above them, the frosty mint-green paint had faded, and the plaster showed through in patches, like mould. The smell was of alcohol and bleach disinfectant, and a naked bulb was dangling from the ceiling, leaking an unforgiving light across the room. The posters on the wall were discoloured and peeling at their edges, or stuck back with

Sellotape that had browned from age. There was a mop and a bucket in the corner by the window, and a bedpan beneath a clutch of skittish flies. He shuddered again and glanced along the corridor. The nurses were gossiping at their station by the exit, scribbling on notepads or sitting on the floor and sorting dirty linen into overflowing laundry carts. When Barrowman had tracked Sein down yesterday evening, Michael's father had offered to pay for his treatment at the private medical centre nearer his family home, but Sein's parents were proud and wouldn't accept it. It did nothing to ease Michael's simmering guilt.

He took an unsteady breath, his eyes wandering reluctantly back to the window, and he coiled the book he had brought for Sein a little tighter in his hands. It was *Return of the Jedi* by James Kahn, dusky blue, with a picture of a Lightsaber and a planet on the cover. He didn't feel sure that Sein would like it, but he hadn't wanted to turn up empty-handed and it was the least offensive book he could find in his suitcase. He held it in front of his chest and bent it double and then back again, unsure of whether to venture inside. The door was open, but his legs were trembling and he felt too nervous to know what to say. Sein was lying on his back on the bed, covered to his chest with a thin patched-up sheet. His eyes were closed and he was perfectly motionless. The flesh around his sockets was purple and his lips were pallid and cracking. His face was swollen like a freshly born child, and on his right cheek the vast, curved gash that Michael had seen so bloodied at the market was stitched like a wonky railroad track. Beside the bed, Sein's father slept in a plastic-covered armchair, his head tilted back and mouth gaping wide. His hair was a mess, not arranged in its usual sleek parting, and the buttons at the neck of his shirt were undone. There was a stain on his breast, perhaps tea or coffee. He had folded his arms across his belly and his spectacles were upturned untidily in his lap.

Watching him, Michael took a step into the doorway, but then hovered there, still not wanting to disturb them, not wanting to have to find things to say. He would creep inside and leave the book by Sein's feet, he reasoned. Just a few quiet paces, then place it down and be on his way. He would come back later, when they weren't so tired. When he'd thought of something worthwhile to talk about. When he'd processed the sight of it all in his mind. He ran a finger between his neck and collar and then hurried forward, dropping the book more heavily than he meant to, panicked almost by the thought of being caught there, but as soon as he turned, he knew he'd been done. The professor had opened his eyes and was sitting up in his chair, straightening his cuffs with a tug to each sleeve.

'Ah, Michael Atwood,' he said, smiling with genuine warmth. '*Mingala-ba*.' He hooked his glasses to his nose and stood up, taking hold of Michael's hands and shaking them in his own. The stubble on his chin was a full night's worth.

Michael flinched at the impact of his voice and the force of his touch in the unfriendly room. He could smell his breath, his uncleaned teeth. '*Mingala-ba*, Professor,' he said, wriggling free from the man's grasp and taking hold of his own arm behind his back, making himself smaller, containing his body so he wouldn't intrude. 'I'm sorry to wake you.'

The professor shook his head, still smiling. 'I wasn't asleep.'

There was a silence that followed, as long and uneasy as Michael had feared there would be, and he felt himself stared at, and he stared at the floor in turn, feeling awkward, feeling the same intense, expectant pressure that he'd felt at the market with Sein's body in his arms.

'I brought Sein a book,' he said after a while, talking to the ground. 'For when he's feeling better, of course. It's science fiction. From a film. Nothing bad. You don't have to worry.'

The professor's eyes flicked to the bed and he picked up the book and examined it half-heartedly, before placing it back down. 'That's thoughtful, Michael. Thank you. He'll appreciate the gesture, I'm sure.'

There was another drawn pause and Michael chipped his toe against his heel, looking up, summoning his courage to ask the question that he only partly wanted to. 'How is he?'

The professor's smile faltered momentarily before resettling, but not quite as comfortably as it had done before. It stopped on his lips, not reaching his eyes. 'They told me he's been unconscious since he arrived here,' he said in his perfectly accented English. He took a handkerchief from his pocket and blew his nose loudly, sitting back down, his eyes roaming now, avoiding Michael's. 'Swelling on the brain, the doctor said. Some debris must have hit him. That's the worst of it. Other than that, he's got a few broken ribs, a collapsed lung. Cuts and bruises. They'll see how he goes over the next few days, but I expect he'll be here for a little while yet. With luck, he'll wake within a day or two and they won't have to operate. He's a spirited rascal though, my boy. As you well know. I'm sure he'll be fine.'

Michael's gaze slipped to the bed, to Sein's unmoving body and his ashen complexion, to the tube in his arm and his bony, rigid limbs. He didn't look fine. He looked appalling. Michael smiled as best he could manage. 'I'm sure he will.'

He looked around again, searching for something to steer the conversation away from their shared unspoken sense of dread.

'My parents send their regards,' he said, trying to sound cheerful. 'My father wanted me to tell you that if there's anything Sein or your family needs, you only have to ask. He'll do his best to arrange it.'

The professor nodded. 'Thank you. That's kind. Please pass on my gratitude for him getting us this room. My wife was pleased to be able to stay the night.'

'How's she doing?'

The professor puffed out his cheeks and shrugged. 'Tired. Worried. Her aunt is watching the children today. The doctor's given her pills to help her sleep. She'll feel better when she's had some rest.' His face darkened slowly, the smile dissipating to be replaced by a serious, fearful look. His eyes twitched to the door and back and he lowered his voice and shifted forward, looking up. 'Has your father heard anything about the bombing, Michael?'

Michael gnawed at the inside of his cheek. He wasn't sure what the professor was after. 'Not much,' he replied truthfully. 'The embassy's asked a few questions, I think, but the Tatmadaw's tight-lipped. We were told that there might be a curfew by the weekend. And extra stoppages at the checkpoints.'

'Has anyone claimed responsibility?

Michael shook his head. 'I don't know. I'm sorry. Not that I've heard.'

The professor's mouth pinched and he looked as though he was about to ask something more, but then he bit his lip and shook himself free from it, forcing an over-eager, insincere grin. He slapped his thighs and stood up abruptly, patting Michael on the shoulder and directing a nod at Sein.

'Would you sit with him while I get a drink, please, Michael?' he asked. 'I couldn't bear him to be alone if he wakes.'

Michael looked at his friend on the bed. He could hear a quiver to Sein's father's voice and see a glint of wetness in his eyes. Sein didn't show any sign of waking. He didn't show a sign of anything at all. Michael nodded, and the professor's shoulders seemed to sag with relief. He turned and strode purposefully away, whipping his handkerchief from his pocket again and rubbing down his face and the back of his neck. Michael listened to his footsteps recede along the corridor and lowered himself into the armchair by the bed. It creaked beneath his weight as he dropped there, and the plastic gummed to his hot, sticky skin. He understood why the professor had seemed so relieved when he had the chance to leave here. The room was a sarcophagus, airless and hopeless. There was something draining about being here. He felt so tired and spent and feeble. His head was aching from the strain of conversation, and a night of fragmented, troubled half-sleep. He shuffled forward and rested his forehead on the edge of the bed, not praying, but willing for something to happen, for the air to change and the room to lighten, for a moment of practical, tangible difference, for a solution to manifest that would fix his broken friend. He closed his eyes, focusing on nothing but enduring the silence and finding that clarity, of passing the time until his world became the same as it had been before.

He wasn't sure how long he had sat there before Sein's father returned with two tiny plastic cups, each filled to the brim with watery black coffee. He held one out to Michael.

Michael shook his head and stood up quickly, embarrassed to be caught in what must have looked like sleep. 'No, thank you, Professor,' he said, dusting down his trousers and stepping aside so the man could have his seat. He darted towards the door, too keenly, he knew. 'I should be going. The visiting hours will be finished soon. I'm not family. They'll ask me to leave.'

The professor looked fleetingly disappointed but he smiled again and shook Michael's hand. 'Thanks for coming, Michael,' he said. 'It would mean so much to Sein if he knew. It does to us all. You're a good friend.'

Michael held tightly to the professor's hand, a new rush of guilt sweeping through him. He didn't feel like a good friend. He felt like he couldn't wait to be gone. He was desperate to abandon him all over again. 'I'm sorry about Sein, Professor,' he muttered into his chest. 'I really am.'

The professor sighed and let his hand drop. 'It's luck, Michael Atwood, that's all. Dreadful luck.'

Michael's heart was pounding as he strode along the corridor. He was walking as fast as he could without running and had sunk his hands to the bottom of his pockets and screwed them to fists where no one could see. Behind him, he could sense Sein's father watching him leave, following his escape and wishing it was him. He passed the nurses' station without a look and shoulder-barged through the double doors beyond them, bundling into the empty stairwell – relieved for the privacy – and hurrying down, two steps at a time. His descent produced an echo that was hollow and unnerving, like a drummer that followed a doomed, losing army, but he wanted to put as much distance between himself and Sein as possible, and though his conscience said that he should do, he couldn't slow down. It was as if the minutes and the metres that separated them were a tonic that would numb his grief.

Downstairs, he tore across the hospital's front lobby and through the open gates onto Thida Street with a desperate gasp. There were colours outside, the scent of flowers and trees and blue sky and the promise of life. *Luck*. He said the word out loud, almost laughing, though nothing about it could lighten his mood. It was luck that the sun rose each day and burnt so fiercely, and that the clouds floated east this afternoon, not south. His own father had used the word as carelessly as Sein's father had done, and it sounded more absurd each moment in his mind. Luck was a lottery. Injustice was different. One was accidental. The other was made.

He cut between the buses on Banyardala Road and headed towards the Kandawgyi Lake, scattering the pigeons on the pavement, feeling the breeze begin to find him as the skyline cleared of buildings and the space opened up. With the sun in his eyes, he traced the southern bank, letting the vendors paw at his arm. There was some luck involved, of course, Michael knew. There was no difference between him and Sein, except that Sein had placed himself in the wrong seat at the teahouse table. He understood the comfort that was meant to come from saying it, but managing to feel it too was beyond him. For Michael, luck was a reason to excuse what had happened. It was a justification to turn the other way. He could feel his cheeks getting hotter and hotter, and his feet moving faster, and his body more tense with each new step. To ignore the truth was to make it possible. More probable, even. Luck was inevitable, but things like this shouldn't be. He had drawn the bombers in with his bright-white skin.

His mouth dry and lungs airless, he stopped at the head of the road by Bahan Market and stared towards the disorder ahead. He had walked here almost without realising he'd done it, or without knowing why at least. It felt strange, being back. Yesterday seemed like so much more than a few measly hours ago. Though the damage was there and he'd watched it happen, he felt detached, like his memory sat crooked, like it leant to the side and distorted his images so they warped and wavered and didn't appear real. The stretch where the market stalls had been was cordoned off by blue and yellow tape, but trade was still happening beneath the awnings; he could see shadows shifting and hear muffled sound. There were a few soldiers patrolling the barriers, looking bored, and three men with clipboards writing notes and taking pictures, though Michael wasn't certain what the purpose might be. The blood had been hosed from the ground and the truck had been moved too, but there were scorch-marks on the road in its place, and little piles of rubble, the decimated stalls collected in their composite parts and stacked along the wall.

Michael shuddered despite the heat and his eyes slipped compulsively to the teahouse. Fifty yards away, a plastic sheet had been pinned across the entrance, a sheath of heavy translucent white, and he could see a man's shape moving from behind. He walked towards it, feeling his heart quicken. For a moment, he dithered on the kerb, but then he peeled apart a split in the plastic and peered inside.

'Teacher?'

In the dim light, tables and chairs were upturned, and shards of glass littered the floor, sparkling in the shaft of new sun as Michael exposed them. A layer of dust cloaked everything, as thick as ash. He covered his mouth. The heat and dirty air were stifling. Instantly, he could feel the sweat start to pool on his lip. From the back of the long, thin room, Teacher looked up. He had a broom in his hand, and his skin and hair were tinted grey. His vest clung to the sinews of his back and his solid belly, drenched. He bent down, picked up a chair and righted it, tucking it beneath a table.

'*Mingala-ba*, Michael Atwood,' he said. He nodded a greeting but kept at his work.

Michael stood in the doorway, watching him, unsure what to do. Why had he come here? In the presence of Teacher's hard glare, formidable size and world-worn appearance, he felt suddenly twitchy, small and afraid. 'I'm sorry about your teahouse,' he said quietly, glancing around.

Teacher turned his back to the entrance and dragged his broom across the floor, throwing an angry cloud around his ankles. 'It looks worse than it is,' he said in his gruff, stunted English. 'The damage didn't reach the kitchen. It's just dust, mostly. Some broken furniture. Nothing I can't fix.'

'Do you need help clearing up?'

The man shrugged an approval, and Michael crept up the step and inside, picking up a chair as he did it too. The plastic crinkled shut behind him and he picked up a dustpan and brush from a table and began to sweep at the glass by his feet, collecting the splinters into a neat pile. He scooped them up and looked around.

'In here?' he said, pointing to a linen sack that was slung from the back of a chair.

Teacher nodded. He wiped his brow with the ball of his giant hand, smearing the grime into claggy grey streaks. 'Do you know what happened to your friend?' he asked.

'He's in the hospital,' replied Michael. 'I just came from there. The Western General.'

'How was he?'

'Asleep.'

'The good type of sleep?'

Michael's chest tightened and he shook his head. Teacher nodded again, more slowly. Michael crouched back to the ground and tried to hide his tremble, but Teacher had stopped sweeping and was leaning on his broom. He stared at Michael, his eyes a thin line. 'Why are you here, Michael Atwood?' he said.

Michael scraped at the floor with his brush. 'I don't know.'

Through the corner of his eye, he glanced up and watched as Teacher dragged his cheeks inwards, still staring at him, assessing him, and he cast his attention to the dustpan, ashamed. Even if his father was right and he wasn't responsible for goading the rebels or the blast or the debris, he was responsible for his actions after, in the seconds that followed, the minutes and hours, and now in the days and weeks that lay ahead. He could pinpoint at once why he felt so guilty, in a way he had strained to but couldn't before. The lucidity had washed through his mind like a waterfall when he'd stood at the crossroads above the market and seen the blackened tarmac where the truck had burst. This guilt was different from the constant, ignorable, low rumble of nervousness he had about Sein being his friend, and from the moment he had let the car drive away with his bleeding body in the boot, and even from the moment that he'd fled from the hospital. He realised now that'd he'd turned away often, in the way he admonished his father for doing – and Sein's father too, though he understood why. Each time he had enjoyed himself in Rangoon, he'd been cheating. Each time he had spoken his mind when his Burmese friends at the table could not. Each time he had left and gone home to England. He had turned away and pretended and forgot. To anyone who asked he claimed to love Burma, but he didn't even know her. He didn't have the right to hope for her like Sein did. She was just a mirage to him, seen through the mist of his privilege and transience. She was real in what she had done to Sein though, and he'd known her potential for cruelty all along.

He felt his heart jar against his ribcage and he looked at Teacher, gripped by a sudden, urgent feeling that somehow an opportunity was leaking through his fingers. Like oil, it was leaving a thick, stinking slick. From the doorway, the plastic sheeting shifted, and he turned and looked to the noise, glad of the interruption to break his thoughts.

'*Mingala-ba*, brothers,' said a man, ducking in. He looked around forty years old and mostly unremarkable, but something about him was sitting uneasy. His body was slender and his hair was neatly parted, and his clothes were clean and freshly pressed. His eyes were stern though, prickly and suspicious. Michael glanced at Teacher. His stance had hardened.

'*Mingala-ba*,' Teacher replied without enthusiasm.

Slipping forward, the man circled the tables nearest to the entrance, running a finger along one of them slowly, scoring the dust. 'Is this your teahouse?' he asked, brushing the grey from his skin.

Teacher raised his chin. 'It is.'

'A fine establishment, I'd heard. Terrible mess now though.' He punted his toe through some fragments of crockery. 'Were many of your customers hurt?'

'Too many.'

The man nodded. 'A shame.'

Under Teacher's unfriendly gaze, he lapped another table then stopped in the centre of the room and Michael felt himself eyed intensely, and his stomach began to twist to a knot. In the broiling heat, the man was sweating, and he wiped his brow and rolled his sleeves back from his wrists before hooking his hands on his hips, studying him. Michael's stare skipped downwards and his heart seized. Terror gripped him. He looked at the man's arm. Along his flesh was a tattoo of an orchid, black and rudimentary. A single eye watched from the petals' heart. Yesterday! *Shit*. The prisoner from the alley. He looked up, aghast – but it wasn't the same man. The scowl was there, but the face had changed.

The man caught Michael's shock and his composure faltered momentarily. He smiled a brief, unfriendly smile then nodded at Teacher and spun on his heels before marching to the sheeting and dipping outside.

The plastic fell shut. Michael clasped his hand to his mouth. He looked at Teacher. 'That man,' he asked, 'who was he?'

Teacher spat towards the door and went back to his sweeping.

'His tattoo . . .'

Teacher's frown deepened. He swiped at the floor. 'Fucking government spies. Always nosing.'

Michael stared at him, horrified. 'It's military?'

Teacher nodded. 'Special Intelligence Department. The police. It's their symbol. The thazin was the first flowering bud of the season. The fables said anyone who picked it before the king would be punished with death. The eye is watching to see who dares. They're ruthless, those men. As unforgiving as starving bears.'

Michael slumped to a chair. 'Jesus.' He shook his head. He was shivering. 'I had no idea.'

'Not many people do.'

'No. You don't understand. I mean I've seen it before. The man who was driving the motorcycle had it. One of the bombers. Fuck, Teacher. He was a Tatmadaw man. I'd seen him with a group of officers earlier and I thought they were questioning him, but they weren't. That's why they let him go. He was one of theirs. It wasn't the rebels who did this, Teacher. The Tatmadaw planted the bomb themselves.'

Teacher stopping sweeping. He rested on his broom, staring at Michael.

'Why aren't you shocked?'

He shrugged.

Michael stared back, the image of Sein's torn, swollen purple face imprinted in his mind. He felt sick. 'Why would they do that, Teacher?'

Teacher shook his head. His nostrils flared and he glanced to the front of the teahouse. There were a few silhouettes loitering outside, walking too slowly to be merely passing by. They were clearing up too, perhaps. More spies. 'Expedience,' he said, speaking calmly and quietly. 'They've stirred up panic, haven't they? Turned the city harder against the rebels. Made Rangoon a little more fearful. Created a reason to tighten control. Created a reason for their own existence even. They're shrewd, Michael Atwood.'

Michael took a shaky breath and fumbled in his pocket to find his tobacco, pulling out his pouch and rolling a hasty, scrappy cigarette. He struck a light and plugged the overflowing Rizla between his lips, drawing deeply, sinking forward and cradling his head in his sweat-slicked hands. He pushed his fingers into his temples and squeezed his eyes shut, daring himself to find a shred of sense in it. That the Tatmadaw could be so callous as to target their own people was almost too much to hold in his mind.

'I thought it was me, Teacher,' he muttered. 'I thought I drew them here.'

He dragged his hands down his face, feeling almost unbearably weary, afraid his emotion was about to overflow. He shook his head and worried the butt of the cigarette in his lap.

'I need to know what happened, Teacher. I feel so useless. I feel like there's nothing I can do to make anything better. I can't stand it. If Sein dies . . .' He couldn't finish.

Teacher let out a heavy sigh and placed his broom down. He pulled up a chair and sat opposite Michael. 'You mustn't talk like that, Michael Atwood.'

'I just wish there was something I could do to help.'

Teacher leaned back and looked at the entrance, then closed his eyes and muttered silently for a moment. When he spoke again, his voice was a whisper. He stared at Michael. 'Perhaps there is.'

NINE

Thuza stood at the top of the guesthouse's narrow stairwell and clutched her satchel across her chest. She was high in the eaves of the building, the staircase having narrowed with each rising level until hardly a feather could have passed between her and the wall at either shoulder, and a wispy breeze was hissing through the rust of the corrugated roof. Across Mogok, the power was out, but an enormous full moon glowed low in the cloudless sky and she'd paced the route here without needing her torch. She shunted her eyes sideways and glanced through the tiny window. The building opposite was close enough to touch and a row of dowdy birds roosted in the shadow of the overhang, their beaks nestled beneath their wings. She could hear the rattle of dice from the gaming tables in the house next door and the odd breathless grunt from the rooms she had walked past, stare averted, as she made her assent. Though she couldn't see them, she knew the street boys would be hanging on their corners, watching for threats, military or rival, as the gangsters had paid them a pittance to do. She recognised most of the faces she had seen on the walk through the alley as off-duty Tatmadaw men themselves. A dog barked and its chain clanked, snapping rigid, and she imagined the beast straining from a doorway, slobbering, gnashing its jaws at a passer-by.

This part of the town was for invisible existence: for the prostitutes and drug dealers, bookies and gem thieves. It was for those who lived at least in part below the surface, and it carried them happily through their vices and impieties, black as open drains. She looked at the clock, nervous but ready. Two minutes to eight.

'Arms.'

The doorman threw his chin at her, brandishing his revolver carelessly. He was overweight and much taller than she was, dressed in a grey-white shirt and black suit that didn't quite fit, and the slant of the roof sat just above his head. His eyes turned slightly outward and his ears were protruding. A heavy-linked choker encircled his thick neck. She lifted her arms and grimaced as he patted her down, lingering over her chest and thighs, the smell of tobacco and toddy on his skin and dandruff on his collar. He dug his hand into her pocket, pulled out her penknife and placed it on the little table beside him, next to the sheet of flypaper and its smattering of sorry insect carcasses, then stepped aside. She threw him a look and opened the door.

A man was sitting in an armchair at the back of the room. There was a flicker of recognition on his face as she entered, and he twisted a flimsy sovereign ring about his finger, eyeing her, and motioned for her sit. Chaiwat Thongsuk was his name – she had heard it just once from a Chinese ruby dealer – though everyone only called him the Thai.

The bodyguard shut the door. Thuza crept towards him and lowered herself onto the stool opposite. She unhooked her satchel and placed it by her side, the thump on the floorboards louder than she meant for it to be. She kept hold of the strap, unable to compel herself to let go. The Thai stared at her with his tiny black eyes beneath limp lids, waiting for her to speak. He was old, as old as Zawtika or Nanna were, but not in the same way. Their age had chipped at them and shown up their frailties. His had turned him imposing and rubbery. He had seen the world and was not backing down. His side table had an oil lamp and a large bottle of unmarked yellowish liquid, as it always did, and he sipped from a tumbler little bigger than a shot glass. There was a revolver there too, freshly oiled and shining. The safety catch was off, she saw. He was wearing a grubby shirt, dark blue and cheap silk, but it didn't do anything to lessen his impact. This was not a man who felt he had to impress. Elsewhere in the little rented room there was a bed and a chest of drawers that was topped with a vase of wilting peonies, though he clearly wasn't staying here. Another minder watched from the gloomy back corner, perched on a chair that was far too small.

Thuza shifted on her stool, sitting there and looking at the Thai as she had done so often before, feeling sick. He knew why she was here – at least to start with. She'd only ever been here for Kyaw.

'The Fifteenth sent me,' she said quietly, gripping the strap of her satchel tighter. She imagined the chants of the monks at the temple, as warm and restful as evening tea. 'They've made the payments you asked for. They want to know about the delivery.'

The Thai sipped his drink and then placed it on the table. He towed a scrap of paper from his breast pocket, and a pen, pulling away the lid with his teeth so their gold caps flashed in the lamplight. He scribbled on the paper, folded it and passed it to Thuza.

'It's an address in Lashio,' he said in his dark, drawn, nasal voice. He leant back, spinning the pen in his fingers. 'A warehouse in the northern district. Their men can come next week. Any day.'

Thuza took the note and tucked it into her own pocket, nodding. There wasn't much she knew for certain about the rebels' dealings, but she'd heard enough from Kyaw to guess that they wouldn't be pleased. Lashio was half a day away, even if the rains hadn't worsened the roads. There were checkpoints every few miles along the highway. Scores of them. How a truck filled with guns and grenades and whatever else was meant to pass between there and here was beyond her comprehension. She couldn't even skip the boundaries of Mogok town with her birds, without a bribe.

The Thai held up his hands, seemingly reading her mind. 'If they want delivery to the forests, they need to pay the extra dollars they promised me. I don't do favours.'

She nodded again. 'I'll tell them.'

The Thai sniffed and looked away, reaching to his liquor bottle and refilling his glass. Thuza stayed seated, unsure of what to do. The rebels hadn't paid what they'd promised. She had thought Kyaw was lying about needing more money but perhaps they were desperate after all. Perhaps Kyaw would be the luckless soul sent on the impossible mission to Lashio as his penance for short-payment. She shook her mind free of guilt. If he was, it wouldn't be her fault. She had done all she could and now she had her own fate that needed her focus: a more immediate, disturbing threat. *I'm only a courier*, she whispered in her head. *Like the Thai is. No different.* She said it again three times, feeling braver. I'm doing nothing worse than anyone else would. I'm doing what I have to do to survive.

The Thai glared at her, pausing for a moment before re-screwing the bottle's cap. 'It's time to go, Little *Naga-ma*,' he said, lifting the glass and taking a sip. 'You're not the only soul I need to see this evening.'

Thuza flicked her head at him, frowning to her lap. She couldn't summon the words to say why she hadn't moved. She felt the same spears piercing through her body as the day before when she'd sat in the bamboo hut in the forest, and opened the note and first seen his name.

He pursed his lips, a slight scowl emerging from behind them, and then raised a gristly finger to his minder in the corner of the room. The man stood and cracked his knuckles, advancing on Thuza.

'Wait!'

Thuza leapt up, panicking, her mind a fuzz as she scrambled to open her bag. She tripped towards the Thai, thrusting it at him, and he saw its contents and sprinted instantly up too, kicking back the armchair and spilling his drink. He grabbed his revolver from the table and swung for her, snatching a ball of her hair into his hand and pressing the barrel of the gun to her head. The minder had found his weapon too and it was trained on her from where he was poised four feet away. She heard herself gasp with the pain of her scalp straining against his clench, and she staggered, feeling the cold, hard metal on her skull and trying to stay still despite her shaking limbs and her impulse to run.

The Thai released her briefly, seizing her satchel and shaking it out before taking hold of her again. The sixteen blocks of creamy clay explosives thudded onto the floor. 'What's this?'

'It's from Htin Soe,' she said through her terror, as quickly as she could. 'Sixteen pounds of C4. Like you ordered.'

She felt his fist tighten on the back of her head and she cried out, squeezing her eyes shut and praying to the spirits, waiting for the bang to come and release her, but then the Thai let go abruptly and pushed her away. Her legs buckled and she fell, scrabbling back from him to the safety of the wall. She hit the skirting and stared up, her heart racing and spine braced to the wood. The Thai stepped backwards too, wiping his mouth and waving at his minder, who lowered his gun cautiously.

'You're working for Htin?' asked the Thai.

'I work for myself.'

He looked at her suspiciously. 'What debt do you have to him?'

'Nothing,' said Thuza. 'I've no debt to anyone.'

He smiled momentarily and pointed at her. 'Ah, you warm his bed, you slippery serpent.'

She spat at his feet.

The Thai glanced at his minder again, the heave of his chest slowing, and then tucked his gun into his belt. He stared at Thuza, appraising her for a long, heavy minute, then spoke to his man in brisk, curt Thai. The minder nodded and lumbered to the bed, digging his hand beneath the pillow and pulling out a briefcase. He passed it to the Thai, who knelt in front of Thuza and clicked open the latches. He raised the lid slowly open, paused, and then turned the briefcase towards her. Thuza's heart skipped. It was more money than she'd ever seen before; ten huge bundles of crisp, new grey-green and white American banknotes, tied with red string.

The Thai stared at her above the rim of the case. 'Have you come to trick me, Little *Naga-ma*? Is this the price of my demise?'

She caught her breath and raised her head to him, dragging herself to sit taller and returning his stare. 'No. I'm here for my money. That's all.'

'Now would be the time to say if you were lying. If you left and the days ahead showed me any differently, I would find you, child, with your blue eyes and serpent's tongue . . . You know that, don't you?'

She nodded, shivering.

'What arrangement did you make with Htin?'

'What business is that of yours?' said Thuza, scowling. She wouldn't tell him what cut she'd agreed to, not give him the chance to steal the prize she'd worked so hard to find and secure and send her back to her old, tricky gem dealer with nothing in the briefcase for her.

The Thai smiled again, still pinning her beneath his stare, but the smile seemed warmer somehow. His shoulders had eased. He clicked the case shut and tipped it up, then slid it across the floorboards towards her and sat back, crossing his legs as lithely as man a quarter of his age. The explosives were scattered on the floor around him, and one by one, he picked them up and arranged them into a pyramid in front of him where the case had been.

'Do you know where these will go?' he said, placing the last block on the top of the tower and rounding its corners beneath his thumb, smoothing it to a curve. He moved to the next, shifting downwards. The plastic coverings crackled like flames.

Thuza swallowed hard. Even through the plastic, she could see her own fingerprints printed on the tackiness of the clay, her indentations smaller and gentler than the new marks he was leaving, but just as deep. Wherever they went now, she was joined to them. Culpable. Whoever they hurt – Kyaw or a stranger – the spirits would know the part she had played. Zawtika would know too, and her parents when they looked at her. Though she wouldn't say why, her face would be different, and they'd know the sins she had committed to set them free. 'Htin said it was for the Tatmadaw,' she replied, glancing down.

'You're not interested what they'll do with it . . . ? Why they need to buy explosive from me?'

She shook her head.

'You're not afraid they'll find out what you've done?'

'No.'

'Perhaps you should be afraid I'll tell them. What's the punishment for treason, Little *Naga-ma*? If the Tatmadaw caught you running errands for the rebels they'd deny they'd ever paid you a wage. By the spirits, they'd deny they paid you one if you were made of nothing but goodness and gold. You don't exist to them. This won't help you be important. It can't change anything about you, except for the worse. You wouldn't be able to hide beyond the border like I could, if they turned. Not that I'd need to hide. I'm protected. What do you have? You're on your own as you're treading this tightrope.' He grinned, leaning in closer to her. 'I'm curious, Little *Naga-ma*. What is it that's making you take such risks?'

Thuza felt a shudder of fear whip through her body, and she thought of her parents alone in their cells. She'd put them there, with her carelessness. She sat on the floor and stared at the Thai, feeling eleven years old again before his ancientness and her memories, listening to his threats and gripped by a burning-hot panic at having been caught, the same way she had been gripped with horror at the sight of the figure closing in on her through the darkness of the forest, and she'd panicked and rushed and torn her father's map. That's how all this had started: her panic. Her weakness. She would stay calm this time. She would do it right. She tensed her muscles and focused on the money. On travelling to Insein. On freedom. The end.

'It's nothing more to you why I take my risks than what I get paid for them,' she whispered coolly. She glared at the Thai, seeing him weigh her up.

He laughed, his lip hooked high above his teeth, and clapped his hands. 'I didn't know there were any souls beside Htin and I in Mogok who dared to earn their suppers from both sides as brazenly as you've done. You're brave. Whatever cut you agreed, I hope it's a windfall.' He gave her a nod of respect and stretched to pick up his liquor bottle from the table and the glass from the floor, then filled it to the brim and slipped it towards her, just as he'd done with the briefcase. With one hand, he fingered the pyramid of C4 blocks stacked in front of him. With the other he drew a circle on her knee. Slowly and lightly he touched her, smiling. He dropped his voice to a murmur and leaned forward, wheezing. 'I heard your brother fights with the rebels. Rest assured, Little *Naga-ma*. This isn't for them.'

TEN

Than leant on the table heavily, peering down at the big, tatty map. Three upturned coffee cups and a can of lentil soup pinned the corners to the tea-ringed wood, and he ran his palm across the paper to smooth it down. Since he'd been home, all he'd done was worry. Though he'd tried his hardest to mark the map with the Mogok zones, the mountains were sprawling, full of ridges and hidden ravines, and each day the boundaries of the safe spaces changed and he couldn't be sure what he'd done was quite right. The kitchen was hot, the oil lamps were low and he'd closed the windows and pulled the curtains so that nobody shirking outside could hear or see in. Though the space was easily large enough for the table and its benches, the two dressers against the wall that Marlar's aunt had given them, Min's bookcase and a half-full sloping wooden larder, and a log store in the corner by the basket of cooking pots, his family was large too. Their supper had been bubbling on the stove for more than an hour, and its steam had fogged the groggy light and the doubts in his mind had grown and grown. He bit his fingernail and tore a strip off, staring at the white chalk circles he had drawn as they wound unsteady rings around the land under Tatmadaw control, and the black rings for the rebels' land, and brown for the areas that were still in dispute. He had wasted enough time on his thinking already. The marks that were there would have to do.

He tapped a stub of chalk on his teeth and glanced to the top shelf of the nearest dresser, to the miniature altar he'd arranged with such care. Though of course Aung San's photo had pride of place in the centre, it wasn't the general who he focused on now. He was still feeling sore from the exchange with Bo Win and he wanted the comfort from something more transcendent – more faithful and supportive – and his eyes slipped over to his two figurines. Milky-skinned and adorned with flowers, and with prickly red rambutan fruits at their feet that he'd laid there that morning, the precious porcelain statues stared steadily down. Almost every home in Burma had ornaments like these. They were the images of the spirits who had died violent deaths, either drowned, murdered or ravished by sickness, or by throwing themselves on open flames. They served as the guardians of dwellings, towns, tribes and possessions across the country, the wind, air, rain, sky, earth, forest, rivers and mountains all within their control. If treated right, they'd protect good men from wild animals and bandits. If treated badly, the havoc they'd wreak would be worse than the plague.

It was Daw Su who had told Than which spirits would guide him personally, the very first time that he'd limped to her door. Thagyamin was the king of all the greatest spirits, the three-headed white elephant who held up a conch shell and a severed yak's tail, and would remind Than how eminence could always be aspired to, and clear his thoughts to pave the way. The other idol was Shwe Nabay, the beautiful queen who married a *naga*, and who would teach him that fortune could twist like tornados, and that whatever misfortune had ensnared him one moment may not be there to ensnare him the next. It had pierced to Than's core when Daw Su called him that *naga*. He had often sensed it, though the feeling then was nameless. Discarded on the outside, he was waiting to come in. He closed his eyes and willed his spirits to help him, as he had every day that Aung San ignored him. They didn't judge him like the generals did, or goad him or betray him. He would always revere them and they'd quietly buoy him. They would always be loyal. They braced his nerves.

He picked up a new piece of red chalk, drawing a careful cross above a cluster of houses on the side of Shwe Hill. A gem thief lived in the shack by the river. His brother was a dissident and everyone knew how he stole from the mines. Of all the existing robbers that Than knew of, this man would be the simplest to catch if decisions were based on location alone. His house was right in the centre of a white zone and Than could stroll to his door and back without firing a shot. He stared at the cross and rolled this thought over, and the ache in his head gave another dull thud. It should have been simple but it never was. There were practical facts that his spirits failed to see. The man had a cousin who was married to a major. The major's father had given Bo Win his most favourite dog. A huge auburn mastiff with a bark like gunfire, he'd brought it home from a trip to China to sweeten a deal about building a house. Than rubbed his neck and a low groan rumbled. He could feel the dog's fangs on his windpipe already. He spat on his finger and wiped out the cross.

From under the table, there was a sudden thump, and a

coffee cup jolted from the edge of the map and shattered on the floor. The sardine can that had propped the table's one stumpy leg spun across the concrete and disappeared beneath the bookcase, and Khine shrieked, throwing herself against Than's shins and clinging to him.

'Daddy!' she wailed as he scraped back the bench and reached down to unpeel her wiry grasp. The little girl stared up at him, eyes wide and watery, her hair a mess of tangled black. 'It wasn't me.'

Than gritted his teeth and dragged her from beneath the table. She slid on her knees, resisting him. A slick of stickiness leaked from her nose and smeared on his sleeve. 'Can't you see I'm working?'

'But Po Chit's chasing me, Daddy,' she said. 'And Thiha.'

'Then chase them back. I'm busy.'

'They were pulling my hair.'

'Tell them to stop.'

'You tell them, Daddy. They're bigger than me.'

'Marlar?'

There was a chorus of coughed laughter stifled behind hands and Po Chit and Thiha emerged from beneath the table and scurried to their mother's side, giggling. Marlar was standing at the stove with her back to the room, one-year-old May hooked up on her hip. She didn't turn around. The boys yanked at the hem of her apron, wiggling their tongues at Khine with glee. Khine wrapped her arms around Than's thighs and started to cry. He muttered a curse and prised her back, bending to the floor and collecting the broken splinters of red and white china in his palm.

'Marlar, did you hear me?'

'I heard you,' said his wife.

'How am I supposed to think in this chaos?'

'I wasn't aware you were given to thinking.' She brandished her ladle at the map on the table, without turning round. 'Can you clear that away?'

'I'm not finished.'

'Supper's ready. I need to lay the bowls.'

'Where's Min?'

Thiha threw himself down on the bench beside Than. 'He told me he had errands to run in the town,' said the boy, watching his father and kicking the table with his little bare feet.

'Yeah,' said Po Chit, grinning. He slumped at Thiha's side and hooked his arm around his neck, dragging him prone and clambering over him, pummelling his fists playfully into his twin's ribs. Thiha wriggled and squealed beneath his weight. 'He'll be polishing his crown, I expect. Shining his medals.'

Than pursed his lips and lifted Po Chit from the table, cuffing the boy's head and shoving him towards his mother. He hadn't seen Min since the incident this morning, but his son had never been far from his mind. Their exchange had swelled in his memory, magnified. It was louder than it had been. Min was more hurtful. Than had been harsh, but Min had been too. He shook his head, nervous of what he would say when he saw him, of how Min would seem when he looked in his eye. 'We're not eating without him,' he said.

'We should, Dad,' said Po Chit, wandering back to sit beside him. 'More for us.'

'Yeah,' said Thiha. 'And Min always gets the best stuff.'

'He's the oldest.'

'He's the favourite.'

'The auspicious son!'

The boys laughed and stretched across the table, picking up the chalk and beginning to scrawl. Than pushed them away again and picked up his map, folding it roughly and ramming it into his briefcase. His wife really was an unhelpful brown trout. They'd been married for almost twenty years and for a few at least, things had been rather nice. When he'd first known her, she'd seemed as good a girl as any from the district, with strong arms and wide hips, and she'd laughed at Than's joke about the snake with the lisp who said he had syphilis, but until the day the vows were made, she never let him hold her hand. The fact that her father had turned out to be a colonel had only sweetened their meeting. It was more than Than had ever hoped, for a boy of his background to marry a colonel's daughter. For whatever reason, the old goat had been fond of Than and he promised to help his career progress quickly, but less than a month after the wedding deal was sealed, he got himself shot in the gullet by a trigger-happy twelve-year-old conscript and died, and he'd been no damn use for anything since that.

Over the years, it appeared that bloody gullet had been a premonition. As the opportunities had flittered past Than, and the children drained Marlar, their love somehow leaked away. To start, he had liked that she'd said what she was thinking – so many of the women he had met were limp dishrags – but then her thoughts had started to wander.

More and more, they roamed further from his. Than had finished being sad about the distance between them or dwelling on his memories of closeness and caring, instead absorbed with Min and their intertwined ambitions, but from time to time he still felt frustrated. It wouldn't have strained her to help him out.

He snatched up his briefcase and spun the one side of the combination lock that wasn't jammed so his children couldn't open it, then forced it into the narrow space between the two dressers. He was slamming his chalk away in the drawer and hoping the beer he'd stashed in the jailhouse's toilet cistern would still be hidden if he went back this evening, when he heard a key in the front door turn.

'Min's home!'

Khine scampered from beneath the table and darted across the room, a smile breaking on her face. She threw herself at her brother as he opened the door, her skinny arms only reaching his waist and her legs around his shins. He hauled her up as she slid towards the floor and he gnawed her cheeks so she screamed and cackled, before plonking her down on the rug by his feet.

'We're having noodles for dinner,' she said, peering up. 'And sausage.'

Than stood by the dresser, his mouth open, as still as the porcelain spirits watching down. He felt as though his heart had stopped. His hand sought out the shelf, steadying him. Min paused nervously on the rug, the street bustling behind him and the last dregs of daylight holding him on the threshold, softening his frame to almost a blur, and then he stepped inside and pulled the door to. From the stove, Than heard Marlar gasp. For once he knew what was in his wife's mind. The twins were staring too from their seat at the table. Their brows were uncertain, riddled by creases. Their brother looked so different. He was taller. Stronger. In the missing hours, Min had grown into a man. Than took him in, this newly formed vision. He was dressed in a full Tatmadaw uniform, his shirt darkest green and starched stiffer than a palm leaf, and the badge on his collar was a crisp, polished gold. The crease in his trousers stood as sharp as the mountains. The shine on his boots made the black look liquid silver. He took off his beret and wrung it in his hands.

'Hi, Dad.'

'By the spirits,' muttered Than. He flicked his head, disbelieving. 'Look at you!' A tide of relief cleared through his veins and he lunged forward and seized his son's hands, beaming. If he didn't move, he was going to explode.

Min smiled awkwardly. 'What do you think?'

'You look like a leader.'

'You look like a thug,' said Marlar. She was glaring at them both from across the kitchen, her face almost scarlet, her eyes afraid. She winched May from her hip and thrust her at Po Chit, striding towards them. She shook her head. 'Tell me you haven't.'

Min threw his gaze at her feet and blushed, nodding. 'I've enrolled, Mum,' he said. 'I'm sorry. It was the right thing to do.' He turned to Than and gave him another clumsy, self-conscious smile. 'I'm sorry about this morning too, Dad. I should have done a better speech. I could have made the general like me. I didn't mean to let you down.'

Than felt a surge of emotion tighten in him. He lifted his arm around Min's shoulder and forced himself to laugh, pulling his son in, hugging him. 'You did fine, boy,' he said, almost choking on his words. 'Better than fine. In fact, as soon as you'd left, the general was saying what a spark you were. Bright as a flare! And how broad your shoulders were. Oh, I've never been prouder in my life.'

He scratched his nose and hurried away, flustered, retrieving his briefcase from where he had just stashed it and fumbling to arrange the dials on the lock. He needed something tangible to snare everyone's attention, to keep his joy and relief from overflowing, and to stop his shame from spilling out in tears.

'It's perfect, see,' he said, taking out the map and flattening it on the table, stabbing it with his finger. He darted back to grab the chalk. 'I was given a very prestigious assignment today and I'm allowed to choose my men. I'm running the first operation in the morning.' He looked up and smiled at Min. 'When do you start?'

'Tomorrow.'

'It's fate!'

Marlar gasped again, chucking up her hands and tearing across the room. She ripped aside the map, and Po Chit and Thiha skittered back from her as she snatched her tray of crockery and cutlery from where it was waiting and started thrusting the pieces into settings on the wood. 'You're not going anywhere tomorrow but school, Min Soe Khaing,' she said, shaking her head. She froze and stared at him suddenly, desperation etched into her expression, then clapped her hands and pointed. 'Take that shirt off. Quickly now. We'll press it again before we give it back.'

Min winced and glanced at his father. 'The paperwork's done,' he said quietly. 'I can't take it back, Mum. It's a five-year term.'

She stared and shook her head again, breathless. '*Oh, Min.*'

Than stepped forward. He reached towards her but she drew herself back as though his touch might burn. 'We've talked about this Marlar, haven't we?' he said, as gently as he could. 'It's what's best.'

'He's seventeen. That's no age for a soldier.'

'It's OK. He knows more than you think and they'll train him, won't they? It's a good life, love. Noble. Secure.'

Her face wrinkled and she blew at the air, disgusted. 'I can't think of any life less secure than a Mogok private. Min needs a proper education.'

She muttered something else beneath her breath and grabbed up May, backing toward the stove, clutching the child tightly and pressing her cheek to her forehead. Than watched, unable to unravel her. No matter how much they had talked it over, he never understood why she wouldn't accept it. Why couldn't she see this was Min's only option? For them all – their destinies – this was the choice.

'Why aren't you happy, Marlar?' he said. 'Honestly. It's the only place a boy his age should be. You know that. The people love and respect the Tatmadaw.'

'They fear them, Than Chit.'

'It's the same thing. They keep us together, sweetheart. What's not to love? Without strong men like Min and me to hold the insurgents at bay — all the murderers and rapists and whatever else they are — the whole country would collapse. Boys like Min are securing our future.'

Min gripped his hands together, looking nervous. 'Do you really believe that, Dad?'

'Of course.'

'Your father believes what he's told to believe.'

'You don't know what you're saying, Marlar. The Tatmadaw gives its blood and sweat for the people. Besides, it's better he's with them than against them, surely? Or would you rather he was sent down the mines? That's the only other job for a Mogok boy, no matter how many days he's been to school.'

'Why would you want to be a soldier, Min?' said Thiha. The brothers and Khine had been watching quietly from the furthest corner of the table. They would never miss a chance to see Min chastised, and as the voices had escalated their eyes sparked too. 'Only stupid boys are soldiers.'

'Yeah,' said Po Chit, cracking a bold, slight smirk. 'They're thieves too. They stole Zeya Aung's vegetables from his garden.'

'And they're drunks. That's why they get shot in the head so often. They never see it coming. What would you want to get shot in the head for, Min?'

Than could feel his whole body convulsing with rage. 'Where did the children learn to speak like that?' he said, his hands clenched to fists. 'The Tatmadaw aren't drunks.'

Marlar looked up at him with a bullet-hole stare. 'Aren't they?'

He shook his head. 'No. And you shouldn't be so careless

as to let them say it. It's lies like that which cost lives. Do you want your boy strung up for treason? Where do you think they'll go when he is, Marlar? A treasonous child has a treasonous parent.' He rubbed the string of spittle from his chin and stepped closer to Marlar, coiling his fingers around her wrist and pressing her against the wall, lowering his face to find her eyes. He dropped his voice to his quietest, most controlled whisper. 'Use your head.'

Marlar recoiled, tugging her hands from his and scowling at his chest. Her lip was trembling. A sob escaped and she clasped her hand to her mouth. 'What were you thinking, Than Chit?'

'I was thinking that this is the very best thing our son can do.'

'Don't lie. You were thinking about yourself.'

'Perhaps I was thinking about all of us, Marlar. Did you consider that? If Min didn't join the Tatmadaw — if our sons don't follow in my footsteps — what would that say? It would say I'm disloyal . . . that my whole family is disloyal. Our children will be marked for life. All of them. Do you want that? I'm keeping us safe.'

'But Min's not safe, is he?' said Marlar, a swell of tears teetering on the curves of her eyes. 'You know the war is escalating.'

'The boy's smart. He'll be fine.'

'What use is being smart when you're dodging bullets? Survival in the forest is nothing but luck. The way things are, they'll send him to the mountains and he'll end up as nothing more than another young minesweeper. Do you want him to have the same journey as you?'

There's been nothing wrong with my journey, thought Than with bitterness. If anything, he'd made it a trip to be proud of. Who else could have forged such success from what he had? He remembered the day the Tatmadaw picked him up, the humidity and the clinical smell of the air in the holding tent at the barracks, the slow advance of the cool blade across his scalp as the sergeant shaved his matted hair, the sting on his skin and in his eyes as they dunked him naked in the vast vat of liquid and the lice that floated to the surface and bobbed like seeds on a river crest, and the stains of orange in his creases and around his fingernails that he couldn't scrub off for more than a week. What he remembered most though was the feeling of gratitude. For their care and approval – for the promise of protection – he would have scaled a thousand snowy peaks. Ever since, he had strived to seize his opportunities, and now his wife had a blade to his wrist-bone, threatening to slit him and bleed him to death. He stared into her face, searching her eyes for something shared in their history, something to remind her of how he had loved her, and the hopes they'd shared when he had sworn to protect her, so she'd know in her heart that he meant what he said. He needed her trust.

He moved closer, gathering her hands in his again and clasping them, pushing her back against the wall, more gently this time. 'Min needs the Tatmadaw, Marlar – like I did. He needs to be part of their family.'

Marlar looked up at him, pain slashing her face. 'He has a family, Than. He admires you more than anything, but he's not the same as you. Why must you force him down a path that doesn't suit him?'

'I haven't forced him, Marlar.'

'You have. And Thiha's right. He'll be nothing but a target for the rebels in the hills.'

'Min won't come to any harm. I'll look after him.'

She sighed, a tear spilling from the corner of her eye. 'You're a second-rate, dead-end officer,' she whispered. 'What protection can you give a front-line boy?'

'I'm not dead-end,' Than spat, releasing her. The words hurt like pelted stones. 'As soon as I get promoted, I'll sort Min out. He won't be on the line for long.'

'And what if you don't get promoted?'

'It's coming, Marlar. I'm certain.'

'How do you know?'

Than felt his expression twist. Marlar glared at him, revulsion smoking in her eyes. 'Oh,' she said, and her head nodded slowly. 'Because the fortune-teller told you. That crooked hag knows you're a fool as much as I do. She says just enough to steal your money and string you along and keep you hobbling back.'

'It's not just her,' replied Than, his eyes skipping away. Raindrops on glass. 'Everyone says it. I've earned this promotion.'

'But you're using your son. You're offering him up to the general as a sacrifice. Do you think this will prove your loyalty? Bo Win doesn't care what happens to Min. You're nothing more than his yapping lapdog. And he's no shrewder than you are. He sits on someone else's lap, all the way to the dog at the top. Don't do this, Than. Don't sell our son.'

He slapped the wall beside her face and she yelped and flinched then scurried away. 'You don't know what you're talking about, Marlar.' He glanced behind. The children were staring.

She dried her eyes and straightened her apron, keeping her back to him. 'I know you more than you think, Than Chit,' she said quietly. 'And the thing I know most that gives me cold comfort? If Min suffers from a scratch or a snake or a demon, the spirits above us will make you pay.'

ELEVEN

Michael sat on the stairs in darkness, drumming his fingers on the backpack in his lap. The curtains at the opposite end of the hallway were fluttering with the wind, revealing the moon and stars in flashes, and the golden spire of the Shwedagon Pagoda cast its glow across the sky. From Bogyoke Aung San Stadium, he could hear a distant warble of tinny music, and from time to time the sound of a train as it left the station, whistling and sighing as the wheels began to turn. The residence, however, was quiet and still. The staff had left for the evening, his mother was visiting a friend in East Dagon Township and his father had retired to his room a good hour before, his book tucked beneath his arm and a glass of water in his hand. Michael had said goodnight and closed the door to his own bedroom too. From the footwell of his wardrobe, he'd pulled out his backpack, stuffing it with clothes as quietly as he could and listening through the wall as his father padded around, opening drawers and clattering coat hangers, before settling down with a creak of the bed. Michael hadn't heard him move for a while now, but a thin line of electric light still trickled from underneath his door. He looked at his watch. It was almost half past ten and his mother would be home soon. He had checked his father's diary on the sly a little earlier. The ambassador had a breakfast meeting at seven. He wouldn't stay up much later than this. His fingers beat on the backpack, harder. He couldn't afford to wait much more.

The bed creaked again and the line of light flickered as footsteps passed it, and Michael lifted himself carefully from the stairs, trying to avoid the loose, noisy floorboards, and crept towards his father's room. There was a cough and a shuffling of bed-sheets from inside and he froze suddenly, but then he heard the book being placed on the bedside table, and the lamp's switch clicked and light went black. He stood there, his hands pressed to the door, waiting to be sure that his father was sleeping, and then he bent to his knees, his bag on his shoulder, and slipped the envelope beneath the door.

Outside, the pickup truck had parked down the alleyway at the back of the residence's gardens where Michael had said it was safest to wait. Teacher was leaning on the side of the cab, burrowing a toothpick between his teeth and swigging from a bottle of Red Cat whisky. The driver inside looked to be asleep. Michael heaved a small sigh of relief. They'd waited.

'Ready?' asked Teacher.

Michael nodded.

Teacher straightened and pounded on the side of the cab, waking the driver with a start. The man gave a thumbs-up and fired the engine to life, and Teacher walked to the back of the truck and unhooked the tailgate, jumping in. Michael followed him, tossing his bag amongst the jumble of enormous white rice sacks. Teacher held out his hand to heave Michael up, then hoisted the tailgate behind him and pinned down the loose flap of thick green canvas that was stretched across the pick-up's frame. They plunged into darkness, and Michael heard Teacher scrabbling between the sacks, and then a torch flickered on. He hung it by its string from a hook above the cab.

The truck veered into reverse, turning in the alleyway and bobbing away along the rutted road, and Michael staggered to keep on his feet. The torchlight swayed, revealing benches along either wall, and Teacher weaved deeper through the cargo to the furthest corner, resting back against the cab and closing his eyes. Michael slid carefully down on the opposite side, without speaking. Neither Teacher nor the driver seemed to want to talk. He tucked his bag between his feet and unzipped the front pocket, pulling out his tobacco pouch, rolling a cigarette and sparking up. He drew on the smoke and his leg started jittering. Had he been rash? A feeling was niggling. His mother never turned on the lights if his father was sleeping; she would tiptoe to bed in the moonlit dark. They wouldn't find his letter until morning. At least until then, he would be on his own.

He shifted back along the bench and tried to relax like Teacher was doing, wishing he'd had the foresight to pack some liquor of his own. Through the canvas's patchworked seams, he could see the city's lights spinning by and hear its movement, but he couldn't see at all where they were headed. The humidity was devilish, the heat of the evening having curdled the fumes of diesel that spluttered from the engine, and he could feel the sweat as it formed on his body. It collected on his lip and soaked his shirt. If he hadn't been paying such close attention, he might have thought that Teacher was sleeping, but every so often he caught the man watching. When their eyes met, he closed them swiftly, or gulped from his bottle and turned away.

Michael closed his own eyes, uneasy with the scrutiny and the unknowns that pinched him, and focused on the pitch and the turns of the truck. As they left the city, the road smoothed, becoming noticeably darker, straighter and quieter, and he felt himself exhale, relieved that a stretch of travel on the highway might give him a chance to let his queasiness drop. The respite was brief. Just a few minutes sped away before an abrupt turn from the long, even highway threw him from his seat, and the smoothness of the tarmac was lost to the thump of a rocky dirt road.

The truck lurched, the undercarriage dragging and cracking against the uneven ground, and Michael clambered back onto the bench, bracing himself against the jolts. Teacher staggered up. He peeled open a corner of the back canopy and tacked it upwards, and a channel of weak, milky moonlight unfurled on the floor. Michael ducked his head and gasped for the air so hard that he coughed. Squinting through the opening, he could see there was hardly a road behind them, just tracks in red dust. On either side of the rubble, the land was overladen with palms, unkempt and unfriendly. They seemed to be cutting a path through the jungle. He swallowed the acid from his mouth and crossed the carriage with unsteady steps, leaning on the rice sacks.

'How long until we reach Shan State?' he shouted to Teacher above the bawl of the engine. The lack of talk was making him anxious. It was leaving too much time to think.

Teacher sat down and picked up his whisky, then shrugged. 'It depends what the rains have done to the roads.'

'Wouldn't it be quicker if we stuck to the highways?'

He shook his head. 'A journey can only be quick if you're allowed to finish it. You understand?'

Michael didn't, but he nodded anyway. The engine was struggling harder against the terrain and with its pummel and the worry that throbbed in his head, it was difficult to decipher Teacher's scrappy English. He had realised too how poor his Burmese was. He could order a coconut for Daw Mar at the market, but when they'd hashed out a plan in the teahouse this afternoon and Teacher's voice was increasingly heated, there were times when he'd hardly been able to fathom a thing. He pulled out his tobacco pouch again and offered it to Teacher. Teacher frowned and closed his eyes, lifting his feet onto the bench and resting his head on the wall. Michael watched him, unsure of what to do. Teacher took another gulp of whisky. Michael tucked his hands beneath his thighs.

'What's the problem?' said Teacher, without looking at him. Michael shook his head.

'Are you scared what the rebels will think of a white boy?'

'Aren't you?'

Teacher hissed a thin, fleeting laugh through the gap where his front teeth should have been. 'Not much. The SSA likes freedom and democracy. White boys like freedom and democracy. There's no need for arguments.'

Michael rubbed the diesel fumes from his stinging eyes and glanced again from the back of the truck. With as much as he knew, he supposed that was accurate. When his father had travelled in rebel territories before, he had left instructions with Barrowman that if he were to be taken hostage, the British government should walk away. The rebels had a penchant for kidnapping foreigners, but a Burmese colleague had enquired discreetly and was assured that the British's refusal to negotiate made bothering with anyone from the embassy pointless. Remembering this gave Michael a scrap of comfort. Still, there was something about the way Teacher was sitting and the tone of his voice that wasn't quite right.

'You don't think they'll be shocked to see me?' said Michael, though he wasn't so sure that he wanted to push. 'What if they think I'm a spy?'

Teacher shrugged again, wider. 'Then we leave and come home.'

'But they trust you, don't they? We're not in any danger.'

'Not much more than we would be at home. Don't worry. You've nothing to fear as long as you're with me. In life there are always big animals and small animals, Michael Atwood. The Tatmadaw thinks they are the only big animals in Burma. They say everyone else is a small animal. In Rangoon, it's true. We are not allowed to have ideas for ourselves. If anyone complains . . .' His eyes sprang open and he jumped forward suddenly, gnashing his teeth together and clamping a hand around his windpipe. '. . . the big animals will eat us. The Tatmadaw are wrong though. In Shan State, the SSA – my friends and my brothers – they're big animals too. They're as fearsome as tigers and as powerful as bears. They can give us a voice. We refuse to be eaten when we fight on their side. You've already

189

proved that you're a big animal by taking this journey. They'll like you for that. You're ready to fight.'

Michael raised an awkward smile and looked into his lap, feeling the tension in his shoulders tighten and digging his hands further beneath his legs. He had heard Sein talk about big animals and small animals too. He wasn't sure he'd done anything to deserve being called a big animal. In fact, he wasn't sure he had ever felt smaller. He certainly hadn't done anything worthy of respect. The note he'd left his parents was cowardly and vague. It didn't say precisely where he was going, just that he was heading north to help Sein. He had told them not to worry. He'd stay in contact as much as was possible, and was sure he'd be home within the week. Of course he knew that when his father read it, merry hell would break loose. His mother would have a stroke when he told her. Barrowman and the embassy staff would have Michael's image pinned to every checkpoint booth by high tea, along with what biscuits he liked with his coffee, and what size under-pants he wore. That's why he'd left a letter. He'd have never got away if he'd told him face to face. It was thoughtless, he knew. Foolish and reckless. What *did* he mean to do, when he got to the mountains? The thought of his friend had clouded his vision. He had hoped clarity would come to him later, or some wonderful bolt of luck might find him, but now in the truck he wasn't so sure. He glanced at Teacher, swigging his alcohol, and a shudder of dread ripped up through his body. He was driving to a warzone with a man he hardly knew and a bright-white complexion, hardly any money and even less of a plan.

'How long were you with the rebels, Teacher?' he asked to break the mood.

Teacher scratched his nose. 'Twenty-three years. I was based in the mountains outside Mogok, not far from where I grew up. It's mining country. Strategic land but tough as elephant hide. I got too old to live in the forests. Another fever would have killed me. I'm still in touch with a few of the commanders though. I do what I can. I send them money sometimes. Information if I have it. Medicine. Organise shipments of essential supplies, like this one. That sort of thing. I haven't been back myself for years.'

'Why are you going now? What's different?'

Teacher stared down into his bottle, swilling the liquid inside the glass. He looked sad suddenly. 'The bomb at my shop sparked memories, Michael Atwood. I'd forgotten what it felt like. The rage. The guilt. I saw the same thing happen many times in Shan State. The Tatmadaw would target the rebels, but they didn't care who got in the way. Once, a bomb was planted on an SSA supply route in a village near where I used to be stationed, but the shrapnel scattered and knifed through a school. I feel for your friend, brother. I feel for every customer in my shop. Every soul in Burma. I want to do more.'

Michael stared into his lap, his own guilt resurging. 'I went to see my father yesterday,' he whispered. '. . . after the bomb when I left your shop. I asked for his help. He said that some problems don't have solutions. That Burma couldn't be fixed.'

'He's right.'

'But you fought to fix it?'

191

'To start with. Later I fought to limit the damage, if I could. There are too many people involved from too many corners, and they've too much at stake to concede or sell up.'

'Do you really believe that?'

He nodded. 'You can try if you must to persuade a lone wanderer, but age has shown me there's nothing on earth to persuade a mob. Nobody who has the power to stop the war truly wants it to end. They've too much money to lose and too much blood on their hands. Too many men are driven more by glory than morals, and they're laced together tightly. They can't be undone. I believe what you said, Michael Atwood . . . that the Tatmadaw did it. Fuck, I'd wager that the same man who sells my comrades in Shan State their weapons had a hand in our bomb too. He's a Thai, toddy-swilling and liver-spotted and as shifty as a snake, and he's been lathering both sides into a frenzy since I was a child. He must be in his seventies now, but he's sharper than a spear and as fit as a fox. He still travels to the mountains every month himself, and he's exactly the type of bandit I mean. Do you think he's urging everyone to strive for peace? All we can do is rub at the edges and numb a little pain.'

Michael looked at Teacher, startled. He must have misunderstood. 'The same arms dealer supplies the Tatmadaw and the rebels?'

Teacher shook his head. 'He doesn't supply the Tatmadaw army. He supplies the secrets. Any extras. The blame they want to apportion elsewhere. Not that the Tatmadaw know what else he's up to. He's probably responsible for half of Shan State's war.'

Michael stared at him and shook his head too, his mind

spinning. 'The fighting in Shan State . . .' he asked, nervous. 'How bad is it?'

A yell from the cab interrupted before Teacher could reply. The driver tore aside the sheath of canvas that separated him from his passengers, turning back and pointing ahead.

'*Ka-myan-myan!*' he cried. 'Quickly!

His voice was snappish, a hasty spat curse. As he shouted again, Michael could see that his eyes were skittering. He brandished a gristly brown hand and the truck pitched left across a boulder, then he barked an instruction, grabbing back at the wheel.

'What's happening?' said Michael as Teacher leapt up. He had thrown down his whisky and torn the torch from its hook, battering it off on the bone of his wrist. His silhouette darted across the carriage and yanked the back corner canopy shut.

'There's a checkpoint ahead,' he replied, tugging at the loops, knotting them.

'On this road?' cried Michael, astonished. He swung around to look through the cab and managed to catch sight of the track ahead before the driver closed the canvas and darkness closed in. Ahead, a booth was illuminated by floodlights, and sandbags formed a staggered wall across two-thirds of the road. A handful of boys in Tatmadaw military uniforms were loitering beside them, some teenagers, but some appearing no older than nine or ten. They were clustered in the shade of a tarpaulin and smoking with their heads bent down. They looked rough and malnourished. Their shirts hung too big from their gaunt, arched backs, and the rifles on their shoulders, oversized against their childish frames, were the only things that seemed to be cared for.

Michael had long stopped counting the number of times his father had told him that Tatmadaw soldiers were not for trusting. Brutes, he called them, the whole rotten lot. The ones that were loyal would arrest a foreigner for little more than a misplaced stare, just to mark their territory like urinating dogs. The ones that weren't would do it for cash or promotion. The ones who looked hungry would arrest you the quickest. The ones who were young would arrest you for less. He looked at Teacher, panicked. 'What are they doing here? We're in the middle of nowhere.'

'They know the rebels take the back roads,' said Teacher, digging through his bag without looking up.

'Then why are we taking the back roads?'

'The rebels take the highways too. Those checkpoints are permanent. These are temporary. Sometimes they're here, sometimes they're not. We took a gamble. A journey is only quick if you finish it, remember?'

He dragged a tatty envelope from his pocket – his identification papers – and tossed them on the bench before throwing his weight into one of the rice sacks and heaving it aside. He bent to the floor and started to tug at the metal hatch that was hidden beneath.

'You need to hide. Help me.'

Michael collapsed to the floor, his heart racing, and pulled at the crack where Teacher had his hands. He had his own papers with him too, though more through habit than anything else. He had known from the moment he'd stuffed them in his backpack that they'd be useless. He had no permission to be anywhere but the city, and they marked him out as a diplomat's boy. He hadn't stopped to think about what this meant though. Denial and adrenaline had hoisted him through.

He tugged harder at the hatch, feeling his panic rise. Teacher cursed and thumped it with his fist until it split from its hinge and lifted up. Michael gasped as he saw inside. Nestled in secret just a metre from where he had been sitting was the biggest, blackest cache of weapons he ever had seen. There were rows of neatly spooning rifles, an open-topped crate of jostling grenades and sticks of long-wicked dynamite. He whipped back his hands and looked at Teacher, reeling.

'Get in.'

'I can't.'

'We're dead if you don't.'

'There's no space for me.'

Teacher grabbed Michael by his shoulders, forcing him flat. Michael threw out his hands, but Teacher was much stronger than he was, and he bundled over him, trapping his legs and rolling him sideways, shoving his struggling body into the tiny compartment. The truck swayed as Teacher dumped Michael's rucksack after him and then hauled the hatch back over the hole. Michael shouted, hearing Teacher's sandalled feet stamp the metal shut just an inch from his face, and then the drag of the rice sack across the floor. In the choking heat and fume-filled blackness, he tried to twist away and press his hands forward, but his limbs were cramped and nothing would shift.

The truck slowed and then stopped and Michael froze, the barrel of a gun cutting into his side. In his ears, the pounding of his heart and his breath sounded deafening. A groaning hinge then a jolt let him know that the tailgate had dropped and the vehicle rocked as a soldier climbed in. Through the narrowest split of metal, he watched a set of muddied boots march across the floor.

'Identification documents,' said a young, tightly clipped voice. He was speaking in Burmese, but now that the truck was still and the words were simple, Michael could hear them clearly. There was a rustle of paper and a pause, and the voice spoke again. 'Your name is Khun Zaw Ye?'

Michael held his breath and listened to Teacher's carefully pitched, compliant reply.

The soldier carried on. 'You own a teahouse in Rangoon? What are you doing in a rice truck?'

'Yes, sir,' replied Teacher. 'I'm visiting family in Pyinmana. My niece's wedding.'

'Why isn't your vehicle on the highways?'

'We heard they were blocked. A landslide on the road outside Taungoo.'

There were a few more steps across the floor, then what sounded like a hand-clap. 'Empty your bag!'

Michael heard Teacher move along the bench and a zip was peeled open, and then the contents of his bag thumped onto the floor. There was another aching pause. The cramp in Michael's legs and head was growing thicker. From the hatch, his own breath spat back in his face, and he closed his eyes and tried to think. If he lived, his father was going to string him up. A burst of chatter followed, but it was muffled and rushed so he didn't quite catch it, then the conversation stopped and the truck rocked again as the soldier stepped out. Michael heard the tailgate slam and the engine turned on and the wheels began to pull away, and he thumped his knee against the hatch and called Teacher's name. The truck gathered speed and the hatch cracked open, and Teacher's tense brown face was staring down. He held out his hand.

Michael clambered from the hole, gasping for air. The stink of cigarettes, diesel and gun oil was swimming in his skull, and he slumped on the bench with his head in his hands. His spine was stiff and his throat was dry, and he needed a drink and he couldn't think straight.

'We're smuggling weapons,' he muttered, horrified.

Teacher smiled a gap-toothed grin. 'I told you we were bringing essential supplies. These are essential.' He closed his eyes and leaned back on the bench, wriggling to get comfortable and turning away. 'Tomorrow will be a long day, Michael Atwood. I suggest you get some sleep.'

Michael dug his teeth into his lip, sucking until he felt the throb of blood. The urge to turn back to Rangoon was gripping him, piercing his chest like a bear-trap had seized him, though he knew that Teacher would never consent. They'd driven too far and it would look too suspicious, and if he asked to get off, where would they leave him? The jungle here would eat him alive.

The truck rocked slowly onwards across the hostile terrain, and Michael slipped from the bench to the floor. He shifted to the tailgate, clutching his backpack and breathing unsteadily, and rolled up the corner of the canopy, just a touch. Outside, the stars were shining in hundreds of thousands and the checkpoint was still visible in the distance, blushing blue. He hadn't seen the bamboo gangway when they'd been approaching earlier, but now it snagged his sight and he couldn't look away. An enormous red banner was strung from its railings, with giant white writing as bright as the moon. A new, hot dread started bubbling inside him. The crisp English print was a noose that was tightening.

Oppose those relying on external elements, acting as stooges, holding negative views.

Oppose those trying to jeopardise the stability of the State and the progress of the nation.

Oppose foreign nationals interfering in internal affairs of the State.

Crush all internal and external destructive elements as the common enemy.

This is the people's truest desire.

He shuddered and snatched the canvas shut, feeling queasy. *Shit*, he thought. He was out of his depth.

TWELVE

It was early morning and the long street of shanty rattan houses was bathed in buttery light on one side, still sleeping in shadow on the other. The breeze was calm and dust from the unpaved road and the mist draped around the buildings and trees, muting their colours like a thin muslin veil. Aside from the dogs, it was deserted. They trotted along the kerb in a pack, sniffing the air and scavenging at the ground, and one stopped and cocked his leg against a cluster of paper flags that guarded a doorway from roaming spirits. Than shooed it away with a brisk, heavy boot. Though he'd shaken last night's bitter row with Marlar from his conscience, the trace of a threat still lingered in his head. Another bad omen was not what he needed. It was crucial today went entirely to plan.

He looked at his watch. It was a quarter to five. At every house around him, the shutters were closed, but inside the sounds of the day were stirring. Doors were being opened and shut, tin cookware clattered. Low rumbling voices were drifting about. The monks would be by for their alms at six and the workers would leave for the mines before seven, so if he wanted to do this, he would need to be quick. It was far better to catch a thief unawares. Far better the street didn't watch him.

A few yards away, Min was finishing his cigarette and

shivering. The four other privates that Than had plucked from their beds at the barracks an hour earlier were all doing the same. Huddled on the corner with their shoulders bunched up and chipping their toes through the gravel, they hardly looked fearsome. A worm of guilt wriggled through Than's gut and he sniffed up the snot from his dribbling nose and spat it to the ground. After the argument Than had with his mother yesterday, Min had slunk to bed early without saying goodnight. When he'd realised, Than had crept into the children's bedroom and perched nervously on the edge of his bed, trying to chat and ease the tension, but the boy had faced the wall and pretended to be sleeping, though Than was sure his breathing was too quick. It had played on his mind throughout the evening. He couldn't stand to see Min trapped between them, even if the fault was all hers. This morning when he woke the boy, he had forced himself to sound chipper, drawing him from the room with a smile and a finger to his lips so he wouldn't wake his siblings, and explaining how he'd got the boy's training deferred by special decree so that Min could come on this most important mission, and Min had smiled back and dressed without protest, but something about his stance had unnerved Than. The boy had seemed to be leaning away.

He sniffed again and hoped it was the misty dawn chill and the anticipation that was making Min anxious now, and not anything else that stood between them.

He finished his own cigarette and tossed it into the gutter, striding towards the waiting boys. 'Are you ready?' He clapped his hands to rile them up.

The boys nodded. Min looked at the ground.

'Good,' said Than, ignoring his snub. He pointed up the road. 'It's the house by the flagpole. Make sure to sweep the rooms quickly when you enter. Secure the exits. I don't want anyone skipping out the back door.'

'Yes, sir.'

'Private Min Soe Khaing?' He squared his shoulders. 'You're going in first.'

Min's head darted up, his eyes flickering. He shifted on his feet as though wading through water. His stare was a jittering, boyish mess. He flashed a panicked glance at the other boys, who looked equally doubtful, and then took a step nearer to his father. 'Wouldn't it be better if someone else did it?' he said, leaning in and speaking low.

Than shook his head, standing straighter. 'What better way is there to get experience than by leading?'

'But I don't know what I'm doing.'

'Just bang on the door and then do as I say.' He gave his son his sternest, most incontestable, most military stare. 'You can do that, can't you, Private?'

Min's chest heaved and he flicked his head obediently.

'Very good.'

Than paused and gave his team a last cool appraisal, then dipped his eyes and began the short approach to the target, muttering a prayer beneath his breath. The boys scurried after him, disorderly as lice. From their approach, the house looked as sleepy as any of the others. Squat and dishevelled, the frame was cracking and splinters of rattan-wall webbing mottled its front and dappled the shadows so where it sat on the kerb and tilted forwards, it looked like an ailing roosting bird.

The idea had come in the hours after midnight as he'd slumped in his kitchen and thought very hard about Daw Su's advice. As always, the old soothsayer was right; a strong man will move the boulders. What she hadn't expressed – but that Than knew was true – was that a smart man would pick which boulders judiciously. This house belonged to the miner Aye Myint. Aye Myint was a middle-sized, blunt-cornered boulder. Through the years, Than had made the occasional deal with him, letting stolen gems pass for a moderate bribe. A pragmatic thief and a fickle salesman, the man was enough of a scalp to appease General Bo Win, but not to disrupt Mogok's established order. His pilfering was small scale and it wasn't political. He didn't care which rebels he dealt with, or even if they were rebels at all. He'd have sold to a drug lord or Mandalay whore with just as much zeal if they paid the right price. Of course, Aye Myint was well enough known in the town that some of the officers would lose a thin trickle of income, but it wouldn't be enough to cause Than any bother. Daw Su had said that he had to be patient, but he knew he had to be cleverer too. This was the very best solution he'd come up with. He was following orders. He would get the job done. He would prove his commitment. What he would not be doing, however, was prodding at vipers and begging for bites.

He waved, ushering Min and the other privates forward, then checked his watch and gave them the nod. In an explosion of flailing black boots, they flew suddenly forward and kicked though the door.

'Officer Than Chit!'

Aye Myint leapt from his seat behind the table in the middle of the room. His bony hips hit the wood as he jumped, tipping up his breakfast. The soup spilled and the plate smashed on the floor, and he backed towards the wall, wide-eyed, his vision fixed on the five glistening gun barrels that were trained on his chest. At the fire, his wife was sitting rigid. A baby howled as it clung to her breast.

Than followed his soldiers inside, ducking beneath the frame of the door and blocking the exit.

'Aye Myint,' he said, 'we are here to arrest you for malevolent and repeated robbery of government-owned gemstones and for using the profits of your thievery to fund activities that are specifically designed to harm the Union of Burma.'

Aye Myint raised his palms and shook his head. His shirt was unbuttoned and sharp ribs ridged his twig-thin torso and his chest sagged just slightly, tobacco-brown and pitted. He kept his face level but a tremor was sounding from the back of his throat. 'I've done no such thing, sir,' he replied, defensive. The *sir* was a cursory glance at respect.

'You've not stolen gemstones or you've not funded terrorists?'

'I've done neither.'

'The Tatmadaw has been informed that you've taken rubies from the mine at Shwe-daing.'

'No, sir. Your informers deceive you.'

Than moved further into the house, his soldiers sealing the gap behind him, and he paced the floor with wilful steps. Though the room was small, it didn't feel cramped; there was so little in it. It was non-committal, he noted with interest, arranged with care to be bland and vague. Beneath the window, the fire smoked gently. The cooking basket beside was stacked as high as the windowsill with earthenware bowls and pans. There were two wooden cabinets, neatly shut with their keyholes empty, an altar in the corner with freshly laid offerings and a bookshelf with a teapot and a portrait of Aung San. His stare hovered on Aung San, then he cracked open the door on the back wall and peered into the bedroom. A wardrobe. A chair. A faded blue quilt that was spread across the mattress. He tugged the door shut and turned back to Aye Myint.

'Do you have rubies in your home today?' he said, feeling bolder. There were gemstones hidden here somewhere for sure.

Aye Myint squirmed and looked at his wife. 'Only the rubies I've bought legally, sir.'

'Do you have your certificates?'

'Yes.'

'Any sapphires or topaz?'

'No, sir.'

Than wandered up to Aye Myint's side, aware of the farce of their conversation. Both men knew well that Aye Myint was a thief. The dance between them was nothing more than posturing – for their pride as much as their ignorant crowd.

'Can we talk about this?' Aye Myint said, lowering his voice and curling his stare to the watching table. 'Outside?'

'There's nothing to talk about.'

'We could make a deal.'

'Are you attempting to corrupt a Tatmadaw officer?'

'No, sir, but there must be an arrangement that can benefit us both.'

'Criminals are not permitted to make arrangements.'

Aye Myint coughed and his shoulders jerked. His palms were still raised, but his expression had hardened and so had his jawline. It was clear to him now that this wasn't a game. 'There are no stolen rubies at my home, Officer,' he said, locking his spine straight. 'I am not a criminal.'

Than shook his head and gave a thin, hostile smile. 'Be honest, Aye Myint,' he said, unblinking. 'Surrender the rubies in your possession and I'll ensure that your punishment is fair.'

He lifted his jaw higher. 'I have no gems.'

Than shrugged in slow, false acceptance, then raised his hand to the nearest soldier. The boy lurched forward, swinging his rifle and thrusting the heavy wooden muzzle into Aye Myint's gut. Aye Myint cried out and doubled forward, crumpling to the floor. His wife began to sob and started towards him, but another of the soldiers had walked behind her and he pressed his hand on her shoulder, shoving her down and holding her still. She bound her arms around the body of her child. From his size and his skinniness, the boy could not have been more than a few months old, and he threw back his head and shrieked to the ceiling, and she buried her face in the pit of his neck, rocking and murmuring.

Than stepped forward and nudged Aye Myint with his boot-cap. 'Do you see what happens when you tell untruths, brother?' he said, raising his voice above the baby's flaming bawl. 'We both know that the gemstones are here. Tell me where they are and I'll help you. Stay silent and the spirits will not be kind.'

Aye Myint dragged himself to his hands and knees and spat on the hem of Than's trousers.

Than shot a breath through his nose. He turned and jabbed a finger to Min and the rest of the soldiers. 'Search the house.'

The boys spread across the room like leaking water, Min the most restrained at first, looking at his father with a tight, worried brow. Than scowled back, pointing to the cabinets, and Min stumbled over to them, tugging at the latch with his trembling hands.

'Open them, boy.'

'They're locked.'

'Break the doors.'

Another of the soldiers charged over, barging Min aside and cracking through each wooden panel with his rifle, snatching the trinkets from the shelves within. Behind him, the others were tearing every cup, bowl and saucer from the baskets beside the stove, shattering them on the concrete and kicking through the pieces where they littered the floor. The fire still burnt as they turned the stove over, and they stamped the smouldering ash to snuff it out, before checking in the brickwork for hidden compartments. On the rush of adrenaline and excitement, they surged inside the bedroom, shouting. Min watched them leave from the centre of the room.

'What are you doing?' hissed Than, grabbing his son's wrist. 'Get in there.'

'I can't.'

'You can – and you have to. You don't want them going back to the barracks and saying you're a weakling, do you? You're a winner, Min. Prove it.'

'But I don't know what I'm doing.'

'There's nothing to know. Those rubies are here. If you find them first, you'll get the glory. We both will. Don't let me down.'

There was a crash from the bedroom like splintering wood and the sound of boots being thrown from the wardrobe clattered out. Than scanned the kitchen again, still holding his son's arm. Aye Myint was on the floor, looking furious but helpless. His wife quivered by the upturned stove. The house had been ransacked. There was nothing left but the windows and walls. Then his eyes fell on the table in the corner; the one with the candles, the flowers and the fruit. Amid the wreckage, it was totally unscathed.

He turned towards it, towing Min with him and pointing with the stare of his widening eyes. 'The altar,' he said as a whisper. 'No one's touched it.'

'Oh no,' said Min, shaking his head and frowning.

'But look at it, boy.'

Than stepped closer, pulling Min in. The wood was polished cleanly, spread with jasmine and freshly cut strawberries, and in the middle sat three pristine, porcelain figurines. He knew them at once when he looked at their faces. A breath caught in his lungs and he sucked in his cheeks, drawing a thread from the dark of his mind. Though every righteous soul in Burma had their altars and their statues, *these* spirits were special. They were pointedly different. Unusual. A set. The one on the left was Pareinma Shin Mingaung, the hunter with the sharpest of all the world's arrows. In the middle was Zawtika Po Tu, the trader who rode on a fiery tiger's back. Nearest to Than was Tabinshwehti, the indisputable warrior king. He thought of his own figurines, at home with their jackfruit, and an invisible smile spread and eased his tense muscles, like steaming water in a rim-full bath. Revere and respect and your spirits will serve you. He thanked Thagyamin for giving him courage. He thanked Shwe Nabay for turning the wind.

'Why haven't you checked the altar, Private?' he said, pushing Min forward, releasing him.

Min froze and looked at his father. 'What are you doing?'

'I ordered you to search the room.'

'We searched it. That's sacred.'

'It's sacred to honest men, not to sinners. Turn it over.'

Min didn't move. 'We can't.'

'We can do what we like. We're the Tatmadaw.'

Than kicked at Min's thigh with his foot, jolting him ahead. The other boys had returned from the bedroom and they loitered in the doorway, watching, out of breath. Than shoved Min again.

'Listen, son,' he said, dropping his voice to a glisten. 'Where would a thief least expect our diligence? You need to search the altar. Find those rubies and you'll earn our reward.'

Min shook his head.

'It's not a choice, Min,' said Than. 'I know you don't want to tempt the spirits, but we'll sort out your karma later, OK?'

'Can't you do it?'

'It's a private's job.'

Than held his stare and Min wrinkled his face and walked towards the table. Kneeling, he lifted the tablecloth and peered beneath it before sifting through the flowers and fruit with a fingertip, as lightly and cautiously as if they might bite.

'The statues, Min,' said Than as he watched him.

Min shuddered and lifted the first of the smiling figurines. He rolled it over his hand, holding the body like it was made of spun sugar, then placed it down and turned to Than, his eyes a weak plea. Than felt a ripple of impatience through his gut. The hunter. The trader. The warrior king. The gems were there.

'Open it.'

Min's frown deepened and he glanced to the other boys, but they all looked away. He picked the statue up again, closed his eyes and brought it down on the edge of the table. The head cracked away and a torrent of bright-red rubies flooded out from the hollow within.

Min's face leapt to Than's, astounded.

Than tried his best not to smirk. 'Break the others.'

Min pulled away the tablecloth and wrapped the remaining statues inside it, bringing them down on the wood. The porcelain broke and from beneath the white lace rubies spilled across the table and floor, shimmering in the light as though the spirits bled. Than's grin spread to fill the whole of his insides. There were hundreds of stones – a thousand even – all uncut and deeply hued. Some were like sand grains but others were bigger, peppercorns and spice seeds, buried amongst the dunes of red gold. He crouched and sunk his fingers through them, and at last his smile began to leak. This wasn't the stock of a small-scale rustler. These were the gems of a man who had plans.

He turned to Aye Myint. 'Who do you work for?'

'I work for myself.'

'A man with this many rubies who worked for himself would no longer be working in Burma.'

Aye Myint was huddled in the corner, scowling. Than stood up, thoughts flitting across like midges behind his eyes. Oh, how the spirits had for once been so generous. If Than had known before that Aye Myint was a player, he wouldn't have let him scurry away for such meagre bribes. But if Than hadn't known, the other officers in Mogok did not know either. Through hard work and ingenuity, he had shifted a river stone and found a whole new breed of fish. Now was his chance to serve up a supper. He could reel him in and claim the glory, without any risk.

'You're funding the rebels, aren't you?' he said.

Aye Myint shook his head. 'No.'

'You've already proved that you're a liar once today, brother. Don't give yourself a reason to suffer any more.'

'It's just me, I swear it.'

'Would your wife swear it too?'

Than slipped across the room to stand beside Aye Myint's wife. Her cheeks were still streaked with wet and her eyes were red and swollen, but the baby had quietened, and Than lifted him from her arms and pressed his tiny weight to his shoulder, bouncing him gently and stroking his hair.

'Put him down,' said Aye Myint.

'I know you're part of the Shan State Army.'

'I'm not.'

'Which division?'

'Give me my son.'

'Oh, the boy doesn't mind it.'

Than bounced the baby harder, rocking him sideways with a twist of his hips. Aye Myint looked to his wife. Her face was panicking, a shrieking, purple mess. At his stare, the woman let off a sob so fierce that she shook.

'He's in the Fifteenth!' she cried, lunging suddenly for Than. She tried to grab the baby but a soldier held her back.

Than's heart leapt. The Fifteenth Division of the SS Army. He could hardly believe that his luck was so sweet! The Fifteenth were the most brutal fighters of any of the rebels, the most persistent and courageous, most successful and most sly. They were also the most elusive men of any Than had ever faced. Every other SS division made enough noise and left enough tracks that the Tatmadaw could find them when they fled to the forest, but the Fifteenth were so swift and wily that the privates joked they had to be spirits; they launched an attack, then they just disappeared. Since their strike on the mine at Dattaw that had left one hundred Tatmadaw men dead and a red-faced general, Bo Win had searched for their camp like a hound. Half of the hillside to the north of Mogok had been scorched on the back of a dodgy tip-off. He'd even requested two planes from Rangoon to hunt in the mountains, but no matter where he sent them, they never returned any wiser.

Than clutched the baby more firmly and tried to calm his thrill as it beat through his head. 'Where's your outpost, Aye Myint?'

Aye Myint glared and Than bent to the floor, hooking up the table with his free hand and tipping it upright. He placed the boy down in its centre, and the child gurgled and wriggled on his back.

'Tell me.'

'No.'

Than plucked his pistol from his belt-strap and Aye Myint's wife screeched as he pressed the tip of the metal into the flesh on the baby's bare thigh. The child smiled calmly up.

Aye Myint shook his head. 'You wouldn't do it.'

'Not if one of you tells me where the camp is.'

'My wife doesn't know.'

'Then it's your responsibility.'

'Tell him, Aye Myint!'

'Yes, Aye Myint,' said Than without flinching. 'Tell me the location of the Fifteenth's outpost or one shot will take your son's leg clean away from his body. If he lives, your wife will have to stitch it back on with her pretty black hair.'

Aye Myint looked at his wife and rubbed his face, panicked. The woman was bawling, fighting against the two soldiers who were restraining her, kicking and biting and throwing her fists. He dragged himself up, stumbling forward and holding out his hands. 'Please, Officer,' he said, 'don't you have children of your own? A son? Think of what you're doing.'

Than swallowed and pressed his gun harder into the baby's thigh to stop his hand from shaking. From the altar, he caught Min staring, ashen, and he dropped his head so he didn't have to see. The boy had to learn that some things needed doing. To get on in life, there were always compromises. And this was different. Than wasn't a traitor.

He clicked back the safety.

Aye Myint's wife screamed.

THIRTEEN

Thuza had been hiding since long before sunrise. With her body braced against the cold stone wall that marked the back perimeter of the temple's grounds, she had watched the sky above her lighten, the dawn mist sweeping away the darkness until nothing was left but a thin sheath of grey. She hadn't dressed for the coolness of the morning, and had pulled her arms from her sleeves and wrapped them against her body as warmly as she could as she fretted and waited, but her cheek-bones and the tips of her ears had still suffered as she listened for the birds rousing from their slumber in the high bows of the tamarinds, and willed the day and its warmth to arrive. When they did, they fluttered awake and stretched their wings so the softly rounded fingers of the damp leaves quivered and icy dewdrops dripped down like rain.

Now it must have been almost noontime. The sun was pricked at its base by the temple's tallest stupa and the tender ripple of the donation gongs was sounding more frequently as the town arrived to pay their respects. Though the chill in the air had slackened and released her, the chill in Thuza's insides was still holding tight. Stiff-limbed, she crawled from her shelter of knotted hibiscus and fiddlewood and crept along the wall to look southwards, and then to the north corner to check the opposite way. In the distance, a few monks were standing in a cluster and talking, and a child danced at their feet with a gap-toothed grin, pointing at the monkeys that swung overhead. She slunk back to her den and stared at the forest. There wasn't a sound or a sight of Kyaw.

Ten more minutes, she thought, feeling nervous. Perhaps a half-hour. He would come like he'd said. He had too much to lose. She picked up the strap of her bag from the soil and worried it through her trembling hands. In part, her fear was that some harm might have struck him, but more it was dread for what harm might come next. She was sure he'd said sunrise – she was sure he'd said Thursday – but it had all been so hasty and the last few days had been filled with such pressure that her memory might lie. If Kyaw thought she had snubbed him, she'd be in for a thrashing; the boy had a temper as red as a fox. His threats to shop her to the Tatmadaw for smuggling were far from empty. Already her Rangoon plan was teetering on a clifftop. She couldn't chance anything that might nudge it off.

The thought had also been playing on her mind about what might happened if the rebels decided that *he* was the fraudster. She slipped her hand inside the front pocket of her bag, flicking the edge of the Thai's little note. If Thuza couldn't get Kyaw the information or the money he had promised his superiors, they'd punish him. She hated giving in to his threats – of him thinking he'd won against her – but the presence of the warehouse in faraway Lashio had stained her conscience. If she could keep him from the journey along the Tatmadaw-lined highway, her parents would want that. It was only right as his blood that she should. Having worked so hard for it, she hadn't wanted to give him a single kyat of the Thai's money, so she'd gone into her tunnels again last night. Not that she knew she had anything like what he was hoping for. One night was not enough time to gather stones of any worth or catch any sparrowhawks and get to her dealer and secure a good price. Instead, she had found herself bartering in the basements of Mogok in the earliest hours of the morning, where the dangers were as high as the Shwedagon stupa and the prices dust-poor. What she had in her bag now was the best she could manage without scuppering her own plan, and it might be enough to buy her brother some favour for a week or two, long enough to let some other poor soul risk his hide on the Lashio road instead. It broke her to do it, to crumble again to Kyaw's ultimatums, and it was true what her parents had told her – the rubies were there to secure her future – but they were also her present; every moment of her day. Without protecting life now, without binding it firmly, what assurance did she have any future would come?

She pressed her fingers into her tired eyes and scowled back at the forest. If Kyaw wasn't coming, she would have to find him; for her sake and his, but mostly for their parents'. She picked up her satchel and climbed from her shelter, glancing each way and spitting bitterly, then stealing towards the dark forest ahead.

The first Thuza knew of the camp was the stink of the latrines. It leaked between the densely packed trees and cloaked across the smell of mud and mouldering leaves, growing with every passing yard. Though she didn't savour the thought of what lay ahead, she was more than glad for her journey's end. For hours she had climbed the steep mountain slope. Enclosed in the forest, the sense of damp was so overwhelming that at times she had been convinced that it rained. Nothing more than her tiredness, the trick came from the squally gush of river-water that spiralled from the mountain's base and the moisture that puddled in the hollows of air beneath the canopy. It soaked her clothes and weighed her down. At her feet, the ground was sludge. It fought her steps until the tops of her thighs and her lungs were burning. There wasn't a path to guide her, just a years' old memory from when she had once been lonely and curious enough to follow Kyaw, and a trail of twigs that snaked along the rugged earth. They were snapped by hand and precisely scattered, but so small and subtle that she almost walked by. It was such a relief to have seen them, however. A wise man never strays from the marked track in Burma. There were more landmines buried in the Shan State jungles than there were green leaves or flowers on the trees.

She pushed on, listening to the shrieks of the birds and insects, following the strengthening stench and covering her mouth and nose with her collar despite her heat, until two broad shafts of bamboo appeared at her feet.

'Shit,' she hissed, slipping from the mossy walkway and landing in the mud.

In the trees, a voice yelled. Young and fearful but barbed with menace. 'Stop!'

Thuza froze. Her heart threw itself against her ribs and her eyes darted through the undergrowth, but the light was dismal and she couldn't see where the shout had come from. She raised her hands above her head.

It came again. 'What are you doing in the forest?'

'Hunting birds!' she shouted back.

There was no response.

She paused and searched again through the trees. 'I've lost my way.'

'Liar,' said the voice. 'A lost girl hikes down the hill, not upwards. Where are you going?'

There was a crackle of shifting foliage somewhere behind her and she spun to see a flurry of crows flee up through the branches. On her every side, the forest was shivering. Had the rebels found her or was it the Tatmadaw? To answer wrongly could be fatal.

She took a deep breath, chancing her side. 'I'm going to the outpost,' she called through the stammer in her voice. Her heart lurched, waiting.

'What's your business?'

'I need to see my brother.'

Where the trees had shuddered hardest and scattered the birds, the barrel of a rifle emerged from the dark. It was followed by two sharp-boned, tattooed hands, two ropey arms and then the body of a spindly SSA private. Twitchy, no older than thirteen perhaps, his face was smeared with deep-green paste and his teeth were black from gnawing betel. The same swollen insect bites and weeping welts covered his skin as did Kyaw's, and a distant, feverish expression spread from his eyes to the whole of his face. Two more matching child soldiers sloped from the shadows and encircled Thuza with their guns raised. She kept her hands above her head but her pulse dropped, just slightly.

The first soldier crept closer, flicking his rifle towards her. Despite his vacantness, he looked as terrified as she was. The sight of him, his youth and brokenness, made her stomach roll. 'Who's your brother?' he said. He stank of sweat and tobacco.

Thuza's mouth was dry. 'Kyaw Lin.'

'Lieutenant Kyaw?' He glanced at his comrades. 'Does he know that you're coming?'

'Yes,' she lied.

'Are you armed?'

She shook her head.

'What's in the bag?'

'Water. And money for my brother.'

'Show me.'

Thuza tugged her satchel around her waist and flipped it open. The soldier peered inside and then nodded to the others. She watched as the two of them lowered their guns and slipped back into the trees, and she was left with the single, fright-eyed boy. He signalled past her with a jut of his head, wanting her to walk. She hauled herself from the sticky mud and clambered onto the bamboo path, feeling the muck slop from her *longi* and the cold jab of his rifle against her kidney. He rammed her forward through the tangled vines and thorn-filled grass for what must have been a half-mile longer, and then – as suddenly as the crows had bolted – the trees fell away and the camp rose up like a city ahead.

Thuza felt a current of hot eyes curling towards her as she

left the dense forest and was marched inside. A mass of tents and crude wicker huts, it sprawled around what felt like a hundred hacked-down tree stumps, and scrawny, coarse-skinned men and boys as young as novices sat in the doorways, polishing their rifles and examining her brazenly as she passed. Only the largest trees remained standing, and vast sheets of tarpaulin were strung out above the structures and alleyways between them, and topped with dead leaves. The ground was rugged, potted with foxholes. Sandbags slumped at every makeshift doorway and she ducked beneath the low-slung, overladen washing lines that sagged above the paths. Rice baskets and rubbish sacks were strung from upright bars beside them to stop their rot on the forest floor, and the dogs prowled beneath them, whining, but what struck Thuza most was the feeling of transience. She couldn't tell how big it was, but it felt tightly crowded. For all the people she passed, it was eerily quiet. They all had jobs and places to be. She let her stare skim over their faces, her heart still drumming inside her chest. She couldn't see Kyaw.

The soldier steered Thuza to a structure that was different from the others. It was a yawning, unwalled rough wood frame with the muted yellow, green and red stripes of the Shan State flag hanging beneath a rusty metal awning, wilting and frayed. Inside, four uniformed men spanned a table and peered at a map. They were all older, cleaner and fatter than the camp boys she had seen so far, and the one with the palest arms and roundest chin stood up at their approach.

'Who's this?' he said to the twitching boy-soldier.

'I found her on the south side of the mountain, General,' the child replied. 'She claims her brother is Lieutenant Kyaw.'

The general paused and looked Thuza over, slowly and steady like a stalking cat. She couldn't see any sign of his rank but, if nothing else, she would have guessed from the cleanness of his fatigues and the length of his fingernails that he was powerful.

'Is this true?' he asked her.

Thuza pushed back her shoulders, staring up at him. There wasn't any benefit to lying.

'What's your name?'

'Thuza Win,' she replied, standing taller. She clenched her muscles. 'I've brought you a message from the Thai. About your shipment.'

The general's eyes narrowed momentarily, a trace of shock just visible. He glanced to his colleagues beneath the shelter and then turned to the soldier and clapped his hands. 'Bring me Lieutenant Kyaw.'

The boy nodded and released Thuza. He scurried away, his rifle bobbing at his tiny shoulder, and darted down an alleyway between two tents. The general twisted back to Thuza. His gaze levelled over her, suspiciously.

'Did your brother ask you to come here?'

'Yes, sir,' she lied.

'And he told you about the shipment?'

'Yes.'

'And the way to our camp?'

Thuza nodded again and a fist grabbed her gut. The ache in her legs was still raw from her journey, and her throat was as scratchy as a thorn bush, and the skin on her arms and neck itched from the grasses in the forest and the teeth of the insects where they'd dug in her flesh. Most of all, her head was throbbing. She'd show Kyaw up for dragging her here and wasting her time and pulling her down.

The general sucked on his teeth and thought for a moment, before holding out his hand. His stance was hard and grisly, as weathered and hostile as the mountain. 'You can give the message to me,' he said coolly.

Thuza frowned and opened her satchel. What choice did she have? Rummaging inside, she pulled out the note the Thai had scribbled and handed it over. The general's stare shot to the little roll of money she had hidden in the pocket for Kyaw too and she thought for a moment that he was going to take it, but then he unfolded the paper and his face stiffened, distracted.

'Is this a joke?' He screwed the message in his fist and glared at Thuza, furious.

Thuza shook her head. 'The Thai said he'll only make the delivery to the forest if you pay him the full amount you agreed.'

The general growled and snatched Thuza's satchel. She thought she saw him slightly blush. He pushed her away and tore inside the pocket, pulling out the money she had bought for Kyaw.

Thuza's jaw ground. 'That's Lieutenant Kyaw's contribution to your effort, sir,' she said bitterly.

The general leafed through, his face still a storm. 'There's barely enough for one rifle,' he said. 'Lieutenant Kyaw promised us ten times as much.'

Thuza's scowl thickened. 'It's the best I could manage.'

'He assured us he had benefactors.'

'He does. I'm the carrier.'

'And where have you carried from?'

'That's my concern.'

The general turned, raising a finger to his colleagues with a sudden, harsh grin. 'Did you hear that?' he said, laughing. 'The little serpent thinks she can roar.'

Thuza swallowed. She should have known better than to speak like she did, but sometimes her temper was quicker than her thinking. She could feel the men in the shelter watching her and she blushed too, casting her eyes to the ground to hide their blueness, suddenly sorely aware of her difference, of her damaged appearance and all that it told them, how it marked her as an outcast, alone and afraid.

'Sir!' Kyaw's anxious voice snapped Thuza from her shame.

With the boy-soldier at his side, her brother scuttled over, holding his hands out to the general and dipping his head. He shot a mean glare at Thuza as he passed her, his black teeth bared, and then he stopped and spat wet betel in the dust. 'I didn't tell her to come here. I swear it.'

The general rocked on his boot heels, frowning. 'And yet here she is.'

'She must have followed me.'

'The error is still yours, Lieutenant.'

'I'll send her away.'

'We can't have our location compromised.'

'She's toothless, sir. No one to tell.'

'How can you be sure? You've already proved that you're careless.'

'It's true, General,' said Kyaw, stepping forward. His eyes

were all pupil, and brimming with fear. 'The town despises her.'

'What do you know of the town and your sister? You're here every day.'

'I know enough, sir. And I can make sure she doesn't whisper a word. Not anything! Even if someone did ask where she'd been. Trust me. I'll make the bitch do anything I say.'

Thuza crunched her hands to fists and glared at Kyaw.

The general leaned in, dragging back her stare. 'Is the lieutenant right, Little Serpent?' he whispered. 'Do you listen to your kin?'

Thuza's fists clenched tighter. She bit her tongue.

'You listened to him about the outpost, apparently. And the shipment. You shouldn't know about either. You shouldn't know about anything at all, except that traitors to Shan State can never be our friends.' He paused and eyed her. 'Is your brother a traitor, Thuza Win, for telling you? He'll be punished, if he is. Did you know that?'

She didn't respond.

'Don't you care?'

'I won't tell anyone,' she muttered, holding his stare. 'I promise. Can I go?'

The general's lips puckered. 'No.'

He gestured to the hovering boy-soldier, who seized her arm and yanked her aside.

'Hey!'

'You'll be escorted back to Mogok when I say so.'

'I don't need an escort,' said Thuza, jerking against his grip.

'And that's just the issue, isn't it, Little Serpent? You know the way. I can't have you wandering through the jungle, leaving a trail and leading the Tatmadaw to our doorstep. Or worse still, telling them where we are. Nor can I have you roaming through our camp. For all I know, you might be a spy. You will remain in our custody until Lieutenant Kyaw has convinced me of your loyalty – and of his – in whatever way he chooses, and then you'll go home when I see fit.'

'You can't keep me,' cried Thuza, struggling. 'I've done nothing wrong.'

'Sir, please!' said Kyaw. He looked at Thuza and the general, panicked. 'I can sort this. Give me a chance.'

The general shook his head and walked back to the table where his colleagues were sitting, pulling out a seat and tucking himself down. 'It's decided, Lieutenant. You've let us down greatly. You do what you have to and then we'll discuss it.' He poured himself a drink from a steaming flask and dismissed the soldier, sipping. 'Take them both to the lock-up. They're under arrest.'

The soldier nodded and swept behind Thuza and Kyaw, brandishing his rifle again and steering them away. He trudged them down the alleyway from where he had retrieved Kyaw, stopping at an empty tent fifty yards or so down the passage, then shoved them both inside with a barked order and shunt of his weapon.

'Well done, Thuza Win,' said Kyaw, snarling as the soldier pulled the tent's front entrance closed. He stuffed a quid of betel inside his cheek and clawed at his forehead, pacing the floor.

Thuza slumped on the cot-bed, spitting a curse beneath her breath. Outside the tent, she could see the soldier knotting up the loops of the canvas, and his shadow was a puppet through the worn khaki screen. She dumped her satchel by her feet and rummaged to find a cheroot. 'This isn't my fault, Kyaw,' she said, lighting up. 'Where were you?'

'I was busy.'

'I waited for hours.'

'You should have waited longer. I would have been there.'

'How was I supposed to know?'

'It was obvious, wasn't it?'

'Not to me.'

Kyaw ground his jaw and glared at her, shooting a line of stodgy red juice from between a gap in his teeth. 'It would have been obvious to anyone with sense,' he said, wiping his scowl with the back of his hand. 'You don't need to be a soothsayer to see that coming here was stupid.'

Thuza stared at the stain where it had landed by her satchel. It was a blood-like splatter at the side of her feet. She sucked on her cheroot. He was going to blame her. He always blamed her. She bit her lip.

'I didn't trust you not sell me up the river, Kyaw,' she said. 'And besides, maybe I wanted to be helpful. Perhaps I thought that if I didn't come, you wouldn't get your message or your money, and then you wouldn't get your guns and your commanders would be angry, and you'd be sat up here on the mountain – surrounded by the Tatmadaw – like sitting fucking ducks.' She drew again to stop her hand from shaking. 'I thought I was doing you a favour.'

Kyaw shook his head and snorted a laugh. 'Bullshit, Thuza. You don't do favours.'

'I did what you asked, Kyaw.'

'You didn't do half of what I asked. How much money did you give the general . . . one hundred kyat? It can't have been more.'

'What did you expect? I had two days, and one of those I was visiting your stupid Thai.'

'I expected you to try harder,' said Kyaw. He stalked towards her and pointed his finger in her face, his eyes bearing down. 'I expected you to recognise something important and work. I should have known that it's not in your nature. You're a lazy sloth, Thuza Win. Always dreaming, never doing . . . I bet there was more though, wasn't there? I bet you had two or three hundred kyat. You've kept it, haven't you? Don't think I don't know what you're doing. I've watched you with your sparrowhawks. I've seen you sitting by the window and dribbling over your cash like an addict or a beggar. I've seen you stashing it too, counting it up and folding it into little paper triangles and flowers and owls and hiding it away in the base of that birdcage. I know you have more than you give me, sister.'

Thuza's stomach turned. How much did he know? Her mind tripped to the Thai, her thoughts groping their way through the dark possibilities, panicking her. 'You've been spying on me?'

'I've been protecting our interests – and you've proved that I need to. It doesn't matter if you hoard ten million kyat, Thuza Win. You won't be able to buy back our past.'

Thuza stuffed her cheroot between her lips, gnawing it. In her mouth, the leaves shred to gravelly dust. 'You don't know anything, Kyaw.'

'I know you want to go to Rangoon. You've been saving.'

'Does it matter if I have?'

'It matters if you're stealing from your own family. You think you can rescue our parents, Thuza – and that's noble – but you can't. Not like that.'

'Shut up, Kyaw. It's none of your business what I do with my money.'

'It is when you waste it. Those rubies are a gift, Thuza. You're throwing them away on a wish and a dream.'

Thuza stood up and glared at her brother. On her tiptoes, she stretched and snarled at his chest. He didn't know about the Thai or her betrayal. He was still obsessed with her pitiful haul. She squared up to him, feeling braver. 'You're the one who wastes them, Kyaw. Those tunnels are ours, brother. *Ours*. Not yours. They belong to every soul in our family, present and past. I've as much right to take my share as you.'

'It's not that you take the rubies, sister. It's that nothing you do with them ever amounts to anything real. You spend your life hiding in the forest, letting the crows peck away the days and thinking the world will right itself if you will it to hard enough, but it won't, Thuza Win. Our parents knew that. They taught you to fight, like I do. Why haven't you listened?'

Thuza shook her head and stared at the ground. 'Our parents are nothing like you, Kyaw. They never touched a weapon.' They never chose to leave me, she wanted to say.

Kyaw waved his hand, dismissive. 'It was different then,' he said. 'A leaflet and a prayer won't change anything now.'

Thuza sniffed, holding back a surge of grief. She remembered folding pamphlets in the backroom with her brother when they'd colour in the Shan flags in the corners of each page. Her mother had bought them the crayons especially, and the gold, green and red wore to blunt waxy stumps. While they worked, writing leaflets to invite the town to learn with them about Shan history, and bake Shan foods and sing Shan songs, her father would recite them his poems about Kinnara birds and the Buddha and the forest, and Shan princes kissing rubies to bring their people luck. While he drummed on a stockpot, Kyaw and Thuza would tap with their fingers, and their mother would laugh when they danced out of time. She shook her head again, more sadly. 'They wouldn't support you, Kyaw. You know that.'

Kyaw frowned. 'And you think they'd be proud of your delusion, Thuza Win?'

'I'm not deluded. Our parents are peaceful people. They taught us to have hope. I've listened to that.'

Kyaw threw up his hands, a froth of red at the side of his mouth. 'I have hope, Thuza, but I'm a realist. You're the hopeless one. How many years have you saved? How much money do you have? Is it enough for a train to Rangoon? Is it enough to bribe a major or a colonel or a general, to buy them a yacht and to break Mumma free?' He laughed and bared his betelblack teeth. 'You're a joke.'

'Fuck off, Kyaw.'

'No, sister. You need to be told. Do you think life will ever be as it was before? I'm the one fighting for our parents' liberation. I'm the one protecting our family.'

'You're not protecting me,' spat Thuza. 'You send me to the Thai, you force me beneath the house, you threaten me, you leave me with Nanna . . . I'm your prisoner.'

'If you're a prisoner, Thuza Win, it's not through my doing. It's the daydreams in your head that keep you trapped. You're like those birds in your cage, like your little hidden banknotes. Every time you tuck another away, you're choosing surrender. You're doing this. Not me.'

She shook her head. 'Your way isn't working, Kyaw.'

'I can hardly believe you sometimes, sister. How can anyone be so passive and weak? After all the Tatmadaw have done to our people – after all they've done to *you*, Thuza Win – I don't understand how you simply ignore them. Why don't you want to fight?'

'I am fighting, brother. I am. Every day.'

'Then fight properly!' cried Kyaw. 'It's the only way our parents will come home.'

'Don't pretend you care if they come home,' said Thuza. 'You know I send them messages. Zawtika takes such risks, to bring us news, yet you never spare a second to ask what it is. You've forgotten them. You don't even want to know how they are.'

Kyaw spat at the floor. 'I'm not feeding your fantasy. You're wasting both our time. What do you actually want, Little *Naga-ma*? What on earth do you think you will ever achieve?'

'I want our family back!' cried Thuza. Her whole body was shaking. She clenched her fists and her heart thrashed a wicked beat. 'You don't understand what loyalty means. You ask what I want, but if you were really protecting me – if you were at home where you should be – you'd already know. You say you're winning, but what have you've done, Kyaw? When I needed you most, you abandoned me. I was eleven when you went to the forest. Eleven! A child. You left me alone. What's loyal in that?'

'You had Nanna.'

'I had her skin and bones, but I didn't have her spirit. I needed *you*, brother. I needed you there to help me fetch the water from the forest when the soldiers were prowling, and to carry it home when my legs were still weak. I needed you help me wash Pappa's blood from our hallway floor, and to fix the bolt on the door so I could sleep at night when the mountain dogs were howling. I needed you when Nanna wouldn't stop screaming and I didn't know how her pipes worked, and when my belly was raw from picking red berries but I didn't have a kyat for potatoes or rice. I needed you there when I woke up in the morning, and when I went to bed, and through all the miserable hours between. I needed you to tell me that flesh would heal and the rains would pass and memories would fade if we stuck together, so don't say I don't fight, Kyaw.'

From the end of the tent, Kyaw's stare faltered, and then he let out a sigh. He stepped towards her, slumped on the cot and knotted his fingers through his greasy hair. She watched his shoulders rise and fall.

'Do you think I like being in the forest?' he whispered, scratching at his scalp. 'I don't want to be thin and ill and sleeping in the mud. I'm tired, sister – like you are. I'm sick of being afraid, of jumping at every snapped twig behind me and thinking a bullet is about to snipe me dead. I was a child too, Thuza Win. I had no choice. Of course I miss our parents. I miss everything about our life as it was. That's why I sit and I watch you sometimes. To remind me why I do this. What still needs to be done.'

Thuza wiped her nose and stared at her feet. It was true. They had both been children when her parents were taken, as alone and afraid, trapped and desperate as the rebel boy that had marched her through the forest, or the Tatmadaw boys at the checkpoint on the highway who had mocked and threatened her to save face. That's why her stomach always knotted so hard at the sight of them. They should have been with their families, like she should have been. Not fighting. Without their parents to prop and steer them, they were nothing more than outcasts and weapons, landmines buried and lying in wait. She felt a runnel of sweat between her breasts. 'You don't have to stay in the forest, Kyaw.'

'The SSA will never let me leave. I've seen too much. By the spirits, there's too much I've done myself to walk safely away.'

'Zawtika said he'd help you get out if you wanted.'

'That old man doesn't know anything about anything. He's always trying to find out our secrets. Nosing and judging and bobbing his bald head.'

Thuza squinted at the floor, feeling the tears welling up in her eyes. With her brother slumped on the cot beside her, his head in his hands, she felt a new pity that she'd never done before. She certainly hadn't ever stopped to give him sympathy in her lifetime, but here he was, looking younger and smaller and utterly broken. He had made himself vulnerable, telling the truth. She thought of the Thai and the money she had from him. Perhaps she could trust Kyaw after all; tell him how much money she had hidden at home and what she meant to do with it. Perhaps even tell him what she'd done to get it. If he knew how close she was now, he might think differently. He might trust her too. She wanted to think all hope was not dead.

She licked her lips, her fingers trembling as they held her cheroot. 'What if we put everything we had together, Kyaw? Maybe we could both go to Rangoon. We could buy Mumma and Pappa from Insein and then leave. We could go to Thailand. Start again. Zawtika would help us.'

'Thuza Win—'

'Just think about it, Kyaw. Please.'

Thuza reached out and touched his hand on the cot beside her, linking her fingers over his and pressing him still. At that moment, she knew from his flinching and the look on his face that he wouldn't, that she couldn't say a thing about what she had planned, but she couldn't feel sad either – it had been this way forever – and he gave a smile, and squeezed her back.

FOURTEEN

Michael's lungs burned and his forehead was dripping as he hauled himself up the steep mountain slope. The trek through the forest had already taken them more than four hours, and the hot, dank air and the sweat of his exertion had glued his shirt and trousers to his skin, and the thorns and burrs of the undergrowth snagged through the wetness, catching his flesh before ripping away. It was darker than twilight though the sun hadn't dropped yet, and his backpack was so tightly crammed with bullets and grenades that its seams strained and its weight bore down through his haunches to his buttocks, and his thighs and the backs of his calves were ablaze. Teacher had told him to keep watch for snipers and his mind was exhausted from chasing shadows through the canopy, jumping at every snapped twig and darting bird. There were landmines too, he was told, well hidden. Each step he took he held his breath.

Teacher was ahead of Michael on the slope, slashing though the branches with a dull-bladed machete. Michael spat the saliva from his mouth and peered at the old soldier as he dragged himself upwards. Like an ape, his hands grasped tree to tree. From where he had cut them a path through the forest, his clothes were smeared with moss and mud, and wetness glossed the sinews of his muscles. He was making no effort to ease Michael's mood. There was a sudden sound and Michael jumped and glanced behind to see a monkey discard his rotten jackfruit from a treetop, droplets of water and seedlings showering down with it, and he hitched up his backpack and quickened his pace.

'Teacher,' he hissed, breathless, 'are we close yet?'

Teacher spun and pressed his finger to his lips, his dark eyes scowling down. He somehow seemed angry, though Michael wasn't sure what it was that he'd done. Since their driver had dropped them at the petrol station on the outskirts of Hsipaw in the earliest hours of the morning, Teacher had hardly thrown him two words. Michael hadn't expected to leave the town so quickly. He had thought they'd eat something, find somewhere to stay. He had hoped that there might have been time to find a telephone exchange somewhere in the centre where he could call his parents and relieve his conscience, but instead, they had only stopped long enough for Teacher to secure a new vehicle, to buy bigger rucksacks and decant all their arms. As their new truck had traced along the banks of the Dutawaddy River, dawn had risen, and Michael had watched the reflection of the mountains on the glass of her surface. Their silence had seemed to feed Teacher's distance. Michael had seen his stare glide between the gold and white stone peaks of the miniature *payas* dotted amongst the fruit trees and rice fields, and they had listened together to the serenade of the prayer chants that had found them intermittently, absorbing and eerie, and he'd felt how odd and opposed the peace outside was, against the tension that hung in the cab.

Of course, it was possible that it wasn't anger. It could have been the distraction of the weapons they were carrying, or the thought of the trek through the landmine-filled jungle, or perhaps he was nervous about seeing old comrades, and a hundred other unknowns that were hiding in the day to come. Whatever it was, Michael judged it was better not to ask questions, but there were so many things that he wanted to know. They'd never make it back to Hsipaw before nightfall now. They wouldn't even make it to the town at the base of the mountain that he'd spotted when they ditched Teacher's truck by the bridge. Now, the deeper they stole inside the forest, the further from the comfort of buildings and people, the more Michael's nerves were taking hold. His dread of not being welcome was mounting. He had no idea what was waiting ahead. In his dreams last night, his father had warned him:

Oppose foreign nationals who dare to meddle.
Crush all our enemies.
Gnaw the marrow of their bones.

It made him wake sweating. His stomach was acid.
You're a fool, Michael Atwood.
You're going to end up dead.

There was a sound from the darkness ahead that snapped Michael back to the present, a thump and the shattering of a branch from within the canopy, and he stopped suddenly, dropping to his knees and looking around, feeling his chest clench and the throb of his pulse in his neck. A bird shrieked and spiralled upwards, and Teacher crouched too, glancing

235

through the tightly packed trees. Michael followed his stare, seeing nothing. Teacher swivelled, wrapping his hand around the rifle that was slung over his shoulder and raising it forward, drawing it smoothly through the line of his sight. With his lips, he made a kissing sound, three times. Michael swallowed, terrified. The forest settled and there was an echo to the kisses, brisker and stickier, and Teacher's stance softened and he lowered his gun. He straightened up again, reaching back and grabbing the collar of Michael's shirt, pulling him up too. Michael scrambled with his hands in the mud. He could feel the unsteadiness of his legs, weakened by adrenaline, and he struggled to find his balance as Teacher dragged him, and then the smell of faeces hit them as the camp rose into view.

Michael clutched his hand over his mouth. 'Jesus,' he muttered, looking around. His heart started sprinting, fear exceeding his exertion. The camp was a wreck. Low-roofed, ramshackle, cramped and stinking, it lay like a maze ahead of his stride. His stomach pitched. It felt like something he had seen on the telly in England, like a squalid refugee camp, not an army winning a war. The huts were decrepit, and rubbish sacks were rotting at the doorways. A dog teased bedraggled chickens that were tethered by their feet. Every few yards there was a dead or dying campfire. The pathways were bogs, spread with straw but still sopping, and the earth made the slurp of hungry quicksand as they passed. A few men and boys were moving through the tent-made alleyways, but more were sprawled on the ground, dozing on their backs with their boots beneath their heads. Many of them looked younger than Michael was — easily so — but their skin had dark liver spots and their hands were gnarled. They were wearing fatigues but they were different from the Tatmadaw's. He could feel the cut of their stares on his cheekbones. There were whispers. *A round-eye.* Cynical and guarded. From somewhere invisible, Michael heard a man groaning. Impulsively, he peered after the sound and two watery eyes shone out from a cage at the end of a passageway. A whip of terror lashed over his body. In his gut was a bubble as big as a football. Nothing about this was feeling right.

Teacher turned down an alley and increased his speed, and Michael followed him, skipping to keep up. In front of them, there was a small clearing with a wooden shelter. At the entrance, a flag hung beneath a metal awning, and a table and chairs were in the centre underneath. A portly, uniformed soldier with a beret clinging to his head was spilling from the sides of one of the seats with his back to their approach.

Teacher walked towards the shelter and then placed down his backpack and ducked inside. '*Mingala-ba*, General Shwe Khin,' he said, standing to attention and saluting.

The man at the table turned, his face alight at the sight of them. Grinning, he pushed aside the notepad he'd been writing on, stood too and saluted, then strode at Teacher and shook his hand. 'By the spirits!' he said, slapping Teacher's face playfully and peering into his eyes. 'Khun Zaw Ye! How many years has it been, brother? I thought the forests were in your past.'

Teacher smiled too, baring his gapped teeth. He batted away the general's hands and hugged him warmly. 'I missed the mountain air.'

'Pah!' cried the general. 'It's all mud and shit and cordite. How's your wife?'

'Pregnant again. A hippopotamus.'

'Of course she is, you virile old dog.'

The men laughed and hugged again, but then Teacher pulled backwards and scratched his nose. The silence was awkward for an instant. His face settled and he gestured to his backpack. 'We bought you supplies, General,' he said, quietly. 'It's not much. Just a token or two of our support.'

The general bowed his head. 'Thank you, brother. We're grateful.' He paused and put his hand on Teacher's shoulder, his expression grave. 'We heard about your teahouse. I'm sorry.'

Teacher shook his head. 'It's not as bad as it appears.'

'You know we didn't do it, brother.'

Teacher nodded. 'Of course.'

Michael loitered outside the shelter, his heart drumming, unsure what to do. He had the sense he was intruding on a private moment, yet he'd nowhere to go and nowhere to look. It was hours since he'd had anything to eat or drink either, and the sun was beating fiercely from the sky in the clearing, and his body was teetering beneath his backpack's weight. In his vision, colours were starting to waver. He unhooked his bag and dropped it heavily to the ground.

The general's eyes arrowed towards him. 'Who's this?'

Michael felt his cheeks prick. He staggered forward, light-headed. '*Mingala-ba*, General,' he said, holding out his hand.

The general stared at him, and Teacher wrapped a strong hand around the back of Michael's neck, hoisting him straight

238

and thrusting him forward. 'This is a friend of mine,' he said. 'He's English. I've brought him from Rangoon.'

The general's stare thinned, suspiciously. 'He's a supporter of the SSA?'

Teacher flicked his head and shrugged. 'Apparently.'

'And he's here of his own free will?'

'Yes, brother.'

'A spy?'

'A gift.'

Michael stumbled momentarily, pinching his eyes, and Teacher's grip tightened around of his neck. The general cracked him a slim, brief smile, but it didn't seem friendly. Not in the same way as when he smiled at Teacher. Michael felt himself being eyed like a bullock at a market and, with his hands on his belt, the general looked like a cowboy, ready to shoot with a flick of his wrist. A wave of doubt and wooziness found him and his vision spotted again. He wanted to lie down, to get rid of his headache, to come back and do this when he'd had time to think. But what time had Sein been given to rest and make choices? Opportunities and accidents came when they came. He cursed himself for his own selfish weakness. He had come this far, so he had to finish. He stood to attention as best he could, trying to look tall and confident and solid.

'My name is Michael Atwood,' he said. 'My father is the British Ambassador to Burma. I was at Teacher's shop when it was attacked. My friend was injured. A Burmese friend. Very badly. I wanted to help, so Teacher let me assist him in bringing your supplies.'

He held his breath, waiting for a reply. The general was staring at him, his appearance unreadable, and then a look of amusement spread across his face. He turned to Teacher.

'An ambassador's son, hey?' he said, raising one eyebrow and scratching his cheek with a long, dirty fingernail. 'We'd heard over the radios that a white man was missing from Rangoon. There are alerts out for him across the country. He's a top-priority find. The Tatmadaw never said who he was, but we assumed it must have been someone important for the wires to buzz so hot.' His eyes slipped to Michael, as thin as they could be. 'Does your father know you're here?'

Michael shivered beneath his stare, a new, icy fear filtering through him. His father had mobilised the cavalry. He had been trying all day to deny that he would have, but now his guilt could not have been clearer. He cringed, thinking of the trouble and worry he had caused and wishing himself back to his Rangoon home. There was something too about the general's voice that menaced him. He swore beneath his breath, livid at himself for being so foolish. He didn't want to stay here a moment more. He paused and rubbed his hands down his trousers. His palms were slick. 'Yes, sir,' he lied.

The general stepped closer. 'Where are you?'

Michael's stomach cramped. He was somewhere in the jungle. He had no fucking clue.

The general's eyes glinted. 'A gift indeed,' he muttered.

He gripped Teacher's hand and Michael looked up to see Teacher grinning too.

'You can use him?' Teacher asked.

The general nodded. 'In a hundred ways.' He shook

Teacher's hand again, harder. 'Your initiative is commendable, soldier. Are you sure we can't tempt you back to the forests? We're crying out for a man as shrewd as you.'

Michael shook his head, too furious to hide it. 'I was trying to help you, Teacher,' he whispered, scowling at the ground.

Teacher looked at him and laughed. 'You were trying to help yourself, boy,' he said. 'Release your conscience. I'm sorry, Michael Atwood, but I don't buy your sympathy, and if you did want to help, this is far more valuable. You heard the general. The British are already shifting the seven seas to get you back unscathed and without being embarrassed. You're currency.'

'You won't get a ransom for me. They'll never pay.'

'We wouldn't ask for one. Your value's goodwill. However grateful your father was, I know your government would give us little more than dry-eyed thanks and an empty promise in exchange for your return, but the Tatmadaw will recognise your price. *British Ambassador's son arrested as spy and rebel agitator*₁ . . . *Evidence of Imperialist plot to destroy Burmese unity and recapture control* . . . They'd love nothing more than to print a headline like that in tomorrow's *Working People's Daily*. Shame your country sweetly. They might even give a man or two of ours back from Insein, for a bounty so rich.'

The general nodded. 'It's true, white boy. And the Tatmadaw will be steaming you got this far without them seeing you. They'll want their pound of meat. By enticement or threat, one side or the other will be sending some favour our way. You're a runaway, a fugitive. We found you. We stopped you. We protected you. We returned you. From whatever direction you look, we're on top.'

He belted Teacher's shoulder, unable to contain his delight, and then motioned to a young soldier who was standing to attention outside a lean-to on the opposite side of the clearing. The boy scampered towards them, slopping through the mud.

'Take him to the detention tents, Private, and keep him safe.' the general said to him, brandishing a finger in Michael's direction.

The boy nodded and took hold of Michael's elbow, drawing him roughly away. Michael let him do it, his head bowed and wincing through his humiliation. The general threw his arm around Teacher, guiding him to a table in the centre of the shelter and pulling a liquor bottle and two glasses from a metal chest, and Michael staggered away from them, useless, bitter, shocked and foolish, watching his feet as they dragged through the mire.

With the barrel of his rifle pressed to the flesh of Michael's back, the boy led him down a quiet, smoke-filled passageway, past an ailing campfire and a soldier plucking chickens, past a man refilling sandbags and one rocking in a hammock, then stopped by a tent at the furthest end. Another soldier was guarding the entrance, perched on a crate marked 'munitions' in bold English lettering and picking splinters from his palm with a rusted penknife. He greeted them in Shan, too dense and foreign for Michael to even begin to decipher, and then heaved himself up at the boy's reply. Michael stared at the shivering canvas as the loops of the tent were deftly unknotted, trying not to cry with the fury that filled him, and then the entrance was opened and the gun barrel nudged him in, and two sets of eyes peered back from the gloom.

FIFTEEN

The guard spat through the tent's open doorway, then pulled the flap shut and slumped back on his crate. Inside the entrance, the boy froze, his body rigid, poise almost animal and the line of his sight firing between Thuza and Kyaw. Thuza stared at him for a moment and then looked at her brother. Her heart jumped.

'It's a round-eye,' she said, shocked. From where she had been sitting on the cot nearest to the door, she stood slowly and backed away towards the safety of Kyaw at the opposite end at the tent. Of all the things she'd expected when they'd heard the footsteps and voices approaching, she would never have envisaged a jasmine-white face. She had seen foreigners in photographs before – there were some at her home of the man who'd once owned it, and her parents would show her from time to time – but never before had she seen one in person. He wasn't at all how she'd thought he would be. White men were supposed to stand tall and be powerful, but this one looked gruesome. His clothes were torn at the knees and filthy, and streaks of blood traced the length of his arm. The skin by his eyes was twitching wildly. His chest was heaving like he'd run through the forest. Already her nerves were spun thinner than cotton threads and her mind sped through the possibilities, but here in the camp in the mountain jungle, not a scrap of his appearance or presence made sense. She kept her eyes fixed on him and lowered herself to sit beside her brother, touching his arm. 'What's he doing here?' she whispered.

Kyaw sucked a breath through the side of his mouth and ground his teeth so the betel soaped. Behind his eyes, Thuza could see that his own thoughts were jerking, and he stretched himself higher and pushed back his shoulders. Like a bear being cornered, he had squared himself up. He frowned. His stare was set on the white boy too. 'I don't know,' he said, quietly. He flicked his chin at Thuza. 'Perhaps he's a gem runner. They use Europeans sometimes. And Americans, I've heard. Less hassle at the borders. Or he might be a spy.'

Thuza's nose wrinkled. 'A spy from where?' She shook her head. 'He's too young to be a spy. And look at him. He's petrified.'

'He's a round-eye in this forest. Wouldn't you be?' Kyaw leant in, dropping his voice. His eyes narrowed and he cupped his hand around Thuza's ear, whispering. She could feel the warmth of his breath on her cheek and smell his betel's menthol tang.

She glanced at the boy in the doorway, with his trembling limbs and his mouth gaping wide. He didn't look like a spy. He looked like a runaway. Like a child who had wandered too far from his home. He glanced at her too, his eyes darting from the floor and catching hers, holding them briefly, but then he let off a violent, penetrating shudder and staggered forward, blinking hard. He grabbed an upright in the centre of the tent to stop from falling and collapsed onto the cot with his head in his hand.

Thuza shot Kyaw a scowl and picked up her satchel.

'What are you doing?'

'He needs a drink.'

'Don't give him our water, Thuza Win. Who knows how long we'll be here.'

Kyaw dived forward and snatched the bag's strap from Thuza's hand, but not before she found a grip on her canister. She yanked it away, unscrewing the cap and holding it out. The boy looked nervously at Kyaw, hesitating, and then reached out. He swigged and passed it back, nodding a thank-you.

Thuza tightened the lid and tucked the canister into her satchel. She fastened the ties. 'It's my water, Kyaw.'

From outside, there was an abrupt hand-clap and a familiar, stern voice cut any response from Kyaw before it began. Thuza's vision fired to the doorway as an order was barked, and the silhouette of the guard darted up from his seat.

'Open the tent,' said the general.

The guard stooped to the mud and started to tug at the row of canvas loops he had knotted behind the white boy just minutes before, and the shadows shifted – three of them – merging together on the quivering khaki-green.

'Shit,' said Kyaw. 'He's coming for us.'

He leapt up, wiping his face and smoothing the breast of his uniform, standing to attention as the soldier towed apart the flaps. He pulled Thuza upright too, shaking her straight. A draught of cooler, lighter air crept in, and with his hands behind his back and an expression of distain on his face, the general stepped forward and ducked his head slightly, peering inside. His stare skidded over Kyaw and the white boy before stopping on Thuza. He nodded to his soldier and then turned away. 'Just the girl.'

Panicked, Thuza spun to Kyaw as the soldier seized her arm. She stumbled in the stodgy mud, pushing the soldier away and grasping for her brother, but Kyaw stepped backwards, beyond her reach.

'Do what he says, Thuza Win,' he hissed. 'Keep your mouth shut.'

She looked at him, pleading silently though she knew he wouldn't help her, and the solider wrapped his arms around her waist, wrenching her sideways, dragging her from the tent and into the fading evening light. Outside, she let him push her forward. The campfires were alight, flaring and smouldering as the men cooked their suppers, and the smell of *nagpi*, cheap whisky and gun oil sunk to the bottom of her surging lungs. The general marched ahead of them, profiled in deepgrey though the cloistering smoke, broad-waisted and striding, ignoring the men who scattered from his path. She could hear the rumble of a drum in the distance, feel it through her body like a shiver that repeated, and men's voices were chanting; a low, dark soldiers' song.

They crossed the clearing where Thuza and Kyaw had been detained earlier, skirting the edge of the shelter and turning down a thinner track on its lowest slopes, where the mud was less churned by the passage of boots. It was darker here too and the smog was thinner, and she hacked the remnants of the chaos from her throat. She couldn't see or hear any soldiers nearby, and dread sunk over her. A tent was illuminated by torchlight ahead, and the general gusted inside it, waving the soldier to the entrance and then stopping him and taking hold of Thuza's wrist.

'Keep watch,' he said, pulling her beneath the canopy and then closing the door.

Thuza bound her arms around her body, trembling. The tent was clean but not friendly or welcoming. A thick, uneven rattan mesh covered the mud and there was a cot along the back wall with a pillow and a pile of folded blankets at its foot, and a tea chest to her left beside two folding canvas chairs. The remnants of an unfinished meal were crusted around the rim and in the base of a soup bowl, and the spoon was upturned on the floor by its side. There was a storm lantern on the chest, the flame simmering low and radiating the faint scent of paraffin, and a bottle of dark rum that hadn't been drunk next to two glasses and a large army-issue flask. Behind them, a jacket was hanging from an old-fashioned coat stand, and a photo of a woman smiling was fastened to one of the arms with a bulldog clip. She had two small children on her lap; one girl, one boy. It curled and browned at the edges like a leaf.

The general stood in the centre of the tent and turned to Thuza. He cracked his knuckles into his chest. 'We need to talk about the Thai.'

Thuza's gut gave a sudden, urgent lurch. She couldn't breathe. She could feel her skin pinking, getting hotter and hotter, see a stack of C4 through a blur of her eyes. The strength in her legs had melted to sludge. She bandaged her arms tighter around her chest. 'What do you want to know?' she replied. She was trying her best to appear calm and steady, but a lilt of panic made her words sound shrill.

The general stepped forward, staring at her. 'I've unanswered questions about your meeting.'

'I don't know what you mean.'

'What else happened when you went to see him? I have contacts in the town. Watchers. They said you were with him for almost an hour. Did some other business pass between you in that room?'

She shook her head, unable to speak.

'Your brother asked you to make the visit?'

She inched away from him. 'Yes.'

'What were his instructions?'

'To collect details of where and when the Fifteenth could receive their next shipment of arms.'

'What took you so long?'

'He gave me a drink.'

The general dipped his stare and rasped the stubble on his chin, nodding slowly as if cooling his temper, before looking at her again. His eyes were small and hostile. He moved closer still and the lamplight caught his sagging face, shadowing his jowls. 'I've already had the Thai picked up, Thuza Win,' he said quietly. 'He was leaving the town, but we stopped him on the Lashio road, a mile or two beyond the checkpoints. My men are bringing him to the camp as we stand here. I know something else happened when the doors were closed, so you may as well be wise and help me. Cast your mind back and decide what you value. What did he say when he gave you the note?'

Thuza clenched her fists beneath her arms and tried to focus through her swelling mist of tears. 'Only what I told you before,' she muttered, holding his eye. 'His men will make your delivery to the forests if you pay the money you owe.'

'Are you certain nothing else?'

'Yes.'

The general clicked his tongue and cocked his head to the side, grimacing. 'Let me tell you a story and we'll see if you can understand my confusion. I sent the Thai seventeen thousand US dollars. It was cash, hidden in a neatly folded *longi*, and it was the full and fair amount we agreed. Lieutenant Kyaw was responsible for passing on the payment. Did you know that?'

Thuza shook her head again, her heart thrashing.

'Your brother left this camp with not a dollar short of what he was meant to. I counted it into his palm myself. So here's the problem I have, Thuza Win: either Lieutenant Kyaw took the money or the Thai did and he's lying, or all three of you are lying and you're snuggled in one bed. You can tell me the truth, girl. If you do, it's better. I can make it so your brother won't suffer quite as terribly. I can make it sure that you won't suffer too.'

Thuza's heart and her mind were sprinting. The fear inside her was a stormy black sea. She didn't know what to say or do. She didn't have a clue about what Kyaw may or may not have done, or who the Thai may or may not have robbed, or even whether a single word that came from the general's thin lips was truthful. She only knew what *she'd* done for certain, and what would happen if he ever found out. He didn't seem to know, but perhaps he was lying. Why else would he prod her and poke her like this? It might have been a trap and she couldn't see the tripwire. And if the Thai was on his way here, he couldn't be trusted.

'I don't know anything,' she cried, a sob leaping from her. 'Please! I'm telling the truth.'

'All of it?'

'Yes!'

The general took a sharp breath and stepped abruptly back from her, turning away. He removed his beret and flattened his hair, then dropped heavily into one of the seats beside the tea chest. He placed the hat down, sighing, and motioned for her to join him. Thuza didn't move.

'I'm sorry,' he said. He threw her an unnatural, toothy smile and brandished his hand, more firmly. 'Sit, please. I'm not threatening you. These are tense times – that's all – and the Thai is as shifty a snake as they make them. Our deliveries are always of the utmost importance. I just want to understand, if I can.'

He jabbed his finger at the chair again and Thuza saw a flicker of impatience repressed behind his eyes, and she slunk into the seat. He was threatening her. No doubt in her mind. He picked up the little glasses from the chest and wiped each one briefly on the cuff of his sleeve, before unscrewing the lid of the flask and filling them with steaming tea. He pushed one towards her. She stared at the grease-smeared glass and the little line of smoke that coiled upwards through the weak light, feeling her nausea rise. The general dragged his chair a little closer to hers, knocking the dirty soup bowl, clattering the spoon.

He smiled again, more awkwardly. 'I've heard the rumours about you, Little *Naga-ma*,' he said. She could see the pores on his nose, big and oily. His teeth were black or missing at the back of his mouth. 'You're special, aren't you? Blue eyes, forked tongue. I'm a superstitious man, Thuza Win. It's no secret in the camp. We could protect each other, if we worked together. You can talk to the spirits for me. Ask them to bring me favour for my gambles and good deeds. I can keep you safe in Mogok, if you'll let me. No one would trouble you if they knew you were with me. There are bigger gems in life than just rubies to play for. I can keep Kyaw safe too, if you tell me you'd like that? And all I'd expect in exchange is your trust.'

Thuza swallowed hard, wriggling backwards and trying to avoid his gaze. She could feel his eyes all over her body, the heat of them, their grope. She sunk back in her chair, making herself smaller, trying to hide there. Her mind was spinning, lost at the unexpected lunge of their conversation. Perhaps this was nothing to do with the Thai. Perhaps she was safe with her lies and deceptions. Perhaps he had never been coming here at all, and the threats were nothing more than the general's bait to get her to his quarters and knock her off guard. His stare was lecherous. His hands wrung together. The tip of his tongue was crusted white. But if that was what he wanted, he could have just forced her. But perhaps he didn't want to feel like he had to. The forest was lonely. She knew that, though differently. Her eyes slipped up to the photo on the coat stand, to the happy family staring down.

'General!'

The slop of boots in the mud outside broke the general from his gawping, and his eyes coarsened as the soldier called his name again. He shook himself and stood suddenly, snatching up his beret and striding towards the door. He pulled the tent open and a boy sparked to attention in the darkness outside.

'The Thai's in the back tent, sir,' he said. 'What are your orders?'

The general paused and glanced back at Thuza, then he ducked into the night and the tent was empty. She could hear his voice through the canvas, see his shadow.

'I'll speak to him myself. Keep her here,' said the general. 'Whatever happens, she doesn't leave.'

Thuza had been awake for hours, listening to the general as he wheezed from his chair. The ache in her head was as dense as the forest. Lying in the cot, wrapped tightly up in the folds of his blanket, she felt too afraid to move or make a sound. Outside the tent, the earliest dawn light was beginning to spread across the sky, softening the shades of brown and green around her and revealing shapes on the canvas above. There were tree boughs swaying, closing her in, and she blinked them into focus, counting away the seconds of her imprisonment, wishing herself to the safety of her tunnels, to where she could hide and be on her own.

Last night, the general been gone with the Thai until midnight, when the moon reached a peak in the navy-blue sky. He was drunk and surly when he returned. Thuza had been exhausted from her previous night of traipsing the town touting rubies for Kyaw and she felt herself slipping in and out of restless slumber, but all the time she still knew she was waiting, petrified to hear his footsteps in the mud. The storm lamp had burnt out, and she'd stayed as still as she could in his bed, the odour of him smothering her, and he'd seemed to forget she had been there at all. She held her breath as he clattered around the tent, cursing in slurs and kicking his tea chest, then collapsing in his chair and falling asleep. She couldn't be sure that she'd slept a moment from then. She had been too afraid he would wake and remember her. Rape or death: one or other was waiting. She prepared herself not to beg or fight him. It all hung on the Thai and the whims of the stars.

She rolled carefully onto her side, wincing with the creak of the cot and her stiff, aching muscles, and then from somewhere on the mountain there came a burst of deafening sound. She flinched instinctively and the tent shuddered with the shift of the earth. The general grunted and woke with a start, and the noise of branches cracking and falling surrounded them instantly like a deluge of rain. He looked at her, shocked for a heartbeat as memory recaptured him, then he seemed to blush and anger. He stood up and turned away from her, ramming his shirt into the band of his trousers and fumbling to buckle his belt.

Thuza squirmed to sit up and smoothed her hair too, drawing her knees to her chest. It was a landmine, she thought as she watched him lace his boots up. The forest was full of them. It was probably a bird that set it off. Or a monkey. The general rummaged in his jacket pocket and pulled out a mirror and a little bottle of water, and he splashed his face as he peered into the silver, ignoring Thuza then drinking the last swig. She sat motionless, eyes fixed to him, pretending she was anywhere but his quarters too. Outside, a dog barked, and Thuza felt its short, harsh yaps reverberate in her chest. The general's radio started to crackle and he picked it up, twisting the dial and muttering beneath his breath as it hissed and snapped and no words came out. He spat a foul curse and snatched his revolver from the floor beside his chair, checking it briefly, then stuffing it into his holster and striding from the exit without a word.

Thuza stayed where she was, deathly still. She felt an odd mix of relief and trepidation. She was glad he was gone, but it was a landmine, wasn't it? It must have been close for the trees to shed their leaves. It couldn't have been dynamite. They were miles from the mines here. It was the general that was making her worry, though she shouldn't. She could tell from his manner that he wasn't concerned. They probably had accidents happen every morning. There's always a racket somewhere in the mountains. She shifted a little, thirst overtaking her nerves, wondering if any tea was left in the flask, and whether she dared to move and get it, when she heard another radio fizzing, louder. From the tea chest, a voice was shouting, panicked. Outside, the dog's cry hastened and another joined in, and at once men's voices were yelling there too. Thuza's heart seized. She could hear feet were running, quicker and quicker. Like the swell of a wave approaching a shore, the commotion grew thicker and more fevered, and she stumbled from the cot, compelled by her horror, and crept to the door and peered from the tent.

A gunshot fired and split the air like shattering glass. A soldier sprinted past her, his thin hands tearing frantically at the catch on his rifle. His eyes were wide and skipping with fear. The roar outside was rising further, a barrage of gun blasts and dog bays and cries. She staggered after him, her own panic rising, moving towards the shelter in the centre of the camp. At the end of the narrow track, she could see a squall of sprinting bodies, and as she reached its head, the sight that met her was almost unreal. Spilling through the pathways of the camp were scores and scores of Tatmadaw soldiers, their faces raging, black and brown with paint. Furiously shouting, line after line of them charged with their rifles drawn and firing wildly, and streaks of light sniped past her face. Everywhere around, the rebels were scattering, grabbing for their own guns and boots and knives. The soldier she had followed was already twenty yards away, his skinny body dodging through the sea of men and burning buildings. The gasp of her breath in her head was dizzying. Her only thought was finding Kyaw.

Around her already, the camp was ablaze. She raised her arm to shield her face, feeling the scorching glow of the flames as they splintered the bamboo structures, and the air quaked with their heat before being swallowed by a swell of thick black smoke. Lungs gummed and eyes streaking, she coughed and stumbled across the clearing, and the heavy crackle of burning wood enclosed her, disorientating her. As the rebels scrambled to their trenches and fired a storm of frantic, aimless bullets, dust and mud ruptured up at her feet where they hit the earth. The voices that had been shouts just moments before had twisted to screams, men's pained bawling and children's shrieks, shrill and laced with the same terror as she had heard from herself when the Tatmadaw came to her home that day. She pressed her hands to her mouth to stop herself from screaming now too, feeling the same uncontrollable panic, and ran as fast as she could, dodging in the direction she remembered she had come.

At the tent's entrance, the guard was gone. She tore inside, staggering to keep herself up, her chest heaving. Kyaw was missing. The white boy stared from the centre like a ghost.

'Where is he?' she screamed in Burmese.

He shook his head at her, body frozen. He didn't understand. She spun away, throwing a desperate glance along the alley where she'd run from and then looking the opposite way, searching for her brother amongst the smog and disarray. He was nowhere to be seen. She muttered a prayer to the spirits to save her, choosing a direction and stumbling out, slipping in the thick mud. She tried to steady her legs and scramble up again, but a hand grabbed her ankle and was yanking her back.

'Get off me,' she yelled, kicking.

The white boy fell to the ground behind her. He groped up her body, dragging her back into the tent. He spoke in Burmese too, but his words were unclear and his accent was terrible. 'You can't go out there!'

Thuza kicked again, thrashing free of him, and she crawled through the entrance and sprinted away. She could hear his voice behind her, high and terrified, bawling, '*Wait!*'

She paused where two alleyways crossed, squinting in each direction for Kyaw and the white boy barrelled into her, shoving her to the ground.

'Let me go,' she cried, pushing him away and clambering back up. Bullets were flying above them and the heat of the fires was on her skin, and she started again for the line of trees at the end of a passage that signalled her safety.

'But I don't know where I'm going,' said the boy.

Running, Thuza glanced behind to watch his pursuit, and she was almost at the treeline when she faced forward again, and she reared up suddenly at the sight ahead. Crawling along the earth were dozens more Tatmadaw soldiers. They were threading through the forest on their hands and knees. The camp was about to be overrun.

'Look out!' the white boy shouted as the first soldier stood and fired.

Thuza shrieked and the boy leapt over her, pulling her down as the bullets skimmed above their heads. He snatched her wrist and wrenched her sideways, forcing her between two burning tents, then darting right and steeply uphill, dragging her with him. She tore her arm free but stayed at his side, and they ran doubled over, barely able to see through the fog and dust. Like shrapnel, the branches were falling around them. A vast explosion sounded and Thuza looked back to see a tower of fire in the centre of the camp, taller by far than any forest tree, pointed and flailing like a fir in high wind. Her vision was spitting and her ears were ringing, full of the gunfire and her horror and the crash of structures as they succumbed to the flames.

The babble and wail of voices circled around her. Dulled by the smog and the sizzle of flames, she could hear the frantic pounding of boots on the earth and see the faceless shadows of men shifting through the peripheries of her vision, and she wanted to shout but felt too afraid. Thick spits of unseen ammunition made her duck, and the heat and her panic soaked her with sweat. The further into the camp she charged, the less she felt sure of where she was heading. Her chest was tight and her legs felt heavy, and her mind was thick with confusion and dread. Another stampede of invisible men raced by and she threw herself aside. At her back, a wall crumbled with the weight of her lurch, and as the dust cleared and she dragged herself up, she saw the form of a body harden – a familiar shape, thin and long, scrambling over the smouldering debris. She went to shout again but all that burst from her lungs was a hack. The body disappeared inside a fold of black smoke and she clambered over the fallen building, chasing towards it. She fixed her eyes on the shape as she neared it and a moment of wind thinned the black and she choked on a gasp as she caught sight of Kyaw. Her brother had fallen a few feet away and was slumped against a tree trunk. His eyes were open and rolling as though he'd been drugged, but they found her stare and hardened, sharp. With enormous effort, he crawled to his knees and hauled himself forward, his head rocking limp like a newborn child.

'Brother!' Thuza cried out and fought towards him, but with one more step her legs started buckling and a bullet shot straight through Kyaw's sad, lolling head.

SIXTEEN

By the time Than arrived at the forest, the fires were all out. It didn't much matter. The bitter musk of burning wood and the warmth that rose through the soles of his boots were almost as good as having seen it for himself. He made his way across the clearing and stood in the centre with his hands on his hips. The camp was bigger than anything he'd ever expected to find from Aye Myint's confession, and the devastation was truly immense. Apart from the very thickest tree trunks, the Tatmadaw had levelled the vast square of land. Nothing was green. Blackened palms stretched towards a smoggy sky, their leaves stripped to spines and swaying in the wind like upturned brooms of wiry horsehair. Only the shells of a few stubborn structures remained, but with their crossbars toppled and their roofs burnt away. The earth was still smouldering, grey and charcoal-white, except where the sandbags had melted and yellow-brown shingle spilled across the ground. There were overturned oil drums and piles of broken bricks, and earthenware urns that were upturned or shattered, and scraps of sheet metal, warped by the heat and tarnished dark red. Most of the injured and dead had been shifted, but amongst the debris Than saw the limbs of a few luckless souls. The smell of singed flesh mixed with the wood in the air and sat on his tongue, like meat cooked in flame. When he went home, he'd tell Marlar to make him a victory feast, he thought as he sniffed it. It was making him hungry, this wonderful pride. The only pity was that Min hadn't seen it. He could have told his mother how well Than had done – and his siblings and the neighbours and everyone else in ungrateful Mogok. They ought to know this triumph belonged to Officer Than Chit.

Looking round, he rubbed a thread of spittle from his chin and raised his hand to a Tatmadaw soldier who was working on the clean-up nearby. 'Is that all of them, Sergeant?' Than asked him.

The sergeant and three other soldiers were laying out the bodies of the Tatmadaw's dead, arranging their sprawled arms and legs neatly and closing their eyes before bagging them up to take back to the town. He stood up and nodded to Than, smearing the blood from his hands to his face as he wiped his glossy brow. 'Yes, sir,' he said. 'We've swept the entire camp.'

'How many?'

'Twenty-eight.'

'And how many insurgents?'

'At least sixty. We're still counting. We've left them where they were.'

Than coughed to stop himself from grinning, and he rocked on his boot heels and glanced around again. A two-to-one ratio was better than decent. The general would accept that as a reasonable loss. Not that any more would have made a measurable difference. Finding the Fifteenth was treasure enough. Than's promotion was sealed – there was no doubt about it – and now all that was left to clarify were the details of his glory.

He wanted each one to commit to his memory, to savour the morsels that had made this day so sweet. He pointed across the clearing to the long line of men in dusty and ragged Shan State Army fatigues. 'And they're the prisoners?'

'Yes, sir.'

'That's the lot of them?'

'There's a few more on the north edge of the camp. Eighteen or so. Perhaps twenty. They're badly injured. We don't expect they'll live. These are the usables.'

'Any good ones?'

The sergeant shook his head. 'Most of them are weaker than kiddies, they've been up here so long, but they'll do alright for porters.'

'How many do we have?'

'Forty-three.'

Forty-three! Than couldn't help but smile as he heard it. Min would laugh too when Than was back home. Their report had been an omen. It didn't matter if the prisoners were scraggy when you roped them up in numbers. Even children work hard when they know what's at stake. They'd be taken to Shewbo and interrogated before being given their postings, and the guards would be clear in helping them learn the fines for dissent. In the jungles, they'd be put to work for the Tatmadaw, clearing the land, digging latrines, shifting supplies and breaking rocks to finish the irrigation grids that were partway constructed outside Mandalay, and when the pressure was on, they'd do just fine.

He smoothed the breast of his uniform and let his eyes wander along the line, sizing each man up with derision and pride. The soldiers had forced them to crouch in *poun-zan*, with their knees half bent and weight on their tiptoes, their backs bamboo straight and hands clasped behind their heads. Their faces were hooded by coarse linen rice sacks, but from the way their legs were shaking, Than knew that they strained. Good, he thought. He wanted them reeling. Shwebo would be ruthless in debriefing them thoroughly but today was already Than's lucky day, and if they left them there long enough so they really were suffering, he might be able to extract something too. The name of a financier or the location of a new outpost could be just the leverage he needed to make sure Bo Win made him major, not captain. He was probably getting it anyway – he knew that – but it wouldn't be foolish to make doubly sure.

'Officer Than Chit.'

From the end of the row of teetering men, an arm raised to shield two eyes. Major Thaw Soe was standing by the prisoners and staring at Than with his arm in the air. His face was straight and typically cynical. The grease on his forehead was flashing bright white. At his side was his despicable captain, Tun Oo. He was smoking a cigarette through the curl of a grin.

At the back of Than's throat, a lump started forming, hard and revolting like a ball of stale rice. Than knew both men better than he'd like to. They had come to Mogok in the same year that he did, at the same low rank, and they'd shared the same dorm. They had all been from street homes and all swept for landmines, and they'd all nicked potatoes from the half-blind old cook. The difference was in how the men had risen, and how callous they were stamping down threats. When they had been privates in training together, Thaw Soe and Tun Oo

262

had teased Than for not running as quickly as they did through the swamp pits. At rifle practice, they had sniggered with the other boys when Than couldn't hit the targets, though he swore at night they tweaked his sights. In front of their superiors, they would laugh at him for not reciting the policies with complete preciseness and for the stammer of his tongue when he yelled the word 'Fire!'

As a youngster, Than had told them to stop it, and once or twice it had come to a brawl. Now that the men were senior there was nothing worth saying. They were the lapdogs that Marlar spat at: the thugs and drunks and thieves and spies. For as long as Than had known them, they had cosied up to the men above them, without shame or excuses, and now they sniffed at Bo Win's crutch like bitches on heat.

Thaw Soe brandished his hand again, calling Than in.

Than's teeth gritted. '*Mingala-ba*, Major,' he said, walking reluctantly over. The charred ground crunched beneath his feet. He saluted. '*Mingala-ba*, Captain. May auspiciousness be upon you.'

'*Mingala-ba*, Officer,' replied the major. He returned Than's salute, then licked his fingertip and smoothed his wiry eyebrows, pausing to examine him. 'What are you doing here?' he asked, suspiciously. 'I didn't see your name on the roster.'

Than shook his head. 'I'm not on the roster, sir,' he replied, 'but I wanted to experience the victory for myself.'

'And what do you think?'

'It's a beautiful sight.'

'The righteousness of the Tatmadaw is always a beautiful sight.'

Than nodded.

The major's stare narrowed. He glanced around the burnt-out camp and then hooked his hands on his hips and cocked his head to the side, just a dash. 'Were you present for the battle?'

Than scratched his nose and looked at his feet, wincing. He could see the path ahead. 'No, sir.'

'So you've helped with the clear-up?'

'Not yet.'

The major's eyes shrank thinner still. 'You have an odd definition of *experiencing* a victory, Officer,' he said. 'It seems to me like you've come to bask in victory's glow.'

A grin burst suddenly onto Tun Oo's face and he stepped forward, slapping Than's shoulder. 'That's just like you, Than Chit,' he said as Than grimaced and swayed. 'Turning up when the hard work's done.'

Than's rebalanced himself and clenched his fists behind his back, hoping his face didn't show his rage. These fools didn't know what they were talking about. It was irrelevant that he hadn't been here firing his rifle. It was irrelevant that he hadn't bagged a body or lugged a log or even been asked to lace up his boots. It was irrelevant too – in the grand scheme of thinking – that he hadn't been able to inform General Bo Win of the Fifteenth's location in person and watch his reaction when he learnt of the prize. Of course Than had been disappointed to start with, but the general was busy and Than understood that, and still, in the end, due credit gets through. He shook his head. He knew he was scowling. 'You misunderstand, sir,' he said. 'I've been intrinsic to this operation from the very beginning. I'm strategically involved. Quite fundamental.'

The major rubbed his chin and looked at Tun Oo. 'Ah, yes,' he said, and a wry smile leaked. 'I remember now that I heard your name. Congratulations, Officer. We do owe you a debt.'

'That's right,' said Than, squaring up.

'What a find. Such luck.'

'There was no luck to it.'

'Aye Myint, was it? The old traitor. Who knew?' Thaw Soe took Than's hand and shook it roughly. He leant in, his face cool and steely, pulling Than forward so their cheeks almost touched. 'Enlighten me, Officer,' he whispered into his ear. 'How did you know there were rubies in his house?'

Than wriggled backwards and extracted his fingers. 'Intelligence, sir,' he muttered.

'From whom?'

'From my own deductions.'

'But you must have done a deal or two with Aye Myint in the past to know he was crooked?'

'No, sir. Never.'

'Go on, Than Chit,' said Tun Oo. 'You can tell us. We've all used jaggery to sweeten our tea.'

Than stared at him, raising his head and standing as tall as his body would stretch. The streak of competition in a street-boy never left. He shook his head again. He was not going to let them ruin his day. 'I love and honour the Tatmadaw better than to steal from her, brothers.'

The major examined Than for a moment more, then clapped his hands and stepped away. 'Well, at least you've made a name for yourself after twenty-five years. We've all been waiting. It was quite a show you put on, so the wind says . . . threatening the baby? We heard poor Aye Myint pissed his pants.'

'A Tatmadaw man uses all resources available to him in acts of persuasion,' said Than. 'Fortitude. Resilience. Persistence. Cunning.' He swallowed painfully, remembering the sight of the little boy smiling up at him from the table, his big black eyes and wavy hair. He was relieved he hadn't needed to shoot the child. He wouldn't have liked to do it with Min there. He twitched on his feet and Tun Oo laughed.

'We didn't know you were capable of such things,' he said. 'Little Thanny Chit Chit! The boy who cried in his sleep for his mother. You've surprised us, Officer. We're almost impressed.'

Than glanced to the long of line prisoners at Tun Oo's side and anger sizzled up in his gut. For what he had achieved here, he deserved to be respected, not teased. 'You should be impressed,' he spat without thinking. 'This attack was my doing.'

The major's face tightened. 'Excuse me?'

'I am responsible for today's splendour. This success . . . these prisoners . . . They're thanks to me.'

Tun Oo glared at Than, half laughing. 'The major planned the offensive, Than Chit. I led the men.'

'The information was mine.'

'The information was the Tatmadaw's. You were a messenger. It was us who acted upon it. We put our lives at risk. Where were you?'

Than's stomach pitched. He had been at home in his kitchen having breakfast, with his feet by the fire and *mohinga* in his bowl. It wasn't until later that he had learnt what was

266

happening, and only by chance when he dropped into barracks to look for Min. 'I was with the general,' he lied, feeling suddenly self-conscious. 'We were working.'

The major's mouth twitched. A slight jealous spark. 'You were with Bo Win?'

'Yes.'

'He invited you?'

'Yes. We had coffee in his Mission Room and discussed how best to utilise the information that will inevitably be gleaned from today's captives in order to maximise the effectiveness of future anti-insurgent operations.'

Thaw Sow and Tun Oo looked at each other.

'He must be pleased with you,' said Thaw Soe.

'He is. Delighted.'

'He must be shocked,' said Tun Oo, spitting. 'I bet after a decade of searching for the Fifteenth, he never imagined the breakthrough would come from you.'

Than shook his head, puffing his chest. 'You're mistaken, Captain. I've been working on uncovering the Fifteenth for a long time. It's been a very prestigious project for which the general selected me personally. We've worked together closely to ensure its success.'

'Why haven't we heard about it?'

'It was a secret mission. An individual objective set in covert partnership with General Bo Win.' He looked at them meanly. 'We couldn't risk leaks.'

'Ha! Rubbish,' said Tun Oo. 'Your find was a fluke.'

'It wasn't. It took months of careful planning, building networks, collecting intelligence and managing spies.'

'The general would have never left all that to an officer.'

'I'm undercover,' said Than. He could feel his cheeks were reddening and his heart was pounding faster, but his mouth was running freely and he couldn't make it stop. 'I've been promoted.'

Thaw Soe and Tun Oo's faces dropped.

'You've had your orders?'

Than nodded. In his chest, his heart was a wild, thrashing bird. He cast his eyes aside so Thaw Soe couldn't catch them. His hands were greasy with sweat and shaking and he tucked them into his pockets. He didn't know where his lie had come from and he felt afraid for what he'd say next, but whatever it was, he wouldn't swim backwards. He wanted these men feeling utterly worthless. He knew it was reckless, but he wanted them green-eyed. It wasn't just for this moment that he'd summoned such bitterness. It was for all the days of suffering he'd lived through; for all the years of being so scorned. 'I'm waiting for the paperwork,' he said, straightening his spine, trying his hardest to steady his shake.

Thaw Soe hesitated, finding Than's eye. 'It would never be that fast.'

'These are exceptional circumstances, Major. I've located a critical enemy hub. The general was especially impressed with the inclusion of my son in the offensive. The boy is a soldier now. He has exceptional potential. He found the rubies that led to my discovery of the camp. Bo Win appreciates ingenuity and loyalty. A new family dynasty in Mogok, he called us. A future force for good and great.'

Tun Oo and Thaw Soe were both still staring at him, and

Than turned along the line of prisoners to escape their vice-like, doubtful eyes.

'You,' he said, flicking his finger to a loitering Tatmadaw private and marching towards him. He glanced behind. The major and captain were watching. 'Who's the fittest captive? Bring him here.'

The boy skipped nervously forward, scampering along the line, scanning it.

'What are you doing?' asked Thaw Soe.

'I'm picking my porter. That's the tradition, isn't it? A new assistant for a senior post.'

'You can't just take one. They haven't been debriefed.'

Than turned his back to them. 'What about him?' he said, pointing. His heart was hammering. 'Remove his hood.'

The private who had been trotting beside Than stopped. 'This one?'

'Yes. Show me his face.'

The private yanked the rice sack from the cloaked head and the prisoner squinted in the sudden light, gasping for air. His face was purple and dripping with sweat. His balance teetered. Than stared down and his thoughts tried to snare him, to follow his body and find what was next. The boy was young – as young as Min was and not unlike him. His hair was thick and scruffy slate-black and his frame was thin, but healthy and tall. His eyes were clear. Their spark was terrified. He couldn't have been in the forest for long.

'Stand up,' said Than.

The boy wobbled and then straightened stiffly.

'You've picked a lion there,' said Tun Oo.

'He's as healthy as an ox,' said Than. 'Look at his arms.'

'That's not an ox, Than Chit. He's spindly.'

Than turned to the boy, ignoring them. His shake was getting worse. By the spirits, where on earth did he mean to go from here? 'What's your name?' he said.

The boy stammered. 'Thein Lwin.'

'Your name is now Puppy Dog,' said Than. 'You work for me, Puppy Dog. OK? You will forget every loyalty you ever had before. I am your master. You will be trained to do as I say, or punished. Do you understand?'

The boy glanced along the line at the prisoners, trembling.

'Did you hear me?'

'Yes, sir.'

'Good. Your first order is to assist my men in bagging the bodies of our fallen Tatmadaw brothers. You will ensure all detached body parts are returned to the correct body, and if a body misses a part that has not yet been collected, you are responsible for scouring the camp and searching it out. Do you understand?'

'Yes, sir.'

Than pointed across the clearing. 'Go.'

The boy staggered away and Than threw Thaw Soe and Tun Oo a curt salute, before striding after him. He had done enough to convince them, hadn't he? His head was a tangled ball of string. He couldn't bear it when they called him stupid. He felt like he was back in his cot in the barracks, nine years old, freezing and lonely, scared of the darkness and of what the new light would bring. He hoped the general would not be angry. What he needed now was to be back in the jailhouse and waiting by the telephone. It was crucial he spoke to Bo Win before they did. He rubbed his head and quickened his walking. He'd spent enough time here to let the shine fade.

Ahead, there was a row of at least twenty fully stuffed body-bags, but there were still a few corpses that had yet to be cleared. The Puppy Dog could pack away a solider or two while Thaw Soe was watching, and then they'd leave the camp and they wouldn't come back. He speeded up again and was about to shout *hurry*, when what he saw stopped him dead in his tracks. Inside, he felt a wind-surge; a blast through his innards. It was white hot and scorching, whipping head to toe. On the soil in a heap, all the bodies were matching, but at the same frozen instant, one was so shrilly not. Thick hair like a wire brush. A long and lean torso. An almost clean uniform. The crease still crisp in its sleeves and trousers.

The Puppy Dog looked around and caught the line of Than's sight. He bent to the body.

'Don't touch him!'

Than lunged forward and pushed the boy away, throwing himself to the ground and rolling over the limp, heavy body that lay at his feet. The corpse had brown eyes and both were still open. Like a marionette doll, he stared at Than with his head slumped to the side. In his skull was a bullet wound, neat and quite circular, a hole that pierced above one eye. It was rimmed in white where the bone was peeping. The blood had dried to a thick, rusty crust. The face looked like Min, but it couldn't be, could it? Min was at home, having tea with his mother. His training was not even due for a week. General Bo Win wouldn't send Than's son to the line before training. He wouldn't send Min to battle ever, surely? Not now. Not after Than had helped him. It wouldn't be honourable. It wouldn't be right.

He rubbed his eyes and tugged at his collar. There was an actual, physical pain inside his ribcage, so barbed and forceful that he couldn't breathe. His bones felt softer than dumpling bread. His senses were reeling, spinning him sideways: louder, hotter, brighter, more acrid. But it was Min before him. Min's clothes. Min's hands. Min's boyish brown face.

The Puppy Dog went to move him again.

Than snatched his gun from its holster and pointed it at the boy. He felt sick. 'Who did this?'

The boy cowered down, his hands raised, terrified.

Than turned his wrist and brought the handle of his revolver into the Puppy Dog's jaw. 'WHO DID THIS?' he shouted.

The boy fell sideways. 'I don't know, sir.'

Than stepped over him, belting the rim of his bone again, feeling it crack beneath the metal. The pain in his chest was blistering, and he grabbed the boy by his hair and dragged him to his knees, pushing him down to look at Min's face. He pressed his gun to the back of his head. 'You have ten seconds to consider whether or not you are telling lies and think about your life.'

The boy started crying. A trickle of urine was soaking his leg. 'I swear, Officer. It was a fire-fight. Chaos! How could I know?'

'What's happening?' Through the corner of his eye, Than saw Thaw Soe heading towards him.

'Stay away!' he cried. His mind was a fog. He could feel that his own tears were starting to form.

272

'Put down your gun, Than Chit.'

'This is nothing to do with you.'

'You're embarrassing yourself.'

'What do you care?'

'You're embarrassing the Tatmadaw. The prisoners are not yours to dispose of.'

'They're murderers!'

'And you're a madman,' said the major. 'Look at yourself. Do you think Bo Win won't hear of your lying? Do you think he won't hear about what you're doing now? You'll be lucky if you don't end up in the gallows.'

Than's legs staggered. He pushed the gun harder to the boy's head. 'I'm not a madman.'

'Then what are you doing?'

'I need to know who killed my son!'

Thaw Soe's expression dropped. He glanced back at Tun Oo, and then Min's corpse where it lay on the ground. 'That's your boy?'

'Yes.'

The major hesitated. He peered forward and covered his mouth, then stood up, sniffing. He jerked down the sleeves of shirt, smoothing them.

'Your son died a noble death, Officer Than Chit,' he said, emotionless. 'The Tatmadaw is grateful for his sacrifice, but this is nothing unusual. There isn't anything I can see here that warrants your reaction. A woman would have more composure than you.'

'I need to know who killed him.'

'The SSA killed him, brother.'

'No!' Than stamped his foot. He was trembling uncontrollably. He knew that his tears had started to fall. 'I need to know who shot the bullet. His name!'

'What does it matter? It's done.'

'I have to punish him. He must be punished!'

Thaw Soe turned, waving his hand to the decimated camp. 'He has been punished, hasn't he? Today the Tatmadaw have won. What more could you want?' His eyes settled back on Than. 'Now, Officer, regain your composure and return to your duties. That's an order.'

The major saluted and walked away and Than stared after him, his whole soul shaking, and he squeezed his eyes shut and took a gasped breath. He could feel his rage twisting, feel it shifting direction. The man was everything Than loathed in existence: his arrogance, disinterest, unfairness and treachery. This should have been Than's day for glory and gratitude. It should have been his rising star. But now Min was gone, it wasn't worth breathing. His past and his future had been swept away. He looked down at Puppy Dog with his young, Min-like features, with his hopes and his innocence and his skull still intact, and his body felt weaker than it had done in his lifetime, but his mind felt suddenly the crispest, most pure. He knew at once all the answers he wanted, and he slumped to his knees and he dropped the revolver.

Bo Win did it.

The Tatmadaw did it.

Than had done it.

He'd killed his son.

SEVENTEEN

The girl ran ahead of Michael, her tiny body dodging through the muddle of trees. Shards of yellow light caught her as they speared through the straining boughs, and her hair and *longi* streaked behind as she ripped across the mountain and fled from his chase.

'Get away from me!' she cried, glancing back. Her face was terrified.

Michael scrambled after her, swiping at the branches as they catapulted back at him, his feet tripping on the uneven ground. Jagged leaves shredded his flesh as he tore them aside and tried to keep up, and his lungs blazed and the humidity of the forest had soaked his clothes, making them heavy. She was shouting in English now, much clearer than his Burmese was, though he doubted it was more than a hopeful guess at his language as the Burmese children all learnt it at school. The stench of death and burning wood still smothered him, and he could taste it on his tongue. Fits of gunfire were rebounding against his eardrums and his heart was sprinting as fast as a cat. All he could think of was not being left here. He needed to reach a telephone. He had to call his father.

'Wait!' he shouted back. 'I need your help.'

Too swift for him, she flew through the bamboo uprights,

thrashing away and emerging into a thicket of waist-high grasses and thorny weeds on the opposite side.

'Leave me alone!' she screamed, wrenching at them with her hands to break herself free and staggering into the undergrowth beyond. Her struggles slowed her, and Michael rammed himself through the narrow gaps between the bamboos, ignoring the blood that it sliced from his torso. He caught her shoulder.

The girl froze momentarily then spun to face him, glaring up through the green and black shadows. Her expression was steaming. She lunged at him, shoving his chest.

Michael stumbled backwards, snatching for an overhead branch to regain his balance. 'Please,' he said, reaching out to her, 'I'm begging you. Just show me the way to the town.'

The girl's face twitched and she lunged again, pushing him harder, and then she threw her head to the sky and let out a wail like an injured animal.

'Shhhh!' Michael hissed. He cast a panicked glance into the forest. 'Someone will hear you.'

The girl howled again and crumpled to the earth, covering her face with her small, muddy hands. She had fallen in the crook of a vast, grey tree root and it coiled about her body like a python, and as she clutched her bloodied knees to her chest, it gathered her in like constricted prey.

Michael staggered back, his lungs heaving, and he rubbed his neck with a shaking hand. The town couldn't be far, he thought, his eyes skittering through the darkness. A few miles at most if he knew which way. A mass of low shacks and towering golden stupas, he had seen it clearly when they ditched Teacher's truck. *Shit*. Teacher. He felt a blazing wave of sickness. He hadn't stopped to think where the old soldier was – or if he was still alive even. He slumped against a tree trunk, trembling. If he got to the town, he could just make that phone call. His father would tell him what he needed to do. But the town would be crawling with Tatmadaw soldiers. There'd be checkpoints, his details on road booths. They'd recognise him. There might be a photograph too, to make sure. His head was hurting, throbbing in drum beats. He didn't trust the Tatmadaw any better than the rebels, and he didn't want to be picked up by either. The only stupid white boy in the whole of Shan State. He was fucked in this forest. He wouldn't spot a landmine or sniper or tripwire any easier than he'd spot a tiger's lair. He looked down at the girl where she had sunk inside the base of the tree, his vision spitting through aching thought.

From the canopy above, the branches were creaking. The forest was whispering, its wind and its water, the invisible shift of its rustle and snap. The shadows danced and his gaze strained further through into trees. 'We should keep moving,'

She wiped her nose on her sleeve and then pressed her legs tighter inside her arms. 'The soldiers haven't followed us,' she muttered. 'We'd hear them.'

Michael's eyes skittered, chasing the sounds. He didn't know what it was he could hear. He leant heavier against the tree. She was shaking too, he saw. 'Are you OK?'

'My brother's dead.'

Michael gagged and spat the bile from his mouth as another vast roll of sickness pitched up in his gut. He knew the boy was dead. He had been right behind her, just a foot away, watched the streak of white light pierce his skull. The blood had smudged and pinked his vision. Though he'd blinked it away, he still felt in a blur. The girl had thrown herself to the ground beside him, her hands frantically scooping at her brother's spillage as though trying to ladle the life back inside. Michael had dragged her away, hoisting her up and hauling her to the safety of the trees as she screamed and thrashed against him.

'I'm sorry,' he said more weakly, and he dropped beside her in the soft, damp leaves.

The girl sniffed. She turned her head to look at him, tears glossing her eyes. 'How will I tell my parents?'

Michael felt a painful cramp of hot, dry guilt. He could imagine what his parents were doing. The ambassador would be pacing behind his great teakwood desk in the upstairs office of their Rangoon home, and he'd be writing letters or speaking on the telephone, or perhaps he'd have a visitor to discuss how to handle this, and he wouldn't have slept for two worrisome days. His mother would be sitting with Daw Mar in the kitchen, mascara streaking her purple-red face. He could imagine them getting a messenger too. It might have been Barrowman with his cheeks extra ruddy, or somebody else from the embassy's staff. They'd arrive to say that they'd found Michael's body, with a bullet through his temple, having met the same fate. He stared at the ground, feeling reckless and selfish. And what was Sein's father doing? Was he still in the hospital? He wanted to go home and say he was sorry. However he got there, he wanted it quickly. He wanted to wash and sleep in his bed. He shook his head, not knowing what to say.

The girl's lip quivered. 'I couldn't help him.'

'You tried.'

'I left his body.'

'What else could you have done?'

'The Tatmadaw will find him. They'll know he was a rebel. They'll punish my parents.'

'And you?'

The slick of tears in her eyes thickened. 'That's different.'

Michael dug his fingers through the leaves by his feet and stared at the ground. He knew what she meant, somehow, without details. In a way, he hoped Sein's parents were still at the hospital. At least then it meant that his friend was alive. In his throat, a surge of emotion caught him. The forest attack had been different from the bomb blast. It was equally terrible – the noise and the chaos – but there was something about being alone that was better, of not seeing the terror in his wounded friend's eyes and feeling his limp, heavy weight in his hands. He took a deep breath and tried to feel steadier. The last few days had been such a folly, but he couldn't be sure he'd not do them again.

'Your parents will know you did the things you thought were right,' he whispered. 'They'll know you loved your brother.'

'Love!' She laughed. It was almost a jeer.

She dried her face and a weary silence settled between them. Michael watched her sighing, through the side of his eye. The girl was about the strangest thing that he'd seen since he'd left Rangoon. Much shorter and slighter than he was, he might have believed she was just a child, if it weren't for the fullness

of her dark-pink lips and the tension in the way she was sitting and staring. There was something feral — a readiness about
her — as if at any time she might turn and pounce. Her steep,
slender jawbone and cheeks worked together to nip her chin to
its harshest point, and her nostrils flared as if she was furious.
At the base of her neck, her hair was tied. Thick and coarse, it
lay along the length of her spine like a black fox's brush. Her
cheeks were smeared with *thanaka* but she'd scored it to lines
before it had set so it looked like war paint. The curve of her
eyes was shallow, flicked to feather-tips at each outside corner,
and a wispy fringe scuffed her lashes when she blinked. Their
most striking thing was their colour, however. Watery azure,
so pale in parts they seemed almost white, they were set against
her dark complexion and glowed as though lit from somewhere inside. When she spoke, she barely moved her lips, but
he'd thought he seen the flicker of a snakelike forked tongue.
From head to toe she was covered in ash, and the black-red
mottle of crisping blood. It was just like his own skin, and his
own shirt and trousers, and it made him feel leaden and dirty
and spent. She was kind though. She had given him water. A
wave of warmth and pity swept up.

'What's your name?' he asked her.

'Thuza Win,' she whispered. She turned to look at him,
resting her head on her knees. 'What's yours?'

'Michael Atwood.'

'Where are you from, Michael Atwood?'

'Rangoon,' he replied without thinking.

Her nose wrinkled. 'Your Burmese is rotten and your skin's
almost see-through. You're not from Rangoon.'

Michael felt himself blush. 'My parents live in Rangoon,' he said. 'I'm visiting. We're British.'

The thinnest crack of a smile broke momentarily on Thuza's lips, before flitting away. 'I'm British too,' she said, pointing at her eyes. 'Do you see? British blue! Why are you in the forest, Michael Atwood?'

Michael gave shuddering sigh. He dragged his hands down his face. 'It was a mistake,' he said quietly. He couldn't bring himself to say *I was tricked*.

There was another silence, easier this time, and then Thuza shook her head. 'You shouldn't have followed me.'

'I didn't know what else to do. I have to get home.'

'To Britain?'

'To Rangoon. I need a telephone.'

She smiled again, gently. 'There's barely a telephone in the whole of Mogok town, let alone in the forest.'

Michael's memory rippled. *Mogok*. Yes. That was the name of the town he had seen. He remembered the signs from the highway approach. An idea snared him.

'Do you live in the town?' he asked her.

She nodded. 'On the outskirts.'

'Alright,' he said. He gave her a smile, as warm and reassuring as he could. 'Why don't I come with you? You can take me to your home and I can tell your parents that you did everything you could possibly have done to save your brother. I'll tell them what happened and how brave you were, and that it wasn't your fault.'

She stared at him. 'Why would you do that?'

'Because it's the truth, isn't it? And I need your help.'

Thuza cocked her head to the side and stared at Michael for a second more, then a frown leaked across her face and she turned away. 'I don't live with my parents.'

'Then I'll go to their house instead.'

'They're not here.'

'Where are they?'

'Rangoon.'

'That's perfect,' said Michael. 'My father can arrange to get us both there, if you help me contact him.'

Thuza's face shot to Michael's suddenly. Her eyes were wide pools. 'Your father can get me to Rangoon? My papers don't say I can travel.'

'He could arrange new papers.'

She paused, eyeing him. He could see she was thinking, grappling with something, but then her face stiffened abruptly, and she squinted her eyes and her lips pinched tightly. 'I can't leave Mogok,' she said. 'My grandmother needs me.'

'We could take her with us.'

'She's sick.'

'Thuza, please,' said Michael. He shuffled closer and dipped his head to find her gaze. 'I know it's wrong to ask you and I'm sorry, but I don't have anything else I can do. I'm lost. I'm so lost, Thuza Win. My parents will be worried, like yours would have worried about your brother being in the forest, and like I'm sure they must still be worrying about you. Please help me. I need to go home.'

Thuza's eyes narrowed further and she drew a deep breath, staring at him. 'Who are you, Michael Atwood?' she whispered.

'What do you mean?'

'I mean, where are you from, British boy? Who's in your blood? Nobody with white skin is ever in Burma without a reason. My brother thought you were a spy. Are you?'

Michael drew his cheeks inward, wary for a moment, but what did it matter? He had no choice but to trust her, and he'd nothing to lose. He shifted on the leaves. 'My father is the British Ambassador.'

Thuza's eyes widened. 'He's powerful.'

Michael looked away, embarrassed. 'Yes, I suppose.'

She clambered to her knees, crawling towards him through the mud and leaning in. 'I'll help you, Michael Atwood,' she said, her skin glinting with sweat, eyes bright. He could see her whole body was quivering lightly. She licked her lips and her fork-tongue flicked, and he wrapped his hand around the root of the tree. 'I'll get you to a telephone and you can speak to your father, but your family needs to make me a more important promise. I want my parents released from Insein Jail.'

Michael pressed himself harder against the tree, holding his breath so his face didn't twitch. Insein was a hell-hole, squalid and infamous. Every soul in Burma lived in terror of its threat. It was where the Tatmadaw sent the murderers and rapists, and where the very worst bandits and thieves were locked away. But it was also a trap, their rotting place for dissidents. It was where men who'd done nothing but dream were hidden, until their fingers were prised from their hopes for the future, ideas abandoned down the drains in tears and vomit and washed away into Irrawaddy streams.

Thuza was glaring at him, impatience wild in her eyes and stance. 'Can you do that?'

Michael nodded, uncomfortable beneath the pin of her stare, afraid to wonder what her parents had done. 'I'll ask my father to make some enquiries. He's got contacts he could use. I know he's found out about other Insein prisoners.'

'That's not what I asked, Michael Atwood,' said Thuza. She stared at him, scowling, just a breath from his face. 'Can he get them out?'

Michael hesitated. 'Sure.'

'He's done it before?'

He paused again. 'Yes. A few times.' His eyes darted away. It was true, strictly speaking. The odd British drunk had been taken to Insein and his father had managed to talk them free. He doubted the ambassador would have much sway with Burmese prisoners though, however minor their crime or unjust the reason they were there, but Thuza was snared and he didn't dare lose her. This was his ticket. There were no other options. She wouldn't take anything less than his word. His hand crept out and his head slowly nodded.

'Alright, Thuza Win,' he said. 'We'll help you. My father will get them out. I swear.'

EIGHTEEN

Sitting on the step outside his home, Than wrapped his arms tighter around his body and buried his head in the folds of his scarf. The night wind felt bitter. The stars were brilliant white. The sun had fled the town for the evening, the power was out, and with the dark had come a chill that settled inside him, bedding down in the marrow of his bones, like a cat for the night. There wasn't a kerb on this part of the street, and worn by the wheels of the sluice-carts that rolled from the mines in their dozens each day, the orange dust track had bowed in the middle like a shallow ditch grave. He lit a cigarette. His hands were trembling. From inside, the sounds were the same as every other night. Marlar was making supper and the tin cookware clattered. His children were bickering. Their shrieks and piglet squeals chipped above the dull pummel of the jail-house generator that echoed from the distant end of the road. In the evening light as he glanced up, Taung-me was visible, deep black against the speckled sky. The mountain was taller than any other in the Mogok hills, and the moon floated low above it, as though snagged on a spur of its ragged peak.

He closed his eyes and tried to think through the ache in his head. In his pocket, he could feel the large shard of shattered porcelain digging into his leg. He had taken it from Aye Myint's house as a memento of his triumph, but now the glass-sharp edge was piercing his conscience. He'd angered the spirits. He'd been punished for his sins. For all of his life, Than had been superstitious. Stories ran in his family, bright as blood through their veins. As often as his parents had told him tales of Aung San's bravery, they'd tell him little fables about dragons and white elephants and princesses too. His father would laugh about the monk who had the cheek to clip his toenails after sundown, and a crocodile ate him as punishment. *Snap, snap!* His mother's sing-song tones would swirl as sweetly as incense as she told of the little girl who had clattered the pan lids and disturbed the spirits' slumber, so they sent a buffalo to trample her rice fields. *Stomp, stomp!*

Mogok was a town with its own superstitions. When Than had been sent here, he thought it was fate. Though all of Burma loved a good crop of fables, there was something about here that made their roots burrow further in. It might have been because the mineshafts were so perilous, or because the shadows that were cast by the mountains never entirely disappeared, or because the forest was so dark and hid so many secrets, but whatever it was, their presence was over-whelming. On every tree at every roadside, the townsfolk had strung little shoots of bamboo to ward away the evil spirits, and their bows were so laden with the sawn-off hollows that when they rocked, they clattered like peculiar chimes. Than had lost count of the number of times he had driven along a remote mountain lane and caught an illicit prospector burying his gems in the earth like potato seeds in the hope they would grow and then he'd be rich. Not a man in the town would have dared to cut a ruby before asking the astrologers. If they picked the wrong day with their hammer and chisel and the spirits were irked, the stones would be sure to split. He had watched pregnant women be chased away from quarries with sticks as bad luck, and whole shafts shut after a single bowl of rice was spilled, and barterers double their prices on allegedly hearing a lion's roar, yet despite their grim sentiments, Than had cherished these stories. At night, as a boy alone and exposed in a barracks of men, they had helped him keep calm. Through the daytime, he stashed away each new tale he heard and then whispered them back as he lay in his cot. In his mind, when he fell asleep to his mother and father's familiar voices, he didn't feel quite so lonely or scared.

It had been a long time since Than had thought of his parents' fables. When Daw Su had chosen his own spirits for him, he had felt such pride at having protectors, and had sworn to always serve them right. They had replaced his parents' stories, somehow. They were something more tangible to focus his strength on. The spirits and Aung San were enough to lead him through. There was one story from his earliest days in the town that had stuck in his memory with more grit than most, however. It told of a little Burman girl, Kyi Pyu. It was summer, and her parents were sick and their stomachs were aching, and the boils on their skin were as big as hen's eggs. All day, they begged Kyi to bring them some water, but the sun had not been so fierce for a hundred years. The streams and rivulets around Kyi's shack were nothing more than parched mud. In the middle of the night, when she couldn't stand the howls of her mother and father any longer, she crept from her home to find them a drink. There wasn't a moon and the night was darker than a dungeon cell, and Kyi was afraid. First she went to her neighbours and knocked on the door, but nobody stirred from the rooms inside, so she travelled to the Mogok River to see if there was a drop or two left for her to take. Finding nothing, she followed the riverbed all the way to the town. When she saw a teahouse with a light still shining, she wept with relief, but the owner was mean and ordered her to pay him, though her family were poor and she didn't have a kyat.

She pleaded, but the man sent her away. Kyi had already searched the rest of the town for someone to help her, and she knew there was nowhere else she could look. The thought of going home empty-handed was unbearable, so she decided to go to the temple instead, but just as she turned to head towards the stupas, an enormous lion leapt out in her way. The lion roared and bared his teeth, prowling towards her. Closer and closer he came and Kyi's heart pumped faster and faster. He stopped and eyed her, as if to savour his ripe, young treat, and she squeezed her eyelids shut and whispered her death prayer, but then — just as the lion was about to eat her — a cough burst out from the hollows of his lungs. The animal leapt back as though she had struck him, retching and spluttering in terrible pain. For all her fear, Kyi was horrified. She couldn't stand to see such a beautiful beast suffering and she ran to his side, patting his back and rubbing his head until the pain passed. Exhausted, the lion lay down, and with one last cough, vomited up little black purse on the kerb's dusty edge.

'What's this?' asked Kyi as she bent down to clean it.

'These are my rubies,' the lion growled back.

Kyi opened the purse and found fifty of the biggest, brightest gemstones she had ever seen in the whole of her life.

'They're beautiful!' she cried, astonished. 'You must be the richest lion in the whole of Burma.'

'I am,' replied the lion. 'And to thank you for being so kind to me, I'd like to give you half my gems.'

Kyi was so happy that she hugged the lion. She told him about her parents and how this meant she could now buy them water from the teahouse. They returned to the teahouse together, but the owner was so surprised to see Kyi again – and with so many rubies – that he didn't believe the lion had given them to her. He said they must have been counterfeit or stolen, so the lion decided to gobble him up in three big bites. He then filled his mouth with water and carried it back to Kyi's home. Kyi's parents were so delighted to see them and to have had such a long, happy drink that they felt much better. The next day, the lion went back to his den in the forest and Kyi went to the hospital to buy medicine for her parents, and then she bought a big house for them all on the banks of Mogok Lake where her parents could rest. In less than a week, their boils had disappeared and their stomachs stopped aching, and they were well enough to eat steak for dinner. They never went hungry or thirsty again.

The day Than heard of Kyi Pyu he felt different. He turned from the past to the future ahead. Whilst the rest of the town had squabbled about the fable's subtle meanings, Than knew in an instant it was written for him. The night before his parents died, he had shared the same fate as little Kyi Pyu. The spirits had brought him her tale to guide him. The lion was the Tatmadaw. The girl was his soldier. Be good to the Tatmadaw – be brave and be selfless – and in turn, the Tatmadaw will be good to you. The story had hardened his commitment to Burma, to serving his superiors and showing his thanks. He knew for the first time in years he belonged here. At last he had something solid and certain. He had direction. He had fresh, new hope.

He dipped his head and curled his body smaller on the step, ignoring the few passers-by as they stared at him and rubbing the balls of his hands into his eyes. What certainty was there now? What hope? Not any. Already, he missed Min too desperately to breathe. The memory of when they first met had trailed him all afternoon, of how Than had held the new baby in his arms, wrapped in a blanket that Marlar had sewn especially, and his squashed eyes had eased open and held Than's own, deeply and completely, and each knew the other right away, right then. It was the memory of how his love had grown day by day that stabbed him hardest, of how it still grew when he couldn't have thought it possible to love anything more, and how consuming it was. How it filled every instant, idea and action. And then came the thought of how consuming his grief was. It was a mirror to his love. A backwards reflection. Every moment he'd given of boundless devotion was returned to him now, unused and useless. Min's future was stolen, his promise wasted. Than pressed his hand to his chest and retched drily, his mouth hanging open in a silent, tearless scream. How was this bearable? How could it ever be? How was he living, without his Min? Their parting had been so swift, too insignificant. He hadn't said he loved him. He hadn't said goodbye.

He dug inside his pocket and pulled out the piece of broken figurine, pausing for a second to scowl at it, then closing his hand and squeezing and squeezing until he felt its edges slice his skin. The wasted promise. Oh, it made him dizzy. He had spent the last hour on his doorstep picking apart the pivots of Min's own life, the days and weeks and months before today's injustice, searching for clues that he should have seen, looking for something that would have told him what was coming and how he could have stopped it, though all the time he knew what it was. Breaking the statues. Forcing Min to do it. That was the moment where life had divided. Before and after. With Min, without. Even before he had seen Min's lifeless body, he had known the world was changed. A heavy new pressure had cast itself over him in Aye Myint's house, and it wouldn't leave and it wouldn't ease. No son should pass before his father. He shuddered with the wind and his newfound terror. It wasn't a panic, but a calm, strange trepidation, like standing in water that was rising and rising, but perfectly still, afraid to move or breathe and cause ripples, in case you disturbed what swam underneath. It was the spirits, he knew, but they couldn't quite see him. They didn't yet know he deserved their wrath too. If he stayed in this moment, quiet and frozen, and if he was lucky, the truth wouldn't see.

This was the trouble with all superstition – the uneven split between hope and fear. At the back of his mind, he knew they were troublesome. They tied him to the Tatmadaw, to his life's only option. They made him promises and stopped him from thinking. They worked their hardest to keep him in line. Inside his scarf, he could feel his own hot, damp breath on his chin, and the wind iced the tears on the curves of his cheeks. He looked again at the dazzling stars. Min's soul was still circling, dipping between them and swooping through the blackness before settling anew. The fear of where it would settle had him petrified. He might be a dog, a rat or a flea. This night, for the first time, Than knew he'd been lied to. The Tatmadaw were not his protectors. They were not his family, not his mother and father. What mother or father could cause pain like this?

'Dad?'

Behind Than's back, the door to his house cracked open and Po Chit stepped outside. Than scrabbled to wipe his face with his scarf, sniffing up the wetness that was dribbling from his nose and glad of the dark to hide his tears. His son slipped past him, throwing his cupped hands towards the gutter, and two fistfuls of yam skins slapped down in the dust.

'What are you doing outside, Dad?' Po Chit asked him. 'It's cold.'

'Nothing,' said Than, not looking at him. 'I'm thinking. That's all.'

'Can I sit with you?'

'Dinner will be ready soon.'

The boy nodded at the ground and moved towards the house, but then hesitated and looked back. His hands wrung together, like Min had done. 'Are you alright, Dad?' he whispered.

Than nodded. 'I'm fine.'

'Are you angry at us? Is that why you're outside? You've

been here for more than an hour. Thiha's watched you. Why don't you want to sit with us? He didn't mean it when he said the Tatmadaw were stupid. Neither of us did. We don't think you're a drunk or a thief, Dad. Honest. We want to be soldiers too, when we're bigger. We're going to make you proud, like you are of Min.'

Po Chit's words tumbled clumsily into the dark, bleak street and the lump at the back of Than's throat started to swell there, so dense and sticky that he thought he would choke. How could he accuse the Tatmadaw of abandonment when the biggest betrayal had come straight from him? No wonder this guilt was a rock on his ankles, and now as Po Chit watched him and waited so patiently, he felt himself sinking, plummeting down through a black, flooded mineshaft to a deep, unseen silt-base, to be swallowed by mud. He had forced Min to join the Tatmadaw though he knew the boy was doubtful, because he also knew Min would never say no. Min hadn't wanted to shatter the statues and anger the heavens. Than wouldn't have touched them – he'd never have dared to – but he made his son do it for his own greedy dribblings. He was stupid and cowardly, like everyone said.

But Than's betrayal was not just of his eldest. He could see that now, as clear as the day. For as far back through Min's life as he could remember, his son had been his sole motivation. The boy had been his only friend. How little he knew of the rest of his children. He hadn't a clue how Po Chit and Thiha worried, or what Khine liked for breakfast, or if they knew any fables, or the names of the ducklings that they kept in the yard. Poor May. He'd barely held her for weeks. All the things he had done and known for Min Soe Khaing, he'd ignored in the others, in bright-white blindness for his son's impending, auspicious greatness. And Marlar. Oh, he'd never wish her such heartbreak. A shockwave whipped through him, violent and sickening, and he clasped his hand across his mouth.

'Dad?' Po Chit looked down, small and sad-eyed.

Than blinked, trying not to cry. He shook his head, unable to speak.

'Po Chit! Where are you? Suppertime!'

Marlar's high voice called the boy inside and Than stood too, leaning on the frame of the door and stepping unsteadily into the light. His head felt giddy at the thought of what would follow, but he needed to confess and unhook this burden. If he waited any longer, he felt he would die. In his kitchen, the high shelf that circled the walls was dotted by candles and they quivered at the gasp of air as he entered. Thiha was sitting at the table with Khine, and Po Chit tidied himself beside them, hoisting May from her spot on the floor-boards to sit on his knee. Marlar was busy at the stove, her apron spattered with brown and yellow sauce as she ladled simmering curry into a row of bowls and passed them out. He glanced at the picture of Aung San and the figures of his own spirits, his gut ablaze. The room was still drenched with Min's presence. His blazer was hanging from the pin on the dresser. His teeth marks were imprinted on the pencil by the stove. He was struck suddenly by the knowledge that this weight would never leave him. For the rest of his life, he'd carry this guilt.

Marlar slid a bowl towards him. 'What's wrong with you?'

she asked. She sat too, lifting May from Po Chit's lap to her own and spooning up a lump of thick slop. She blew it until the steam settled, then dodged the spoon between May's babbling lips.

Than looked at the table, shivering. 'Min's not coming home.'

Marlar's mouth puckered and she went back to stuffing May's podgy face, and the baby grizzled and tried to shove away. Khine and Thiha were squabbling over a cold egg dumpling, Khine shrieking as her brother pulled it apart and gave half to Po Chit, ignoring her.

Than stared at his wife. 'Did you hear me, Marlar?'

Marlar nodded. 'I heard you,' she said. 'I already know. He's staying at the base tonight.'

'He's not.'

'Yes, he is. He told me. His training starts in the morning, not next week. They've changed it.'

'No, Marlar.'

Marlar grabbed May's hands as they flailed about her face. '*Yes*, Than Chit,' she said, shooting him a sour, exasperated glare. 'You're not the only one who speaks to that boy, you know.'

'Min's dead, Marlar.'

The table fell silent.

'What did you say?'

'Min's not coming home,' Than whispered. 'He's dead.'

Marlar let out a noise that was almost a laugh, but her eyes were wide and skittering. 'Nonsense,' she said. She shook her head.

'I'm sorry, Marlar,' said Than. 'It's true. The rebels shot him.'

'How would the rebels shoot him?'

'He was in the mountains.'

She shook her head again, more fiercely. There was panic in her voice. 'He wouldn't have gone to the mountains. He knows it's not safe.'

'It was an order.'

'It must be some other boy.'

'It's not.'

'They wouldn't have ordered him anywhere. He hadn't had training.'

'I know.'

'So you're wrong. Who told you?'

'Marlar, please,' said Than. He rubbed the sides of his aching head. 'It's Min. I saw him.'

I can see him now, he wanted to say. *Behind my eyes, I can see his face.* All afternoon he'd been trying to shift the image of his son's sparkling new uniform and ruined skull from his consciousness, but every time he was forced to blink, it flashed through his mind as crisply as a lightning bolt through the monsoon rains. At the table, his family were staring at him, and Marlar was frowning. Her head was still shaking – slowly and heavily – but her breathing sprinted. The children were pinned to their seats by fear. Their eyes darted between their parents. With a quaking hand, Than reached into his pocket and pulled out his cigarettes.

Marlar leapt from her seat. 'Murderer!' she screamed, slapping the packet from his grip.

She lunged at him again, striking his face, and he staggered up and tried his best to push her away, but he felt so weak. The children had scattered from the table and they threw themselves in his way as they tugged their mother's skirt and tried to drag her back. Khine was wailing, clawing at the flesh on Than's arm and Thiha and Po Chit grabbed him too, straining to haul him away from Marlar – or into their own brawl, Than couldn't be sure.

'Marlar! Stop!' He swung for her wrists.

'You killed my son!' she sobbed, struggling against him.

'It wasn't my fault. I didn't know they'd send him.'

'He was seventeen, Than Chit,' she cried. 'A child! He shouldn't have been in the Tatmadaw.'

'Do you think I wanted to see him dead?'

'You wanted glory. You don't care about anyone but yourself.' She screamed again, prizing herself away and pushing him, cursing, jabbing her hand to the door. 'Get out! GET OUT!'

Than backed away, breathless and tripping, and he looked at his children, their streaked wet faces and the panic in their eyes, and at Marlar and her hatred. *The spirits will make you pay*, she had told him. He knew he deserved it. He felt himself stagger and his vision was blurring, and all of his thoughts felt cold and unfamiliar, and they wouldn't line up and they didn't make sense. He didn't care if Burma dissolved now – if the rebels won and chose to shatter her. If he dissolved too, it would only be a mercy, for death would mean rebirth as a cockroach or a locust, or an eel in the river or a worm in the earth. The things he had done were all unforgivable. Every outcome he'd fought for had been a waste. He felt as though his whole life had been pointless. He seized up his cigarettes and stumbled to the exit. All he had wanted was to never feel lonely, and now, in his home with his family around him, he was the most alone he had been in his life.

NINETEEN

The south gate of the temple compound was not like the other gates; this was the reason why Thuza had chosen it. At the north, east and western entrances, the paths were freshly swept. Crowded fruit stalls and the warm, fiery glow of torchlight lined the approach to each painted gate, and as evening fell and the town arrived with their stockpots of rice and curry for the monks, she knew the piles of dusty sandals on the steps outside would be growing fast. Empty greetings, gossip and sly, sideways glances would burble along with the women and children and drown out the bells that topped the pagodas like the wash of a stream.

The south gate, however, backed on to the forest. There wasn't a path, just overgrown scrub. Her body half ducked, silently she weaved through the thickets and thorn trees that covered the land at the base of the mountains as they flattened towards the temple, and the white boy breathed heavily, keeping up at her side. At the back wall of the compound she stopped, crouching low, and glanced beyond the stupa spires. She couldn't hear voices, just the thin singing of chimes, the cry of the odd unsettled crow, and the faraway purr of the Sangha inside. The setting sun had cast the clouds gold, pink and greyish purple, and the deeper dusk gathered, the more she felt its weight pressing inwards, like the smoke above the burning camp.

'Hurry up, Michael Atwood,' she hissed as a whisper, looking back and kicking her sandals into the cover of a bush. She gripped the rickety gate, wrapping her hands over the vines that covered its bars and pulling herself up, before dropping down to the clean white tiles on the opposite side.

Michael stared at her through the gaps in the metal. His eyes were as wide as the rising moon. 'We're breaking in?'

Thuza stared at him, scowling hard. White boys were supposed to be clever, she thought, but this one was thicker than a month's worth of pig-muck, slowing them down when they had to be quick. She didn't want to be here any more than he did. With the soot of the gutted jungle camp still in her lungs and Kyaw's blood crisped on her skin, the stickiness of nerves in her stomach and the pain in her head, she wasn't sure how long her own thoughts would stay cleanly laced together. Bloodied and filthy, she knew what she looked like and the danger in bringing him here. She needed to get him inside and get him gone, and help her parents. Thuza had heard stories about the white men who lived in Rangoon, their links to the government and the power they held. She'd been told they had enough money to pay off officials and do as they pleased. An image of her parents sparked in the space behind her eyes. A white man as an ally, especially an ambassador, was more valuable than any money she'd managed to save. He'd have a far higher chance of success than she would. And she'd still have her money in her pocket as insurance. She could pick up her plan if it all went wrong. There wasn't time for hanging around. The longer she left it before finding Zawtika, the more she felt terrified. Already she knew what the old monk would say to her. Already she felt so completely ashamed.

The boy threw a last nervous glance at the forest before nodding and climbing over the gate. It rattled beneath his weight and Thuza winced and yanked him away from it, nudging him along in the shelter of the wall and stubbing at his heels.

'Where are we going?'

She shot him a glare that threatened for silence and skipped ahead, dipping down a passageway that dropped them into almost pitch dark. The warren of monastery buildings around them was unlit. Thuza dodged left, passing the slumbering library, the empty schoolhouse, the deserted teakwood dormitories, and a gong reverberated somewhere in the distance and a light melted slowly into view.

'Thuza Win?'

'I'm looking for someone.'

'A monk?'

'A friend.'

A friend, Thuza muttered again in her head. A ripple of fear spread through her body. She hoped Zawtika would still be her friend once she told him. She dropped lower and crept into the shadows beneath a building, weaving between the stilts towards the brightness and rumbling sounds at the opposite edge. Michael followed her. Before the light touched them, she stopped and peered out. In the courtyard ahead, the Sangha were assembling, the elder monks shifting calmly into lines in their dark maroon robes, the tiny bare feet of the novices slapping on the tiles as they scurried between them, their white cloaks fluttering through the torchlight like doves' wings, their alms bowls and tin pails clutched to their chests. One by one, the lines shuffled past the waiting Mogok residents, who filled each empty, upheld bowl. The monks filtered away towards the refectory, settling in rows on the floor, and the trill of crockery and jumbled voices rose in the air.

Zawtika was sitting at the back of the ranks, against a wall on the furthest side. He had already finished his supper and was stirring, nodding in conversation and dabbing his mouth with his handkerchief as he collected his belongings. He gave a last, slight bow to his companions and picked up a candle before slipping away through the refectory's back door.

Thuza grabbed Michael's wrist. 'He's leaving,' she said, sprinting beneath the building.

She pushed him into the alleyways, chasing around the edge of the courtyard, finding the little floating light of Zawtika's candle as it disappeared around a corner and following its thread through the slumbering dorms. Zawtika reached a doorway, gathering his robes to climb the steps, and the light vanished when the door swung shut. Thuza shoved Michael below the building on the opposite side of the path, and the light reappeared in a downstairs window as a pale yellow glow.

She turned to him. 'Wait here.'

'I want to come with you.'

'No.'

'I can explain myself.'

'I can explain you better.'

She shifted him further into the gloom, pointing. The boy glanced back, chewing his lip and looking scared. She didn't care. Her own stomach had knots that were tighter than lynch ropes, and there were things that Zawtika needed to hear before she could get to mentioning the round-eye. Her confessions would be sore enough for them both without him there. She pointed again and scowled, waiting until he stepped backwards and crouched down, and then she slipped away and crossed the path.

'Sayadaw,' she whispered, climbing the bottom steps and peering through the window. The old monk was alone, crossed-legged on his bed-mat. He was reading by candlelight and it caught the lines of his dark-brown skin and scored them deeper.

He looked up. 'Who's there?'

'It's me, Sayadaw. Thuza Win.'

'Thuza Win?' Zawtika scrambled up from his seat, squinting after her. He pushed the shutters wider open. 'Heavens, child!' he cried, seeing her. His face was horrified. He rushed from his room and threw open the front dormitory door, stealing an urgent glance each way and ushering her inside. He shut his own door, locking it, and slammed the shutters tightly closed.

'What happened, Thuza Win?'

'I'm sorry to come here, Sayadaw.'

'You're covered in blood! Are you hurt?'

She shook her head.

'Sit down! Sit down.'

The monk was scurrying to clear his tea chest of books and pencils and he motioned at it, flustered, his cheeks flushing red.

Thuza slumped to the seat, trembling. The tears were forming at the back of her eyes. She caught her reflection in

Zawtika's propped-up mirror and tried to wipe the dirt from her cheekbones but her cuff was as grim as her own frowning face.

Zawtika knelt at her feet. 'Thuza Win,' he said, pleading, 'you have to speak to me. Who did this?'

'I was in the forest.'

'Oh, Thuza.'

'I know, Sayadaw.'

'I've told you, haven't I? Those birds aren't worth the risk to your life. Did the rebels do this?'

She shook her head. 'The rebels were there, but Tatmadaw ambushed them. I couldn't escape.'

'You were caught in the attack? We saw the fires, Thuza. They were wild. How far into the forest did you roam?'

'I went up to Taung-me.'

'By the spirits, child. Why would you wander so far from the town? You know it isn't safe.'

'I was at the camp.'

'*Thuza!*' Zawtika drew a sharp, shocked breath, stepping back. Thuza stared at her hands in her lap. She couldn't bear to look at him.

'I went to see Kyaw,' she whispered. 'I've been helping him. I've been smuggling rubies . . . in the sparrowhawks. I've been taking them to the dealers at Blue Stone Pass and selling them, and giving the money to the rebels.'

Zawtika stepped back again and stood up, shaking his head. His face was a pane of shattering glass. 'You lied to me, Thuza.'

She flicked him a nod and tried to swallow away her guilt, but her throat was too dry. With all that he'd helped her, the hurt was suffocating. She wanted to throw herself across the room, to drop at his feet and scream that she hadn't meant to do it, but her limbs felt so heavy and her heart was aching, and she knew if she parted her lips, she would cry.

'I've looked after you, Thuza,' Zawtika whispered, staring at the ground. 'I've tried so hard to keep you safe. Why would you come here so often and ask my opinion, then hide from me?'

'I wasn't hiding. I listened to you, Sayadaw. I always listen.'

'Then you'd know the risks I've taken for you.'

She nodded.

'You should have told me what you were doing. There were so many times, Thuza – so many times. You could have said where the money had come from. I deserved to know the truth.'

'I was ashamed.'

'You were cowardly.'

'I didn't know what else to do. You wouldn't have helped me.' Thuza sniffed and wiped her nose, standing up and stepping after him. 'I'm sorry, Sayadaw,' she said, holding out her hands. 'Please forgive me.'

The monk's head shook again and he took another retreating step. 'How can I?' he said. 'You've used me, Thuza Win. What years of our friendship have ever been real?'

'No!' cried Thuza. 'I wasn't using you. I never would. You're my friend. I need you.'

'Oh, child,' said Zawtika, sighing. He cracked a pained smile and dragged his hands over his face, looking at her. 'How can I help you now, knowing this? There's been peril enough at my shoulder for rooting around Insein, but if the Tatmadaw were to discover I'd been doing it on behalf of rebel sympathisers . . . of their financiers? Think what they'd do to me, Thuza Win. Think what they'd do to the temple. Oh, Little *Naga-ma*. How could you?'

A sob escaped from the bottom of her lungs and she collapsed to the tea chest, burying her face in her filthy black hands.

The monk's voice dropped suddenly. His anger had changed to shock and fear. 'Where's Kyaw?'

'He's dead,' said Thuza, looking up, her tears streaking. 'They killed him, Sayadaw. I saw them. They shot him.'

Zawtika gasped, his hand clutched to his chest. From where he was standing in the centre of the room, he closed his eyes and tipped his face to the ceiling, blowing a thin-drawn, wavering breath. 'Oh, Thuza,' he muttered.

Thuza wiped her eyes and tucked her shaking hands inside her sleeves. The day hissed in her mind like rotten meat.

'Please help me, Sayadaw,' she whispered. 'I know I've betrayed you. I'm not worthy of a moment more of your kindness, but I don't have anyone else in the world to ask, and I'll never want anything from you ever again.'

The monk paused, then staggered over and slumped at her side. Through the corner of her eye, Thuza saw him shaking too. 'What do you need?'

'There was a white boy at the camp,' she said, slowly. 'He was from Rangoon. He says he can help my parents.'

Zawtika's expression crumpled. 'A white boy in Mogok? Who is he?'

'His father is the British Ambassador. He needs to get home. If I help him, he'll ask about my parents. He says he can get them released.'

'From Insein?'

'Yes. It's happened before.'

'So why have you come to me?'

'The rebels have threatened him. He's scared. He needs a telephone. Somewhere safe to stay until he can talk to his father.'

'Where is he now?'

'Outside.'

'Thuza Win!' Zawtika shook his head, squeezing his eyes shut again and frowning hard, his fingers pressed to the ridge of his brow. 'The danger you cause, Little *Naga-ma*. If the Tatmadaw hears of a white boy at the monastery, we'll be punished. They'll turn us out.'

'Where else can I go?'

'You could have gone anywhere.'

'We'll leave if you help us.'

'Don't threaten me, child.'

'That's not what I meant. I just need a telephone, Sayadaw. You can arrange that, can't you?'

The monk's eyes thinned and he sighed again, looking at Thuza. She thought she could see the faint gloss of tears. 'The boy promised to help you in exchange for a telephone?' he said wearily.

Thuza nodded. 'Yes. We made a deal. This is my chance, Sayadaw. I can put things back – like they were before. No more bribes to Insein guards. No more smuggling. No more whispers and notes. Please! My parents can come home. They'll be safe again. I won't be alone. I can't let this pass.'

Zawtika bowed his head for a long, aching minute. Thuza watched his thoughts ticking through, and then the old monk patted his thighs as if to brace himself, and heaved his body stiffly up. He moved to the window and unbolted the shutters, cracking one apart and looking from the room. Thuza stepped beside him, peering into the shadows beneath the building ahead.

'Do you trust him?' Zawtika whispered as the breeze swept around them.

Thuza paused and gazed at the darkness. Two white eyes were glistening. 'What choice do I have?'

TWENTY

Michael sat on the floor in Thuza's front room and stretched his palms to the small, restless flame. He didn't know what time it was but night had settled heavily over the mountains, cloaking the house in deep, silent black. There were just a few pieces of wood on the fire – not nearly enough to chase away the cold and gloom – and their sizzling splintered the brittle air like knuckles being cracked. Thuza padded through the space behind him, busying herself with he knew not what, and he watched her shadow through the corner of his vision as it slipped from the table to the bureau and back. The room was vast but almost empty, and the smell was of damp and neglect and decay. He flicked his glance through her meagre possessions. There was a chair by the window, a birdcage, a rug. With a twist of his finger, he tugged a yarn from its unravelling fringe and a shudder fizzed hard up the bones of his spine.

'Jesus,' he said without thinking. 'It's freezing.'

Thuza had stopped at the back wall and was peering in a mirror, rubbing the grime from her forehead and cheeks. 'The windows are broken.'

Michael looked up. In the dark, he hadn't noticed, but now he could see the jagged edge of shattered glass as it snagged the moonlight at the rim of each pane. He sucked in his cheeks.

Outside, the leaves were shivering. 'You need to get them fixed.'

Thuza shook her head, shoving shut a bureau drawer with a thick wooden thud. 'There's no point.'

'But winter's coming.'

She threw him a blanket. 'You'll be long gone by then.'

Michael gathered the coarse woollen throw towards him, tucking his feet beneath its bristles with a guilty flush. He had meant for Thuza; it was too cold for her to live through the winter in an unsealed house. At night in the mountains, the temperature plunged like it didn't in Rangoon, and after the humidity of the sun-speared forest and scold of the fires, it already felt as bitter as a frosty English day. The chill would only worsen as the months rolled past.

Thuza tiptoed beside him and placed down her washbowl, nodding to it, and he smeared his face with the murky water and dried his eyes on the hem of the blanket. She crouched, her knees creaking as she leaned towards the fire and lifted the pan that was lynched at its peak. She scored the metal's inside edge with a spoon and folded the contents, before holding it out.

Michael paused, watching the smoke tease from its brim. 'Where's yours?' he asked.

Thuza shook her head. 'I don't need any.'

'We can share it.'

'There's not enough.'

'Won't you be hungry?'

'Not as hungry as you. I can hear your belly moaning. Besides, you don't know when you'll get to eat again.'

Thuza thrust the pan at Michael, pressing it into the knot of his wrist so he had to grab the handle to stop it from burning, and then she sat back and peeled a long, sharp splinter of wood from the uneven floor. She drew her legs to her chest, wrapped her arms around them like she had in the forest and rested her cheek on her shoulder, digging the wood between her teeth. It was true, he thought as he dipped his eyes downwards. He didn't know. He didn't know when he had last eaten either, and his hands were trembling and his muscles felt weak. The monk had promised to send them a message as soon as he had sorted things and found a telephone that was safe to use, but that could mean days of waiting and the temple couldn't keep him, and Thuza had been the only choice for a host that they had. As she sat calmly watching him and gnawing her splinter, he felt like a burden for the first time today. The strands of hair around her face were damp from where she had splashed them, and they clung to her skin and enclosed her expression like a lacquer-wood frame. Her stare was fixed, but not unfriendly. The blanket. The washbowl. Her last bowl of supper. There was more kindness than he had any reason to expect.

He scratched his nose and scooped the spoon inside the pan, throwing her a thin, awkward smile. 'Thank you.'

She shrugged. 'It's just potatoes.'

'I meant for letting me stay here. I know you're not allowed to have foreigners in your home. I don't want to get you in trouble.'

Thuza shrugged again but her blue eyes never flinched. 'The temple has more to risk than I do.'

Michael shoved the spoon between his lips and forced the hot, powdery starch down his throat without chewing. He knew it was odd, but tonight at the temple when he met the monk – and somehow more so than at any other time through the sprint of the last few days – he had felt the risk that Thuza spoke of more acutely than he ever had in Burma before. There was something about seeing such intense shock on the face of a grown man when he learnt of Michael's presence, of not being able to follow the meanings of his quick, hushed mutterings but chasing the inflections of fear as they darted through the words that terrified him too.

'He doesn't support the rebels like you do?'

She shook her head again, fiercely, and brandished her shard of floorboard towards him. 'We'd never support the rebels. Zawtika is like me. We don't take sides. If the Tatmadaw comes to us, we fear them. If the rebels come, we fear them too. We do not love or hate either. We are only afraid. Burma is selfish, Michael Atwood. You must never trust anyone. They only fight to survive for themselves.'

Michael winced and glanced away, embarrassed. *Trust.* The word struck. He had trusted Teacher blindly, without an instant's caution. Thuza had trusted him too now, with her parents. Teacher was an error, borne of emotion, but Thuza was different. He had made a decision and put himself ahead of her. The thought was a whip-crack across his chest. 'Can you trust the monk?' he asked to distract himself.

Thuza nodded. 'Zawtika's different.'

'The monks are good people.' Michael nodded too, but Thuza scowled.

'Not all of them,' she replied. 'Some are as crooked as the Tatmadaw. Even fewer would do the things that Zawtika has done for me. When my parents were taken and Kyaw gave himself to the mountains, Zawtika looked after me. He was the only person in Mogok who cared.'

Michael's gaze gave the room another skittish once-over. There wasn't a sign of her family anywhere; no photographs nor teacups, no jackets nor shoes. There was only one chair at the table by the window. 'How long have they been gone?'

'Nine years.'

Michael rammed another spoonful of potato into his mouth to hide his shock. Thuza had said she was twenty-one years old, hadn't she? The same age as he was. She had been alone nearly half of her life. 'It's a big house, just for you,' he whispered. He didn't know what else to say.

Thuza shook her head again and smiled, almost. 'I could never leave.'

'You wouldn't feel safer, closer to the town?'

'The town doesn't like me. That's why I don't fix the windows. The Burman boys would only break them. The soldiers too. They think I'm bad luck.'

Michael glanced at the forest, shuddering at its cavernous blackness, and the shout of an owl slipped out through the trees. Thuza looked at him, seeming to sense his incomprehension, and she drew her lips away from her teeth and the two tips of her tongue slid through their middle then disappeared again, as quickly as a snake. She shivered too and closed her eyes.

'This is Burma,' she whispered. 'Superstition is king. The Tatmadaw don't like my blood.'

'Are your parents rebels,' Michael asked. 'Like your brother?'

Her forehead crumpled. 'They're nothing like Kyaw.'

From inside the house, there was a sudden crash and Michael jumped and turned towards it, his vision straining across the shadowy back wall, searching it. Somewhere beyond his sight, there was scratching, the slow, determined drag of fingernails on wood. His heart quickened. 'What was that?'

Thuza's body had snapped rigid. 'Nothing,' she said, shaking her head.

The sound came again, and then her name. A groan. She scrambled up and scampered away from him, grabbing a key from where it was hung on a ribbon at the corner of her mirror and digging it into a bolted back door.

'There's someone in there,' said Michael, shocked.

'*Thuza Win!*' the voice wailed, and Thuza slipped through the slimmest opening she could manage. Michael bounded after her, but she rammed the door shut against his hands.

'Go away,' she cried.

She pushed harder but he was stronger than she was, and the door flung open. A mouthful of sickness swamped up from his gut. The air stank worse than burst drains. Thuza stumbled backwards towards a dresser, her eyes pinned to his in distress. There was a body at her feet, filthy and fleshless, grey skin and sharp bones. From the way the old woman was sprawled by the side of the mattress, she might have been dead, but her naked ribs were heaving, fast and laboured, each curve of raised bone spooning the next. He had seen skeletons like her on the streets of Rangoon occasionally, addicts in the alleyways by the backdoors of teahouses and restaurants when the sun dropped, picking through bins or sniffed at by mongrels as they passed out and spilled from their cardboard boxes, though the Tatmadaw cleared them away if they knew.

A rash of panic bubbled on Thuza's skin. 'She's my grandmother,' she said, frozen.

Horrified, Michael shook his head in disbelief. 'Why was the door locked?'

'You don't understand.'

The old women whipped out a hand and snatched Thuza's ankle. 'My pipe, Thuza Win,' she said. 'Get my pipe.'

Michael looked at the tray on the dresser. Thuza hadn't moved. Her grandmother's fingers flexed and tightened, pulling her in, and Thuza tore her eyes from Michael's and grabbed the tray up with all its contents, dropping to her knees at her grandmother's side.

'Get out,' she said to Michael, striking at a match.

'You said she was sick.'

'What's it to you?'

'She needs help.'

'She has me.'

'You're keeping her prisoner.'

'I'm protecting her. I'm protecting us both. She'll go to the town. She'll cause trouble. They'll come for us.' Thuza paused and looked up. Her head was tipped back and the steep angle of her jaw and cheekbones drew lines with the light. 'Get out of the room, Michael Atwood.'

He didn't move.

'It's not her fault,' said Thuza, fumbling with the match. 'Don't judge her.'

'I'm not.'

'You are. You're judging us both. I know that look in your eye. My brother had it. Life isn't as simple as you want to make it seem.'

She struck the match again, but her hands were trembling and the old woman was clawing at her arm, and the spark wouldn't take. Michael smeared his own hands on his trousers and glanced back to the safety of the fireplace before dragging himself from the doorway and crouching at her side. There was something about the fear on Thuza's face that outweighed his repulsion and he took the box and ignited the match with a single brisk flick. Thuza lit the lamp and her grandmother grabbed the pipe and wheezed in the perfumed smoke, and Michael watched the rage dissolve from her eyes as her head eased back on the wooden floor.

'Why didn't you tell me she was here?' he said, slumping back.

Thuza slumped too, rubbing her face. Her whole body was shaking. 'She'll need more soon.'

'Don't you have it?'

Thuza shook her head. She stared at the flame on the little spirit lamp and turned the pipe in her hand, then shook herself free of whatever dark thought had snared her and picked up her grandmother's hand. She held it on her thigh, stroking the brittle, baggy skin beneath her dark thumb.

'My grandmother worked in the poppy fields,' she said, quietly, 'before the land was given over to the mines. For years, she did it . . . for as long as my life. The Tatmadaw paid her in drugs, not kyat. They paid everyone that way. A dependent workforce is a loyal one. She doesn't deserve this. I know she doesn't, but what else can I do?'

She shrugged and looked at Michael.

'Do you know, Michael Atwood, she said with a sigh, this house is British, like you are? It was a gift to my great-grandmother – to Nanna's mother. I never knew her, but when I was a little girl, I used to dream about meeting a British man one day. I imagined I'd invite him here for *laphet* and tea to say thank you, and to show him how well we'd cared for something so special, how much we prized this beautiful gift.' She looked around the room and laughed sadly. 'Can you believe it? What you must think of me – of my family.'

'I don't think anything.'

'Don't lie. Addicts. Convicts. Insurgents. I know how we appear.' She sniffed and struck a tear from her cheek with the back of her hand. 'I tried so hard not to be angry at Kyaw, or at my parents – to not think that my family had abandoned me – but every day I feel so alone. It's stupid and selfish, but I can't help it sometimes. It's not their fault any more than it's Nanna's. My parents aren't criminals, Michael Atwood. They're teachers. They didn't trouble the government or hurt anyone or do anything half as bad as the rebels or all the other Mogok bandits. They just wanted me and Kyaw to know about our heritage, to let us sing Shan songs with the children from the town, and be proud of all the tiny different parts of our history that had made us who we are. They smuggled a few rubies to put food in our bellies, but who here hasn't? They love Burma, and they love Shan State, and they don't see why they can't do both.'

Michael shook his head. 'How can they be sent to Insein for nine years for that?'

'They have bad blood, Michael Atwood. I wasn't lying in the forest. My blue eyes are British. My great-grandmother loved a white man. He was the manager at a gem pit on the east side of the lakes when the rest of the foreigners came here, and Nanna was his child. Her eyes were blue too, before their grey-ness. And my mother's . . . they were beautiful. Like sapphires set in ice. My great-grandmother's choices — her frailties — they'll never leave us. They drip and drip like water down walls. The drops of my blood that are British are threatening. They've sailed across oceans. They've known what it means to be rich and free. The Tatmadaw don't like it. That's why they tell everyone to keep away. They spread rumours, and they've had their suspicions about Kyaw for years. They tell the town we're traitors. Sometimes I believe them. We were given this house to try to protect us, but it's been as much our curse as our guardian. We must be bad luck.'

On the floor, the old woman twitched and Thuza linked her fingers through her grandmother's more tightly, squeezing them and closing her eyes.

'It was my fault they were taken,' she whispered. She was rocking. 'My great-grandmother was given a dagger too, for her safety. It was beautiful teakwood, encrusted with rubies along the handle. Her name was carved on it, and when I was little I would rub the ridges with my fingers and imagine what she looked like and the life she'd lived with the man she'd loved. I was eleven when the Tatmadaw came here. They'd been looking for reasons to punish us, Zawtika said; to rid the town of our poisonous blood. I was the one who showed them the way. The rebels had snatched Kyaw. My father worked in the mines and they threatened to kill Kyaw unless he helped them. He drew them a map, and I was supposed to take it to them, but I was weak and scared and I tore it in the forest. I lost our dagger too. My father had given it to me for protection, but when I panicked I left it, and the Tatmadaw found it, and it let them trace the map to our home.

'I cried when they came. I screamed and yelled and fought them, though my mother told me not to. She was pregnant. I was going to have a sister. Perhaps if I'd listened, the baby might not have died. My father tried to comfort me. He tried to pick me up and carry me with him as he pleaded and reasoned, but the soldiers beat him. They dragged him from our house and I swore and shoved them, and I bit one, and he took my great-grandmother's dagger and slashed my tongue. A vicious little serpent, he called me. Now everyone for ever and ever would know.'

'Jesus,' Michael muttered. Her eyes were glazed and there was a detachment between what she was saying and the way she was saying it that scared him, almost as though the only way she could speak was to make it all just a matter of fact. 'What did you do?'

She shrugged. 'I did nothing. How could I? I was a child. Nanna had been in the valley-fields when it happened and I had no idea whether Kyaw was alive. Zawtika found me the next day. He bathed me, calmed me. He made me bowls of soup and lit candles at our altar. Sat with me each evening until I slept. For the last nine years, he's been my only friend.' She moved across the room, tidying the tray.

'The officer that took my parents stole our dagger too. He hung it above the highway checkpoint without washing my blood from the blade. Nanna had to walk past it every Sunday when she left for the valleys and every Saturday evening when she made her way back. It tortured her, poor spirit, seeing the last memory of her mother defaced. It tortured us all.

'Everyone in Mogok still calls me a serpent. They might not remember where it started, but it's stuck. Zawtika tells me it's a good thing. Who'd fight with a *naga*? I want to believe him, Michael Atwood, but I'm weary. I don't want to be the outcast, though I know I deserve it. That's why I have to help you — you're the pass to my future. I need to say I'm sorry. I need my parents before anything else.'

Thuza looked at Michael with her dry red eyes, and the shame in his stomach was hot, bitter bile. He knew how it felt to be guilty of errors. He had caused his parents such worry and trouble. Worst of all, he felt raw for lying to Thuza. He knew a little too about being the outsider. He had always felt apart from the boys he grew up with in those frosty English classrooms, having seen so many glimpses into his father's shifting world. As a teenager in England and a teenager in Asia, he had found himself stranded between East and West. He had wanted so badly to fit in with Burma's romance, to stem the frustration that he felt in boring England, and though he'd never said it aloud or even consciously known it, that's why he had forced his friendship on Sein. But he'd never belonged here. He looked down at his hands and folded them over, steadying them, staring. 'You'd be fine without me,' he whispered, guiltily. 'Your parents will be out soon.'

Thuza shook her head. 'You don't know that.' She clutched her grandmother's fingers. There was fear to her voice. 'No one knows.'

Michael swallowed and stared harder at his hands. 'I came to the forests because I felt guilty too, Thuza Win,' he said quietly. He told her about the bomb and Sein and leaving the city, and how foolish he felt at travelling north. He sniffed a brief, hostile laugh through his nose. 'I'd only wanted to help.'

He looked at her, expecting to see her laugh at his childishness, but instead she listened patiently and shook her head. 'There's no helping anyone but yourself in Shan State,' she whispered. 'Mogok is a beast, Michael Atwood, and she's sick. Just when you think you've found a way to soothe her, she writhes and wriggles and breaks herself free. I tried to be clever, working the rebels and the government at the same time, but somehow the spirits always seem to see it coming. My brother. The generals. That shifty weasel Thai.'

The Thai. Michael's mind flashed back to the truck. Teacher had mentioned a Thai man too as they'd travelled and he'd sipped on the whisky in his hand. Teacher. Jesus. Even though later he spoke nothing but bullshit, Michael felt he'd been honest then about his thoughts. Inspiring, even. Michael hadn't given him a thought since the camp was attacked. It didn't matter that the old soldier tricked him; if Teacher was dead, that was Michael's fault too.

'The Thai,' he muttered, rubbing his face.

Thuza looked up, surprised. She chucked him a nod, her brow furrowed. 'Chaiwat Thongsuk,' she said. 'Do you know him?'

Michael shook his head. 'I heard him mentioned once.'

Thuza's face stiffened and she spat at the floor. 'He was at the camp yesterday. If he wasn't killed, I hope the Tatmadaw have picked him up. He worked for both sides too. They'll be furious when they know it.' She spat at the floor again, harder. 'Good riddance to him. Good riddance to them all.'

She slammed the top drawer of the dresser shut, but then her head spun suddenly to the front room, and the light that slipped from the dwindling fire. She cleared the stray streaks of tears from her cheeks, quickly, creeping to the door.

'Did you hear that?'

She glanced at Michael and waved him with her, grabbing the key from where it had fallen on the floor and bolting the door behind them, before rushing to the window and peering briefly out.

'It's Zawtika's messenger,' she said, rushing into the hallway.

Michael peered outside too and saw the shadow of fluttering robes in the darkness as a young monk rushed from the forest and along Thuza's path, the gravel crunching beneath his sandaled feet. Thuza opened the door and the boy met them. The look on his face was urgent and scared.

'Sayadaw U Zawtika has made arrangements for the white boy,' he said to Thuza. 'We need to go.'

'Already?'

'Yes.' He stole a look behind him, into the trees.

322

Thuza stepped aside and nodded at Michael. He hadn't moved.

'What are you waiting for?'

He stared at her. His heart was spitting. The wrench he felt at leaving her so soon had shocked him, and he felt in her debt. He couldn't just leave. 'I'll help you, Thuza Win,' he said. He stepped towards her, aware of the feeling that he wanted approval, the hint of a plea at the base of his tone.

Her eyes flickered, surprised.

He shifted closer, dipping to find her stare. 'Please, Thuza Win, believe me. I may not be able to do anything for Sein, but it's not too late for me to do something for you.' He threw her a smile, as sincere as he could muster, but he knew it looked strained. He didn't know why he wanted to tell her, but he felt that he had to; that he owed her a truth.

Thuza held his stare for a moment, weighing him, and he thought he saw just the smallest smile. She nudged him to the door and he took a nervous breath and dug his hands in his pockets, searching for something he could use. He had lost his wallet, but there was a screwed-up tissue at the bottom of one. He pulled it out, tearing it as he flattened it. He thrust the scrap at Thuza. 'Write down the names of your parents.'

She hesitated.

'Go on.'

She wrinkled her nose and he thought for a moment that she knew he'd been lying, and he grabbed her hand and pressed the tissue inside it, embarrassed.

'You're really going to help them?'

'I'll try my best, Thuza Win,' he said, and he meant it

this time. With all he had seen and all she had told him, how could he stand to possibly not? He would ask his father to find Thuza's parents. He would write a letter to the British government, if he had to. To the very, very top. He would ask one of the staff at the residence to write a letter in Burmese too, and he'd send it to the Tatmadaw and every newspaper in Asia. He would do all he could because that was what's right. He watched as she took the tissue to the bureau and scribbled across it, and then she padded back and passed it over, without speaking. She nodded, and he thought for a moment that he wanted to hug her, but then he caught himself.

'Goodbye, Thuza Win,' he said, stepping outside. 'Thank you.'

The monk scurried away and Thuza closed the door. Michael drew his hands into the warmth of his sleeves and wrapped his arms around his chest as the chill of the night closed in. The monk had already vanished beneath the black forest canopy, and Michael ran after him, his heart a thick thunder, and as the last of his steps before the forest ate him too, he glanced behind and saw Thuza's face through a shattered front window, the moon on her cheeks and eyes like melted silver, and on a wash of the wind he heard the hiss of her grandmother's curse.

TWENTY-ONE

'Good Morning, Officer Than Chit.'

From behind his vast desk, Bo Win looked up. He straightened his aviators on his nose and tided the papers he had been writing on, pushing them aside.

Than fumbled to close the door behind himself, clunking the heavy wood clumsily shut and walking the few paces across the private Mission Room with nervous steps. He hadn't shaved. He had slept at the jailhouse. He felt hungover, though he never drank a drop. The general's stare skimmed him, slipping from the tufts of his uncombed hair to the scuffed-up caps of his unpolished boots, and he dipped his eyes to the worn shag-pile carpet beneath his feet, at the geometric maze of mustard, beige and caramel, wishing himself to be lost inside. Beyond the open window, the sky was hazy grey and the wind was light. In the trees, the crows were quarrelling. In his head, the pressure was fit to burst. His eyes were dry and tired and itchy. His limbs felt as though they were packed full with mud.

He gathered himself and stood to attention, clearing his throat and offering up a wobbly salute. 'You requested to see me, General?'

The general nodded. Than knew what it was. He had waited so long for this moment to find him, but now it was here, he was so disappointed. It tasted so acidic that it made his lips curl inwards. It was not at all how he thought it would be. He wanted to be quick, just to pick up the stars that would pin to his epaulettes, and then he could leave and return to his sadness. He could go to the jailhouse – or home if Marlar let him – and hide in the bedroom and bury his head there, and mourn his beautiful Min in peace.

The general linked his fingers together and placed his hands in the centre of the desk. He smiled at Than, his thin mouth stretching momentarily before settling flat.

'I wanted to congratulate you for your work this week,' he said, looking up. 'Your contribution to the Union of Burma has been exemplary, Officer. Your loyalty has been noted and commended throughout the district's most senior ranks.'

Than stared ahead. His vision fogged.

'I've informed Rangoon of your commitment too. They send their sincere gratitude.'

'I appreciate that, General.'

'They have asked me to inform you that subsequent interrogations of Aye Myint and his wife have resulted in their permanent internment as Traitorous Conspirators. Your actions and their imprisonment have directly improved the safety and honour of your Burman brothers and your Burman homeland. The Union is grateful.' The general paused and Than felt his eyes on him, as hot as white coals. He pulled his glasses from his nose and rested them on his paperwork, staring. 'I heard you lost your boy yesterday, Officer?'

Than felt a prickle at the back of his neck. His eyes faltered down. 'Yes, sir.'

'I'm sorry. I'm sure the boy had every bit of promise you attributed to him.'

Than said nothing.

'How is your wife?'

'She is as you would expect any mother to be, General.'

The general nodded again. He lifted his pen and scratched at his nose. Last night Than had felt Marlar's howls much worse than he'd heard them, and the noise seeped inside his dreams. He glanced at Bo Win, at his crisply starched uniform, and thought of the general's sons at home in their beds. If a spirit had asked for Than's feelings this morning, he'd have said they'd all left him; that his tears had been spent. Now, in his belly, a new weevil was wriggling. The vision of the general's boys snuggled up in white bed-sheets had goaded his anger. His words were respectful, but worthless somehow. There was something about them that felt insincere. It wasn't just Than's fault that Min was departed. The general had guilt as deep as his own. He would never have sent his own sons to the front line. Than knew in his gut that the man didn't care.

He clenched his teeth to hide his resentment and pinned a note to the front of his mind. As he worked the days and nights of his new job, he'd remember this moment; he would make sure it paid. He wouldn't be cruel and he wouldn't be unscrupulous. He'd give something to the temples from the extra in his wages. If he did things right, he could mend his karma. He could fix Min's too and beg his soul some mercy. Marlar's hate was too far beyond saving, but his other children would see he was decent, and he'd keep them safe and make them proud.

He rebalanced his weight on his aching feet, waiting as the

silence in the room thickened. The general waved his hand at the chair across the desk.

'Sit down, Officer.'

Than scraped the chair out and half sat, half slumped.

The general leaned aside and pulled open a drawer. 'Your son fought for a great cause,' he said, rummaging around where Than couldn't see. 'His contribution was not in vain. The capture of the Fifteenth's outpost was a significant achievement and our prisoner interrogations have provided us with excellent new information. We've learnt a great deal about the SSA's activities, including the names of previously unknown financiers. As I said, you've done very well.'

The general sat up, pulling a map with him. He unfolded it across the desk. Than glared at the dog-eared, browning paper, and then to the general. The general paused, eyeing his confusion, and then he hooked his glasses back onto his nose.

'We understand the key rebel sympathisers live at the following locations,' he said, standing up and circling three miniature hamlets with a bright-red pen. He leant on the desk and pointed at Than. 'Take your men and make arrests. We need it done as quickly and quietly as possible. Today, please.'

Than felt his heart quicken and he stared at the map, shaking his head. 'Today, sir?' He didn't know what else to say. 'I can't. My boy isn't buried.'

'Your wife can manage the arrangements. I've sent someone to assist her.'

'Sir, please.'

The general shook his head. 'I'm sorry, Officer. I recognise your situation, but this is a busy time and your commitment to

328

Burma must come before everything else. It is crucial that we capitalise on the evidence discovered as a result of the attack, and we must mobilise swiftly to maximise its benefits. I trust you understand this?'

'Yes, sir. Of course I do, but isn't there someone else who can be entrusted with my duties . . . just for a few days?'

'You wouldn't want your son's death squandered, would you?'

'No, sir.'

'So it's your duty as a soldier and a father to honour him in the best way you can – loyalty to the Tatmadaw's cause.'

Than sat forward and gripped the edge of the table to stop his hands from trembling. The panic inside him was starting to rise. How could the general expect him to do this? He opened his mouth to throw out a protest, but all he could manage was a dry cough of shock.

Across the desk, the general was staring. 'I hear you were expecting promotion for your actions, Officer Than Chit?' he said quietly.

Than's heart skipped. He'd forgotten the lies he had told in the forest. His cheeks felt suddenly, searingly hot. 'No, sir.'

The general's face twisted to a frown. 'You made no such claims to Major Thaw Soe?'

Than shook his head again, more fiercely.

'Nor to Captain Tun Oo?'

'I was only informing them of my involvement in the operation. If they made assumptions, I'm not to blame.'

The general let off a tut and straightened abruptly, and Than stood too, almost leaping up. The general squared up to him, looking directly into his eyes.

'I've recognised that you did an admirable job, Officer Than Chit, and you've earned my respect, but you must recognise that you just followed orders, not anything more. If everyone was promoted for following orders, there would not be anyone but generals in the Tatmadaw. Do you see that?'

'You told me to find the ruby thieves, sir.'

'The rebels are the ruby thieves, aren't they?'

Than opened his mouth to protest, but the general cut him short.

'Under typical circumstances, you would be reprimanded for making such claims in my name, but your son's spirit has rescued you today. Don't let me hear of your duplicity again.' The general pressed a long, strong, threatening finger to Than's shoulder and then folded it away and stepped back to his chair.

Than leant on the side of the desk as he gathered up the paper. Dizziness had pitched him and his head was fizzing. Hatred was scuffing at his skin like rats' feet. Never in his life had he felt so humiliated. He hadn't been called here to get his promotion – nor would he ever; he realised that now. It was clear as a diamond, as topaz ocean waters. This was his lot. He was damned to stay here. Than Chit was a dog who'd forever be owned. His children wouldn't see him being thriving and successful. His karma would stay tattered and his soul would be punished. For the rest of eternity, he would always be power-less. He would never be paid in kyat or kind for giving up Min.

TWENTY-TWO

Zawtika arranged his robes in his lap and leant slowly forward, lifting the teapot from the tiles at his feet. A line of smoke coiled from the thin metal spout into the fresh morning air, thickening, skipping and then scattering into invisibility as he poured Michael another glass of powdery green tea. Michael stared down, absently chipping the mud from his bare feet and frowning at the dust as it settled through the cup. Zawtika hadn't told him anything that was happening. It didn't do a thing to relieve his anxiety. Their conversation was proving tough.

'Are we waiting for someone?' he asked to break the stillness.

Zawtika gazed into the distance and sipped his tea.

They were sitting in a tiny pagoda building at the very back of the temple grounds, just a few paces from where Thuza and Michael had stolen in the night before, and he lifted his eyes to the bolted gate and the forest beyond. He could see why the monk had chosen to hide here. No wider than a washroom, the pagoda was barely large enough to squeeze the two men and a Buddha inside. Far away from the hum of the dormitories and refectory, it didn't have the feeling of being cared for like the others, or that monks or worshippers ever stopped by. Bird droppings spattered the floor beneath nests at each inside corner and the stone had been blued by a layer of mould. No offerings of flowers were laid at the idol. A candle had sunk to its stub at the door. Cramped, quiet and facing the boundary, the pagoda felt to Michael like it might have been a secret, like nobody else might have known it was there.

He shuddered from the thought and squinted to the sky above the wall. Since leaving Rangoon, all grasp of time had escaped him. Lost to the chaos and his near-constant terror, it had streaked wildly as he fled through the forest and then ground so slow that it almost stopped. Wherever it sat now though, the new day was arriving. A chorus of birdsong had risen with the sun and warmth was beginning to fracture the clouds. As the air stirred, the scents of slight, tepid sweat and musky-sweet sandalwood circled. Infused in the threads of Zawtika's maroon robes, they fanned when he moved and collected beneath the pagoda's low steeple as if he were incense, smouldering himself. Michael took him in through the corner of his eye. His anger wasn't visible, but it had to be simmering. He had never felt quite so unwelcome before.

'Do you know what time it is, Sayadaw?' he asked again.

The monk swilled his tea. 'Seven,' he said. He shrugged faintly with his eyes still elsewhere. His English was perfect, as crisp as the queen's. 'Or a little before.'

'How long will we wait?'

'As long as we have to.'

'I only need a telephone, sir.'

Zawtika batted a mosquito from the air around his face. His expression hardened and he peered at Michael, sidelong. His mouth was tight and the skin around his eyes was crumpled.

Sharp disapproval had pierced through his stare. He smoothed his robes and knocked back his tea.

Michael squirmed on his low wooden stool and looked away, embarrassed. There was the ire that he knew had been rumbling – not that it came without reasonable cause. It was stupid to keep apologising, but he couldn't help it. He had caused so much trouble and put everyone in danger. For hiding a foreigner the price would be prison, but Thuza had risked it on only his promise. He had grabbed her misery and desperation and he'd dragged Zawtika and his entire temple into his foolishness, and he'd ruined their friendship without a thought.

'Please don't be angry at Thuza Win,' he muttered at the ground. 'It was my fault we came to you, not hers.'

Zawtika's eyes sloped away. He poured himself a new glass of green tea. 'My relationship with Thuza Win is nothing to do with you.'

'But it's terrible what happened to her,' said Michael. He shook his head. His hands were trembling. He kept talking, if only to distract himself from his mounting nerves.

'Terrible. I can't begin to sort it in my mind. If I'd heard her story when I was still in Rangoon, I wouldn't have believed it. I wouldn't have thought she was lying, but it might not have stuck in my memory, you know? Before the bomb, I thought it was pantomime, all these things that I'd heard. They weren't real. I used to turn my nose up at the other embassy kids, criticise them for never speaking to any Burmese people, never seeing the real city. In the teahouses, I'd listen too keenly when my Burmese friends told me about the horrors of Shan State, but I never really thought about it. At times, it was almost a contest between us . . . who'd found the most grisly rumours. Perhaps I enjoyed it even. It was exciting. Nothing like England. When my father had news of new intakes to Insein, sometimes I'd ride my bike along Hlaing River Road, hoping to catch a glimpse of someone being marched inside. It makes me feel sick when I think of it. That's why I came to Shan State. I said I wanted to help my friend, but it was guilt more than anything.'

Michael paused and wrung his hands together, staring down as hard as he could.

'The deal I made with Thuza Win . . .' he whispered. 'I never meant to keep it. I want to fix it now though. I don't know if I can and I'm worried that I can't, but I'll try. I'll ask about her parents. I'll do my best to bring them back. I feel horrible, Sayadaw, I'm ashamed for being so thoughtless and for leaving here when Thuza's still trapped. I'm embarrassed that I'm safe. It's absurd, isn't it? I hardly know her, but I feel that I'm abandoning her, like everyone else.'

The monk sipped his tea and gazed at the gate. 'Guilt is the most selfish of all the dogs, Michael Atwood. It's not for Thuza you feel this way.'

Michael rubbed his face. It was in part, at least, he reasoned. He did feel guilty for his lies and naivety, but he also felt shaken by the shadows of last night. By the fire in her home, Thuza's stare had been a bear-trap. When he'd looked in her eyes, his reflection unsettled him, the way he was smeared through the blue of her iris, a watery smudge that warped in his view. He scratched his face again and glanced into his lap, willing his blushing to fade. 'I owe it to Thuza,' he said, '. . . to try and help her.'

Zawtika drained his drink, impassive.

Michael scraped his stool closer towards him, peering up. 'I'm grateful to you, too, Sayadaw,' he said, holding out his hands, bowing almost. 'If there's anything that I can do for you when I get to Rangoon, anything I can give you or the monastery in return, please – you only have to ask.'

The monk didn't answer. Instead he cocked his head, listening. From beyond the temple walls, the wind threw in the rumble of a distant engine. Zawtika's poise sharpened. He stood, and Michael heard the sound rebound from the mountain slopes around them, swelling as the vehicle approached. Zawtika snatched a look from the pagoda's arched doorway before hoicking his robes around his knees and padding out.

At the gate, he turned. He clapped his hands at Michael. 'Come.'

Michael grabbed his shoes from underneath his stool and rushed outside. Thick spits of rain had begun to drop and the tiles were slippery beneath his feet. Zawtika was rummaging inside his many folds of material and he produced a key from some hidden pocket and forced it into the rusty lock. The metal bars clattered and Michael hurried to knot up his laces as the gate creaked open and the monk shoved him through. In the scrub, a dark-blue Mazda was idling. The windows were glazed with tinted glass. Its bumper was filthy and streaks of mud criss-crossed the bonnet as though it had driven its whole route without going on a road.

'*Mingala-ba*, Sayadaw,' said a man as he emerged from the back seat. He was smartly dressed and tall, perhaps pushing fifty, but his body was lean and muscular despite his creeping age. Large tinted aviators straddled the bridge of his nose.

Michael grabbed Zawtika's wrist, pulling him back impulsively. 'Sayadaw!' he whispered. 'It's the Tatmadaw. An officer!'

Zawtika peeled away Michael's grasp with his long, cool fingers. 'He's a general,' he said.

Two more men stepped from the car. They were uniformed as well but much younger than the general, both holding rifles, looking bored but mean. The raindrops fell and soaked their fatigues so they looked like camouflage. Michael tried to move but his muscles weren't shifting. He was rooted by dread to the dampening earth.

Zawtika dipped his head to the general, pressing his hands together in a slight, brisk bow. '*Mingala-ba*, esteemed General Bo Win.'

'What's happening?' said Michael.

'The general has arranged for your travel to Rangoon.'

'You said I'd be safe.'

'Who in Burma is safer than a general? Get in the car.'

The general was watching with a hint of amusement and he reached into his pocket and pulled out a clump of folded banknotes, nodding his head. He slobbered on his thumb and rolled it though the blue-green corners of the paper, peeling aside a hefty wedge.

'For the temple, Sayadaw,' he said, holding it out. 'We're as grateful as ever for your continued support.'

Zawtika bowed again and took the money, counting through and then stashing it away beneath his robes.

336

'We're picking up the *naga* girl this morning. You've served your country well.'

Zawtika nodded and scratched his chin, and then he let slip a faint smile and waved to one of the general's waiting henchmen. The soldier leapt forward and seized Michael's arm and Michael tripped as he was wrenched towards the car. He slammed his hands against the bonnet to steady himself, feeling like his sickness was going to spill. Shock was rattling his mind like a dice-shake, and he couldn't quite get it to land on a thought. Last night, Thuza sat in the old monk's dorm room and she'd cried and begged and he'd teased out her secrets, like sharp wooden splinters from soft, supple flesh. He heaved a nauseous breath and tried to think clearly, but the only image in his mind was of Thuza. *Zawtika's the sole person who cares*, she had told him, but the monk was a gangster. This was worse than abandonment. This was betrayal.

He turned to Zawtika, furious suddenly. 'What are you doing, Sayadaw?'

'I'm collecting my payment.'

'You lied to Thuza Win. She trusted you.'

'I'm not to blame for Thuza's poor judgement.'

'Don't you care what they'll do to her?'

'The spirits will protect her if they view it as fair.'

The general snorted a laugh and wrapped his hand around the bone of the monk's shoulder. 'Ah! The refrain of a man who sleeps without worries at night.'

He squeezed and Zawtika waited calmly until he released him, before dipping again and stepping away. The soldier holding Michael yanked him, opening one of the car's rear doors and shoving him downwards with a hand on his skull, forcing him into air-conditioned iciness as Zawtika headed back toward the temple's gate.

'Wait!' Michael cried.

He pushed against the soldier, but the general was bundling inside too, squeezing Michael back with his tough, wiry bulk. Outside, Zawtika was sweeping his footprints and the gate-grooves from the dust with a drooping palm leaf, backing into the temple and lifting the fallen hinges to cover his path, and he tossed the leaf through the bars and locked the bolt quickly with the key from his chain. Michael turned and pulled at the door behind him but it wouldn't open, so he scrambled back across the seats, trying to reach over the general to stop the door from shutting, but the general was powerful, and from the front seat a rifle was pointing, and the engine was revving and the noise was thunder, and the monk was gone and the car door slammed shut.

TWENTY-THREE

Do you trust him?

Zawtika's question bobbed along the surface of Thuza's sleep like feathers on the crests of a softly tidal stream; not enough to break the surface and wake her, but enough to cast a shadow below and tint her dreams. She didn't trust the white boy. An undertow to his voice unsettled her. A slight lack of patience gave his motives away. By the time they sat at her fireplace last night, Thuza had almost let go on his promise being kept. As he ate and a few careful words were batted between them and the night hours grew thicker, her doubt had crept over her, steady and silent like crisping ice. Perhaps, in an odd way, her nanna had saved them. Though she would never have dreamt to seek it, what truth would they have shared without her being there? Thuza had never told anyone her memories – not even with Zawtika had she spoken so plainly – but if she was ever going to be able to wash the colours of her past from black to white, now was the day and she needed to try. If she was honest, maybe, Michael Atwood might be honest too. She hadn't thought she would tell him everything, but it felt a relief to be speaking somehow, and once she'd begun, like sand through her fingers, the words started spilling and she couldn't make them stop. For the first time since she'd met him, his face seemed different, and he listened and waited, and his restless eyes calmed. When he spoke about his friend in Rangoon, he looked young and innocent. Thuza's chill warmed; just one sun-ray of yellow. She never trusted anyone, though she always longed to. She slipped inside a deep, drained sleep.

The knock that woke Thuza was as loud as gunfire. Her eyes leapt open. No one ever called at her home. She lay still and glanced to the window. The pace of her heart was sparking fast. Outside, morning had arrived and the trees were rustling, being teased awake from the dance of a breeze. The night had draped their bows with a shroud of cool white moisture and the crows sat amongst it, flexing their wings and cawing with glee.

'Open the door!'

Thuza scrambled up from the rug at the fireplace, her head still groggy. On the wood, the fist was hammering again, so hard and brisk that her house seemed to quiver, and she stumbled into the hallway and shunted the bolt aside, the man's voice still shouting and adrenaline streaking through her veins. The door was thrown open from the opposite side and a flash of green fatigues and dark flesh pushed her, and she tumbled from the entrance and crumpled against the wall behind as six more soldiers surged through her doorway, filling the corridor with their boots and rifles and noise and musty stink. They fanned across the floor, their heavy feet scattering between the rooms on either side of the hallway, and she heard a crash and the sound of splintering wood and she staggered up and into the front room to see the little glass door being ripped from its hinge on the front of the bureau and a soldier emptying the contents with a drag of his gun-muzzle through the space inside.

'Stop!' cried Thuza. 'Please!'

Her head felt dizzy from where she had cracked it and she glanced back – first to the hallway and then to the windows, as though looking for escape or someone to help. The Tatmadaw had found out what she was doing. They had come here to take her! She had thought she'd been careful but someone had seen her. No, she thought, and her eyes started blurring. Of course she'd messed up. Like before, she was reckless. Her mind had been spitting. She had been too eager to think of her parents and blinded by the white boy's skin that had glowed brighter than moonlight. She hadn't hid him properly and she'd gotten herself shot. She slumped against the door frame, reeling, feeling her heartbreak with a palm to her chest. A soldier shoved beyond her, pounding up her staircase. There wasn't any furniture remaining in the bedrooms – it was years since she'd sold all the wardrobes and drawers – and it wouldn't take long for them to find that he'd already left, but it didn't matter anyway. Clearly they were looking for him and knew that he'd been here. They knew that she'd helped him and knew she was done.

'Thuza Win?'

An officer was standing at Thuza's shoulder. Between his tight lips, a cheroot smouldered. He didn't look like officers usually did. His shirt was untucked and his chin was coated with grey-black stubble. The tone of his voice was distracted and quiet. He was watching his men with half-hearted, blood-shot eyes.

Thuza gripped the doorframe tighter and nodded weakly. Still her fear was scolding hot.

'By the will of the Tatmadaw,' he muttered, 'I have been instructed to search your property for evidence of criminality.'

From somewhere inside the depths of her home, a mirror shattered. Thuza could feel that her tears were swelling, brimming up at the cusp of her eyes. The officer stepped into the front room, sinking in her chair by the broken window as two wiry privates ransacked Thuza's possessions, emptying her drawers and discarding her *longis*, throwing her bowl of *thanaka* roots, shattering its earthenware, clattering through the cookware on the shelf above the fire. The officer licked the end of his cheroot. He nudged her birdcage and set it swinging, then stared from the window. A corkscrew of wind flicked the strands of his hair.

Thuza staggered forward, snatching up a tiffin box from the floor. 'I'm a seamstress,' she said, tripping towards him, thrusting it out with both hands. She poured the knotted thread spools from the metal to the table and pointed at the needles with their brown cotton tails. 'See!' Her hands were shaking. 'I'm not a criminal.'

The officer frowned and drew on his cheroot, holding the smoke in his mouth for a long moment and looking at the pile of spools. 'We have cause to believe that you are a thief and a benefactor of insurgent activity.'

Thuza's heart gave a kick. It was worse than just the white

boy. They knew about her rubies. They must have found something of Kyaw's at the camp that had led them to her, or perhaps a prisoner had coughed up her name when they stood on his chest. Her eyes twitched to the rug – to the little ridge beneath the threadbare material, almost imperceptible, where the trapdoor nipped shut and all her rubies and her secrets hid. 'I'm not involved with the rebels,' she said, gripping her hands together and trying to sound confident. 'I'm loyal to the Tatmadaw.'

'We have information that names you as a ruby smuggler.'

'It's lies.'

'Our witness accounts link your activity directly to that of the SSA.'

'No!'

Thuza stood beside the table and braced herself, tensing her muscles, looking at the officer and waiting for his interrogation to start, for his questions to fire across and encircle her like a swarm of hungry insects, and she wracked her thoughts for one to protect her, for one she could offer up to buy his mercy, but instead he sighed and leant stiffly forward, holding his weight on his forearms and taking a breath with his eyes closed.

'You are not a smuggler of gemstones?' he mumbled, sounding weary.

Thuza glanced at the privates on the opposite side of the room. They weren't watching her or the oddness of their officer. They were absorbed in the thrill of their destruction, their eyes black rounds of anticipation as they tore her home apart.

Thuza shook her head. 'No.' He was making her nervous – not just in the way that all Tatmadaw men did, but there was something in the strain of his voice that felt unpredictable, like some scraps of his presence were discarded elsewhere.

'Sir!'

There was a shout from one of the soldiers and Thuza turned to see him rattling the handle of the backroom door. Her stomach turned. The key was on the ribbon that she wore as a necklace, tucked beneath her blouse, invisible and secret, but that wouldn't stop them. The soldier tugged the handle harder, ramming his shoulder against the motionless door, and then he raised his hand and waved.

'Officer Than Chit,' he called. 'It's locked.'

The officer dragged himself from his stupor and wafted his hand across the room. 'Leave it.'

'But, sir, who locks a door inside their own home? She's hiding something.'

'It's rubies,' cried the other soldier.

'Are there rubies in there, girl?' asked the officer.

Thuza shook her head again, panicked.

'Unlock the door.'

'I don't have the key.'

'She's lying.'

The officer shrugged and nodded to his private. 'Fine. Break it down.'

The boy sprung forward and planted his boot on the door, belting it fiercely. The house shuddered and the hinges buckled. The door cracked open and Thuza went to run towards it, but the other soldier seized her back.

The officer heaved himself up and wandered over, stepping into the doorway, covering his mouth. 'What is this?' he said, peering inside the room where her grandmother slept.

'Leave her,' said Thuza, a tremble in her throat. 'She's sick.'

'She's a poppy fiend. Look at her hands . . . and her feet. They're purple,' cried the soldier holding Thuza.

'She's no trouble to you. Please. Don't touch her.'

From where he was keeping her captive, Thuza could see that her grandmother was stirring, twisting to a ball on her mattress and starting to moan as she came around. *Stay sleeping, Nanna*, Thuza begged in her head. *Don't wake! Don't wake!* The old woman snuffled louder and rolled to her side, drawing her knees to her waist and whimpering, and the sound and her stench leaked out from the room.

The officer edged forward to examine her closer and then coughed and began to walk away. He pulled a handkerchief from his pocket and wiped his face. 'Forget her,' he said from behind his hand.

The soldier who had kicked down the door seemed shocked. 'Don't we have to report her?'

'We are looking for rubies, not junkies. Just check the room and then we'll go.'

'*Rubies* . . .'

Thuza's grandmother squirmed, muttering from the floor. The officer's stare leapt to Thuza. 'What did she say?'

Thuza shook her head. 'Nothing.' Her pulse was racing. She couldn't be sure of the last time her grandmother had left the back room – it was two years or more and her brain was pickled – but she might have remembered about the tunnels or where Thuza stashed the gems.

The officer's stare narrowed and he crept slowly back towards the room. At the last moment, his eyes slipped from Thuza's and he crouched by the side of her grandmother's mattress. 'What do you know about rubies, old woman?' he asked her quietly.

Thuza's grandmother flinched and stretched out to his hand. 'I want my pipe.'

He edged back, just beyond her reach. 'Are there rubies in this house?'

'Do you have my medicine?'

The officer nodded. 'Yes. We have plenty of medicine.'

'I need it.'

'If you tell me about the rubies, I'll ask my men to sort you out.'

Thuza's grandmother shifted on the mattress, straining to touch him, and he moved further back. Her expression crumpled and she growled in frustration, her hand dropping to the floor and clawing the wood.

'Tell me, old lady, where does your girl keep her gemstones? Be honest and my men will give you all the medicine you need.'

Thuza's stomach cramped as her grandmother's stare roamed from the officer to the tray on the dresser, then settled vacantly somewhere in the air around where she stood. She shook her head and begged her silently – *Don't tell them, Nanna! Please don't. They're lying!* – but her nanna's attention sloped gently away.

She closed her eyes. 'The birdcage.'

'Nanna, no!'

Thuza let out a howl and her legs buckled. The soldier held her up, ramming her against the wall, and the officer stood up and dusted his hands down his trousers, scowling. He marched from the back room, passing Thuza without a look, and hoisted the birdcage from its stand. He yanked open the latch and peered inside before dropping the cage to the floorboards and trampling the bars. The thin metal bowed, creaking and straining until at last it gave way underneath his weight, snapping from the base with a loud hollow crack. He wiped the powdery rust from his boot-cap and squatted down, prising apart the layers of metal where the bars had split, and Thuza struggled to keep herself from sobbing as he pulled out the treasures that she'd hidden inside. He pocketed her three precious bundles of banknotes – her savings and the money the Thai had paid her – with nothing more than a second of dim scrutiny, and then rummaged back inside and dragged out her navy velvet pouch. In the back room, her grandmother was crying, cursing the officer's name and shrieking at the soldier who tried to restrain her, clawing at his trousers with her hair across her face. A deep, breathless cry escaped from Thuza's lips now too, and she dragged her hand to her mouth to catch it. After all she had struggled to keep Nanna living, her nanna had done this to knock Thuza dead.

The officer weighed the pouch briefly in his hand and Thuza watched miserably as he tipped the contents into his palm and weaved his finger through the gems. There were only a few miniature red stones there, not enough to buy her a cockerel even, but one alone would have sealed her fate. She looked to the window and stared at the forest, at the white peaks of the stupas glinting through the trees, and the last nine years floated up like prayer chants, and all of her future trailed up behind them, in wispy drags that rose to the clouds and melted away to nothing but grey. She dipped her head and looked at her gemstones, and they disappeared too through the haze of her tears.

The officer sniffed and closed his fist tightly. 'You're under arrest, Thuza Win,' he said.

Thuza huddled in the corner of the jail cell, leaning her head on the cold concrete wall. She had been here long enough for her limbs to have stiffened, and she guessed it must have been almost noontime as the streak of light that cut through the window had crawled from her left side, almost to her right. There was no one else in the cell beside her, but the previous tenants had left their stains on the floor. Spits of red betel juice splattered the stone like squashed spiders, and the tide-marks of urine skirted its edge like a dried quarry stream. From inside the wall, a pipe was dripping, marking the seconds with a blunt metallic trill. A pressure was floating inside her temples, borne from exhaustion and throbbing in waves. Her parents' lives had become hers too now, but she didn't feel fearful or angry or sad. She felt a weight of inevitability, like a decade of grief had at last settled onto her, and the hope that had buoyed her was now kicked away. Despite what she'd worked for, this felt oddly fitting – like she'd known all along it would end up the same. Whatever the route a soul walked through Burma, the

Tatmadaw would wait at the head of the pathway. Whatever you argued, fought for or valued, destinations were fixed, pre-determined as fate.

Across the room, Officer Than Chit had his elbows on the desk. He was chewing his cheek with his head in his hands. He'd sat that way for what felt like an hour. The table was strewn with disordered papers and his coffee was undrunk in its cup, and he was reading something, slowly and carefully, and the scores on his brow were burrowing deep. It might have been her charges or her interrogation order, the forms he would fill with her thieving and lies. She closed her eyes and tried to imagine the weeks and months that were waiting ahead. If she made them as terrible in her mind as the day the Tatmadaw came for her family, nothing that followed could be any shock. She breathed heavily, readying herself for the unknown horrors, and peered again at the silent man. There was something about him that was oddly compelling, despite the threat of his uniform. Since his privates had left, his slump had become thicker, and his skin was as grey as the monsoon rain. He'd shown no interest in her. Two enormous horseshoe shadows sagged beneath his bloodshot eyes. His fingers were jittering on the side of his scalp.

He looked up and flicked his chin at her, suddenly. 'You,' he said, seizing a sheet of creamy yellow paper and brandishing it in the air.

Thuza stared at him.

'Can you read, girl?'

She nodded.

'Well?'

349

'Well enough.'

He rammed his chair away from the desk and stood up, marching to the cell and pressing the paper against the bars. 'What does it say?' he barked, glaring at her. 'You read it.'

Thuza clambered up and hurried forward. It wasn't her orders – she could see it was a letter. Her belly had a twitch of nerves at the sight. The address was Rangoon, the writing was formal and the Tatmadaw's flag was embossed at its top.

The officer shook the paper, rushing her.

'*Dear Officer Than Chit . . .*'

His frown hardened. 'Not that,' he said. He prodded his finger to the bottom of the page. 'There. Tell me what it says.'

Thuza's eyes scanned downwards, skimming the sweeping, flowery coils of ink and settling on the line above the man's filthy nail. '*His sacrifice was chivalrous*,' she said, mumbling as she tried to keep her voice from a tremble. '*The Tatmadaw appreciates the gallantry of his fight.*'

The officer seized the letter from the cell and rasped the stubble around his lips with a drag of his palm. He stared at her, still scowling. He smelt unwashed; stale sweat, rotten breath. 'What does chivalrous mean?'

'Brave,' replied Thuza.

'And gallantry?'

'The same, I think. It's noble. Bold.'

The officer paused and held her stare briefly, and then he turned away and collapsed back to his desk.

Thuza wrapped her hands around the cell bars, her knuckles whitening. That was a letter that was sent to soldiers' parents; a non-specific gesture of solemn, false regret. The SSA would have done something similar for Kyaw if they had a place to deliver it. Her brother would have wanted a letter – he would have felt honoured – but she knew that it wouldn't give her parents any solace. It wouldn't have done a thing for Thuza either, except perhaps to rekindle her rage. She looked at the officer as he gawped into his coffee. He didn't seem comforted. A glint of damp was showing on his eyeballs. How thin the thread to stitch both their wounds.

The officer's nose wrinkled. 'My son was seventeen,' he said. 'The SSA killed him.'

In her chest, Thuza felt a drag of hard, unexpected pity. Though she hadn't meant for any of the last day to happen, her intent was irrelevant. Her guilt was what mattered, in all of its forms. The roles she had played when she clung to her brother had forced her grief – the grief of her family – to leak from her gemstones and drown someone else. There wasn't any anger in his voice where there might have been, but instead there was tiredness. The man was as empty and worn as Thuza was. She glanced at her fingers, at the scars on her knuckles where her birds had hooked her and torn through her flesh.

The officer sighed. He reached across the table and plucked up an apple from his filing tray, examining it, and then scraping a speck from its waxy green skin. 'Have you eaten today?' he asked her.

Thuza shook her head.

He bent forward and placed the apple on the floor, nudging it with the cap of his boot. It wobbled sideways and bumped through the bars. 'My boy was smart too,' he said, and he almost smiled. 'He was good at reading. The best in his class, the teachers told me. Ever since he was little.'

Thuza stared at the fruit by her feet and her stomach growled. She could feel the officer's stare on her body as she crouched to pick up the apple and took a small bite. He sat for a while and watched her eating. She couldn't tell if it made him pleased.

A minute passed. He stared at the image of Aung San on the wall. 'Are you a Mogok girl?'

Mouth full, she nodded.

'Shan?'

She nodded again.

'How old are you?'

'Twenty-one.'

His forehead creased. 'You look younger.' He sat forward and squinted, studying her. 'Do you have a son?'

'No.'

'Any children?'

She shook her head again. He seemed disappointed. 'I had a brother though,' she said. She paused. 'He was shot.'

The officer hesitated too, and then sniffed. 'What was his name?'

'Kyaw Lin,' replied Thuza.

A memory flashed across the man's face. Thuza watched it spark. 'My son was called Min Soe Khaing,' he said, smiling suddenly. 'Did you know him?'

Thuza squinted a little to show she was thinking. She might have, she supposed. It wasn't unlikely. Mogok was not as big as the seas. She wanted to tell him that she knew him, to lessen her guilt by sharing some pain. Her mind riffled back through the boys in her schoolyard and most of their faces peeped out from a crevice, but she hadn't been to lessons since her parents were taken and so much since had happened that there wasn't much space left to stash away names. 'I don't know,' she said, truthfully.

The officer's smile faded and a long, sad yawn replaced it. He rubbed his face, resting his head in hand again, staring down. 'I bet their bullets flew faster than lightning,' he muttered at the desk. 'My Min and your Kyaw. Even the stars can't foresee such suddenness. That's the only relief that I have.' He looked up at Thuza, red-eyed. Exhaustion had broken the poise of his features so they seemed to droop and have slipped from their place. 'It's less than two days since Min died. Did you know that? Rangoon – they found the time to write me a letter, but not a man to cover my work. It's a crisis, they said. We need to act swiftly. They couldn't spare me a moment of time to grieve with my family. Not a single night to mend and sleep. Instead they sent me to search your house. My wife, the rest of my children . . . they think I'm the reason Min joined the army, that he's dead. They hate me for leaving them and abandoning his soul. I can't blame them.'

He wrenched at the breast of his uniform, disgusted, and then caught himself and wiped his nose and eyes, blushing, folding the letter briskly and tucking it away in the pocket of his shirt.

Thuza buried her teeth in her apple. The Tatmadaw had sent him to her, but why would they do that? Standing in the cell, an idea had pricked her, sharp as a pin in the grey

353

of her brain. She had spent enough years with smugglers and addicts to know when a man was poised on the edge. If she was heading to Insein Prison, her only joy was that her parents would be with her, but they would want to know every turn of her story, every stone she had stepped on to find her way there. They would want to know about Kyaw's journey too. She needed to discover exactly what had happened to make sure she could tell her parents just right. There might have been a gift hidden somewhere inside the last rancid day that she could pass to her parents and soften their sorrow; a forgotten memento that was found on Kyaw's body – a photo or a note that led the Tatmadaw to Thuza's home but could act as a sign of Kyaw's lingering love. She looked at the officer and felt her thoughts firming at his slight uneven tilt against the desk.

'The tide flows both ways, sir,' said Thuza. She pushed her eyes onto him, watching him squirm, fixing him beneath her will. 'It's heartless to make you work. Your generals should be more understanding. How can a soldier be loyal to his bosses if his bosses have nothing but cruelty for him?'

She smiled, as sincerely, kindly and sympathetically as she could, and she waited, watching her words seep in through his sadness, watching his shoulders begin to sag. She paused, gently. 'Did the general send you to me, Officer? Did he pull out my name?'

A nod.

'What reasons did he give you?'

'He knew you had rubies.'

Thuza nodded. 'Yes,' she said, pushing carefully. 'But why me? Why this morning? How did he know to search my house?'

The officer looked at her. Beyond his stare, she could see a thought forming; a hint of confusion, perhaps even guilt. He arranged himself upright, as if gathering himself. 'We captured your brother at the SSA camp,' he said. His voice and face were perfectly flat. 'He gave you away and then he died from his wounds.'

Thuza's heart lurched. She clutched the bars tighter. He was lying. She had seen Kyaw killed. She shook her head. 'No one questioned my brother,' she said, without thinking. 'He wasn't captured. I watched him be shot.'

The officer glared at her, clearly shocked at the strength of her confession, but his mind was still tacked to his own sticky pain. Thuza's stomach was fizzing. She didn't care that she'd exposed herself. Her thoughts were quick fragments, not joining up. Of all the lies the man could have told her, it didn't make sense he would chose this one. 'Who was it?' she asked. 'Who said I had gems?'

'The general,' he replied. 'Bo Win. I told you.'

'Who did he hear from?'

He shrugged.

'No. There's more,' said Thuza. 'I can see it. There's doubt.' She pressed herself harder against the cell bars. 'Please, why won't you tell me? What difference does it make when I'm already captive? Isn't it fair that I know what was done?'

The officer glanced away, wriggling in his seat.

Thuza held out her hand, reaching to him. 'You asked my brother's name earlier, but you already knew it.'

He shook his head. 'I wasn't sure.'

'Yes, you were,' said Thuza. 'You must have been. You

knew my brother was a rebel, but you didn't make me say it. You knew he fought with the SSA. Their men killed your boy, but you didn't need to throw me in with them . . . . You showed me mercy, Officer. You're a good man. You understood what I was feeling. My loss. You don't want others to suffer like you've done. That makes you more chivalrous than the Tatmadaw deserves. More gallant. Show me mercy again. Who sold me out?'

There was a long, thick silence and then the officer shivered, frowning. 'It was a monk,' he said. 'Sayadaw U Zawtika.'

Thuza's heart threw itself against the cage of her ribs. 'Sayadaw U Zawtika,' she asked. She felt sick. 'Are you certain?'

He nodded. It was brief slip of a nod, barely visible but as loud as a thunderclap. He said something jumbled, but Thuza couldn't hear it. She felt as though she was plummeting through a well shaft. There must have been some clear explanation, a plan or reason that she didn't understand. She glanced at the window and its yellow-white radiance and then at the exit with the heavy wooden door. Zawtika was her friend. He wouldn't deceive her. She had to get out. She needed to see him. By the stars and the spirits, it couldn't be true.

She dragged herself across the cell, placing her body as close to the front of the desk as she could manage, squeezing herself against the cold metal bars. She could work this man. She knew she could use him. His grief made him pliable; weak and soft. She would offer him a sweetener and tempt him to free her and then she'd find Zawtika and everything would be clear again. And her parents too! Her plan was still possible. If she didn't quit now, they could still be free.

'Please, Officer,' she whispered. She braced herself but she tried to not to beg him. She had to sound calm if she wanted to do this – or at least not as desperate as the pounding of her heart. She reached out again with an open palm. She was daring him to trust her, drawing him in. 'You and I are the same. The Tatmadaw has robbed us both. Your son was a soldier, but he was a brilliant boy. Smart . . . such potential. It's all been wasted though, hasn't it? Doesn't that make you bubble inside? You've nothing to be ashamed of, being angry at the generals. They sent you to work before your child was buried. Worse than that, they signed his murder warrant. They killed Min as eagerly and easily as they killed my brother. They don't care about you, Uncle. What right do they have to keep giving you orders? What right do they have to make you suffer any more?'

The officer drew his lips tightly inwards. His cheeks were flaming red. 'You can't speak of the Tatmadaw that way.'

'I can't speak the truth? Your family would tell you the same, wouldn't they? Your wife would. She knows it.'

The officer was glaring the desk. He was shaking. He wasn't speaking, but she could see he was listening. His eyes had thinned to hair-cracks. His mind was active.

She was standing on her tiptoes. 'The Tatmadaw men are cockroaches. I've heard it said a thousand times. Your general's orders are what cause your trouble. His orders, his superior's orders, the orders that rise all the way to the top. Aren't you tired of living in his shadow? Wouldn't you like to step into the sun?'

Officer Than Chit stared at Thuza. A tear had dripped from

the middle of one eye. She licked her dry teeth and reached out through the cell bars further.

'If you let me go, Officer,' she said, 'I can do things to help you.'

His hand twitched hard on the top of the table.

She pointed to the desk and a vigour kicked through her. 'Pass me the keys, sir. You won't be sorry. Pass me the keys and turn your eyes sideways, and I promise I'll punish them all for us both.'

TWENTY-FOUR

The car weaved through the narrow lakeside streets at speed, throwing Michael sideways along the leather back seat. He clutched the handle on the inside of the door, bracing his boots into the footwell and trying to keep from bumping the general, who was somehow sitting perfectly still at his side. His stomach churned and he glared through the window at the early afternoon sun, drawing his eyes into wavering focus and biting down on the edge of his nail. Mogok was busy with people. They were washed in sunlight turned sepia by the dust, and each occupying themselves cutting in and out of the little rattan houses and shops with business to attend to, or navigating the throngs with their baskets and pushcarts, or sweeping their porches and shooing the dogs. He watched them, envious of their simple, oblivious freedom – of the lack of despair in their moments of routine – and focused on the sounds of the children playing to block out the whistle of the general's nose. Like a bullock, he was snorting, breathing too heavily. He was staring ahead through his crimson-tinted shades.

The driver swung a sharp, unexpected right and Michael's head cracked against the glass. He winced, pinching his eyes between his finger and thumb and firming his grip on the door, but then the car slowed and the potted concrete smoothed. Outside, the town's commotion had vanished abruptly. In its place was quiet, disconcerting calm. This road was broad – three times as broad as any they had driven to get here – and brighter and emptier and colder and bleak. There weren't the trees that grew everywhere else in Mogok, just weeds that skulked along the deserted, cracked pavements and stole up the telegraph poles where they stood. Giant colonial villas hid behind razor-wired walls, beige, faded peach and crumbling as though they were made of pastry overcooked by the sun. The guards at every gate were standing to attention. The lake winked between the buildings. *You've no idea what's coming next.*

He gnawed his fingernail again and wriggled at the blast of steaming air that thumped him as the driver rolled down his window and flashed a pass before pulling into a courtyard at the head of the road. A few soldiers were criss-crossing the barren concrete plot, alone or talking in fast-paced couples, and the car rounded the statue of Aung San in the centre of the space and stopped outside the doors. Michael heard the locks shunt open and then the general slid out and snapped his fingers. Michael followed him, the polished leather shrieking beneath his clammy skin. The general took hold of his arm to hurry him, and he heard the car roll away and glanced back to see it park up and the barrier being lowered across the front entrance, and a stone sunk down to the bottom of his gut.

With his hand clawed around Michael's bicep, the general led him inside and along a whitewashed corridor, airy with the echoes of their footsteps on the tiles and muffled conversations from behind closed doors. They skipped up a tall staircase and along another upstairs hallway before stopping at an office at the very furthest end. A clerk was tapping at a typewriter on the desk. The general gusted past him, dragging Michael behind.

'Get Rangoon on the phone, Sergeant,' he said in clear Burmese.

The man leapt up, clearly flustered and gawping at Michael as he scrambled to salute and mutter a reply. The general unlocked the door in the back wall, entering the room beyond with Michael before slamming it shut behind them. He released him and swept to the desk in the corner, sitting down and sorting through his files with a thick frown entrenched on his face, but without a word.

Michael hovered awkwardly by the door, rubbing his arm. His skin felt hot and damp and sticky, and he was still gripped by nausea from the lurch of the car through the narrow alleys and the stink of its leather. He shifted his weight on his feet, glancing around. The room was large, grand and not unlike an office in the embassy, but everything inside was just slightly off colour, like a piece of fruit that had started to turn. There was a sofa beneath a slightly wonky portrait of a uniformed man that he didn't recognise, the spongy cream velvet encased in thick plastic, and the curtains had moth holes and the floorboards were faded, patched light and dark where the furniture had been placed and then rearranged. The books on the shelves were speckled with mildew and a plate of stale sandwiches curled on the finger-smudged coffee table. Rotten wood framed the open windows and someone had splodged on a brush-full of gloss paint to cover them over and stuff up the cracks.

He squirmed again and his legs started jittering, and the bleat of the telephone made him start.

'Yes?' the general answered. He waited for a few seconds, levering his glasses to his forehead and pinching the furrow of his brow before breaking into a brisk Burmese greeting. From the other end of the line, Michael heard a voice that sounded like a rail-car, low and rumbled, pausing and then jolting, and he felt his discomfort continue to mount. He could understand the odd passing sentence and passage from the general. He heard his name mentioned more than once – and his father's. They were talking about how to send him back.

Michael's eyes cut to the door. For all its haste, the car journey had seemed to pass slowly, and certainly without information, and his dread for Thuza was sharply prickling, like pins and needles beneath his skin. He stared at the little china plate on the table, at the small triangles of dry white bread with their crusts cut off and the slices of fatty ham and pale, watery cucumber that drooped from their sides, and he pushed his hands to the well of his pockets and looked at the doorway once again. He couldn't stand the thought that Thuza was hungry. It was stupid, he knew, considering what had happened, but he'd eaten her last supper and at Zawtika's betrayal the Tatmadaw had picked her up already, and he didn't know where they'd taken her or what was going to happen and the fact that her stomach was empty and aching was the final cruel barb to the trap that he'd laid. The intermittent drone of the general's voice was still reverberating, swilling beneath the high ceiling with the turn of its fan, though Michael didn't care what the words were any longer. His eyes slunk down to his feet and stayed there. It was all he could do to stem his despair.

The slam of the telephone's receiver jolted Michael from his guilt. He looked up as the general rammed his chair away from the desk and stood up, tidying the stack of brown paper files he'd been skimming through and collecting them in a stack on the corner of the wood before walking away.

'Tie up your laces,' he said, addressing Michael in curt English and pointing at his boots. He stepped to a bureau beside the opposite window, whipping his cap from a large bronze bust.

Michael dropped obediently to his knees. His boots were still filthy with mud and ash, and he wrenched at the tatty black rat-tails quickly, feeling the heat of the general's scowl. 'What's happening?' he asked.

'We're leaving.'

The general checked his appearance in the mirror, dusting a few flecks of dandruff from his epaulettes before levelling his cap on his side-slicked hair.

Michael's stomach crunched. He should have felt glad he was finally leaving but his thoughts were a siren shrieking instead. 'What will happen to Thuza Win?'

'To who?'

'The girl you picked up this morning. The one the monk told you about.'

'The serpent? She'll be questioned, charged, tried, convicted and imprisoned. As well she deserves.'

'She doesn't deserve it, General.'

'Many souls in Burma suffer, Michael Atwood, but they don't all steal, conspire and harbour a fugitive.'

'I'm not a fugitive.'

'Do your documents give you permission to travel to Shan State?'

Michael swallowed. The General tweaked his hat again and turned to him slowly, his eyes contracting to thin, wry lines. He wandered back to the desk and tapped a finger on the mass of files.

'Did you know her brother was a murderer? I have the evidence here. From the capture of his division, we know that he was amongst the most notorious insurgents the Fifteenth had. He was a sniper, a bandit and a critical money-cow. There were forty honest Tatmadaw men against his name this year alone, apparently. Do you think Thuza Win has clean hands despite this? There are always choices you can make to be righteous. She could have come to our offices, confessed her brother's sins on his behalf. Instead she chose to stay away.' The general blinked heavily, and Michael saw his pupils shrink behind his glasses. 'Anyway, white boy, why do you care?'

Michael didn't answer. He looked at his feet and wondered why he did care so much. The general considered him for a moment more and then swung around, heading towards the door and cracking it open. From the corridor, Michael could hear footsteps and distant, muffled voices of soldiers and clerks as they scurried like insects and went about their chores. They were all Thuza Win, in their own little guises, all terrified and lonely, injured and hopeless, trapped within the bars of the Tatmadaw's cage.

Michael leapt after him, harrowed suddenly at the thought of this. 'I'll pay you!' he shouted.

The general stopped. The light outside was glinting, and it held him on the threshold like a web of spun gold. 'I can't be bribed, Michael Atwood.'

'It's not a bribe, General,' he said carefully. Fear coursed through him. 'It's a thank-you. You've arranged for me to get home. That's kind of you. My father will be grateful. Let me call him before we leave. I think he'd like to know that I'm on my way. It would give him the opportunity to prepare your gift, and I'm sure he'd be pleased if he heard that you hadn't punished anyone else that had helped me too. You could do that, couldn't you . . . you could let Thuza Win go? Nobody needs to know about it.'

The general licked his lips.

'I can see you're a wise and powerful man, and she's no one to Burma. Rangoon wouldn't notice if she slipped through your fingers. What difference would one little Shan girl make?'

The general's stare hardened. 'I'm not doing this for Burma.'

'Then take my offer,' said Michael, inching closer. 'I want to reward you.'

The general stepped back and spat at Michael's feet. 'You want to buy me, you arrogant child. It's just like the British to assume that they could. I'm less foolish than you think, boy. Far less foolish than you. There are prizes more valuable than kyat in Burma. I already have *you*. I'm playing the longest game, Michael Atwood. You can't give me what the Tatmadaw can. Your money can't buy me what I want.'

'What do you want?' Michael said. He was shaking.

'I want what every rational man is seeking,' the general whispered. '. . . to be floated upstream. Every soldier in the Tatmadaw serves his country, but he serves his own special kingdom first. The rebels saw your value, then the serpent did, and now I do. I'm the only man smart enough to cash you in though. Handing you to Rangoon is your best possible use. They'll send you home to your poor, fretting father, and he'll be so grateful that your heart is still beating that Rangoon can demand what they please in return. Cheap loans, trade deals, lobbying and favours. I don't know what they'll ask for, but your government will bend.'

Michael shook his head. 'They won't. As I told the rebels, General, the British don't pay ransoms. They couldn't. It wouldn't be a choice.'

The general smiled. 'What did I tell you about choices, Michael Atwood? When we tell them how we found their ambassador's son in Shan State without permission to travel, how you'd been hanging around at the home of a known ruby thief, taking sides and playing soldier with the rebels in a battle against the Tatmadaw . . . what else could they do? We have enough evidence of your misdemeanours to lock you away for a hundred years. Your government couldn't allow that. If they dared, we'd make your pale face the pin-up of dissension. You'd be the biggest coup we've ever had. Your government can't have headlines about spies and conspiracies. Whatever they do, you're priceless, little round-eye. Your father and your country are indebted to the Tatmadaw, and the Tatmadaw now are indebted to me.'

Michael swallowed hard again as the general released him. He knew in the pit of his gut it was true.

Behind the general, there was a cough and a brief clatter from the clerk's desk. The general turned and Michael looked up to see the clerk scampering towards them with a piece of paper in his hand. The general stepped back, glowering at him.

'I've just had a message from the Operation Hall, sir,' said the clerk, stopping at their side, flustered and pink-cheeked. 'They need to you to authorise the remaining prisoner interrogations before you leave. The cells at the barracks are full and they can't ship anyone else to Shwebo without your signature.'

The clerk handed the paper to the general, who read speedily and let off a growl. He thrust it back at the clerk, who flinched, and then nudged Michael backwards into the office. He pointed to his man.

'Guard him,' he said, already beginning to march away. 'I'll be five minutes.'

The clerk looked at Michael, his fear as clearly spread over his face as Michael felt his own was, and then he took a few wary steps backwards and pulled the door to. Michael held his heart in his mouth and listened to the sound of the general's boots receding down the corridor. He crept to the door and peered through the gap. The clerk was pacing by the window, looking anxious. His hands were screwed to a twitching ball. Michael padded away and kept his eyes on him. An idea was clawing through his head. He turned to the desk, to the pile of brown folders in the corner by the lamp. There must have been fifty. All the same. All neatly stacked, looking innocently up. If he could find Kyaw's file, Thuza might not be punished. He cast his eyes down and riffled quickly through them. Each had a label at the top, a name tag. His pulse sped a little faster as he saw them. They couldn't punish her parents either. If the general was sending these files to the capital, they wouldn't ever notice that Kyaw's was missing, and then they couldn't make a link to Thuza's parents at Insein, and at least just one of her fears could be allayed. He dug through them quicker, feeling his heart kick. He had found Kyaw's name! Kyaw Shwe Min said the label. But another said Kyaw, too; Kyaw Lin. Then another. *Shit.* Burmese names were all so similar. He tore the pages from each of the folders he could see marked Kyaw, creasing them in half as fast as he could and stuffing them into the band of his trousers. He tightened the buckle of his belt, glancing to the door and leafing through the files again, checking for any stray names he might have missed, when suddenly one was different from the others. *Chaiwat Thongsuk.* That wasn't a Burmese name. His breath snatched. His heart jerked like lightning. That was the name that Thuza had told him. This was the man who was known as *the Thai*.

He shot a look at the door, tearing open the file and staring down at the pages within. Thuza had said the Thai was at the camp yesterday, hadn't she? He skimmed the paper. It was all in Burmese and he couldn't read it, but it didn't look like a death certificate. It looked like a transcript. A conversation of some sort. Perhaps an interview? There were reams and reams of it. His eyes scanned downwards and his thoughts started galloping. If the Thai had been captured, the Tatmadaw would be seething. Both Thuza and Teacher had said the government had no idea he worked for the rebels. To find him in the jungle would be a loathsome betrayal. Fuck. If Michael was right, this could be evidence that the Tatmadaw had bombed their own people in Rangoon – that they'd bombed Sein – and if Michael could prove a link to the bombing, perhaps the world would have to take notice. It would give his father the power to act. Make a difference. He could hardly believe it. He stared at the paper, adrenaline sparking.

A flurry of movement outside the room and the clerk's nervy voice made him start, and he rammed the sheets of paper inside his trousers too, slipping the empty brown Chaiwat Thongsuk file back into the centre of the stack and tidying it quickly. He spun around as the door opened.

The general flicked a finger at him. 'Move.'

Michael held his breath and walked to the door, feeling the sweat pour from his temples. The general ignored his clerk and paced away, swallowing the corridor with his long, sturdy strides. Michael darted after him, following him along the upstairs hall and down the staircase, running his hand over the thick, teakwood beam. They cut through the lobby, and the soldiers seemed to scatter around the general, aborting their paths and scuttling away, then he marched outside and down the steps to the courtyard, brandishing his hand at the car parked by the gates. It fired to life and swung around the statue, pulling up. The general opened the back door and motioned for Michael to get in. He ducked inside, wincing at the sound of the paper as it crumpled inside his clothes. The general shoved into the car beside him, oblivious.

'Take us to the Mandalay airfield,' he said to the soldier who was driving.

'Yes, sir.'

The boy nodded and the car pulled away. Michael leant back

in his seat, feeling the air conditioning blast on his face. They were on their way to Rangoon. They were leaving. He'd actually done it. This wasn't a waste! The car reached the gates and a soldier dragged the barrier from their path and he let himself smile inside, catching a glimpse of the Tatmadaw's flag in the rear-view mirror, fluttering and then folding upon itself above the guard booth, when a hand struck hard to the window beside his face.

He started, and the general did too. Outside, a young monk was running beside the window, his robes hoicked over his arm, wide-eyed and shouting the general's name. He looked terrified.

The driver glanced in his mirror. 'Sir?'

The general's eyes narrowed and he glanced at Michael suspiciously. 'Pull up.'

The car slowed and shuddered to a standstill, and the boy skipped around the bonnet, his bare feet catching on the hem of his robes. He slapped the window beside the general this time, pressing his hands and face to the glass, searching through its tint. The general rolled down his window.

'What do you want, child?'

The young monk was perspiring. 'It's about the white boy,' he cried, breathless. 'Sayadaw U Zawtika sent me. He needs to see you.'

The general looked at Michael again, his stare as hard as granite. Michael felt his muscles clench.

'Can it wait?'

The boy shook his head. 'No, sir. He wouldn't have sent me here if it could.' He glanced fearfully sideways and whispered,

'There's danger ahead for you both, he said. Black clouds.'

The general's mouth puckered and his stare sidled over Michael's face again – slowly and with the heat of a thousand reservations – and then settled back on the waiting boy. He sucked in his cheeks. 'Alright,' he said. 'Get in. We'll go to the temple.'

'No!' cried the boy. He wrenched at the door and his eyes started sparking. 'We can't take your car. No one must see us. We have to be quick. Get out. Follow me.'

TWENTY-FIVE

Thuza lay with her body on the mud and her chin on her knuckles, peering out to the clearing ahead. She hadn't moved at all for what felt like an hour and, pinned so still by her anticipation, her joints felt stiff and her muscles ached. Despite the shade, it was still only the middle of the afternoon and hot where she lay, and a dribble of sweat ran from her forehead into the corner of one eye, stinging her, and she blinked it away and wiped her brow with the slightest, quickest movements she could. So close to the earth, the breeze had no way of reaching her, but it fingered through the branches in the canopy above and the sound of their rustling fell down like rain. If she tipped her eyes upwards, she could see their leaves dancing, and darts of swift light like fish in a pond. The fruit bats were gathered in clusters beneath them. Too heavy to sway or be bothered by the wind, they hung instead like the shadows of the cormorants who sat in the treetops and flexed their wings.

Beside her, a twig snapped. The man had shifted. 'We need to go.'

His voice was muffled, its clarity lost to the folds of his scarf. From above the wrap of tight red cotton, two deep-set black eyes jerked impatiently towards her. Like Kyaw, he smelt of cigarettes and mould.

Thuza shook her head, just the smallest amount. 'Not yet,' she whispered.

The man fired an angry breath through his nostrils and squirmed again, his finger hovering on the trigger of his gun. He nudged the barrel with the ball of his hand, dipping his head and realigning his sight. The clearing was a broad, shallow oval of land that had once been a gem crater, but abandoned now, it had grown to be a lush green spread of thigh-high grasses. Thuza's vision skimmed their rippling peaks, resettling on the men in the centre of the bowl. Ten minutes must have passed at least since the general marched from the narrow gap in the trees at its distant end. She shivered. Her hiding place was too far away to hear what he was saying, but his stance was hostile. His hands were on his hips. At his side, Michael Atwood looked boyish and nervous. The messenger's face was perfectly calm.

Her stare skimmed back to the concealed path. 'It won't be much longer,' she said, feeling nervous.

'We don't have much longer,' replied her companion. She could hear the scowl in his voice. 'The general will leave. Look at him. He's itching already.'

'The monk isn't here. We made a deal.'

'We'll miss our chance.'

'You won't. The general's not going anywhere. He thinks there's a problem. He's scared.'

The man's stare narrowed and he edged closer to Thuza, pulling his scarf from his face and leaning in, studying her, a threat flashing in his eyes. His skin was as rough and pitted as an elephant's hide. 'You'd better be right, Thuza Win,' he hissed, baring his betel-black teeth at her. 'Bo Win never goes any-where without his minders. He's paranoid. This is the first time I've seen him without another soldier in almost a decade. If he slips away now, we'll never get an opportunity as good again.'

Thuza gritted her own teeth, frowning. 'You'd never have had an opportunity at all if it wasn't for me, Myat Zaw,' she said, and she glared back bitterly. 'Remember that. And if history and brotherhood mean anything to your karma, remember Kyaw.'

She stared for a moment longer before looking away, then heaved a breath gently in to calm herself and tried to shrink her body inwards, drawing it back from his stink and doubt. She hoped it was more than the strength of her wanting that made her sound sure. Myat Zaw was one of Kyaw's oldest friends. His father had died in a landslide at the quarries when his mother was pregnant and his mother had followed him to the spirits just a few months later, hanging herself from a banyan near the government tea fields; the baby could not mend her broken heart. Myat Zaw had been brought up by his miserable grandmother, and as boys he and Kyaw had played together in the forest, swum in the lakes and dived for fish. He had stayed at her house sometimes on Saturdays, when he'd eaten his one good meal of the week. When her family went to the temples, Myat Zaw went too. Thuza had watched him rage the same way that Kyaw had done at her parents' detention – as though he had lost his own family again. When her brother decided to stay with his SSA captors, Myat Zaw decided to join them too. Over time, they drifted to different divisions and Thuza had hardly seen Myat Zaw for years, but he was a commander of some sort now, far above any height that Kyaw had reached, and she always kept half an eye on his whereabouts. He'd never paid much attention to Thuza, but she knew one day she might need a favour, and a tenuous ally was better than none. Today, it had taken her an hour to find him, and almost as long to persuade him to come. In the end, it wasn't his loyalty that had swung him to help her. The promise of Bo Win was too sweet to miss.

Myat Zaw sniffed hard and stared at Thuza, then his eyes sloped away. He rocked his weight sideways, digging into his pocket, pulling out a fresh roll of betel and tucking it into the pouch of his cheek. He ground his jaw and cleared the froth from his lips with the back of his hand.

'I don't know why you didn't run, Little *Naga-ma*,' he said, without looking. 'You could have done, you know? When the officer let you out, you could have gone anywhere. You could have skipped into the forests and headed for Thailand. Disappeared. Forgotten. Never come back. Kyaw wouldn't have thought any less of you.'

Thuza bit her lip. 'I'm not doing this for Kyaw.'

'What else would you do it for?'

'I need to speak to Sayadaw U Zawtika.'

'Why didn't you go to the temple?'

She shook her head. 'There'd be too many people. Besides, you're not the first deal I've made today. The officer who released me hates the Tatmadaw as much as you do. He couldn't say, but he's ambitious and angry and wants rid of the general. It was only right I kept my promise.' She shot him a look. 'Like you should for me.'

Myat Zaw spat a streak of bright red juice into the grass and went back to his rifle, closing one eye. Thuza linked her fingers harder together, pushing them down on the cool, supple mud. There was another reason too, though she tried not to think it. Somehow, she felt the need for a witness. Around her chest was a rope that was tightening, a sense of unfinishedness that burnt as it constricted, that had looped in the jail cell and kept drawing firmer, and was stopping her breathing and wouldn't release. Since Than Chit had told her, she'd felt such confusion. There had to be a reason why Zawtika had done it. There had to be something she couldn't quite see. She needed to find him so much that her stomach hurt. He might have been captured and forced to betray her. He might have been threatened or tortured or worse. Or he might have a plan that she couldn't quite fathom, and he needed to tell her to make it all work. He might still be angry she was here with a rebel, but she'd have to tell him there'd been no other way. This was the need that had kept her from fleeing, though her head had screamed for her to run.

Across the clearing, the forest's shadows leapt. Thuza grabbed Myat Zaw's wrist and pressed her finger to her lips to quiet him, pointing at the trees as the stooped, billowy silhouette of Sayadaw U Zawtika emerged from the path. The monk stepped into the sunlight, mopping his brow on a swag of his robe and the bald arc of his damp head glistened. Relief shuddered through her. He wasn't hurt.

'Look!' she whispered.

Zawtika was moving towards the general, one hand raised to shield the sun. Unsteady on the slope and in the long grass, the old monk was resting his other hand on the arm of a soldier, a young man dressed in Tatmadaw clothes. Thuza's heart jolted. At nothing more than the sight of him, tears were heating her eyes. She wiped her nose with a rub of her palm. She hadn't expected to feel so afraid. Her relief was still pulsing but her dread was more powerful, a current beneath it that was tugging her down. She wanted to trust him – she wanted so badly – but now he was here and the general was waiting, and though he had been her friend forever, there was something about him that seemed unfamiliar, like all of his details had been softly upturned. The men met in the centre of the clearing and spoke briefly, and she watched the bewilderment as it seeped across each of their faces, and their uncertain glances at their loitering messengers, then they looked to the trees in a flittering half-panic as a gunshot resounded and the truth abruptly dawned.

Above Thuza, the cormorants bolted with a squall of shrieks and beating wings, launching into the empty oval of grey-blue sky and scattering. With his rifle smoking, Myat Zaw leapt up and stormed from his trench into the clearing, shouting, kicking dirt into Thuza's face, and she blinked and scratched her eyes as three dozen men or more spilled from the trees around her too. Her head felt giddy from the shock of the action and the suddenness of the sound, the ringing in her ears and the sprint of her breathing, and she scrambled forwards after them, dragging herself upwards and into the sun. Ahead, SSA soldiers were encircling the general, brandishing their guns and yelling furiously. Zawtika and Michael's hands shot above their heads, and the two young messengers slipped inside the ranks of their SSA men.

'I'll have you executed!' yelled the general. 'You're dead, you dogs!'

He swore and whipped his pistol from his belt, firing as the soldiers charged and bundled over him, wrestling him into the grass, forcing the gun from his fist and trussing up his flailing limbs. They stuffed his mouth with a rag and pinned it there with a strip of black tape that was pulled from a pocket, and his eyes were frantic bulging whites.

Thuza staggered down the hill, reeling. 'Sayadaw?'

Zawtika spun around. There was moment of fleeting astonishment on his face, and then he gathered up his robes and rushed forward. 'Thuza Win!' he cried. 'What are you doing here?'

Before she could stop them, the tears had burst from Thuza's eyes. She balled her hands inside her sleeves, wiping her face. 'I was scared that they'd taken you, Sayadaw,' she said. Her legs were shaking and she couldn't control it. 'I thought it was my fault. I didn't know what to do.'

Zawtika stepped closer, lowering his voice. 'I don't understand,' he hissed as a whisper. He threw up his hands. His face was pained. 'What are the rebels doing here? What am I doing here, Thuza Win?'

She drew a shuddering breath, heaving up what little strength she had left to speak. She felt exhausted. Entirely drained. 'They told me you did it, Sayadaw,' she whispered. 'You were the one who gave me up.'

Zawtika's lips pinched. 'What nonsense.'

'Why would they say that?'

'Because they're lying, cheating, bullying gangsters.'

'But why was the white boy with the general?' said Thuza. She clawed at the skin inside her elbow and stared at Zawtika. 'It doesn't make sense. And I could see it on your face when you came through the forest. You were afraid, Sayadaw, but it wasn't of the Tatmadaw. You walked right up and bowed your head.' Thuza stepped back. She was breathing heavily now, and her heart was pounding so fast that she jolted, and her words were slipping before she had formed them, tumbling from her lips before she could think them, before her mind had pieced them together, before she had realised what each of them meant. She looked up, dry-eyed suddenly.

'You did tell them, didn't you, Sayadaw?' she said, speaking slowly. 'Why else would you come when the messenger called?'

Zawtika's stare crisped. 'They threatened me, Thuza.'

She shook her head. 'No. You know the general. You have to.'

The monk straightened, shifting away. His eyes had slimmed to the finest of slits. 'It was for your own protection.'

'How could it be?'

Zawtika fired an anxious glance around the clearing. The soldiers were still consumed with their bounty and he rasped his chin and turned his back to them. He paused and tried to hoist a smile to his lips, holding out his arm to steer her awkwardly. 'This isn't the place for explanations,' he said through his lopsided grin. 'Come back to Mogok with me, Thuza Win. Please. We can discuss this in the temple – away from unfriendly ears and eyes.'

379

Thuza shook her head again, angrily this time. Her stomach felt hollow, an echoing black. 'No. I need to understand now, Sayadaw. Tell me why you did it?'

From behind the monk, Michael Atwood staggered forward. 'He was paid.'

Zawtika shook his head. 'The white boy's lying.'

'I've no reason to lie,' said Michael. 'I was there. I saw it. The general gave him money. It must have been at least five hundred kyat.'

Thuza's eyes darted between Michael and Zawtika. Michael had his head high and his eyes were holding hers, steady and firm. His skin was as pale as dusty cool ash. Zawtika's face was scowling, all wrinkles and divots. She clasped her hand to her own breathless mouth. 'You sold me. How could you?'

The monk's eyes hardened. He spat at the ground by the white boy's feet. 'This is Burma. You know that. Everyone does what they must to survive.'

'There's always a choice, Sayadaw. Was this really survival? You took money.'

Zawtika jabbed his finger towards her. She could see the rage was reddening his face. 'The facts are not entwined, Thuza Win,' he said, leaning in. She could smell tobacco smoke on his robes, overpowering the sweet scents of the temple's incense, smothering them. 'They are tied, but they are not dependent. One is not because of the other. You're too young and simple to see that. My motivation was not to harm you.'

'But you didn't care if it happened anyway?'

'I do what I have to do to serve the temple. If it isn't the

Tatmadaw after us, it's the rebels, or the meddling round-eyes . . . I'm protecting the *Sangha*. I'm securing our safety. That's more important than any one soul.'

'But I trusted you, Sayadaw. How were you protected by betraying me?'

'The day you stop selling is when someone sells you, Thuza Win. I would have talked you out, in time. I wouldn't have left you.'

'You're lying, Sayadaw. You are! Please stop. You couldn't possibly have saved me once I was taken. What did I do to you, Sayadaw? What changed? I thought we were friends.'

A gasp burst from Thuza's lungs before Zawtika could speak. *Her parents*. The realisation struck her, hard and powerful, like a fist to her chest.

Nothing had changed.

Today wasn't different.

Today was the same as everything else.

She stared into the depths of his eyes. 'What more have you lied about, Sayadaw?' she whispered. 'The letters I gave you for my parents . . . did you send them?'

The monk lifted his chin, blinking. He shook his head. 'No.'

'And the money? Did you keep it for yourself?'

'It went to the temple.'

Thuza's chest thumped again. Why today, after nine years of hoping? He could have left her dreaming. It would have been less cruel. Faintness rushed to her head and she staggered, and Michael stepped forward to support her quickly, and as she clung to his shirt and looked at his whiteness, the truth fell on top of her as crushing as rock. Around them, the SSA soldiers were curling their eyes towards their voices, muttering.

She looked up. 'Where are my parents, Sayadaw? They're not at Insein, are they? You know they're not. Michael Atwood would have found out. He'd have told me. The town would have learnt you were a liar and a thief. I was no more use to you. I was only a threat. That's why today. You needed me gone. I'm right, aren't I, Sayadaw? That's why my parents never wrote a word in return to my letters. Do you even know where they are?' She shook her head and clutched Michael tighter, staring at Zawtika. 'Tell me truthfully, Sayadaw. I can't stand any more deceit.'

The monk raised his chin higher and his nostrils flared. 'Your parents are beneath the ground, Thuza Win. They were dead the first day that the Tatmadaw came.'

Thuza let out a cry. She lunged for him. 'Liar!' she screamed, tearing at his robes and pulling him into the grass. He struggled, and she clambered onto him and struck his face, a slap that pinked his cheek instantly and stung her palm and all of her insides, and he raised his hands to try to protect himself as she howled and thrust her fists back down. Michael grabbed for her and she kicked and shrieked and sent him tripping. He scrambled up to find Myat Zaw standing, clutching Thuza's arms and together they dragged her back.

Zawtika staggered up, straightening himself. He was shaking, furiously so, and his face was a twist of shock and rage. He stepped towards her, as if to say something or strike her back, but then he shook his head and snarled, turning away.

'You can't leave!' cried Thuza, wrenching against Myat Zaw's grip.

'I can do what I like.'

'Tell me they're not dead, Sayadaw. Tell me!'

'It's the truth, Thuza Win.'

'How do you know?' She pulled again with all of her muscles and Zawtika continued to stride from her thrashing, his back to her begging, heartless and cold. She yelled at him, planting her heel into Myat Zaw's crotch, and she ripped the pistol from the knot of his belt as he cried and doubled over. She fired into the air.

Zawtika's steps stopped. His head curled back.

Thuza lowered the gun to point at his chest. Her mind was fogging. 'Answer me, Sayadaw.'

'I'll answer nothing.'

'How could you possibly, *possibly* know?'

The monk scowled, studying her, and then he squinted and began to walk away again. Before Thuza's mind had caught up with his movement, Michael had leapt and seized his arm.

Zawtika jerked against him. 'Let go of me.'

'She deserves to know.'

'It's not your concern.'

Thuza stepped forward. The sunlight glistened the gun barrel in her trembling hand. She didn't know what she meant to do next. 'Tell me, Sayadaw.'

'Be careful, Little *Naga-ma*.'

She sniffed. 'Get down.'

The old monk frowned more thickly but he didn't move, and Michael shifted behind him, wrapping his own quivering hands around Zawtika's shoulders and pushing him to his knees. Thuza's eyes met Michael's briefly, and she felt steeled by their solidness despite his throbbing ribcage, and she stepped forward again, pressing the tip of the gun to the base of Zawtika's throat. Nothing in her life had such solidness any longer, and yet for once she felt perfectly steady. Beneath the drum of blood in her head, she could hear the birds in the trees and the wind in the rushes, and somewhere a voice was speaking – perhaps Michael's – but she couldn't drag her eyes from Zawtika. Michael stepped back; she and Zawtika were alone now. She knew precisely what she needed to ask him, though the answer was clearer than spring water too. She pressed the pistol firmer to his throat, forcing it down in the soft dip of his flesh.

'Did you do it, Sayadaw?' she whispered calmly. 'The day the Tatmadaw first came to my home . . . did you send them? You found my satchel at the temple, didn't you? The map I'd left. Great-grandmother's dagger. Are you the reason my family is dead?'

Zawtika didn't answer. Instead he stared up.

Thuza rammed the pistol harder into his neck. 'Tell me, Sayadaw. You murdered them, didn't you?'

The monk's eyes closed slowly. 'You're a foolish child, Thuza Win. Don't you know that?'

His voice was dry and she felt her tears swelling, and his face started blurring behind their hot veil. She would never have thought she could feel such disappointment, or breathe beneath its crippling weight. It was as though all her years had been stacked against this moment, and the crutch that had held them had been kicked away. A flood of vomit swept up through her gullet and she felt herself gag as she squeezed the trigger, but she didn't blink as the gunshot sounded, and Zawtika toppled backwards and his blood burst over her, and from where they'd resettled, the cormorants all fled.

TWENTY-SIX

Last night in his sleep, Than had dreamt of this happening. Though he couldn't have known the new day would bring the serpent and her offer, and the details were different of course – more fluid – the most important fact was the same. He stood at the entrance to the main Lay-Bauk mineshaft, the dusky evening covering him, and pressed his handkerchief to his mouth, swallowing back his shock and the sticky saliva that was pooling and re-pooling on his tongue, feeling it trickle down his dry, wordless throat. In his chest, his heart was thrashing madly, as wild and stunned as a bird in a net. The wind had turned. The girl had done it. Thuza Win, the *Naga-ma*. His guardian spirit. She'd kept her promise. Her golden oath to him. The general was dead. His soul had fled him. Not a doctor or shaman from anywhere in Burma had enough skill or voodoo to bring him back. Now he had to do his bit.

The private at his side was shaking. 'What happened?'

Than leant forward to peer inside the railway cart, but his feet wouldn't budge from where he had planted them on the muddy earth. The rebels had chosen Lay-Bauk on purpose, clearly. There were no quarries in the district more central or prominent. It was the only one floodlit, that worked through the evenings. Bo Win had gloated about its fearsome protection. There was nowhere to humiliate the general more. Tipped off as he was, Than had been the first Tatmadaw man to arrive, of course, but now a large, clamouring crowd was gathered and his soldiers were struggling to shoo everyone away. He snatched a juddering breath and glanced to the ridge above the quarry and the line of murky silhouettes that crouched and watched with invisible eyes. There must have been a hundred workers or more, perched like vultures. His soldiers were all watching too. They were scattered about the dip of the quarry, shifting their weight and fondling the triggers of their rifles, aware that the balance of Mogok was teetering, of the storm that was swelling and threatening to drench them, but not what had caused it – not of the man who had willed it to happen – and not of which way the clouds would now turn. They made him feel anxious, like he might be discovered. Like it wouldn't take much to give him away. He shook his head at the boy and arranged his eyes to their most officious, regretful squint. 'The SSA are animals, Private.'

'They're monsters, sir. Fuck. Shall we round up suspects?'

Than clutched his handkerchief harder to his lips to hide his reaction. He nodded. 'Bring them in.'

The boy was right. This was more than a murder. In his wildest imaginings, Than had not foreseen this. It was barely half a day since he'd let free the *Naga-ma*, and it was astonishing the damage the rebels could do to a body with so much resolve yet so little time. Only a few yards away, the general was not so much laying inside the cart, as suspended above it. Each bluing limb had been lashed to a corner and the ropes pulled him tight like a pelt being dried. His shirt was gaping open. There wasn't a thread torn anywhere on it, but instead it had been carefully, calmly unbuttoned, and a clean, straight cut ran from the well of his neck to his navel, parting his flesh so precisely that it almost looked like another open shirt. The crease was still crisp in both of his sleeves. He didn't have his trousers on, but wherever they were Than felt sure they would have their creases too. They were probably with his underpants – and his testicles and penis. They were probably all bubbling in a pot of rebel stew. He forced himself forward, stumbling over the tracks as he did it and flashing his torch into the base of the cart. He wanted to escape the private and his muttered incantations, but he also knew that he had to face this. He stood on his tiptoes and his heart-rate quickened. Bo Win's spectacles were shattered on the bottom, the shards of glass on his gold and beige hat. There were also two kidneys, two lungs and a liver, a stomach, intestines and a pudgy black heart.

He snatched another sharp breath and gripped the rim of the cart. For a moment, he couldn't be sure what was pitching him; the horror of the sight, the blood or his secret, or the niggling hint of a thrill: *what next?* It was true he was dead if anyone discovered him, but there was more to this feeling than guilt or anxiety. Like a single gem in a landslip of shale, he could see the reason, buried but glittering. He couldn't deny his excitement was there. Bo Win's eyes were the sirens that called him. Their lids were slack and sleepy but open, and their whites had turned to reddish-brown. From the centre of each, a gold star was shimmering. The general's rank had been plucked from his epaulettes, placed on his pupils and forced down with a thumb until they were embedded, and the pressure had made his eye sockets leak. In the torchlight, the gold seemed to be singing, and Than had the urge to reach out and take them. To pluck them up and slip them in his pocket. To carry them home and wash and polish them. To love them dearly – because he had earned them – once Marlar had stitched them to his own starched green shirt.

This was how the Tatmadaw worked, wasn't it? For each fallen comrade, a man took his place. The longer Than stood there, the more he felt giddy. Nothing that arises ever does so by accident. No outcome is borne from anything but action. He lifted his head and looked into the mineshaft. The slope was steep and black and empty, plummeting like a cliff-edge just after the railway cart, as if ready to tip the general away. Than had caused this beauty, though he couldn't have planned it. His actions had made it inevitable and right. More than that, he was sure he deserved it. He was serving his son with an act of sweet karma. Min's spirit was watching. He had brought him this favour. Everyone knows that evil begets evil. Everyone knows that good begets good. Bo Win's death was the only fair outcome. Min would have been so proud if he'd seen him. At last, Than was poised to take his proper place.

He glanced to the hillside and the spine of grey miners, feeling a new strength in the sinews of his legs. He stuffed away his handkerchief, defiant. He was pleased they were here to see him be crowned. There wasn't much time though, if he wanted to finish this. The majors would be here soon, and the colonels and captains, but his moment of rebirth was still just beyond his fingertips, and he needed to move swiftly to pull it his way. *A strong man will move the boulders, dear Officer.* It made him smile as he remembered Daw Su's lessons. He'd found the rock that was lighter than air.

With this thought in his mind, he turned to the private, standing up straighter and jutting out his jaw. 'Bag him up,' he said, and he clapped his hands briskly. He marched away with his chest almost bursting.

The boy called after him. 'Do we need to call Rangoon, sir?'

He tipped his chin higher. 'They already know.'

TWENTY-SEVEN

'We need to be quick, Thuza Win,' Michael whispered.

He glanced back as he shoved his way through the dark, damp forest, his feet slipping on the steep, rugged slope. Through the trees, he could hear Thuza's sobs but he couldn't see her. She was slipping further and further behind. There was a clearing ahead and to the right, small but with enough moonlight breaking through the overhanging boughs to set it aglow, and he made for it, slumping forward into the oasis, his legs and lungs searing. On every side, the mountain looked the same and he threw his eyes urgently around, unsure of where to go.

'Thuza?' he called as loudly as he dared. 'Where are you?'

Thuza tore through the undergrowth and staggered into the clearing, collapsing to the ground.

Michael rubbed his face and looked around again, shaking. He stumbled to her side and wrapped his arms beneath her, trying to pull her to standing. 'Get up, Thuza Win. I don't know where we're going. You have to lead the way.'

She pushed him back. 'Leave me alone.'

'We have to get out of here. The Tatmadaw will be looking for us.'

'Let them find me.'

'What about your grandmother?'

A howl burst from Thuza and she rocked forward and buried her fingers into the earth, pained. 'The Tatmadaw took her when they arrested me. She's dead. If not now, any day. She'll have gone to Shewbo. Or to Mandalay. To the prisons. That's where they put the addicts. There won't be a doctor and there won't be judges. There wouldn't be anything a girl like me could do.'

Michael shook his head, more forcefully. 'But you can't stay here.'

Thuza's face shot up to him. Her eyes were wide and sparking water blue. 'Where can I go, Michael Atwood?' she cried. 'Don't you know what I've done? The Tatmadaw will have already found the general's body. It won't be long before they find Zawtika too.'

Michael felt a roll in his stomach and he swallowed down a surge of bile. Of course he knew what Thuza had done. They had left the monk in the forest where he fell, his body doubled back on his knees, arms splayed to the side and staring to the heavens as if he waited for rain. He hadn't died instantly, but once he had toppled, he hadn't moved either; he just lay on his back and gasped for air. Blood had leaked from his throat with the throb of his pulse, spilling sideways and soaking into his robes where they bunched at his collarbone, darkening and darkening until it disappeared. The flow of redness ebbed into bubbles, spitting like breath being blown through a straw, and his eyes had shifted as though he was furious; as though he had cursed them all until the end.

The image was scalding and Michael's stomach heaved

again. He fell to his knees and wretched, vomiting through the grass to the black mud below. 'It wasn't just you, Thuza Win,' he muttered, wiping the spittle from his mouth, trembling. 'I killed him too.'

'I pulled the trigger.'

'We could have let him go.'

Thuza spat at him. 'What for? So he could scurry back to his life at the temple, and his three fat meals of curry each day?'

'You didn't need to kill him.'

'Don't put your guilt on me, Michael Atwood. You knew what I was going to do.'

'I didn't.'

'Don't lie. You saw what was happening and you didn't move an inch to stop me. If Zawtika was robbing me, he was robbing half the town. I swear it. In the moment, you did what you knew was right.'

Michael dried his eyes, catching his breath and licking the sourness from his teeth. It was true. He had known from the instant she stole the gun. He had seen it in the steadiness of her glare, in the coolness that had settled despite her trauma, and he'd known with all clarity how her actions would end. More than that, he had willed her to do it. He had wanted her justice as though it was for him. In a way it had been – and for Sein. Zawtika was the Tatmadaw too, in his disguises. This was what made Michael feel sicker than anything; the realisation of how wrong he had been. He understood now how Burma was different. Justice could be grey and fickle here, and selfish. The earth where his feet had been rooted was pitching. *Life isn't as simple as you want to make it seem.*

He pushed himself up and turned to Thuza, sniffing. 'The Tatmadaw won't know it was us for certain,' he said, wringing his hands together. It was all he could think to say to reassure her.

Thuza shrugged. 'Whispers fly on the wind.'

The briefest flash of peace passed between them, and Michael tipped his head to the star-strewn sky. He paused, breathing deeply, and then stepped towards her, bending down and lifting her more gently, letting the weight of her body lean on his. An apology, perhaps, or an admission of complicity at least. She allowed him to guide her up and balance her.

'Please, Thuza Win,' he whispered softly. 'We need to escape. Which way do we go?'

The nearer they travelled to Thuza's home, the more she regained her pace and resolve. They didn't speak to each other, but Michael heard her whispering to herself, muttering beneath her breath what sounded like a cross between encouragement and scolding, in a clearly determined, punishing tone. By the time the house appeared in the moonlight ahead, her lungs were heaving but her shoulders were set steelily as she sprinted along the path and ripped through the door without breaking her stride.

Michael chased her inside and collapsed at the doorframe with his hands on his knees. He dried his face, breathless. The house was astonishing, utterly destroyed. From the hallway, he could see to the fireplace where they'd sat the night before, but the table and chairs had been tipped and thrown over and there were clothes on the floor that shouldn't have been there, and the bureau was smashed with its papers all emptied, and the birdcage that had hung by the window was mangled. It had fallen to the ground and was rolled against the skirting, and its bars had all been bent and snapped. Bowls, saucepans and utensils were scattered five feet from the stove, and the glass and shattered mirror shards that speckled the floorboards threw the chaos further, along the walls and over Thuza's body, making her glitter like an underwater dream.

He staggered up, looking at Thuza. Though she must already have known what the damage was – she'd been here when they'd done it – she seemed in shock to see it again. At the threshold to the living room, she had frozen, staring in. He saw a shudder throw itself across her shoulders and then her vision sunk to her feet and she picked up a tattered scarf from the floorboards and wrapped it around her pallid, injured face.

Michael gathered himself and pushed past her. He kicked aside a chair and picked up the satchel that was hidden beneath, thrusting it back at her.

'What are you doing?'

'Hold this,' he said and he dropped to his knees and sifted through the chunks of red brick, scrabbling to gather the potatoes and onions from where they were strewn amongst the wreckage of the stove. He grabbed a blouse, a *longi* and a few loose cheroots, and a pan and the matches, and shoved the bundle into Thuza's arms. 'We're going to Rangoon.'

'You don't owe me anything, Michael Atwood.'

'You have to leave Mogok and I have to get home. The

journey's too long to travel alone. It's safer with two. We need each other, Thuza.'

Thuza stared at him, grappling with her dark thoughts, and a firm, distant intent settled onto her, stiffening her shoulders and the line of her jaw in a way that gave the impression of her body turning into itself, hardening and hardening, battening down. Her eyes shadowed and her glare deepened, disconcerting him further, and he felt himself weighed; his truth and lies. She growled suddenly and looked away, dipping to the floor too and beginning to stuff the possessions that Michael had given her into the bag, and then she stood again and hurried across the room, sweeping it with her eyes, and she crammed her pockets with an apple and some soap.

'OK,' she muttered, carefully at first but then again, quick and hard as if to whip herself. 'We have to hurry. As soon as they find the general, they'll start rounding up suspects in the town. They'll come for me soon. They always do. We'll stay off the roads. I know my way to Lashio. There are men there who can help us. Gem dealers. I've sold to them before. We'll have to chance our luck getting through the town, but they'll know the smuggler routes to Rangoon.' She paused and then rammed another bundle into the satchel and pulled a little roll of money from behind the buttons of her blouse. She brandished it at Michael, wild-eyed. 'We can use this. The officer returned some of my savings when he released me. I don't have much, but there's enough to buy the smugglers' maps. They'll tell us which ways are safest to go.'

Thuza's expression tightened and her eyes shot beyond Michael. Michael turned, following her line of sight through the window. There was a noise — a voice and then another. They were almost imperceptible and he mightn't have heard them if Thuza hadn't alerted him, but then the boots started stamping, and there were shadows of movement at the brink of the treeline in the deepening dusk.

'They're here!' Thuza hissed at him, teeth bared.

She grabbed his arm and pulled him down, and as he thudded to the floor beneath the window, a scream of panic in his head, he caught sight of the men as they emerged through the trees. There must have been ten of them. More even. Armed. Even though he'd known they'd be looking for them both since Thuza went missing from the jailhouse and he'd disappeared on a whim with Bo Win, this was still so much quicker than he'd even dared to dread they would be. He looked to Thuza, wanting her to say that his vision had tricked him, but she was scrabbling away, grabbing her satchel and dragging it with her, pressing herself low and crawling across the room. At the fireplace, she threw the rug aside and Michael scrambled to his knees and hurried after her, watching as she turned out her pockets and rammed a key into a tiny trapdoor lock.

'Get in' she cried, throwing the door open.

Michael clambered inside the pit and Thuza pushed after him, shoving him down before he found his feet. He tried to shift from under her as she whipped the rug back over the evidence and wrenched the hatch shut. The darkness gripped him instantly. He could hear what sounded like the lock being re-turned and the shriek of his breathing, and then Thuza struggled over him, her limbs in his face. He lifted himself up and his head hit the roof with a hard, solid thump, and he felt the cold, damp earth sloping beneath him and curving around him where his hands were groping to find his balance. A shaft of thin yellow light flickered and he blinked and saw Thuza ahead of him, crawling along a narrow tunnel. The light settled and she turned back and beckoned to him, a torch between her teeth. Michael squinted and fumbled towards her, feeling his way down the shallow slope. The air was cold, soggy and stale, and there was a smell like fire that sat below the mud. From the house, two gunshots sounded. He ducked instinctively, and there was a pause and then another, and then there was shouting, feet running and pacing, men throwing their weight and crashing around.

They scrambled away from the noise, Michael following Thuza deeper into the tunnels until she stopped and collapsed against the wall. She dropped the torch and her cheekbones shimmered.

Michael edged towards her, his heart thrashing. Above them, the shouting continued, muffled but fierce. He looked at her. Her sleeves were sodden and blood was running down her arms. 'Thuza!' he whispered. 'You're dripping.'

Thuza looked down and flicked her head, shaking. 'There was glass by the trapdoor. On the floor. It doesn't matter.'

'It's in your skin, Thuza. I can see it.'

'I'm fine.'

He picked up the torch and reached out to touch her but she recoiled and dug her palms into her armpits, scowling. 'Stop it, Michael Atwood,' she said. Her voice quivered, angry. 'You don't have to help me. I can't stand your guilt.'

She squeezed closed her eyes and two thick tears fell from their corners. Michael put down the torch and shrank away too, staring at his own hands, embarrassed.

'You knew I'd lied to you,' he said. 'Didn't you? About getting my father to ask after your parents. You knew I wasn't going to do it.'

Thuza drew her legs to her chest, binding her arms tighter around her folded body, drying her eyes on the curve of her knees. She didn't look at him. 'Not when you first said it.'

'But later?'

She nodded.

'Why did you keep helping me?'

She drew in a long breath, shrugging. 'I took a chance,' she said. 'I wanted to be wrong. Besides, you needed it, and there are different types of tricks. I've lived enough years and met enough men to know the difference. Your lies weren't proper ones. They just sat on your surface. They didn't go deep. Some people have lies that go all the way to their middle bits.'

Michael paused. 'Like Zawtika?'

'I suppose so.'

'But you never saw it.'

'I never looked. I never thought I had to.'

From the house, there was a shout and a gunshot, and the sound of fragmenting, falling wood. Thuza winced and buried her head in the crook of her arm.

'They'll bring down this house if they have to,' she whispered. 'My family's history will end on my watch. My great-grandmother started digging these tunnels – when her white man went home. My grandparents made them longer and my parents did the same. I only came down because I had to. I needed money for food and Nanna's medicine, and to give to Zawtika and keep Kyaw quiet, but there's hardly anything left that's worth selling now. This house is everything I have of my family, a home for their spirits as much as my memories, but I've picked our rotten carcass dry.'

A new tear slipped out and Thuza left it to trace the ridge of her cheekbone.

'I was going to dig a new tunnel and not tell Kyaw,' she said. She waved her hand along the passageway, into the dark. 'This way. Towards Spider Mountain. The government were there last summer, assessing the land. They said it was better than any site Mogok had ever seen before, so I thought if I dug towards it, I might be able to pinch a few rubies from its edges too. I could use them to get to Rangoon quicker. I hadn't found a moment to start doing it though. It was something I said I'd do one day, when Kyaw and Nanna were gone. I knew I wouldn't have to wait for long. I was impatient though, Michael Atwood. I've done things for the Tatmadaw as sinful as the rebels have in the name of desperate cash.' She curled her eyes to the earth. Ashamed, perhaps. 'I've never told anyone about these tunnels,' she said. 'Not even Zawtika. Nobody outside my family knows.'

Michael scratched at the dirt with his fingernails. It would have taken Thuza a hundred years to dig a new tunnel. 'I won't tell anyone,' he said, and he tried to force a smile.

She glanced at him briefly with the same detached, resolute stare that told him nothing of what she thought. He reached into his pocket and pulled out the pieces of paper he had stashed there, unfolding them, smoothing their creases. He passed them to Thuza.

'What's this?'

'I'm not sure,' he replied. 'They might be rebel profiles, or debriefs from prisoners arrested at the camp. Something like that. I took them from the general. I saw the name Kyaw and I picked them up. I thought that if the Tatmadaw didn't have your brother's name on their files, you and your family might have been a little safer. I don't suppose it matters now, but you should have them anyway.'

Thuza looked through the pages slowly, tears glinting newly in her eyes. She hesitated. 'Thank you.'

Michael paused too, then rummaged in his pocket again and passed her the last piece of paper. 'I took this as well. It has the Thai's name on it. Can you tell me what it is?'

Thuza took the sheet from him picked up the torch. 'It looks like the transcript of an interrogation,' she said, reading. 'They must have picked him up from the camp. Alive. He wasn't killed. The Tatmadaw are calling him a traitor. A duplicitous spy.'

Michael exhaled into his lap. It was a breathy laugh almost, a gasp of relief.

Thuza held it out to him, staring. 'Why does it matter?'

He shook his head and tucked the paper back into his pocket. 'I was right,' he muttered. He hardly believed his luck. Possibilities flooded through him. 'The bomb that hurt my friend was planted by the Tatmadaw, not the rebels. This is all the evidence I need to show that the Tatmadaw have been arranging strikes against their own people – if not the bomb I saw directly, then others at least. My government can do something maybe. Tell the world. I'd never have managed to find it without you. You gave me his name, Thuza Win. Thank you.'

Thuza nodded. 'I hope it helps your friend.'

He hesitated, looking at the ground. 'Thuza, are you sure you want to do this?'

'Do what?'

'Leave.'

She shook her head, frowning. Minutes seemed to pass before her thoughts became words. 'There's nothing in Mogok for me now.'

'What about your grandmother? There might be a chance for her. Something we can do.'

'There isn't, Michael Atwood. I'm an outlaw, remember.'

'What will you do in Rangoon?'

She shrugged, unable to meet his eye. Her voice sounded thin, beaten perhaps. Unconvincing. 'I don't know, but I'll blend in a little better there. I'll find a job. Save what I can and then travel to Thailand maybe. I don't want to stay in Burma any more. I love my home – no less than my parents or Kyaw – but I just don't know how to make her work.'

Michael shuffled forward, dipping his head to her. 'If all you want to do is go to Thailand, I can help you. I can buy you a plane ticket.'

Thuza's lips tensed. He couldn't tell if she was angry. 'I don't want your pity.'

'It's not pity, Thuza.'

'Your charity then. I don't want to be in your debt. I don't want to be in anyone's debt, Michael Atwood.'

'I could help you get a job though, couldn't I? Perhaps even at the embassy. That's not charity. Let me do that, Thuza. Please?'

Thuza laughed. 'What can a serpent do at the British Embassy?'

'What are you good at?'

She grinned. 'Mining. Thieving. Poaching.'

Michael let go a grin too, at his lap. He left it there and it hung in the silence until it started aching, and he felt it wane and fizzle out. 'I'm sorry, Thuza,' he whispered. He rubbed his face. He felt exhausted. 'I'm sorry for lying to you and for judging you, and I'm sorry about Zawtika and your grandmother and Kyaw and your parents. I'm so sorry for them all.'

Thuza rested her head on her knees, looking at him, still unsettling and unfathomable and she wriggled a hand out from where she had hidden it and brushed the strands of hair from her face. He thought he saw the slightest trace of warmth lingering in her eyes. 'You know,' she said, 'in a way, I feel different, knowing they're gone. I mean – I feel happy. Perhaps I shouldn't. I don't know. Of course I wish my family were alive and that not a day of the past nine years had happened, but since they've been taken, I've had such a weight on me, Michael Atwood. I can't explain it. Sometimes I felt like I was buried in sand. Everything I did – every moment of every day – it was all for them. Looking after my Nanna, and taking Kyaw's lashings. Lying, smuggling, stealing. They were all tiny grains, but heavy, each of them piling on me, one by one. I didn't want to do these things, but I had to, because I thought if I did them the world might change. It's strange, knowing that I can't fix anything now, so I don't need to try. I feel lighter. That's why I want to leave. The tide has washed me out. It's cleaned me. I want to see how far I can float.'

Michael stared at her, deep into her bright blue eyes. 'Are you lonely, Thuza Win?'

She closed her eyes. 'I'm tired.'

He paused again, biting the skin from the rim of his finger-nail. 'For being different, I mean,' he mumbled.

She shook her head. 'I don't want to be like them.'

Michael took a long, hard breath. He had always been different in England – always distant – but Thuza had found the words that he'd struggled for. It was not being lonely. It was just being lost. That was why he had clung so tight to Burma when he came here. It was the chance for a purpose so much richer than was plotted before him: of London and office blocks, and living for paycheques and Fridays and piss-ups. He understood now though, and he felt lighter also. The last few days had unclogged his mind. Perspective, perhaps, his father would have called it. He wouldn't go back there. Not now. It wouldn't matter. Whatever came next, he'd make a change.

Without thinking, he moved his hand across the floor, finding Thuza's, and he lifted her fingers and turned up her palm. She let him hold her this time, gently. He rested her hand on his thigh and took the torch, shining it downwards, examining her and pulling the large, dirty dagger of glass from her swollen flesh, fumbling with its slipperiness, feeling her flinch but then ease back. He ripped a strip of material from the hem of his shirt, binding her up and knotting it firmly, and then he linked his fingers through hers and waited.

Above them, it was silent. The house had fallen still.

'How long shall we stay here?' he said, looking at her fingertips where they rested on his knuckles.

'A little while longer.'

She turned away and placed her head back onto her knees, and Michael felt her hand holding back. The dark, the calm and the quiet were soothing. For a moment in the turmoil, they had both felt safety. Neither of them wanted to ruin the peace.

'Michael Atwood!'

Michael groaned as he woke. He shifted, turning towards the voice and feeling at once that his joints had seized. His left leg and side were numb, the full weight of him having settled through the bone of his hip and bedded him into the freezing earth. The air was thin and his head was groggy, still mired in the thickness of his sleep, and he prized his eyes open and blinked them into focus. Thuza was a few yards away along the tunnel in the direction of the house. A weak grey radiance was framing her and she looked as though she was crawling back down.

Michael dragged himself to his knees. 'What time is it?'

'I don't know,' she whispered. 'It must be after midnight. The house is empty. We need to leave.'

She beckoned to him, and he watched as she shuffled backwards and hauled herself up through the ceiling's trapdoor.

Outside, the stars were luminous. A fat, low, mottled moon

sat above the treetops amongst them, lilac almost and peering down, so crisp and close that it made Michael cower, as if at any new moment she might swing and strike him, as if the breeze alone might cause her fall. In her glow and against the vastness of the sky, and after the solid, airless embrace of the tunnel, he felt exposed and reckless and woozy. He was glad for the darkness and the denseness of the trees.

They moved through the forest and Thuza gripped his hand, though he couldn't see her. She was a spirit ahead of him, guiding his way. Like wicker, her fingers linked through his as she led him over the hard, raised ridges of roots and the ankle-turning sunken divots, and she pulled him deftly through the barbs of the thorn trees and then he felt the brush of thick, velvety grass on his ankles instead. Beneath his feet, the dead leaves were crumbling. The wind was hissing between the branches and the insects creaked, scratched and clawed. Somewhere, a fox howled like a crying baby and there was the shrill call of an agitated bird. He couldn't measure how far they had travelled by the minutes or the miles, only by the pounding of the blood in his temples and the strain of his vision as he staggered after Thuza, following her blindly with his stumbling steps.

Soon they would reach the highway to Lashio, and at least the tracks would be smoother and straight. It was one hundred and fifty miles to the city, Thuza had told him. They would stay in the forest and trace the road's edge by foot until they were far enough from Mogok town, and then there were bound to be a few rest stops that they could hide at and where they could steal soup, and they'd wait for a truck to pull over for water then stow away in its wheat or its maize. They'd look for the ones that might smuggle poppies, with linen sacks nestled between vast golden bales. Those drivers paid their way through the checkpoints. Only the honest ones stopped to be searched. Give or take, they'd be there in a day. It was details like this that Michael clung to for comfort. He felt relieved to be travelling with Thuza. He wouldn't have known these things alone.

Ahead, Thuza's grip tightened. She stopped abruptly and stepped nearer to him, so much so that he saw her outline harden against the shadows, and she tilted her head to the side, listening. Michael stopped behind her, his heart drumming. He had heard it too. Somewhere close, an engine had fired. She turned to him and pressed her hand to his mouth, warning for his silence with her eyes in the moonlight, and then she pointed away, down the slope of the hill. She stooped and he copied her, creeping beside her for a stretch, and the sound of the idling vehicle became louder, and as the trees thinned, he saw the lights. They were stationary, two broad strips of yellow, headlights streaked along the peppery concrete.

She pressed her fingers to her own lips and glared at him again, then edged forward, her vision raking in front of her, urgently but carefully, trailing him with her.

Michael's stare skittered along the road. There were buildings, black in their slumber but at least four or five of them, standing in a row on the opposite edge.

'We need to turn back, Thuza,' he said, tugging against her.

'*Shhhh.*'

'We haven't left Mogok. Someone will see us.'

He felt her pace quicken.

'Thuza? Where are you going?'

He tugged again, sharper, and she spun back and grabbed his shirt with her both her hands, yanking him suddenly – surprisingly strongly – and he tripped in the dark where the bank harshly steepened, tumbling them both through the last of the trees. He landed over her, hearing her yelp and striking his shoulders and skull on the hard ground. She bucked beneath him, shoving him aside, and in the brightness of the headlights, Michael rolled away from her, squinting. The pain in his head blurred his sight. It was bigger than a car on the road in the distance, but not as big as a truck or a van. A jeep. He lifted himself to his knees and looked at it, struggling to clear his vision and mind. It was beside a checkpoint. There was a booth and a barrier. Signposts. Threats. Above them, a rope was slung across the street and strung with charms of guns and knives. There were two boys with rifles and bored expressions, sitting slouched back with their feet on the sandbags. Soldiers! He willed his stare to harden, panicking. They hadn't moved. They hadn't seen them. He looked at Thuza, feeling dizzy. She was scrambling up with unsteady steps.

'Get down, Thuza!'

Michael staggered up too, just enough to swipe for her, to pull her towards him and keep her still, but she pushed him away, harder than she needed to, flattening her palms in his face and slapping him.

'Let go of me, Michael Atwood,' she cried, fighting him.

He lunged at her a second time, trying to drag her to the shelter of the trees, but she dodged him and snarled like a tiger, pounding his stomach with a thrust of her knee. He stumbled back. His head was spinning. The engine cut and the jeep's door opened. Michael plunged to the tarmac. Thuza held up her hands.

'Officer Than Chit,' she called. Her voice was breaking. 'Where's my Nanna?'

An officer stepped from the jeep and started towards them, fully uniformed, stealing nervous glances into the forest and pulling his jacket tighter around his body. Michael glanced too, thrown by the panic and confusion in his head. To one side, the trees were dark and rustling. At the other, the windows on the buildings were still shuttered up. His heart thundering in his ears, he watched the officer toss a nod to the checkpoint boys and they gathered their hats and rifles and slunk inside the booth, closing the door. Their faces turned blue in the crude electric light and he heard a radio crackle to life and the soft, high warbling of a woman's song seeped through the Perspex. Thuza Win was walking along the road unsteadily. She looked like a spirit, miniature and blazing, staggering the line of the headlamps' light.

The officer squinted, raising his hand at her advance. 'Where's the white boy?'

She turned and pointed to Michael where he lay on the road. His heart skipped. He watched the officer's hand twitch to his holster and clutch the barrel of his waiting gun. With his other hand, he rooted clumsily inside his breast pocket and pulled out a wad of money.

Keeping her distance, Thuza snatched it. 'Where is she?' she hissed, backing away.

'She's at a clinic outside Shwebo,' he replied. He glanced again along the street. 'They'd already taken her to the jailhouse by the time I asked questions, but she wasn't there long. My wife's cousin runs the clinic. He's an honest man. She's being looked after.'

'I want her home.'

'Tomorrow. I'll drive and collect her personally. I'll bring her to you.'

'Do you swear it?'

He nodded.

Thuza's glare thinned and she held the officer's stare as she dipped her head, then at last she let go of his eyes and riffled through the money he'd given her, checking it. Michael staggered up as she stuffed it into her satchel.

'What have you done, Thuza Win?' he cried, stumbling toward them.

The officer seized his gun from his waist, aiming it. Michael halted, his palms up and head spinning. Thuza stared at him for a moment and her nose wrinkled slightly, then she looked at her hands, re-buttoning her bag.

'I'm sorry, Michael Atwood,' she muttered, fumbling with the straps.

'Sorry for what?' he said, angry. 'For selling me? Did you do this because I lied to you?'

'I did this because I had to, Michael Atwood,' said Thuza. A hint of bitterness was crisping her tone. 'It's nothing to do with you. The Tatmadaw will take you back to Rangoon. You'll go home. You'll be safe. That's what you wanted, isn't it?'

'I wanted to help you.'

'You are helping me.'

'Not like this.'

Thuza was still grappling with the fastenings on her satchel, but her fingers were shaking and she couldn't do them up. 'What difference does it make to you?' she cried, wrenching the bag from her neck and throwing it to the ground, lunging at him. She was crying suddenly. Big glistening tears. 'Nothing, Michael Atwood,' she shrieked, striking him. 'Nothing! Tomorrow your life will be just as before.'

He ducked, grabbing for her wrists.

'I need this, Michael Atwood,' she sobbed. 'I need life to be different. I can't live another cold day of the same.'

'It was going to be different, wasn't it? What about Thailand?'

'I lied about Thailand. I needed to get out of jail, Michael Atwood. I wanted to face Zawtika for myself and confront him, and I'd planned so long and worked so hard and risked so much to get to Rangoon and rescue my parents that I couldn't just trust you do it for me. I was going to find them. Set them free. I had to make a deal, Michael Atwood. You were the only bait that I had. Now that I know my parents are dead, how could ever I leave Burma, my home? I'd be no one. It's my blood. And Nanna! Who else does she have? Who else do *I* have, Michael Atwood?'

'But it's dangerous in Mogok. You said yourself. The things you've done . . . You can't stay.'

'Officer Than Chit will protect me. He's promised.'

'And you believe him?'

'Yes.'

'How can you trust him, Thuza? He's pointing a gun at us.'

'At you, Michael Atwood. He's pointing it at *you*.'

Thuza yanked her body free from Michael's grasp and threw herself back from him, scowling, straightening her clothes with a shrug of her arms. She smeared her streaming nose and wet cheeks on her sleeve, and her chest was heaving beneath her torn blouse. She glanced at the officer for the briefest instant and the hairs on the back of Michael's neck started needling.

'I've no choices, Michael Atwood.' She cried as though she begged him. 'I thought I did, but I've never had choices. You have to see.'

Michael tripped back and rubbed his face, exhaling. He dropped his head. 'You could have run.'

The officer took a cautious step towards them. 'Listen,' he said, raising his hand to the white boy and ducking in a brief bow. 'I'll look after her. On my son's doomed soul and my own wretched karma, I swear it. I've already secured my new position with Rangoon, thanks to you. It's done. Everything's done. There's a driver waiting at my headquarters to take you to the Mandalay airfield. You'll be on the plane before the sun comes up, and the moment you touch down, Mogok is my district. For as long as Thuza lives here, she won't be troubled. No Tatmadaw man will knock at her door.'

He took another slim step forward and nodded to the boy, smiling nervously, then he lowered his gun and tucked it away. He pointed to his jeep by the blue-glowing checkpoint and Michael sniffed and scratched his nose.

'After all the Tatmadaw's done to you,' he whispered,

staring at Thuza. He shook his head. His insides felt empty. 'And to your family . . . ? I'm afraid for you, Thuza. I hope that you're right.'

Thuza straightened her back as if standing to attention, and she tipped up her chin and widened her eyes. She drew her cheeks softly inwards, breathing deeply, steadying herself, and her stare wandered past him and sloped gently upwards, to the row of little carvings that were tangled together and swinging like vine threads. To the single, hardwood, stub-handled dagger. To the shimmering blade of a thin silver knife. Michael turned to see it too as it rocked with the wind's gust, flashing in the moonlight like liquid wishes, and then as quick as a snake, Thuza darted for her satchel. She looped it round her shoulder and started striding to the forest.

'I'm not going to bury my head, Michael Atwood.' She threw her hands to the sky as she left them. 'I don't want to hide in the mud and the darkness. Survival comes first and tomorrow comes second, but who would I be if I lost my hope?'

Michael stood, watching her body as it shrank into the distance and her colours melted to grey, then looking back up at the charms, heart racing. Sein had once told him that hope was a tonic. *All regimes will eventually fall.* He sunk his hands to the bottom of his pockets and clenched his fists, his eyes on the ground. A smile was spreading on his lips. He could feel it. It was light as a breath, the faintest shiver of relief. The officer was speaking to the soldiers at the checkpoint, and he finished with a last, curt nod and then opened the jeep's passenger door. He waved to Michael and walked to the driver's seat, ducking inside. Michael paused, looking back at Thuza's shadow, and then there was a rumble of sound – the engine starting – and he held his breath and clambered onto the bonnet, and the metal bowed as he ripped down her dagger, then he jumped to the ground and ran towards the treeline. He had wanted to help her, to free what she needed.

'Thuza!' he shouted into the dark of the dogleg, but the trees were shivering and the serpent was gone.

EPILOGUE

Than stood at the mirror in his kitchen and turned his face to the thin dawn light. He tilted his head and stuck out his jawbone, running his hand across his skin and checking for any stray prickles that his razor might have missed. His scissors were sitting on the dresser and he picked them up and snipped a strand of unruly hair from one pepper-grey sideburn, then leaned in and squinted with a thick-set frown. Jaw still raised, he smoothed his tongue slowly across his teeth and clipped again at a wiry black nose hair. The itch was sudden and his shoulders shuddered, but he sniffed it away and scratched at his nostril, then he plucked up his hat, tucked it on his head and levelled the brim so it sat precisely straight.

He took a step back for a wider impression and tried to feel pleased with how smart he'd become. His uniform still looked like a flawless new outfit, perfectly fitting and crisply pressed. The stars on each of his epaulettes shone like gems. Today was a day it was worth looking smart for, he knew with a flicker of anxiety in his gut. The generals were visiting Mogok from Rangoon. They were due to arrive in just a few hours and their plane was probably already setting down on the Mandalay airstrip. He riffled in his trinket box for his favourite gold cufflinks, threading them into the holes in his sleeves and muttering to himself that being tired was for women, but beneath his eyes were deep purple crescents. For another night, he had not slept well. It was the first time that the generals had come to the district since he'd been awarded his promotion, and the month that had passed since he'd known they were coming was almost more tense than his battered heart could bear.

After more than twelve months of Than being in charge, Mogok was still in shock at his appointment. Shock was not enough to prevent things from moving, however, and for once Rangoon were as good as their word. As soon as the white boy had arrived in the capital, Than had received a telegram to say it was official. His papers were signed and the deal was done. Oh, it made him burn as he thought it. He worried then as he worried now that the *Naga-ma* had found a way to trick him, that at any new instant his life may come toppling down, but instead she had done every deed that she'd promised. When he'd telephoned Rangoon after leaving the quarry, he'd made certain to let them know exactly how incompetent their former general had been to let the white boy slip through his fingers. But they needn't have worried, he said with his chest puffed. Than Chit had already captured him back. If Thuza had deserted him, Than would have been a dead man, yet there she had been: a spirit indeed. Perhaps that was why he felt so nervous. This new unknown was still stretching ahead. The days that led to his meeting with her had streaked past his vision, but this was his doing as much as it was Thuza's. When the girl had begged for his mercy at the jailhouse, the glitter of her offer had blinded him, almost. On another day, on a

morning when the sun had risen more warmly and his mind
had turned freely, he would have glanced away, but fate – that
day – was what kept him staring. The spark in her eye was as
though she had known him. It was just like Daw Su, the old
soothsayer, said. *Commit to the path you have chosen, Officer. Do
what's required. Be brave and focused. Winning will follow if the spirits
deem it right.*

There were more days than not when Than didn't feel sure
that he really had won. There was still fighting in the mountains, and as many thieves, landmines and ambushes as in Bo
Win's era. No worse perhaps, but no better for sure. He had
to show Rangoon that their trust wasn't wasted, but being
inside was more strain than he'd anticipated. He was always
wary of the men around him, above, below and on every shadowed side. Loyalty is fickle and power is finite. It's not for
sharing, Daw Su had also told him. The image of Bo Win's
spilled innards never retreated far from his consciousness, and
he could never shake the feeling that he walked along a knife-
blade. It hurt his head as he tried to find the balance. Keeping
the town from slipping to the rebels. Making men afraid to
screw him over. Keeping them happy so they didn't feel the
need.

He levelled his hat in the mirror again, feeling his heart thud
a beat in his chest. Today at least the mountains were quiet.
He hoped it would stay that way. Though he'd kept his guests
as secret as he could manage, whispers leaked like water and
the rebels still might know. No amount of mythical captured
insurgents would undo the carnage of an SSA attack. At least
he didn't have to lie about the rubies. The new shafts at Spider

Mountain were delivering gemstones as red as August sunsets. They were fatter and more lucid than beads of monsoon rain. When the Ministry of Mines had first started digging, Than had taken a huge, brilliant ruby and set it in silver as a gift for his wife. He still wasn't sure what had nudged him to do it. A peace offering, perhaps, or a clumsy apology. Of course, Marlar had refused to wear the ring, but he kept it with his cufflinks and one day she might feel different. One day if he was lucky, she might bring his children back.

He hadn't expected to miss her when she left. He had thought he'd miss the boys and Khine and May, but she was the one he had found a surprise. It was ten months and four days since his family had gone to the city, and he still found the house an echoing cave. Regardless, he was glad he had let them go. They were safe in Rangoon. Marlar's sister's flat was roomy, and he sent money each month for their schooling and clothes. In his letter, Po Chit said they ate beef and fresh fish almost daily. At his own lonely suppers, Than's stomach might have ached from the grief that stopped him eating, and he knew in his heart that they might never truly love him, but if nothing else he had earned the finest sliver of respect. He saw it now; their lives were different from how his was. They had always been different, and he was different too for knowing it. He had thought that the Tatmadaw was the only way for all of them, and the only way for Burma to exist in the world. Now he saw how the chains were binding. Though he knew he'd never sever them – as much as anything, he deserved them – he could cut them for his children. It was right to set them free.

He rubbed at his nose again and glanced from the mirror,

and his eyes slipped up to the photograph on the shelf. Min was wearing his own spotless uniform. He was standing as tall as he could and saluting, as proud as the lion that had marked his day of birth. Than had left his figurines and the picture of Aung San beside the one of Min, but his son was bigger. More important. Real. It was taken on the afternoon he'd enlisted, and despite it all, Than felt proud too. They had travelled here together, whatever the stars said, and their souls would meet in another new life. Than was working on his merit to ensure it would happen. He had promised the Sangha a year of his wages and they were building a temple on the old Lay-Bauk ridge. It wouldn't be as big as some others in the hilltops, but he'd make it the grandest, most beautiful and regal. It was a palace for Min – a dedication to his promise – to rebuild both their karma and help them find peace. Perhaps this was really why Than stayed in the valley, despite his worries and his absent kin. As much as he longed to be a part of their futures, he missed Min more, with all his heart. Even if it weren't for his debt to the Tatmadaw – even if he were freer than the highest soaring eagle – he couldn't have left the Mogok hills. This was his rightful place and he knew it. Solitude, fear and threats were his penance. Whatever happened with his comrades or the rebels or the townsfolk, he would stay with his boy until his own gloomy end. He closed his eyes and begged an entreaty to the spirits and his karma, then snapped to attention and saluted the photo, spun on his boot-heels and marched from the room.

*

Michael shot a look down the heaving Hong Kong road, first left towards the hum of the distant evening market then right through the neon glow of Kowloon. The motorbikes were streaking in both directions, pummelling their horns as they weaved between the Mercedes and Peugeots with swift, slanting wheels. Dusk was starting to settle over the city, a smoke of it rolling thickly down the high-rise towers. Rows of jumbled Cantonese hoardings buzzed against the greyness, blazing blue and pink in the speckled, dimming light. The reek of diesel seeped out from the bikes that had cut their engines and parked in the alleyways, but the food at the booths that lined the main drag smelt delicious, dim sum and bean curd and pungent fried fish.

He licked his lips and skipped quickly forward, following a group of schoolchildren as they trotted over the busy crossing, the girls linked at their elbows as they chattered and laughed. There was the sound of sizzling fat ahead of him, spitting grease from the eateries that made his mouth water, and high-pitched pop songs that blared from TVs. As he passed each hotel reception, a blast of cold air on his skin made him shiver, before the broiling heat gripped back. Every shop overflowed with people. There were clothes stores, cobblers and a hawker selling beepers. And then there were the jewellers. There must have been thousands. In Kowloon alone, there might have been a hundred, with their gold, jade and gems in the window. He dipped down a side street and caught himself rushing. He felt such drive and energy at being back here. How different it was from the hush of Rangoon.

Not that the wonder of that hush would ever leave him, with

its secrets and promises and desires and hopes. When the aeroplane had sped along Rangoon's potted runway this time, a slight, cool regret had prickled on his forearms and he'd wished he had stayed for more than one week. As the wheels lifted and he was carried into the cloudless air, Michael had unlatched the clip of his seatbelt and leaned to the window, peering out, watching the shrinking buildings and the rivers as they stretched into thin silver twine, and the vast, soaring peak of Shwedagon Pagoda was so brightly lit that its goldness seemed to rise above its tip and edges, reaching up to the warm purple sky. Long after the land had flattened to sparkling paddies, its radiance left a trace in the darkening night. He couldn't help thinking how special it would have been to have shared the view with Thuza, or at least have seen her in the time he had spent there, but he knew it wasn't possible and he hadn't tried to push it. Maybe next time he'd think of a way that was safe.

Bittersweet Burma, such contradictions, where beauty and risk were so neatly aligned. To arrive and to leave each held their weight. When the Tatmadaw had delivered Michael to his father, the ambassador's anger was matched only by his relief. A string of demands had already been made and agreed in principle for Michael's safe return, but the details of the goodwill negotiations were still being finalised when Michael and his parents had gone to visit Sein the same afternoon. His friend was awake, his bruises fading and the huge scar on his cheek that curved like a sickle bulbous and red as it melded together. Most of all, Sein was groggy but cheerful – the only way he knew how to be. Michael had presented the transcript of the Thai's interrogation to them all with pride, recounting his story and showing them the evidence of the Tatmadaw's guilt clearly printed in black ink, indisputable. Though his father was wary, they had all been steaming hot with elation and details were left like mosquitos at the windows; butting and twitching and never let in.

It was in a telephone conversation at the embassy later that evening that the ambassador mentioned the transcript's existence to the Tatmadaw. At that moment, all goodwill fled. The deal that ended up being struck was at best a shady one, but it was *Even Stevens*, his father had said. To Michael's disappointment, the ambassador had been forced to keep quiet about the Thai. The Tatmadaw didn't give two shits what the world thought they had done or not done and, in truth, the world was indifferent too. To out them was more than pointless; it was foolish. The Brits would be expelled. They'd be exiled and useless. At least from the inside they could chip at the edges. They knew Michael knew now, and that was some slight leverage. They wouldn't want the hassle of denying to their people or cleaning up protests. It still made Michael sad, but he'd resigned himself now to Burma's realities. He had been naïve, but he wouldn't be again, and what could he do? His father was right.

His stomach knotted at the thought of it, his anger as fierce as the moment he'd first felt it, and he turned down an alley and quickened his step, glancing at his watch. If these were the rules of Burma's game, he would play them. He would roll his own dice and count the spots. He had told his parents he would spend the year travelling, getting over his ordeal and riding his savings before settling back to a London life. Happily, they had bundled him on a plane, nervous of what his ire could amount to if left unchecked in Burma, but he'd known from the start what he intended to do.

He squinted ahead at the Blue Falcon jewellers, with its door propped open and the big, flashy sign. Inside, a handful of customers were milling around and he slipped through the doorway and browsed beside them, the hairs on his arms prickling in the cool, air-conditioned air. From the back wall, the proprietor nodded a greeting. He waited for the last shopper to leave, then walked to the front of the shop and locked the door.

'So what do you have for me this time?' he whispered.

Michael pulled the drawstring pouch that Sein had given him just a day earlier from his pocket. It was navy-blue velvet, heavy and full. He unknotted the strings and tipped the contents onto the counter. A slick of red rubies spilled out on the glass.

Thuza sat in her chair by the window, a little limp bird resting back in her hand. The candle was flickering with the breeze and she bent closer to the light and strained her vision, slipping the thread through the needle's eye. She had fixed the broken panes now, but she'd become so used to the sounds and movements of the forest that she liked to keep them open still. It was dusk and the mountains were starting to settle into their rhythms of slumber, closing around her, and though she felt relieved for how the dark hid her, her heart kept her senses sparked to alert. Her needle readied, she sat up straighter and started to stitch the bird's sleek feathers, and a fresh sense of purpose made her fingers work quickly. The sparrowhawk was dense and his stomach was bloated. Stuffed full with rubies, he would buy her escape.

A swirl of wind rustled the leaves and Thuza shuddered and drew her candle nearer, tugging the bird's eyelid gently closed, then coiling the thread around her finger and snapping it before licking the frayed end and re-lacing the needle, moving briskly to stitch up his other vacant eye. It had taken six months of blistered knees and bleeding fingers to dig her new tunnel. Though she'd bought better tools with the money Than Chit returned to her, the work remained tough and she had lost count of the number of cold, damp nights she had spent carefully planning where her burrowing would take her, then chipping away her precarious route. Not that it mattered now. Every moment of effort had been worth it when at last she saw that the rumours were true. The gems at the base of Spider Mountain were bigger, brighter and more plentiful than anything she had ever known to come from beneath her home before.

She peered through the window again, feeling nervous. The graves she had dug were guarding the twilight. There were four of them at the treeline, neat mounds of earth topped with white and red flowers, though only one had a body beneath. The officer had been as good as his promise and returned her nanna safely, though the brittle old soul did not then last long. Thuza had buried her with a ruby in her fingertips. She had buried a stone in the other graves too – for the spirits of Kyaw and her mother and father. It felt like the honourable thing to do. She lay the sparrowhawk down and paused at the memory before picking up her dagger. When she looked at the graves, she felt less guilty. She had done the right thing coming back to her blood.

Holding firmly to the dagger's heavy teakwood handle, feeling its balance and the carefully re-laid gemstones beneath her grip, she tightened the length of unused thread from the bird's eye across its polished silver blade, cutting it crisply. She ran a knuckle across his glossy brown breast and then a flash of irregular movement yanked her attention outside. Blood and fear thudded in her head and she clenched her fist momentarily, but then her wary eyes found the boy who was waiting in the shadows of the canopy at the end of her pathway. It was the boy who'd returned her dagger from Michael. The one with the scar on his cheek like an arced moon.

She exhaled, tucking the sparrowhawk inside the bag with the rest of his brothers, then buttoning up the leather fastenings and creeping into the evening air. On the gravel, her footsteps seemed to crunch and crackle as loudly as the insects arguing around her, and the wind pawed her and hissed like a warning, and she glanced behind and from side to side. The boy took the bag and slung it around his neck before throwing her a nod and digging into his pocket, passing her the money and stealing back into the dark, thick trees. Thuza stood alone for a moment. They never spoke. There wasn't a need.

Turning back to the house, she looked at the stars above the mountains, judging the time she had left to prepare. The night was bulking up and she hurried herself, rolling the wad of notes through her fingers and counting as she went. There was more than last time, easily so. Enough to buy a dozen blankets and hammocks as well as the usual stash of supplies. Perhaps even antibiotics if she could find them in the Lashio bazaars. Inside, she knelt at the hearth. The curry she'd made had cooled and she spooned it into the little row of tiffin cans, screwed on their lids and dished them out alongside the piles of clothes she had washed and darned, the aspirins, the quids of betel rolled up in their glossy, heart-shaped leaves, the tubes of cream she had bought from the apothecary to ease the insect bites and stop them turning septic, the potatoes they could cook themselves, the rain macs, the clean bottled water, the cigarettes and lighters and tins of yellow fuel. She bundled each stack of treasures into a mosquito net, knotting them tightly with loops that small, raw hands could carry with ease. Every time that she did this, she thought of Michael Atwood. She wouldn't have been able to help without him.

The last time they had seen each other on the road through the forest – and for all her relief that her plans had served her – she hadn't expected to feel so sad. Though they'd only known each other for a few days, so much had happened and she'd laid herself so open that to know that she'd betrayed him felt like one more bereavement. Despite her lies about leaving, she had meant almost everything else she had told him; about feeling lighter and about feeling free. Their oath was unspoken but true – a friendship – and she'd tricked him the same way that Zawtika had tricked her. The thought had towed her down like an anchor, and a fierce, fresh resolve had started to simmer. Though it didn't have a shape or a weight or a name yet, it was there at her insides, stirring her up. She had knifed the boy, but the act was an ending. *I'm not going to bury my head,* she had told him. That was the instant that she'd known things were new. If she wanted to feel safe and proud and worthy, she would need to be different from all those who'd punished her. It wasn't enough to mouth the words meekly. She wasn't going to be like them.

Picking up the bundles and slinging them over her arm, she coughed to ready herself and tiptoed outside again, towards the trees. At the ridge behind her family's graves, she hid the packages, and then rushed back inside and sat by her table at the window, staring out. An hour must have passed before she saw the first watery eyes spark in the moonlight, young and wide and feral with fear. The child's thin limbs scrambled through the gloom, snatching a package before stealing away. They came quicker after that, one boy-soldier then the next, scurrying rat-like from the forest until all the packages had disappeared. From this distance and in the dark, she couldn't see how many were rebels and how many were Tatmadaw, but she didn't care. They were all as doomed as Kyaw was . . . and as her parents. They were all like she'd been, trapped and desperate, no older than the day she had found herself alone. Her stomach tangled as she watched each one fleeing. She had no idea what the future would bring her, or how long she'd stay safe and be able to do this, and the dread of it kept her awake through the night-times, but for now at least she was more than the *Naga-ma.* This was what was becoming her escaping — not miles or borders, rivers or hills. For the first time in years, she wasn't the outcast. Escape didn't mean she'd abandon her history, but it did mean at last that she felt she had choices. At the thought, a smile surged up from her insides. Despite it all, she was glad to be back here. The spirits of her parents were holding her tightly. There was nowhere else that could ever be home.

AUTHOR'S NOTE

'In Myanmar there are big animals and there are small animals.
The government are the big animals. We are the small animals.'

It's still not easy to have a conversation about the past in
Burma. In the early 1980s, when *The Road To Rangoon* is set,
Burma – or Myanmar as she is now more commonly known
– was deeply isolated from the rest of the world, embroiled
in bitter fighting on many fronts, stagnated by decades of
economic ineptitude, political repression and human rights
violations. For many, the country remains a frightening place,
a society of insiders and outsiders, relentlessly competitive,
where people feel trapped, exhausted and silenced, where fear
defines actions and interactions, and where rumour and sus-
picion are powerful kings. It's understandable, therefore, that
people are reluctant to share their thoughts and experiences. In
writing this novel, what I tried to capture most faithfully was
the spirit of the conversations I had when travelling there, the
moments of fleeting truth that slipped almost imperceptibly
from person after person I spoke to – such as the above quote
from a taxi driver – concealed inside innocuous, everyday chat.
The story and the characters I've created are fictional, but the
context through which they wade is real.

Today the country is synonymous with Aung San Suu Kyi, but it was her father, Than's hero General Aung San, who was perhaps the real architect of modern Myanmar. Burma's history is replete with conflict. The kings of old brawled endlessly for land and power, slaughtering any rival with a claim to the throne. The Portuguese mercenaries who came to exploit Burma's immense natural riches in the sixteenth century were drawn into these battles between kings and warlords, forced to choose sides. In the eighteenth century, the British Empire absorbed Burma into India after a succession of bloody wars, exiling the last king and queen before making her an independent crown colony in 1937. Though they wrought great improvements in the country's infrastructure, building ports and railways, transforming Rangoon from a swampy scattered settlement into a majestic thriving port town, they were dictatorial too, and countless nationalist and ethnic movements sprung up in opposition. The cooperation of some of these groups with the Japanese in the Second World War temporarily expelled the British, but when Japanese brutality became apparent, they switched support to the Allies and a return to British rule followed. It was General Aung San's tenacity that finally secured Burma's independence in 1948. He was assassinated before the handover was complete, however, and in the chaos that ensued, the seeds of *The Road to Rangoon* were sown. In 1962, a military coup seized power from the delicate fledgling democracy, making Burma a one-party, military-led state. The new government abolished the federal system and introduced the 'Burmese Way to Socialism', a push towards socialist totalitarianism. The movements that had emerged under the British mushroomed and the country descended into civil war.

It is estimated that more than a million people have been killed in Myanmar's civil war since independence. There are dozens of active ethnic armies across the country – including the Shan State Army with whom Thuza finds herself embroiled – and some of the insurgencies are the longest-running conflicts in modern history. The rebels are experienced, organised and heavily armed. They are not amateurs. The government's army is a fighting one, potent and practised. Ordinary people like Thuza are often trapped between the sides, unable to extricate themselves and doing what they must in order to survive, suffering 'taxes' on their goods passing through the areas, road tolls for free movement, threats, coercion and even kidnap.

As has been the case so often throughout Burma's history, disputes over natural resources – teak, oil, fish, rice, opium and gems – have both fuelled the battles and funded them. As much as ninety per cent of the world's rubies originate in Myanmar and their quality is unparalleled. In real life, as in this novel, their value extends far beyond the price of their sale. The mines have become a petri dish for all Myanmar's ills. Her social, political, economic, cultural and environmental challenges are magnified in the presence of the promise and tension that rubies bring. Whilst researching, I focused on sources offering real-life accounts of existence in Burma under military rule, and of people caught in the crossfire of the civil war and the gem trade. Where I have used creative licence or simplified complex subjects and cultural quirks to aid the story, I have tried to do so delicately, being mindful of authenticity. Mogok is real, however. Violence, corruption, smuggling, trickery, secrecy and superstition are the hallmarks of the ruby business, and prevalent there like nowhere else.

Similarly, my portrayal of the conflict between the Burmese government and the Shan State Army is based on fact, though at times embellished. In the early 1980s, the Tatmadaw was waging a propaganda war against the disparate ethnic insurgent groups, as well as a military one. Bombs were commonplace throughout the country, and though most were discovered unexploded, they were frequently deadly too. Little has been proved, but there was speculation that some at least may have been planted by the regime themselves to justify their existence and keep a fearful people subdued. The British retained a sparse diplomatic presence in Burma at this time also, and whilst Michael and his father are works of imagination, the ambassador would have dealt with similar challenges and frustrations.

A last point worth noting regards place names. In the 1980s, the Burmese government prioritised eradicating Western influences, and amongst other changes, they switched the official name of the country from the Union of Burma to the Union of Myanmar, and the name of Rangoon to Yangon, apparently neutralising any colonial associations. An increasing number of countries are recognising these names today, though controversy remains. Since *The Road to Rangoon* is set several years before the change was decreed, in the story if not this note, I've stuck exclusively to the old naming conventions.

When writing *The Road to Rangoon*, I often returned to the conversations I had in Myanmar, remembering their context and searching for the giveaways that betrayed their hidden truths. In most, I realised, the nervousness – and at times even the despair that I sensed – was matched by a soaring hope. The period after this novel is set was famously dark. In 1988, mass uprisings – the first genuine effort of a repressed population to speak out – were ruthlessly crushed. Thousands of pro-democracy protestors were killed in clashes with the government and Aung San Suu Kyi was thrust to prominence. She won the 1990 presidential election with eighty-five per cent of the vote, but spent fifteen of the next twenty-one years under house arrest. The military denied her party the right to assume their seats in government and imprisoned most of the leadership. Human rights violations and ethnic conflict spiked. The country is changing, however. A series of unexpected reforms followed 2010's election. The military government has been officially dissolved, Aung San Suu Kyi has taken a seat in parliament and other political prisoners have been released. Laws providing better protections for basic human rights have been passed and controls on the media, association and civil society have gradually reduced. Ceasefires have been struck with rebel armies, and Western countries are lifting economic sanctions. Foreign investment is pouring in. Further elections in 2015 were roundly praised by international observers for their fairness and transparency and the country's gradual progress towards freedom was evident in a newly-confident electorate which turned out in record numbers to award a landslide victory to Aung San Suu Kyi's National League for Democracy. Commentators remain wary, but this feeling of optimism is what I now remember most from my travels there, particularly amongst the younger generation.

The people I met were excited, as eager to talk about their new country and the progress it was making as they were uneasy to speak about its past. They were welcoming, generous, full of humour. Though they knew too that any improvements were embryonic and fragile, and that words should still be watched and shoulders glanced over, and though never was I offered an explicit solution to any issue or grievance, there remained that constant undertow of promise. Like Thuza, they believed real change would come if they willed it – one day.

ACKNOWLEDGEMENTS

Of the many resources I plundered while researching this novel, most invaluable in helping me understand the complexities, legacies and pressures of Burmese history, culture and politics were *Living Silence: Burma Under Military Rule* by Christina Fink, *Burma/Myanmar: What Everyone Needs to Know* by David I. Steinberg and *Nowhere to be Home: Narratives from Survivors of Burma's Military Regime* edited by Maggie Lemere and Zoe West. For insights into the Burmese government's human rights abuses, the reports of the Assistance Association for Political Prisoners (AAPP), available at www.aappb.net, were as enlightening as they were horrifying. In learning about the Mogok mining region and the ruby trade, I would have struggled greatly without the extraordinarily detailed *Mogok: Valley of Rubies and Sapphires* and *Gems and Mines of Mogok*, by Ted Themelis. The discussions that former British ambassadors to Burma, Sir Nicholas Fenn and Martin Morland, had with the British Diplomatic Oral History Programme at Churchill College, Cambridge, were beyond fascinating, and sparked my imagination like little else. The transcripts of these are available via the Churchill Archives Centre's BDOHP Biographical Details and Interview Index, here: www.chu.cam.ac.uk/archives/collections/bdohp/

These key texts were my starting points, though any missteps are entirely my own.

Many individuals have also helped me shape this book. Thanks go to the friends I made in Myanmar for taking me to the most magical bookshops and talking so passionately about their home. Some know they helped and others probably never will, but all were generous in sharing their thoughts and stories, however brief. Though I can only imagine what life is like living under a military dictatorship, I hope to have done their experiences justice, at least a small amount. In the UK, thank you to MiMi Aye for helping me navigate the intricacies of Burmese names.

A big thank-you is also reserved for Jon Watt, Susan Watt and the team at Heron Books for their incredible patience and consistent belief, and to my agent Robert Dinsdale for his incisive feedback and guidance on all things publishing. As ever, I am grateful for the continued unqualified faith of my family and friends, in particular my husband, who has read more drafts than anyone should have to and whose carefully-struck balance of encouragement and humouring keeps me on the straight and narrow. This novel is dedicated to our son, without whom it would have been finished much sooner, but whose birth – in some miniature way – will always be linked to the birth of this book.

Also by
LUCY CRUICKSHANKS

Vietnam, 1980s — propelled by greed, fear and hope,
three desperate lives are about to collide....

Shortlisted for the *Guardian* Not the Booker Prize
and the Authors' Club First Novel Award

HERON
BOOKS
www.heronbooks.co.uk